THE
BEST LAID PLANS

"This is a funny book that could only have been written by someone with first-hand knowledge of politics in Canada, including its occasionally absurd side. This is a great read for anyone thinking of running for office, and especially reassuring for those who have decided not to."

—**The Hon. Allan Rock**, former Justice Minister and Canadian Ambassador to
the United Nations

"Bravo! This is a wonderful book with a clever and funny storyline. Humour and heart run through these pages. The parliamentary setting and the backroom shenanigans reel you in. Readers will never look at a finance minister the same way again! I can't wait to buy copies for my friends. I loved it!"

—**The Hon. Paddy Torsney**, veteran MP and Parliamentary Secretary

"Terry Fallis's novel has two things that kept me hooked: characters who I cared about and a story that made me want to find out what would happen next. And often, very often, there was a line that made me laugh aloud or think twice—sometimes at the same time."

—**Mike Tanner**, author of *Acting the Giddy Goat*

THE
BEST LAID PLANS

A Novel

TERRY FALLIS

iUniverse, Inc.
New York Lincoln Shanghai

The Best Laid Plans
A Novel

Copyright © 2007 by Terry Fallis

iUniverse books may be ordered through booksellers or by contacting:

iUniverse
2021 Pine Lake Road, Suite 100
Lincoln, NE 68512
www.iuniverse.com
1-800-Authors (1-800-288-4677)

Because of the dynamic nature of the Internet, any Web addresses
or links contained in this book may have changed
since publication and may no longer be valid.

This is a work of fiction. All of the characters, names, incidents, organizations, and dialogue in this novel are either the products of the author's imagination or are used fictitiously.

Author photo by Tim Fallis.

ISBN: 978-0-595-42872-4 (pbk)
ISBN: 978-0-595-68535-6 (cloth)
ISBN: 978-0-595-87211-4 (ebk)

Printed in the United States of America

For Nancy, Calder, and Ben

The best laid plans of mice and men
Often go awry
And leave us nothing but grief and pain
Instead of promised joy!

—Robert Burns, *To A Mouse* (1785)

ACKNOWLEDGEMENTS

Writing seems the most solitary of pursuits, particularly late at night when you're clacking away on the laptop as your family sleeps. But eventually, it dawns on you that, in fact, your ability to bind up your story into a book turns on the support of so many others. My thank-you list is long, and I'll be forever grateful to the family members, friends, and, yes, to several strangers who helped me.

For being brave enough to read my words when I was barely brave enough to share them, I thank Christine Langlois, Catherine Shepherd, Tom Allen, and Kathleen Naylor. For advice and comfort in trying to navigate the publishing labyrinth, John Lute, Steve Paikin, Beverly Slopen, Ben McNally, Mike Tanner, and Bill Kaplan were there. Camille Montpetit, retired Deputy Clerk of the House of Commons, spent time with me to ensure that the parliamentary procedure portrayed in this story honoured the Standing Orders. I'm grateful to him and to Audrey O'Brien, the current Clerk of the House, for bringing us together.

While I would never suggest that you judge any book by its cover, I'm thankful for the early design work of my friend and colleague Steve Palmer on both the novel and the podcast blog page. Ron Boisvert was also generous in allowing a perfect stranger to use his amazing photograph, which I found while trolling the Internet. Many podcasting and blogging friends helped to promote the podcast version of *The Best Laid Plans* (www.terryfallis.com), which, in turn, should help to promote the printed version. I owe a debt to Shel Holtz, Neville Hobson, Donna Papacosta, Mitch Joel, Bryan Person, Scott Sigler, Dan York, Joe Thornley, David Jones, Keelan Green, Mark Blevis, Bob Goyetche, and many others. Novelist Mike Tanner, veteran Member of Parliament the Honourable Paddy Torsney, and the Honourable Allan Rock, former Justice Minister and Canadian Ambassador to the United Nations, were very kind to provide glowing quotations to help promote the novel. Tom Allison also played a role in this. They all have my gratitude.

Thanks to my father, Dr. James C. Fallis, for passing on to me a love of our language. To all my friends and colleagues who endure my passion for proper English, you can't fight DNA, so blame him. I'm quite sure my mother would have loved this book—regardless. As for my identical-twin brother, Tim, I certainly appreciate his support and encouragement, but wish he would stop telling people it's his book (unless of course they don't like it, and then, by all means, he should carry on).

Writing—a solitary pursuit? Hardly.

To my wife, Nancy, and our two sons, Calder and Ben, who gave me the time, space, and inspiration to write—this is for you.

PROLOGUE

I could take no more. With the backroom boys still driving Machiavelli's motor coach, I was just a helpless, hapless passenger as they tossed the public interest under the wheels yet again. Just to be sure, we stopped, backed up, and rumbled over it once more. It was time to bail out.

There's little point in recounting the specific incident that pushed me over the edge. Let's just say polls trumped policy. Politics pummeled leadership. And in the main event, the four-year electoral horizon crushed long-term vision—again. You get the idea. My camel's back was broken. Don't misunderstand me. It wasn't the crazy hours, the impossible workload, or the wrong-side-of-modest salary. I signed on for all of that—willingly, gratefully. No, I had to get out because of what flowed beneath it all, relentless as the tides—cynicism, manipulation, self-interest, ego, opportunism, duplicity, deceit, and cowardice.

I am Daniel Addison. When I escaped Ottawa the first time, I was head speech writer for the Leader of Her Majesty's Loyal Opposition. But after five years in the crucible of Parliament Hill, my public-service calling was battered beyond recognition. I sent for the dental records. Naïve, innocent, and excited when I arrived, I was embittered, exhausted, and ineffably sad when I left.

Still, I remained liberal and a Liberal—in that order. I had come by my liberalism the hard way—by slowly and steadily shedding the expectations and assumptions inflicted by my family's five generations of leadership in the Progressive Conservative (PC) Party. I had canvassed for PC candidates when the staples in my diet had been puréed chicken and strained peaches. My stroller had been a Tory campaign sign on wheels with a cramped space underneath it all for me. In those days, the candidate-kissing-the-baby shot had been *de rigueur* for campaign leaflets. Well, I had served as the local baby until I was old enough for it to be creepy. Check out the party's photo archives and you'll find my smiling mug over and over again, my snowsuits or sunhats festooned with Tory paraphernalia according to the season.

When I arrived at university, I decided that family tradition was one reason to be a Tory, just not a very good one. Then, I stumbled upon a radical approach. I decided to read about ideology, liberalism, socialism, and conservatism and what they really meant in theory, in practice, and in our history. I majored in English but also pursued my personal political science minor on the side. The more I read, the more of what had been my family's bedrock cracked and crumbled. After literally a lifetime of blind support for the Progressive Conservative Party, the family veil fell, and I realized in my heart and in my head that I was actually a Liberal. My forebears are still dizzy from subterranean spinning.

My parents seemed amused by my conversion and considered it to be a predictable manifestation of late-onset teenage rebellion. Their tolerance of what some of my relatives considered a knife in the family's back or, at least, a slap in the face was couched in the sincere belief that I would eventually come to my senses. Even then, I felt certain I'd be a Liberal for life. I still believe that.

To me, the challenges now facing nations, societies, and economies are simply too complex to be resolved by pat solutions of the Right or the Left. The Tory mantra of "less government is better" and the socialist maxim that "more government is better" just don't fly in the real world. I simply believe that "better government is better." Our policies should be enlightened, pragmatic, progressive, compassionate, and leavened with foresight. In some cases, less government and a greater role for the private sector may well be the right approach. In other instances, government intervention may not only be appropriate but required in the public interest. Within reason, we should be doctrinaire about our destination but not necessarily about the vehicle that takes us there.

In the first year of my master's program in English—after much soul-searching—I capitalized the L and joined the Liberal Party of Canada. Uncle Charlie stopped speaking to me. Had I known, I'd have taken the plunge years earlier.

I landed in the Opposition Leader's office after completing my coursework for a PhD in Canadian literature at the University of Ottawa. I started in the correspondence unit and within eighteen months, wrote my way up from letters to speeches. For most of my thirty-two years, I had lived with what I called my "completion complex." I was bound to finish what I started. I couldn't leave any food on my plate even if the meatballs were hard as golf balls. I couldn't start a book, hate the opening chapters, and discard it until suffering through all 569 pages of it. I would sit through far more very, very bad movies than someone with at least average cerebral capacity would ever endure. So leaving U of O one dissertation shy of my PhD was a therapeutic breakthrough, of sorts. After all, an opening as a wordsmith for the Leader of the Liberal Party (arguably, the Prime Minister in waiting) did not beckon often. I took the job. But in twisted, Herculean tribute to my completion complex, I somehow nursed along my dissertation on Canadian comedic novels at night while turning phrases by day. After enduring Liberal caucus meetings, I found that defending my dissertation two years later was like making dinner conversation in the Cleaver household. Juggling my time and the demands of both poles of my life was not easy. Some of my colleagues thought I was very committed while others simply thought I should be. I languished somewhere in the middle. I was glad the PhD was done but was unclear about the implications. Clarity came soon enough.

On Parliament Hill, the pendulum of power swings between the cynical political operators (CPOs) and the idealist policy wonks (IPWs). It's a naturally self-regulating model that inevitably transfers power from one group to the other—and back again. It can take years, even multiple elections, for the pendulum to swing to the other side. It was just my luck that I—a member in good standing of the idealist-policy-wonk contingent—would arrive in Ottawa just as the backroom boys were starting their swing back up to the top.

To be fair, governments work best when the pendulum is somewhere near the middle—with the CPOs and IPWs sharing power. When the CPOs are dominant as they were when I arrived in Ottawa (and when I left, for that matter), they tend to erode public confidence in the democratic process and infect the electorate with the cynicism, self-interest, and opportunism that flow in their veins. In the mind of a hardcore CPO, the ends always, always justify the means. At least, that's my balanced, impartial view.

On the other hand, when the IPWs are at the helm, however well-meaning we may be, we often lack the necessary killer instinct and political acumen to push our vaunted policies across the finish line. We can't seem to accept that selling the policy is just as important as coming up with it in the first place. We seldom get to the ends because we mess up the means.

But even the staunchest policy wonk cannot work in a CPO-controlled environment without absorbing and assimilating the overtly political approach we wonks philosophically abhor. It's insidious and inexorable. One day, you wake up and find you're instinctively reviewing polling data in a different way; you find yourself thinking about the election cycle and how to isolate the weak Cabinet Minister from the rest of the herd in order to move in for the kill. I felt sick when I realized how my perspective had changed. I kind of felt I had inadvertently crossed to the dark side and that all the backroom boys were waiting just across the threshold to present me with monogrammed suspenders, shove a cigar in my yap, and welcome me into the fold. It really was time to go.

But in the interest of full disclosure and transparency—concepts sadly absent in government these days—I confess there was more to my hasty retreat from Ottawa than a near fatal case of political disillusionment. Something else also played a role. Around the time of my crisis of conscience, my two-year relationship with Rachel Bronwin flamed out in much the same way as the space shuttle *Challenger* had exploded over the Atlantic Ocean. When I replay our last encounter in my mind, I always accompany the scene with the public-address voice of NASA Mission Control, uttering that now classic understatement, "obviously a major malfunction," as burning wreckage fell into the sea.

Rachel was serving as senior political adviser to Dick Warrington, the youngish and, some would say, handsome Opposition House Leader. I had met Rachel at a political-assistants' meeting, and we had clicked in a way that had left me somewhat unnerved. She was wonderful in every way. It was as simple and rare as that. She was intelligent, thoughtful, committed, ambitious, and beautiful—so beautiful that our relationship violated the accepted order of the universe. The match just wasn't credible. Someone like me was not supposed to be dating, let alone sleeping with, someone like her. But I was. I wore the perpetual, loopy grin of a lottery-ticket holder who wins big his first time out.

When we would walk hand in hand down Sparks Street on a Saturday afternoon, I could almost feel the skeptical glances of passers-by. Modesty aside, I'm a far cry from ugly. But admittedly, I was not exactly in Rachel's class. Pierce Brosnan would have just barely made the cut.

For those two years, I'd never been happier. By the end of month six, I had a toothbrush at her apartment in the Glebe. On our first anniversary, she gave me the bottom drawer in her dresser. After two years, I was frequently noting the folly of paying rent for two apartments when only one was really being used. I really thought the big search might be over. I'd also finally stopped looking over my shoulder, waiting for some uniformed relationship bureaucrat to tell me that there'd been some mix up with my paperwork and that I couldn't see Rachel any more. He never showed up, but someone else did.

Nothing really seemed amiss at the time. I thought she seemed a little distracted, even distant, but I blamed that on a spike in her workload. Looking back now, I realize she was pulling a few more all-nighters at the office than might be reasonably expected of the senior adviser to the Opposition House Leader. It was mid-July, so Parliament wasn't even sitting at the time. Hindsight is a cruel companion.

One night, after Rachel told me she'd be working late again, I unexpectedly found myself back in Centre Block, picking up the car keys I'd managed to leave on a table in the Library of Parliament earlier in the day. No wonder I left my keys there. I usually became misty-eyed and foggy-headed in the Library of Parliament, so I often forgot things there. I thought of the library as one my favourite places in the world. In one of Canadian history's few spasms of generosity, the fire of 1916 spared the library and its immaculate woodwork while razing the rest of the original Parliament building. A new and equally majestic Centre Block was erected to house the two chambers of our democracy, grafted onto the original library in all its august glory.

I like to think that the best speeches I wrote for the Liberal Leader were penned and polished in the Library of Parliament. My preferred spot was a varnished, wooden table under the watchful gaze of a white plaster bust of Sir Wilfrid Laurier. When words would abandon me, I'd stare at Laurier or read his speeches from Hansard, which lined the shelves behind me. Canada has spawned precious few orators and even fewer leaders of Laurier's calibre. I fear he'd be disgusted and depressed were he to return to the House of Commons today for the tabloid TV of question period.

After leaving the library's security desk, keys in hand, I thought I'd surprise Rachel and, given the hour, perhaps even drive her home. I strolled through Centre Block, feeling the history, as always, seeping out of the walls. I pushed open the door to the House Leader's office and found the reception area empty and dark. I could look right down the hallway to Rachel's office, which was bathed in light from her black, halogen desk lamp. I was surprised to see the House Leader himself sprawled in Rachel's chair with his hands on his head like he was about to be handcuffed. He had quite the rapt expression on his face, which left me somewhat perplexed—for another two breaths. That's when I caught sight of Rachel.

For me, Centre Block is hallowed ground. I'm reluctant to defile its image with tawdry descriptions of infidelity. On the other hand, what happened that night gave me the strength to reject the path of least resistance and get the hell out of that netherworld. So I'll recount the story, but out of respect, I'll at least honour the strictures of parliamentary language.

Rachel, my Rachel, was on her knees in front of the Opposition House Leader. Let's just say she was rather enthusiastically lobbying his caucus. Stunned and devastated, I turned away—to get a better view in the lee of a well-endowed rubber plant. Rachel jumped into her advance work with both hands before moving to what seemed to be his favourite part of the proceedings—Oral Questions. Eventually, he pulled her up off the floor and onto the desk where he begged leave to introduce his private Member's bill. Clearly, there was unanimous consent as the cut and thrust of debate started immediately—well, mostly thrust. By the look on her face, second reading was proceeding satisfactorily with just a few indecipherable heckles thrown in for good measure. The House Leader occasionally shouted "hear, hear" and slapped her backbench in support. At one point, she amended her position on his bill, and the debate continued.

They were hurtling towards royal assent when I regained my faculties. I considered rising on a point of personal privilege, but, abhorring confrontation of any kind, I simply threw up on the rubber plant and stumbled back out into Centre Block's arched and awe-inspiring main corridor. Portraits of former prime ministers mocked me as I hurried by, searching for answers and some industrial-strength breath mints. At that moment, I was sure that Rachel and the Honourable "Dickhead" had no idea I was their vomiting vestibule voyeur. Damn my weakness for alliteration.

By the time Rachel arrived home in the wee hours, I'd already cleaned out my drawer and repatriated my toothbrush. I left her a crumpled leaf from the rubber plant, which I was surprised to find still clenched in my hand, along with a terse note, breaking it off and suggesting that she invest in a deadbolt and a DO NOT DISTURB sign for the office. I resigned the next day.

Before meeting with the Leader and his chief of staff to consummate my escape from federal politics, I made a phone call to the head of the English department at the University of Ottawa, who was also my dissertation supervisor. I couldn't exactly just throw in the towel and live off my savings and investments until I found gainful employment. Given the state of my finances, that would mean finding another job by the following Tuesday afternoon. So I decided to advance plans I'd already intended to pursue—just not so soon.

Professor Phillip Gannon not only ran the English department but also chaired the faculty-appointments' committee. They'd recently had a transfer appointment fall through and weren't happy. The committee was short one junior professor for the fall term, and they were scrambling to find a replacement. He'd already called me some weeks before to gauge my interest. At the time, I was still planning on staying with the Leader through the election expected in early October and perhaps becoming speech writer to the Prime Minister should the campaign unexpectedly go our way. But much had changed in two weeks, and I prayed that in the dead of summer, the committee members would be more interested in their Gatineau cottages than in searching for a newly minted PhD to teach Canadian literature 101. After the way my life seemed to be unraveling, I fully expected this opportunity to have been shut down already. I was wrong.

Professor Gannon was thrilled to hear of my interest in the position. Apparently, I was saving his bacon, not to mention his summer. He did a quick call around to his vacationing committee members, and by noon, I had paperwork on my home e-mail. In the minds of the dock-lounging committee members, I was more than qualified to teach undergraduate English. After all, I knew my ABCs and had never been in prison. As for the approval of the Senate Committee on

Appointments, my years on Parliament Hill and proximity to power at a time when the university was seeking federal funding for a new economics building seemed to grease the wheels.

The university usually operated in geological time but not that day. By three-thirty, it was official. I was the English department's newest faculty member. In courtesy of a practice common in many universities when easing in a new and untested faculty member, I wouldn't actually be teaching until the second term, freeing up some time in the fall to orient myself to the rigours of life in academe.

Despite appearances, joining the faculty wasn't a precipitous decision on my part. I'd already decided to pursue teaching after completing my PhD. I just didn't think it would happen for another few years. In politics, leaving your options open is standard operating procedure.

My final meeting with the Leader and Bradley Stanton, his chief of staff, went as expected—at least until the end. In other words, they were mad as hell. How could I abandon them on the eve of an election? After all they'd done for me, how could I leave just as the battle beckoned? I calmly explained that I'd already produced the election kickoff speech, two stump speeches (one of them down and dirty, which hammered the Government, and the other one high-road, which sounded more prime-ministerial), opening and closing debate remarks along with witty and thoughtful repartee in all policy areas, a victory speech, and a concession speech. Stanton had been so busy planning diabolical campaign gambits that he knew nothing of my election prep work.

I apologized for the short notice and pledged my support during the campaign, provided it didn't interfere with my new faculty responsibilities. I also offered to participate in debate prep when the networks and the party leaders had decided on timing and format. As the meeting wound down, the Leader seemed to soften and asked me if I was moving out of Ottawa. I replied that I really wanted to get out of the city as part of my reintegration into normal Canadian society. Escaping Ottawa's gravitational pull was a big part of my plan. I relayed my intention to find a place on the water in Cumberland, about a 30-minute drive east of the capital on the Ottawa River. Several U of O faculty members lived there and made the short, sedate commute to campus every day. The Chief of Staff's left eyebrow lifted in a Spockian arch, and a wave of unease washed over me.

I had made a big mistake mentioning Cumberland. Since birth, I had had great difficulty saying no. Though I was already guilt-ridden for bailing on the imminent campaign, I was determined to make a clean break. But like a thin crust on new-fallen snow, my resistance looked solid enough but gave way at the slightest touch. I left the Leader's office and Parliament Hill, not quite free of politics. The Leader gave me his sad-eyes routine, and I swayed, vibrated, and collapsed like the Tacoma Bridge. One last favour; then, I was out.

My parting gift to the Leader? I promised to find a Liberal candidate for the riding of Cumberland-Prescott and then manage the local campaign. I'd be free and clear by mid-October.

No problem. Piece of cake. How hard could it be?

Cumberland-Prescott—a Tory stronghold since before confederation and currently held by the Honourable Eric Cameron, the most popular Finance Minister in Canadian history. He was young, good-looking, widowed, and blessed with an eloquence that, while honed and rehearsed, sounded as if he were talking off the cuff—a wonderful gift in politics. In other words, Cameron was as close as any politician came to the elusive "complete package."

People actually believed he was honest and a straight shooter. I saw through him. I loathed him in a partisan way. But I may have been the only person in Canada who did. I had watched him at close range for five years and was convinced he was not what he seemed. He couldn't possibly be. Nobody could be. Yet, he'd won the last election by over 36,000 votes, up from a 31,000 plurality in the previous campaign. His most recent budget, introduced in February, gave Canadians a 10 per cent cut in personal income tax, a one-point cut in the goods and services tax, and higher RRSP limits while still paying off $10 billion of the nation's debt. Masterful.

Skyrocketing favourability ratings for the budget, the Tory government, and the Finance Minister himself had the pollsters checking and rechecking their field and tab operations. No one had ever seen anything like it. The unprecedented numbers cemented an autumn election call. And we weren't ready. Cumberland-Prescott was the only constituency in Canada still without a nominated Liberal candidate. Only seven weeks remained before the Prime Minister's quadrennial drop-in at the Governor General's to dissolve Parliament and call an election.

Despite an unprecedented Tory lead in the polls, we had many, many hard-fought Liberal nomination battles across the country. We were optimistic, had attracted some star candidates, and had put little stock in the pre-election numbers. Inexplicably, most Liberals across the country were feeling good. Why? Well, during an election period, seemingly rational people commonly take leave of their senses and replace reason with hope. Political parties have practiced the mass delusion of their members long before the Reverend Jim Jones took it to the next level. Despite this ill-conceived Liberal optimism in many parts of the country, Eric Cameron's utter invincibility cast a pall over the handful of Liberals living in Cumberland. The Liberal riding association was not just moribund, it was very nearly extinct.

So I packed up and moved to Cumberland, choosing a clean but inexpensive local motel as my home base until I could find permanent accommodations. But that wasn't my first priority. I had seven weeks to secure a Liberal candidate for Cumberland-Prescott, no doubt to be led once more to the electoral slaughter. Otherwise, I'd be struck from the Leader's Christmas-card list—political excommunication at its zenith.

PART ONE

CHAPTER ONE

After an impressive hang time, I plummeted back to the sidewalk, my fall and ego broken by a fresh, putrid pile of excrement the size of a small ottoman. I quickly scanned the area for a hippo on the lam.

Before I quite literally found myself in deep shit, my day had actually been ripe with promise. I'm a big believer in signs. After six straight days of rain, I believed the sun burning a hole in the cloudless, cobalt sky was a sign—a good one. It somehow lightened the load I'd been lugging around in my mind for the previous six weeks. I lifted my face to the warmth and squinted as I walked along the edge of Riverfront Park. Even though it was a Monday morning, I hummed a happy, little tune. Maybe, just maybe, things were looking up. Unfortunately, so was I.

My foot made a soft landing on the sidewalk and shot forward all on its own, leaving a brown, viscous streak in its wake. Congenitally clumsy, I was well into the splits before I managed to drag my trailing leg forward and slip the surly bonds of earth. Airborne, I surveyed the terrain below and, with all the athletic prowess of a quadriplegic walrus, returned safely to earth, touching down in the aforementioned crap cushion.

Just after I landed, I counted twenty-four witnesses, who stared slack-jawed before many of them split their sides. Fortunately, only a handful of them had video cameras. I expect you can still find me on klutzklips.com. Everyone seemed quite amused by the prominent sign planted three feet to my left: KEEP CUMBER-LAND CLEAN. PLEASE STOOP AND SCOOP. The owners of whatever behemoth produced this Guinness-book offering would have needed a Hefty bag and a snow shovel.

And what an unholy aroma. I've always believed that English is better equipped than any other language to capture the richness and diversity of our daily lives. I promise you, the *Oxford Concise* does not yet have words to describe the stench that rose like a mushroom cloud from that colossal mound. Stepping in it was one thing; full immersion was quite another.

Bright sun in a clear blue sky—good sign. Russian split jump into a gigantic dog turd—not a good sign. Good form, good air, but not a good sign.

An hour and a shower later, I retraced my steps, eyes fixed on the pavement, ignoring the two township workers in hazmat suits at the scene of my fall. I quickened my pace, pumping myself up for the important encounter ahead. After nearly six weeks of intensive searching, I was down to my last seven days. I'd tried flattery, threats, cajolery, blackmail, and bribery, but had come up empty and bone-dry—nothing.

In the first two weeks after my arrival in Cumberland, I'd spoken to the mayor and every town councilor, including the lone Liberal, as well as the head of the chamber of commerce. No dice. In week three, I had pleaded with prominent business leaders, local doctors and lawyers, the head of the four-bus transit authority, and the high-school principal. They're all still laughing. In fact, one of them needed two sick days to rest a pulled stomach muscle. Last week, I had bought drinks for the local crossing guard, baked cookies for the chief instructor at the Prescott Driving School, and shared inane banter with the golf pro at the Cumberland Mini-Putt. No luck, although the crossing guard at least listened to half my spiel before holding up her STOP sign.

I like to think that one of my few strengths is a keen sense of when I'm doomed. None of this "the glass is half full" stuff for me. I know when I'm in deep. And in deep, I was. So I gave up and returned to the no-hope option I'd rejected at the outset as cruel and unusual punishment. But what else could I do? I had splinters from scraping the bottom of the barrel.

The Riverfront Seniors' Residence loomed on my left just beyond the park. Built in 1952, it had that utterly forgettable but, I suppose, practical architecture of that era—early Canadian ugly. Two wings of rooms extended along the river-bank on either side of a central lobby. Everything looked painfully rectangular. The only architectural grace note, just adjacent to the dining room, was a curved wall of windows, overlooking the Ottawa River. For the residents, the panorama provided a welcome distraction from the steam-table cuisine.

The lounge next to the dining room was populated with 30-year-old couches and chairs, sporting strangely hued upholstery from the "shades of internal organs" collection, accessorized by protective, plastic slip covers. I saw a couple of dozen or so residents camped out in the lounge. Some were reading. Others were locked in debate over what vegetables would accompany the pot roast that night. A few simply gazed at nothing at all with a forlorn and vacant look. The scent of air freshener hung heavy, only just subduing that other odor sadly common to many seniors' residences. I loitered in the lobby, surveying the scene and deciding on my approach. Evidently, I was too slow.

A grizzled, old man in a peach safari suit and a lavender, egg-encrusted tie looked me up and down a few times, wrestling with his memory. Finally, recognition dawned on his withered face. "Hey, it's the doggy doo-doo diving champ!" he shouted. I glanced at the aging alliteration aficionado before taking in the rest of the room. All eyes turned to me. I saw heads nodding and smiles breaking. A wheelchair-ridden centenarian gave me a thumbs-up. I heard a smattering of applause that slowly gathered strength and culminated some time later in an osteoporotic, stooping ovation. I felt compelled to take a bow. When the commotion abated, the guy in the peach safari suit approached.

"I gotta tell you that was some performance this morning. After that horse of a dog dropped his load in the middle of the sidewalk, we were all gathered by the window there, waiting for some poor sap to step in it. We even had a pool going."

"I'm certainly gratified that I could brighten your day," I answered with an inferior replica of a genuine smile.

"We had no idea someone would actually throw himself into it. What a show-stopper! What chutzpah! We haven't had that much excitement around here since the great Arnie Shaw flatulence evacuation in '94."

"My pleasure," I said. "I'll work up a new routine for next week. Perhaps you can help me. I'm looking for Muriel Parkinson. Do you know where I can find her?"

He surveyed the room and pointed to the far corner. I followed his crooked finger to see an attractive and well-dressed woman, trying to conceal herself behind an anemic *benjamina ficus* that really wasn't up to the job.

"Thank you," I replied and started towards her.

From behind me, I heard, "No no, thank *you*. You made our month, young man."

I recognized Muriel Parkinson immediately. I'd met her four years earlier at a Liberal Campaign College prior to the last election. She had attended a workshop that I had led on election communications for campaign managers and candidates. We had eaten lunch together that day, and I had gotten to know one of the grand old dames of the Liberal Party. She'd been acclaimed as the Liberal candidate in Cumberland-Prescott for the previous five elections, never once gaining enough support to get back our deposit. Now, that redefines dedication.

During World War II, Muriel had actually worked as Mackenzie King's head secretary. Some historians believed she served as his sounding board and confidante when his dog, Pat, was unavailable. She was Liberal to the core. I clung to the fact that for five consecutive campaigns, with no hope of winning, she'd stood as the lone Liberal in the safest Tory riding in the land. I harboured a faint hope that she might have a sixth left in her.

I was expecting at least to have the element of surprise. I didn't think my mission was well known beyond a small circle at national campaign headquarters back in Ottawa. But from her reaction, I had a faint inkling my cover was blown. She peeked through the sparse, nearly naked branches of the ficus and saw that I had a lock on her. Resigned, she sat back in her chair and waved her hands in front of her face in the universal gesture for "get the hell away from me."

"No no no no no!" she yelled. "Do not even think about it! Do not pass go! Do not collect two hundred dollars. Security! Security!" She yelled just loud enough to vibrate the picture window behind her. What a voice.

The room once again turned to me while I held my hands up in the universal gesture for "I'm harmless and just want to talk." Fortunately, the celebrity conferred by my morning acrobatics had not yet waned, and I was permitted to continue. I approached her as an asylum orderly might inch towards a violent patient.

"Hello, Muriel, I'm Daniel Addison. We had lunch together a few years back at the last candidates' school. How are you doing?"

"I know who you are, and I know why you're here," she said. "You really have your nerve. I told the Leader's office that under no circumstances would I stand again. I've done my part. Get somebody else to fall on their sword this time."

"Look, we really think Cameron's ripe for the picking this time around," I countered, wondering how plugged-in she still was to the local political scene.

"Look, college boy," Muriel said, "I'll lay it out for you. Eric Cameron is so high in the polls he starts each day with a nosebleed. I've run against him in the last three elections and have never even come close to seeing his dust in the distance. He's smooth, courteous, educated, articulate, widowed, for mercy's sake, and so right wing that the middle of the road is in a different time zone!" Her tirade aroused the interest of everyone in the room and several who weren't. "I'm eighty-one years old," she continued. "I've got the shakes, and I've been in the bathroom 13 times in the last three hours. I would not run again if the Leader promised to name me ambassador to Bermuda. And looking at the polls, he won't be able to offer me a Canadian flag for much longer. I am not your candidate!" she harrumphed with finality, crossing her arms.

I lowered my voice in a vain attempt to lower the temperature. "Is that why you think I'm here—to persuade you to run again?" I asked, giving her my best wounded look.

"Well, I don't think you're here to ask me on a date." I paused, unsure of how to play it out. Concern clouded her face. "Oh, please, tell me you're not here to ask me out," she blurted, mortified.

"I'm not here to ask you on a date," I conceded. "My two-year relationship with a philandering girlfriend just ended, and I plan to lay low for a while." I thought I'd open up a little and go for the sympathy vote.

"Then, I'm agog. You really are here to get me to run again, aren't you?" she pressed.

I really had no idea how to handle her, so I just rolled over. "Okay, okay, I thought I at least owed you the right of first refusal."

"Consider it exercised, Danny boy. I'm not your girl this time around. Am I coming in loud and clear, or should I speak slower?"

I crumpled into the chair beside her and buried my head in my hands. I toyed with the thought of convulsive blubbering, but she'd have been unmoved, and around the room, a dozen gnarled hands would've shot from sleeves, offering used tissues.

"What am I going to do?" I wheezed. "If I don't find a candidate to run against Cameron in four days, my solemn promise to the Leader will be broken."

"A broken promise in politics? Stop the presses!" she quipped. Now, she looked like she was officially enjoying herself.

"I just want to do the right thing and leave with a clear conscience," I stammered and fell silent.

I could feel her eyes on me, and when I looked up, they seemed to soften. I knew she'd never run. I think I knew that before I'd even arrived at Riverfront Seniors' Residence. But Muriel Parkinson was a loyal Liberal.

"Look, Daniel, I'll work on the campaign, but my name will not be on the ballot. Is that clear?" she asked gently.

I was very much in a "take what you can get" frame of mind. I was also filled with affection and gratitude, and I told her so. A topic change was in order before she reconsidered.

"How long have you lived here?"

"About two years," she replied. "Ever since God's sense of humour simply made living on my own too difficult for me and too onerous for my daughter." I was puzzled and must have looked it because she carried on. "It's my lot in life to suffer with a disease whose name I share. I was diagnosed with Parkinson's ten years ago and became debilitated to the point that getting around my house wasn't possible any more. I suppose I should be thankful I wasn't christened Muriel Melanoma. Anyway, after a fall, a broken hip, a stint in Cumberland

Memorial, and much debate with my saint of a daughter, here I am." I nodded in sympathy and thought of my own name and how JFK had suffered with Addison's disease.

"My daughter and I nearly came to blows over my move here," Muriel continued. "She really wanted me to live with her and her daughter, Lindsay. I love them both, but they have their own lives." Her words faded.

"I'm sure their offer was genuine and well-meaning," I suggested.

"I'm sure it was, too. That's why I insisted on coming here."

For the first time, I noticed the book in her lap—*Home Economics and Free Labour*, Marin Lee's groundbreaking treatise on the unrecognized economic contribution of women working in the home. Lee's book was the first solid analysis of how society in general, and the economy in particular, benefited from the services typically provided by housewives day in and day out, ostensibly for no income. It was a classic in feminist theory that had first opened my eyes to women's equality issues during my involvement in student politics at university. In fact, I'd heard Marin Lee speak once at a Canadian Federation of Students conference at Carleton where she taught. She'd even signed my copy of her book after her talk.

I pointed to the book. "A little light reading?" Muriel's face brightened as she turned the book so I could see it and stroked the cover the way book lovers do.

"Light? No. Liberating? Yes. The way she writes, the way she puts her arguments, the positions she advances—it all makes so much sense to me. She actually uses humour to make her point even more profound; so many before her simply used anger and rage—not that they weren't justified, mind you. You should really read it." She was surprised and, I think, pleased when I told her I already had. Policy wonks read stuff like Marin Lee.

So this was Muriel. Eighty-one years old. She'd put her neck on the line in five consecutive elections. She was battling Parkinson's while fending off my entreaties to run yet again. Undiminished intellectually, she lived in a seniors' home where only a handful of her fellow residents could match her mental acuity. And she read Marin Lee instead of playing bingo. I liked this tough old warhorse.

I swept the room with my hand. "Have you made friends here?"

"I was born and raised in this town and only lived in Ottawa while working on Mr. King's staff," Muriel explained. "I returned here in 1950 after I refused to take minutes for one of his creepy seances. Anyway, the point is, I knew everybody in this place long before I ever signed up to live here. See that guy over there in green-plaid shorts and the orange-striped shirt?" she asked. I looked over at a group of men playing cards, all of whom seemed to buy their clothes from the bargain table at the golf pro shop.

"Which one? Half of them are wearing plaid shorts."

"The one on the left, leering in my direction. When I was 18, I used to date him. He had the same avant-garde fashion taste back then, too, not to mention a penchant for wandering hands, which he has yet to outgrow."

"Would you like me to have a word with him about his manners? I'm not about to sit idly by as the honour of a former Liberal candidate is challenged by a dirty old … fashion train wreck."

She laughed. "Thank you, but I fear he could take you," she chuckled. She was probably right.

I was suddenly hit by the smell of lunch wafting in from the kitchen; I felt queasy. "How's the food?" I inquired with my nose in full wrinkle.

"The view of the river is lovely," she said, closing down that subject.

Muriel brought us back to politics and the millstone that still hung around my neck, feeling heavier with each passing day. As we reviewed my exhaustive four-week odyssey, she seemed impressed by my methodical search. I had left no stones unturned in Cumberland. Every person she rhymed off, I'd already crossed off or pissed off. She sighed and leaned back in her chair, the plastic slipcover protesting.

"You know, before Mr. King lost himself in the occult," Muriel said, "he used to say 'if you've really done absolutely everything you can and you still come up short, fate will smile on good people.' He called it King's axiom. That's what accounted for his serenity in the face of such daunting challenges. Are you a good person, Mr. Addison?"

I didn't know how to respond, so I just dialed up the wattage of my smile and nodded.

"I'll tell you something else," she went on. "There is more to Eric Cameron than the world sees. I can feel it. He's been under my microscope for the last 15 years, and something's amiss. Ever since that harlot Petra Borschart took over his staff, I've been waiting for the wheels to fall off."

I filed this insight away for further analysis. I'd met Petra a few times on the Hill, and she reminded me of a rattlesnake—scary, slimy, aggressive, loud, and poisonous. That's where the similarities ended, because rattlesnakes were also ugly.

We talked a bit more about how the campaign might unfold and what role she might play, assuming I found a candidate. When we appeared to have run our conversational course, I rose. I squeezed her hand and told her how much I enjoyed renewing our acquaintance. She squeezed back and told me to call on her any time now that we'd resolved any confusion over her potential candidacy. I turned to go.

"Daniel, I'm sorry about your recent breakup. That's never pleasant. And I regret your search so far has been fruitless. But do not despair. It sounds to me like you've done everything humanly possible to draft a sacrificial Liberal lamb. Lord knows Mr. King was wrong about many things, but he was not wrong about fate honouring good people just when they're dangling at the end of their rope."

I smiled—the genuine article this time—placed my hands in prayer, and looked heavenward. I waved good-bye to the others in the room and noted return waves from all but the two residents jousting to be first into the dining room. Wheelchair bumper cars seemed a common activity as no one else appeared to notice. I paused to retrieve a fallen newspaper for an old man on one of those electric scooters and then headed for the main door. Just in time, too. The lunch bell rang, unleashing the midday rush. Like a running back with a very bad offensive line, I dodged and deked the stampeding residents while holding my breath against the encroaching aroma.

With Muriel's parting comments still fresh in my mind, I walked over to the bank, eyeing passers-by and half-expecting one of them to walk right up and tell me it was my lucky day. None did—although in the preceding weeks, I'd struck up quite a friendly rapport with one of the bank tellers and wondered whether she might be interested in becoming this riding's Liberal. I needed to certify 12 postdated rent cheques to convince my new landlord that I was, indeed, solvent. Apparently, a tenure-track position at the same university that employed him wasn't adequate assurance. The friendly bank teller handed me the certified cheques with nary a whisper of a latent interest in federal politics—so much for Mackenzie King's axiom. I picked up my car in the public lot where I'd parked it earlier that morning, twice, and headed back to my still-new digs.

I'd really lucked out on the apartment front. I'd always wanted to live on the water, and through some shrewd maneuvering, laced with luck, I'd landed the upper floor of a boathouse built mere metres from the Ottawa River—hence, the term *boathouse*. My landlord's workshop occupied the first floor, and I occupied the spacious, one-bedroom apartment on the second floor. The apartment was nice enough to call a suite, but saying "suite" and "boathouse" in the same sentence just didn't ring true. My living room, with hardwood floors and a wall of built-in bookshelves, was much nicer than the downtown bachelor apartment I'd left back in Ottawa and only cost two-thirds the rent.

In my mind, nothing furnishes a room like books, and I had plenty. A raft of non-fiction—Canadian, American, and European politics and history—betrayed my ideological predisposition. An extensive collection of comedic novels—mostly Canadian, American, and British—rounded out my inventory. A chocolate brown leather couch and two matching armchairs guarded the perimeter of a small, family hand-me-down Persian rug. An old wooden desk bought at an Arnprior auction filled the far corner of the living room and supported a desk lamp, a green blotter, and my Fujitsu Lifebook laptop computer. A picture window offered an unobstructed northern view across the Ottawa River. Very soothing. The Parliament buildings were about an hour's boat ride upstream—just far enough for me. Out of sight, out of mind.

The galley kitchen was large enough and more than well equipped to meet my modest needs. At this stage in my budding culinary career, I had mastered the kettle and was well on my way to conquering the toaster. For me, making dinner usually meant making a phone call. I could already make Kraft Dinner and spaghetti carbonara and was poised to add beef stroganoff to my burgeoning repertoire thanks to the August *Reader's Digest* I'd nicked from my dentist's office.

The refrigerator was one of those side-by-side units, which initially left me flummoxed. When you've spent the first 32 years of your life with the freezer on top and the fridge on the bottom, switching all of a sudden to the left/right configuration required some acclimation.

The bedroom was a good size with a view up the hill to my landlord's house. My queen-sized bed took up most of the space along with a bedside table, a small dresser, and a chair that held as much of my wardrobe as the closet in the corner. Finally, the bathroom had all the traditional apparatus save for a bathtub. I preferred to shower, anyway, so the glass-doored stall suited me just fine. My lonely toothbrush stood on the shelf over the sink. I'd retired the Rachel-toothbrush in several pieces before vacating Ottawa.

Two ceiling fans, one each in the living room and bedroom, kept the summer air circulating while the Ottawa River moderated the occasional heat wave. No need for air conditioning. When the temperature dipped, a small gas furnace stationed on the ground floor of the boathouse delivered warmed air to my apartment above via a generous network of ducts and vents.

I loved that apartment. Nothing before or since has lulled me to sleep like the tranquil rhythm of the flowing river an arm's length away. On the flip side, the lapping water completely baffled my bladder. The bathroom beckoned every two hours. Yep, I loved that apartment and was lucky to have landed it. I'd learned from an initial phone call to the off-campus-housing office that I had some competition, so I'd resorted to the kind of tactics that drove me from Parliament Hill just to ensure I'd be the chosen tenant. I wasn't proud of my subterfuge, but I really wanted that boathouse.

My first step was to Google my prospective landlord. In a matter of minutes, I had learned that Angus McLintock was a widowed, 60-year-old mechanical-engineering professor. He'd written esoteric papers on affordable third-world water-filtration systems as well as a number of articles on innovative propulsion systems for small, recreational air-cushion vehicles, more commonly known as hovercraft. Interestingly, he had contributed a number of book reviews (mostly, on works of fiction) to the university newspaper and had even appeared once on a book panel on the local cable station. McLintock was no typical engineer. I also dug up a letter to the editor in the *Ottawa Citizen* wherein McLintock decried the decline of proper English usage in the newspaper and cited several recent heinous affronts to the language. Finally, on an obscure Ottawa-area chess-club Web site, I found a reference to his stellar play in an open tournament three years earlier. Beyond a passion for war on the battlefield of 64 squares, I could find nothing else about his personal life. He was an engineering, book-loving, chess-playing grammarian—a rare bird, indeed.

Twenty minutes later, I'd elevated my knowledge of hovercrafts from nothing to next to nothing, which I hoped was enough. I needed no remedial grammar work as I, too, was, and remain, a stickler for proper usage, courtesy of my father. Some people contend that the English language is a living, breathing organism wherein the definitions of words and rules should change to reflect their mass misuse. I contend that English is already an extraordinarily difficult language to teach. Monkeying with English to legitimize common errors would not make the language easier to learn and love. English should not stoop to embrace the lowest common denominator. Rather, society should step up and grant the language the respect and reverence it deserves.

Finally, I played several games of chess online to reacquaint myself with the ancient board game. I'd played a lot of chess in my youth. In fact, I was quite obsessed for several years. Chess can do that to you. In any event, I discovered to my satisfaction that I could still play without embarrassing myself. I felt ready for my interview with Angus McLintock, landlord in waiting. I love Google.

I showed up in his office on campus with the most recent issue of *Chess Life* magazine rolled up in my back pocket, the title conveniently facing out for the world to see. As I had planned, he didn't notice it until I was leaving the interview, and by that time, I figured I had it in the bag anyway.

Angus McLintock looked like the quintessential engineering professor—an archetype. A Scottish émigré, he was of middling height but solid build. His longish, wavy, grey hair was not burdened with a part, a style, or even the slightest trace of organization. His hair looked as though he'd gone to the Ontario Science Centre, put his hand on the Van de Graaff generator's shiny silver ball, shaken his head, and accepted the result as permanent. In succinct terms, his hair looked Einsteinian. Combined with his unruly grey beard, McLintock looked like a stunt double for Grizzly Adams. Something about him, however—perhaps his clear, blue eyes—betrayed deeper waters.

Angus McLintock was articulate, if a little gruff, and clearly took delight in the English language as his letter to the editor foreshadowed. Even though he'd been at U of O for the last 25 years, his Scottish brogue decisively won its daily battle with the dull, flat Canadian tongue.

In the interview, I talked about my faculty appointment in the English department. I mentioned that I was a nonsmoker and that I spent most evenings in the company of my beloved books. I mentioned, only in passing, that reading the newspaper daily had become a habit while on Parliament Hill though I lamented the sad decline in writing standards. With a deft push of his button, he was off. Fifteen minutes later, we were kindred spirits, united in the preservation of the English language. When he mentioned his interest in hovercrafts and told me he was actually building one on the ground floor of the boathouse, I casually offered, "Ah, Christopher Cockerell's contribution to the world." Home run.

Professor McLintock called back that night to give me the good news and let slip that he'd cancelled two interviews scheduled for the next day. Grand slam. I moved out of the Cumberland Motor Inn the next day.

Upon arrival at the boathouse, I carefully placed my newly purchased, wooden chess set on the coffee table. Anyone who carries *Chess Life* magazine around in his back pocket must have a board set up and ready to go. The classic Staunton-style pieces stood ready to advance. The set brought a welcome, old-world charm to the room. I was careful to orient the board appropriately with a white square in the bottom, right-hand corner. I'd seen too many movies, TV commercials, and magazine ads, featuring chess players deep in thought over boards set up incorrectly. Politics teaches you to sweat the small stuff.

I was still thinking about Muriel Parkinson. I looked forward to spending more time with her. She had seen it all during a period of unprecedented Liberal dominance and unparalleled change in Canada and the world. In the Liberal Party, and in society in general, we have a nasty tendency to cast older people aside and then to repeat their mistakes as if we're exploring uncharted waters. I made a pledge that night to plumb the depths of Muriel's knowledge as a way of inflicting historical perspective. While Parkinson's disease may have slowed her down physically, her intelligence, wit, and reasoning seemed undimmed. She also had a heart to balance her brain—my kind of Liberal. Unfortunately, she was not my candidate, but she was my kind of Liberal.

I put the twelve postdated rent cheques into an envelope and ambled up the slope to the McLintock house about 30 metres away. As I raised my hand to knock, I heard from behind the door a pseudohuman cry of anguish that seemed to cross an air-raid siren with a water buffalo in labour. My inner voice suggested a hasty retreat, but curiosity mugged my better judgment, and I rapped on the door. I heard Angus McLintock's footfalls charging from within, and far too soon for me, the door opened with considerable violence. Note to self: Next time, listen to inner voice, idiot.

CHAPTER TWO

"Whaaaaaaaaat!" Angus McLintock screamed as he materialized in the doorway, intimidation incarnate.

"Er, hello, Professor, sorry to bother you, but I … I just wanted to give you my rent cheques for the year if I … I'm not catching you at a bad time," I stammered, wishing I were at the dentist's on the wrong end of a root canal.

In his right hand, I saw a crumpled letter on university letterhead that I reckoned had prompted his meltdown. His knuckles were white and his face, well, it was almost purple. The folks at Crayola might have called it "Violent Violet."

"I'm happy to come back later," I persevered. Perhaps, much later. He took a moment to collect himself and dialed back his facial hue to "Crazed Crimson."

Through grinding teeth, Angus grunted, "You're lucky you're not the dean of engineerin' or you'd not still be standin'." He paused as if deciding what to do and then continued.

"You might as well come in and sit down. I could use the distraction." With that, he turned and stomped down the hallway as expletives ricocheted off the walls.

I entered the house like James Bond infiltrating Blofeld's lair—minus the tuxedo and shapely accomplice. I found him flopped on a fluffy chintz couch, hands on forehead, with his eyes—no, it was really his whole face—clenched. The mangled letter, finally free from his choke hold, convalesced on the coffee table. I placed the envelope of rent cheques next to it and confirmed that the letter was from the dean of engineering. On the couch, Angus sustained a quiet, baritone moan.

I looked around the room as I settled into a matching armchair across from my supine landlord. I saw bookshelves with standing room only on opposite sides of the room and a large bay window, opening onto the river. Hardwood floors gleamed. A vintage single malt stood guard over two glass tumblers on top of a small, oak liquor cabinet in the corner. I noticed that an antique chess table with a game in progress was framed in the bay window with two rather uncomfortable looking, arrow-back chairs.

The interior architecture was open concept, so the living room bled into the dining area, which featured a small fireplace, an antique harvest table and eight chairs, a modest chandelier, and a couple of landscape paintings on the pale yellow walls. I couldn't see the kitchen from my perch but assumed it was off the dining room. I wanted a look at his books, but that would have to wait.

His face-clenching and low moaning abated. I would like to have used the word *stopped* but *abated* was regrettably more accurate. Social convention compelled me to say something as several minutes had elapsed since I'd sat down.

"Are you feeling all right? Can I get you a glass of water or something?" I offered.

"Water won't cure what's ailin' me. But three fingers of Lagavulin would be a start."

I wasn't much of a drinker, but my father's dedicated exploration of single malts made Lagavulin a familiar name. Pleased to have something to do that took me a little farther away from him, I poured a generous portion of the peaty-scented scotch and placed the glass within his reach on the coffee table. I waited until he'd taken a few swigs to take off the edge before I lifted my head above the trench.

"Did you just receive some bad news?" I said, gesturing to the letter. He fixed me with a steely gaze as if contemplating bringing me into his circle.

"You're a young English professor. Have you ever taught English to engineers?" he asked.

"Never. The closest I've ever come to engineering students was when a group of them swarmed me one day early in my freshman year. Apparently, I had set off some kind of artsy alarm by walking too close to the metal lab," I replied with little or no thought. "Ah, no offence," I blurted.

To his credit (and my good fortune), he seemed nonplussed by my moronic response. In fact, he was looking at the ceiling and almost seemed to be somewhere else at the time. He turned his head so that I was again in his field of view.

"Every five years or so, I'm sentenced to a term of teachin' introductory English to first-year engineers. I did it last year, and it near finished me. What sustained me through the unbounded ignorance of me young charges was the knowledge that I'd never have to do it again. By the time me number was to come up again, I'd be retired."

"Surely, it can't be that bad."

"For a man of letters, it's utter torture!" he spat. I thought he was a man of wrenches. But putting this conversation together with Google's biographical offerings, I clearly saw that Professor Angus McLintock was one of a rare breed of

Renaissance engineers who actually read outside of his field. "These kids are so fixated on engineerin', beer, and nurses that they wouldn't know literature if they threw up on it. Their idea of a pleasin' read is *Kinematics and Dynamics of Planar Machinery*. Such myopia I cannot again endure. I cannae do it again. I won't."

"But you did it last year. Are you not off the hook for a few more years?" I inquired.

"I was until that infernal missive arrived." With purpose, he extended his middle finger towards the letter. "A bizarre confluence of life-threatenin' illnesses, ill-timed sabbaticals, and retirements in our department has put me very firmly back on the hook," he moaned. "I cannae do it again. I just cannae."

I feared we were seconds away from a crying jag. "Just your luck that you didn't contract a life-threatening illness." Had I actually expressed that last thought out loud? Think, then speak.

His icy stare was remarkably intimidating, but eventually, his face softened to an almost plaintive countenance. For the second time that day, I felt the need to change the subject. I stood up to eye the books on the east side of the room. The six-shelf bookcase harboured what looked to my amateur eyes to be a rather comprehensive collection of feminist theory, literature, and criticism, both popular and academic. Betty Freidan, Susan Brownmiller, Kate Millet, Simone de Beauvoir, Gloria Steinem, Andrea Dworkin, and many others in the pantheon of the women's movement, were all represented. I even saw what looked like a first edition of John Stuart Mill's *The Subjection of Women*. The entire bottom shelf showcased the dozen or so books of Marin Lee, including, coincidently, the classic I'd seen in Muriel Parkinson's lap earlier that morning. I was puzzled, which is not an infrequent condition for me.

"Impressive collection. I didn't think engineers were allowed to have feminist literature." Out loud again. Clearly that whole "think before you speak" mantra really wasn't working for me that night.

"Kind of you to promulgate a popular but not universally valid stereotype," he intoned, eyes closed, from his horizontal position of authority on the couch.

I winced. Damage report, Mr. Scott. "I apologize. I simply meant that engineering students have a very onerous course load with few academic opportunities to expose themselves to more enlightened and progressive social attitudes."

He smiled. He actually smiled. Then, he chuckled; at least, that's what it sounded like. With his brow at last furrow-free, he took on a completely different appearance.

"A clunky but well-meanin' recovery, Dr. Addison, but you should choose yer words more carefully. No one in their right mind when talkin' about engineering students would use the phrase 'expose themselves.' It strikes a wee bit too close to home." He took a long draw on the Lagavulin then continued in a more sober vein.

"The books you're lookin' at belonged to me wife. She succumbed four months ago to breast cancer."

"I'm so sorry. I knew you were widowed but had no idea it was so recent," I said, hoping I sounded as sympathetic as I felt. "It must still be a very difficult time."

"Aye, it is and I fear always will be," he conceded.

The conversation was losing altitude fast. I thought another abrupt topic change would be inappropriate, so I tried at least to ease back on the stick and slow our descent. "I see she was a fan of Marin Lee." I motioned towards the shelf full of her works.

Angus smiled. "Yes, me wife seemed to agree with everythin' she said and wrote."

"I actually heard Marin Lee speak at a student conference," I babbled. "She certainly made a compelling case for equality. And she graciously signed my copy of her last book." I watched the ground racing up to meet me.

"She would be pleased to know that a fan was livin' in the boathouse," he concluded.

On instinct, I nodded in sympathy and then proceeded to process his last sentence. I hit Rewind and played back his comment. It still seemed like a non sequitur to me.

"Sorry?" was all I could manage. His smile then turned wistful.

"I was married to Marin Lee, and she loved that boathouse. You're lookin at her bookcase. Mine is over here," he said, pointing.

I was thunderstruck. Stunned into silence, I searched for a thoughtful and respectful response. I found it but, instead, went with, "No shit! That's amazing!" Damn.

"Yes, Dr. Addison, it was—for nearly four decades."

I was relieved that he seemed almost chuffed by my reflexive enthusiasm. "Forgive me, I just had no idea. I'm very sorry for your loss. She was a remarkable woman, who made an enormous contribution," I said with due reverence, enunciating as well as I could around the foot lodged in my throat.

"Kind of you to say." Angus seemed to be enjoying my discomfort yet, at the same time, seemed clearly pleased that I was familiar with his wife's work. Most men weren't. Eventually, he showed mercy.

"Dr. Addison, enough of this depressin' talk. I propose the tonic of chess." At that moment, I would have given him a foot rub had he asked, so playing chess seemed like a big win to me.

We sat down at the chess table. Angus shuffled one black and one white pawn under the table and presented me with two clenched fists. I chose his left and was handed the white pawn. I opted for the standard Bobby Fischer opening (e2-e4), moving my king pawn up two squares. Angus responded with c7-c5, and we were off with the standard Sicilian defence. I won't bore you with a move-by-move analysis of my expedient demise though it wouldn't take long. Let's just say I was clobbered and leave it at that. Actually, by the third game, I was holding my own, and we stalemated the fourth (which I considered a well-earned victory under the circumstances). I seemed to pass this initial test as there was talk of future matches.

I was reasonably pleased with my performance on the board after a slow and embarrassing beginning. I was, and still am, quite capable of stringing together several solid moves in something resembling a strategy before executing a spectacular blunder and losing my queen. But there's nothing like playing a superior opponent to elevate your own game. We talked about chess for quite awhile after we finished playing. Angus spoke in hushed and reverential tones. He'd been bitten by the chess bug at the age of 12 and had played ever since. The advent of Internet chess had resolved a perennial problem for the avid player—lack of opponents.

"I've played over 500 games of chess online in the last four months," said Angus. "Modesty aside, I think the concentrated game time has made me as good as I've ever been. But it certainly was refreshin' to have an adversary before me in the flesh. Chess is a mind game, and it's hard to read yer opponent through cyberspace."

"Delighted to be your punching bag," I replied, hoping to shift the focus away from my lacklustre play. Angus had a different view. He was not yet finished with the postgame show though I was certainly ready to roll the credits.

"In that last game, you brought yer queen out too early, you crippled yer pawns, you marooned yer knights on the edges, you castled too late, and you split an infinitive when I took yer bishop. Other than that, you were flawless," he decreed.

"Thanks, I think. I'm a little out of practice. Give me a couple of days, and we'll line them up again."

"Aye, we will," he concluded.

Now done, Angus hoisted himself from the board and left the room to write out a receipt for my rent cheques. While he was gone, I headed over to his bookcase. You can learn a lot about people from their books. The overflowing shelves confirmed that this engineer was cut from a different cloth. Yes, he had science and engineering books, many of them on the topics of fluid mechanics, thermodynamics, and something called finite element analysis—whatever that is. But he also had many more volumes from many more fields—philosophy, history, art, politics, and an excellent complement of novels from around the world. Easily a better collection than mine. I also saw a special shelf dedicated to Alexander Graham Bell. The library of Angus McLintock revealed a man of culture, science, intelligence, and sensitivity with an enlightened world view. At that moment, an earthshaking fart, long, loud, and almost melodic, ripped through the house. On instinct, I buried my nose inside the neck of my shirt. Angus didn't just break wind, he tortured it first.

"Blast that damn turnip! I'm swearin' off it!" Angus offered from two rooms away. *Blast*, indeed, seemed the appropriate term.

When Angus eventually returned to the living room, my rent receipt in hand, I saw his eyes fall again on the coffee table and the letter bomb that had detonated an hour and a half earlier. He looked as though he had completely forgotten about it and was now seeing it for the first time. He stopped short and groaned. I watched him slide back down into his couch and his blue funk. "There's not much I wouldna do to let this vile cup pass me by," he breathed in a voice so low I barely heard it.

Idea approaching at ramming speed. I don't know why I didn't think of it before. It all came to me in a matter of moments. It seemed fated. I don't even remember how I broached it with Angus, but I knew that if my idea were to fly, I had to move quickly. I didn't know how long his descent into the depths of despair would last. The man was desperate, and so was I.

Within 20 minutes, the deal was done. Pending the university's approval, I had an extra class on my teaching schedule, to which I gave barely a thought that night. More importantly to me, Cumberland-Prescott finally had a Liberal candidate—at least in name—no doubt to become yet another forgotten footnote in the political history of the safest Tory seat in the land.

Angus McLintock was a tough negotiator, and with three days until the gun would sound, I wasn't exactly in a strong bargaining position. Secure in the knowledge that a Liberal could never win this riding, Angus agreed to let his name stand with the following stipulations:

- He would make no campaign appearances.

- He would do no media interviews.

- He would do no door-to-door canvassing.

- He would attend no all-candidates meetings, debates, information sessions, coffee parties, or individual voter meetings.

- He would take no phone calls from anyone other than me.

- There would be no Angus McLintock lawn signs.

- There would be no Angus McLintock campaign Web site, blog, or podcasts.

- There would be no Angus McLintock campaign song (I just threw this in as a freebie to soften him up. I had no plans for a campaign song, anyway—just good, old-fashioned, shrewd bargaining).

- He would have no contact with the campaign workers (either of them).

- Finally, he would not even be required to be in the country, let alone in the riding throughout the campaign.

In other words, he had to do absolutely nothing, diddly-squat, nada—other than sign his nomination form to put his name on the ballot. But rest assured, this was not a lopsided, one-way negotiation. No, siree. He gave up stuff, too. Here's what I negotiated:

- We could produce one inane pamphlet for soft-drops.

Yes, I know. It was hardly worth a bullet point. Finally, Angus did accept that while defeat was assured, we needed to preserve at least the pretence of an active campaign. Or as my former colleagues on Parliament Hill might have put it, we needed to ensure the "optics" were good. I, at least, owed my party good optics.

We signed the napkin on which I'd written up our little agreement and shook hands to etch it in stone. Though poker-faced during the negotiations, Angus looked ecstatic now that the deal was done. He kept walking around, saying, "I cannae believe this is happening. Free at last, free at last, thank God almighty, I'm free at last." Or words to that effect. To my chiropractor's great disappointment, Angus stopped just short of locking me in a bear hug and waltzing me around the room. I managed to maintain a calm and dignified demeanor befitting a junior faculty member and limited myself to two loud "woo-hoos" and a little end-zone touchdown dance of my own creation—win-win personified.

After three games of chess and the excitement of the deal, I was exhausted. The events of the evening seemed to have the opposite effect on Angus. He continued to pinball around the room, sporting a face-fracturing grin that was clearly beyond his control.

Eventually, Angus walked me down to the boathouse in the dark to spend some time in his workshop. More accurately, I floated half asleep, and Angus jitterbugged down to the boathouse, the two of us united in relief. He slipped the key into the ground-level door and waved me inside. I would much rather have climbed upstairs to bed, but he would not be denied. He turned on the light, and I stuck my head in. The skeleton of what I assumed to be the hovercraft—but to my untrained eye looked to be a boat—rested on two sawhorses in the middle of the room. Two large doors formed the north wall and obviously opened onto the river. A workbench, with what looked to me like tools of some kind strewn on it, stretched along the western wall.

It's probably worth noting that I'm not exactly what you'd call a handyman. For instance, four years earlier, I'd won a fancy, chrome-and-steel gas barbecue at a charity golf tournament. The barbecue required assembly. I gamely tried my hand at putting it together and worked steadily at it for my entire two-week summer vacation. In the end, it never became the barbecue pictured on the side of the box. In fact, when I gave up, it looked more like a miniature Frank Gehry opera house. I was left holding a bag with 37 forgotten parts, some of which I figured must be important. I let the good folks at the Salvation Army figure it out and have since limited my do-it-yourself projects to replacing lightbulbs and setting up the card table, which I can now do inside of 14 minutes (though I need assistance putting it away). I'm still several years away from venturing anywhere near IKEA.

Along the back wall, I saw a small desk, on which lay a large, brown, leather-bound notebook, open to what I assumed were the personal scrawlings of Angus McLintock. A battered, wooden stool rested on the floor beneath. He discreetly closed the notebook and slid it into the top drawer. A small gas furnace squatted in the southeast corner with ducts heading up to my apartment. Two smallish windows in the east wall and four bright lights, suspended from the ceiling, completed the functional and cheerful workspace.

I looked for a long time at what Angus had been building, trying like hell to divine which end was up. I also fought valiantly to keep my eyes open. Lateral ribs stretched across the vessel at two foot intervals, leaving only an open compartment in the middle that I took to be the cockpit (if *cockpit* is the right term in a hovercraft). Plywood covered the bottom as well as parts of the upper surface of the craft. An engine of some kind was positioned just behind the cockpit on a raised mounting bracket of some kind. I could see a fan housed in a duct beneath it. Two vents, open at either end, ran longitudinally from stem to stern on either side of the hovercraft and seemed to open into the middle of the chamber immediately beneath the engine and fan. I noticed twin vanes in both ends of the two longitudinal vents, which, I assumed, were there for directional control. A rubber material had been sewn and attached to the periphery of the vehicle, making it look a little like a deflated Zodiac boat minus the Greenpeace activists.

"I'm glad that you know something about hovercrafts. So few do," Angus remarked as he rested his considerable keister on the edge of the workbench.

My 20 minutes of Internet research on hovercrafts had fed me the Christopher Cockerell card (which, at that moment, I regretted playing) but in no way equipped me with even the slightest idea of what I was looking at. Nevertheless, I stepped closer and feigned unparalleled interest, running my hand along the smooth plywood decking and battling the urge to sleep.

"So this is it?" I said as I eyed the half-finished craft but visualized my bed.

"Aye." Long pause.

I yawned towards the engine. "And this would be the motor, no doubt."

"Aye." He was smiling now.

"I see." I nodded and pursed my lips in a gesture of understanding. Angus just let me twist. After a few minutes of this, he must have grown bored.

"You have absolutely no idea what you're lookin' at, have you," Angus declared, the second and third tumblers of Lagavulin taking their toll on his enunciation.

"Absolutely none," I quickly conceded, relieved to be put out of my misery. I was exposed, but nothing could dampen his mood.

"It's actually very simple," Angus explained. "Simplicity is one of the hovercraft's primary assets. Whether it's cars or boats or bicycles, friction is the arch enemy of efficiency and locomotion. The greatest friction of all is that which exists between the vehicle and surface on which it is movin'. Hovercrafts virtually eliminate this friction by supportin' the vehicle on a cushion of air."

I was exhausted. I was struggling. I was halfway to coma town.

"Hovercrafts are really aircraft that fly just above the earth, benefitin' from what we call the ground effect," he mercifully concluded.

I had to hold my end up. It was the only honourable thing to do. I stumbled back into the fray. "Does your hovercraft do anything differently?" I asked. "Are there any advancements or noteworthy innovations?"

"Kind of you to ask. Yes, there are two principal innovations staring you in the face. First of all, most small hovercrafts are powered by two engines. One for lift, stationed at the front, and one for thrust, positioned at the back. Two engines mean twice the noise, twice the likelihood of breakdown, and with two propellers fore and aft of the driver, twice the danger."

How absolutely riveting. Drifting … drifting, I could no longer feel my legs.

"Are you still with me, Dr. Addison?"

My eyelids had drooped, so I reached down to inspect the bottom of the craft as if I'd been concentrating on it while Angus had been spouting off.

"Of course," I countered with only a hint of resentment, "I'm just checking out the finish."

"That shouldn't take long. There is no finish, yet." Angus barreled ahead. "This hovercraft is a single-engine design wherein both the lift and the thrust are supplied by a single multi-wing fan," he droned.

By that time, I had a pretty good idea of what it must be like to live with narcolepsy.

"Secondly—"

Oh, sweet mother of mercy, he was only halfway home. I nodded mechanically.

"Controllin' and stoppin' hovercrafts have always been difficult as there is no contact with the ground when you really need the friction. These twin vents provide more precise steerin' and better braking as I can direct the thrust totally frontwards or through just one side vent or the other. I can even apply forward thrust through the port vent and reverse thrust through the starboard vent at the same time and rotate the hovercraft about its axis while stationary."

I'll alert the media. I gave silent thanks that Angus had only two major advancements to describe. If he'd been any more innovative, I'd have been out on my feet. I sidled towards the door. Casual. "How long have you been working on this?" I thought this was an innocent enough question, carefully designed to elicit an answer I could understand without a master's in engineering. I also thought his response might get me to the door without dragging on too long.

"I've had it on the drawin' board for years but only started to build it about four months ago—shortly after Marin passed on." He looked at his feet briefly before returning to the present. "Anyway, I figured if me hammerin' and sawin' are goin' to keep you awake from time to time, at least you should know what's takin' shape below you."

Hammering and sawing my left knee wouldn't have kept me awake that night. I took that as my cue to leave him. I shook his hand and thanked him for the chess and for showing me his hovercraft. I ascended the outside staircase to my apartment above.

As sometimes happened to me, by the time I'd shed my clothes and crawled between the sheets, I was still bone tired but no longer sleepy. I opened Stephen Fry's *The Hippopotamus*, which was always good for a late-night laugh, but couldn't focus on the novel. Stephen Fry requires concentration, and I had none at my disposal. My mind, or what was left of it, kept returning to the night's developments and how much closer I was to extricating myself from the clutches of politics. Yes, Angus McLintock drove a hard bargain, but at that late date, not to mention hour, I really didn't care. I was saved. I had actually found a Liberal candidate. In Cumberland-Prescott, we Liberals calibrate success in very small increments.

Through the air vents, I could hear Angus working away and talking though I was certain he was still alone. I turned out my light, surrendered to the fatigue, and eventually, drifted off to what I could have sworn was the sound of weeping beneath me.

◆   ◆   ◆

Diary
Monday, September 2

My Love,

I have been delivered from hellfire and damnation by a most unlikely angel. You'll know if you've been near that Dean Rump Roast once again had me in his crosshairs to teach E for E again this term even though I'd suffered through it this past year. When I read the letter, I truly contemplated early retirement, that is, after ruling out homicide (I doubt any fair-minded jury would have convicted me) and then suicide. Rumplun is an asshole, plain and simple. Aye, he is.

Just when the black clouds threatened to envelope me completely, Dr. Addison, the young politico turned English professor now living in your boathouse, alighted in our living room and delivered me. I will never again teach the wonders of English to first-year Cro-Magnon engineers. However, in quid pro quo, your dear husband's name will appear on the ballot in the upcoming federal election as the officially nominated Liberal candidate. I can hear your unbridled laugh from here. I know it's incredible and incongruous but no more so than expecting me to spend another year babysitting illiterate engineers who think Robertson Davies is a Toronto law firm. Dr. Addison promises me that a Liberal simply cannot win this seat, so in five weeks, I'm scot-free or, a free Scott, as the case may be. Do not trouble yourself. I know what I'm doing. And more importantly, I know what I won't be doing for three hours every week in the main auditorium of the engineering building. Forgive my hand; my feet are dancing a quick highland reel as I write these words.

Baddeck 1 is progressing nicely and taking shape. I knew that if I could just get started on the infernal thing, the work would sustain me. And it has. The skirt is attached, the engine is mounted, and the integrated lift/propulsion system is nearly complete. I need to finish the plywood decking and then set to work on the cockpit controls. I haven't quite figured out how to connect all four rudders to the steering system and whether I'll go with a wheel or a stick. I'm tending towards a wheel.

As I work on the hovercraft in this boathouse, I think often of Bell in his workshop on the shores of the Bras d'Or Lakes as he built his record-breaking hydrofoil. What a man was he. He was driven by a curiosity so fierce it could barely be contained and never ever extinguished. It still burns in those who follow.

Tomorrow, I'll hold my nose and take young Dr. Addison—Daniel is his Christian name—to meet the dean if I can keep my breakfast where it belongs. There is paperwork the dean must attend to if I'm to slip the E for E noose. I won't hesitate to invoke Montebello if required. Daniel seems a good lad. Beneath some rust, his chess game is adequate and likely to improve. His experience on Parliament Hill should serve him well in navigating the shoal-infested waters of the university.

By God, I miss you. Every day, I expect to turn the corner and find you in the garden. Every day, I expect this great hole inside me to get just a little bit smaller. Every day, it seems to grow. By God, I miss you.

AM

CHAPTER THREE

At ten o'clock the next morning, Angus and I entered the office of the aptly named Roland Rumplun, dean of engineering. It took about 30 seconds to appreciate the contempt in which Angus held him. What a grade A, 100 percent pure, no preservatives added, free-range prick. I detest that word and reserve it for a precious few. Rumplun had earned it in record time. Angus had warned me that Rumplun had been born with a severe mirth defect; the long-term effects were obvious.

"Yes, Angus, please come in," Rumplun said. "Can we please keep it brief? I'm due in the president's office shortly. He's asked me for my advice on a rather tricky little matter." I lost sight of him briefly until the pomposity dissipated. Angus ushered me in and made a show of closing the door with great deliberation.

"Good mornin', Roland. I do hope yer hemorrhoids aren't too inflamed these days," replied Angus with an utterly straight face. Both Dean Rumplun and I winced, I assumed for different reasons.

"You can stow the adolescent insults, McLintock. Just sit down and tell me why you're here. I'm very busy. And who is this?" The dean jabbed a finger in my direction. Angus stood beside me and gestured like Vanna White showcasing parting gifts.

"I give you Professor Daniel Addison, faculty of arts, English department, and a specialist in teachin' English to Neanderthals." I flashed a sheepish smile and offered my hand. Rumplun ignored it and looked puzzled, instead. I sat down in one of the two rather low chairs positioned in front of his raised power-play desk.

"Just get to the point."

Angus sat down, awash in congeniality, and lifted his smiling face to the dean. "Yesterday, I received yer poison-pen letter, throwin' me to the wolves again even though I taught English for Engineers last year. You know how much I despise teachin' that course; yet, you could arrive at no solution other than to dump it on me again," Angus said in a quiet and measured voice.

"I had no choice, and you know it," Rumplun said. "Baxter is in chemo, Shamadri is on sabbatical, and we've just put Hollingsworth out to pasture. You're the only one left who knows anything about English." He smirked. "Look,

Angus, let's cut the crap. I don't like you. I never have. A lot has happened between you and I over the years—"

"Me," interrupted Angus.

"What?" said the dean in a hissing tone.

"You meant to say a lot has happened between you and *me*, not you and *I*. Carry on," Angus invited.

The warning light on Rumplun's head gasket seemed to flicker on. "Don't you correct me in my office. I'm fed up with your incessant pedantry. You're nothing but a grammar-Nazi," Rumplun grunted through gritted teeth.

"But, Roland, I only correct you when you make a mistake, so the frequency is really up to you. In any event, you're single-handedly justifyin' the need to teach English to engineers." The smirk had emigrated from Dean Rumplun to Angus.

"I'm running out of time, McLintock. State your business."

"Professor Addison here has kindly agreed to teach E for E in me stead, and I'm just offerin' you the courtesy of meetin' him before you file the necessary paperwork to make it so," Angus explained, the very embodiment of equanimity.

"What audacity!" Rumplun sputtered. "It's impossible. Absolutely not. I will not have it. The course must be taught by an engineer, and that means you, McLintock."

I just sat there in the middle of the bellicose exchange and shifted as necessary to evade projectile spittle. I worried that this buffoon might put the kibosh on my bargain with Angus.

"Daniel is a first-rate lecturer, understands his audience, and will get all the support he needs from me," Angus replied.

"I don't care if he has a Nobel Prize; it's out of the question. Don't even think about it. End of story. Now, I'm nearly late, so if you'll excuse me."

Angus paused and looked to the ground as if deciding how to proceed. Then, he looked out the window with a distant look in his eyes. "Montebello," Angus said in a voice so low I barely heard it.

"What did you say?" Dean Rumplun spat. His face turned the colour of rust, and his jowls vibrated. I wondered what an aneurism looked like.

"You heard me. You've left me no choice," said Angus. His eyes were two slits trained on his adversary.

"You wouldn't dare!"

"Just sign the faculty-transfer form, and you'll never have to find out," concluded Angus the ice man.

For what seemed like minutes, they stared each other down through tension so thick it would have snapped the knife.

"You are a bastard, McLintock. And after all I've done for you. Who got you your appointment in the first place? It was me!" Rumplun shouted.

"It was I," whispered Angus as he smoothed a wrinkle in his pants.

"What!"

"A copula verb takes a subjective completion. It was *I*, not it was *me*. You might want to audit Daniel's course." Angus rose, and I followed suit, in awe of the master.

"Get out this instant before I phone security. Calling you a bastard is a high compliment you're unworthy of."

"Of which you're unworthy. All right, all right, we're goin', we're goin'. A pleasure as always, hemorr-Roland," Angus soothed over his shoulder as we hustled out just ahead of the slamming door.

The campus looked beautiful in the dappled light of a second consecutive sunny day. Angus said nothing as we left the building but whistled as we walked. I think the tune was "Zip-A-Dee-Doo-Dah" but, then again, it might have been "Onward Christian Soldiers." Music was not his gift.

The suspense was killing me. "Okay, spill the goods on Montebello," I implored. He was silent for a moment, pondering, which I much preferred over his atonal whistling.

"It's a private and delicate matter involvin' documented academic dishonesty at a major scientific conference at Montebello. Discretion prevents me from identifying the perpetrator, but his initials are Roland 'the rumphole' Rumplun."

"You mean you caught him plagiarizing a scientific paper?"

"Worse. I caught him claimin' credit for research he did not undertake, theories he did not conceive, and a paper he did not write," Angus intoned.

"That is a serious accusation. Why didn't you take it through the formal channels and have him drummed out of the university?" I asked.

"It wasn't worth it to me then. Instead, I confronted him. He denied it until I showed him the evidence. He then broke down. At the time, I felt a pang of sympathy, so I pursued it no further. But I did keep the evidence. I dust it off every ten years or so when it's important," Angus replied.

"Like today, for instance," I suggested.

"Aye, like today."

"What arrogance," I observed.

"Aye, he's always suffered with a self-esteem problem," Angus noted.

"Self-esteem problem?"

"Aye, he has too much," Angus explained. We walked on in silence for a moment or two.

"So do you think he's going to sign the form and let me take your class?"

"I have no doubt the deed was just done. The class is yours. All yours."

Later that day, I received an e-mail from the Faculty of Engineering, confirming that I was, indeed, teaching English for Engineers. I thought I'd better check with Professor Gannon to make sure I wasn't violating some obscure regulation by having an engineering course on my teaching schedule. When I reached him, he already knew about it, having received the faculty-transfer form from Rumplun's office. Very efficient. The power of Montebello. There was no problem beyond a concern he expressed that I might be dulling my intellectual acuity by fraternizing with lower life forms. The arts-engineering enmity was not confined to the undergraduate population.

That evening, I drove back to the Riverfront Seniors' Residence to confer with Muriel. I had in my hand the official Elections Canada nomination form, completed and signed by one Duncan Angus McLintock. With a candidate locked up, Muriel greeted me with a warmth and an enthusiasm that were in stark contrast to the reception I'd received the day before.

"Daniel, congratulations! I knew you could do it!" she said as I joined her on the shiny, slippery couch that looked out over the river. The evening was beautiful, and the sun had begun its descent off to our left. A couple of boats puttered up the river, and a lone windsurfer leaned into the breeze as he cut across the water. She gave my hand a squeeze as I sank in beside her. I felt like we'd been friends for years.

"Hello, Muriel. Yes, I'm certainly feeling better today than I was yesterday. Wow, that's some view you have," I said, taking in the scene.

"Trust me," she replied, "it gets old fast. So don't make me wait any longer. Who won the great Cumberland-Prescott Liberal Candidate Sweepstakes?"

I beamed and held up the envelope. "And the winner is," I announced with theatric flair as I slipped out the nomination form. "Dr. Angus McLintock, a stoic Scot of an engineering professor who kind of looks like Karl Marx." That got her attention.

"That's odd," she said. "I thought I knew all of the Liberals in Cumberland, and I've never heard of him."

"Well, to be frank, I'm not certain he is a Liberal. But I am sure that this is his signature on the bottom of this nomination form, and with three days before the writ drops, that's what really counts," I gushed, hoping Muriel would get on board. She looked noncommittal. I continued, saying, "Muriel, he's a nice guy, a smart guy, and he's prepared to have his name stand to help the party." I hesitated but then decided to bring her into the tent where I needed her. "He won't exactly participate actively in the campaign, but we're still going to hit the hustings as if he's right there with us. I can make this work, and nobody will be the wiser."

"Did you save his life or something? What's in it for him?" she asked.

"Why he agreed is not important. What is important is we've got a candidate, and we'll have a campaign ... of sorts."

She persisted. "How are you going to manage the canvassing, the all-candidates meetings, the media interviews, and the rallies if you don't have a candidate in the flesh?"

"I've got it all covered, Muriel, but it simply won't work if you're not with me on this. I need your local knowledge and your experience if we're going to pull this off." She looked out over the river. "Muriel, Angus is a real character. He's thoughtful, intelligent, and very funny. He's also going through a rough time personally, and I really think this campaign might be just the distraction he needs. You see, his wife of 40 years died at the beginning of May. On the surface, he seems to be handling it as well as can be expected, but beneath the veneer, I can see he's still in a great deal of pain." Her eyes softened though they were still on the water. I paused for effect before delivering the coup de grâce. "I discovered quite by accident that his wife was Marin Lee." I gazed out over the white-capped river and waited.

I could feel her turn and look at me. "*The* Marin Lee?"

"None other," I whispered. "Muriel, even though the terms of his candidacy are somewhat ... er ... irregular, he has a good heart, and he's agreed to stand. Unless you or I are prepared to run, his name is all we've got, and time is nipping at our heels." I took her hand, rearranged my face, and gave her the most pathetic visage imaginable. "Will you help us?"

Ten minutes later, she signed the nomination form as the only existing executive member of the Cumberland-Prescott Liberal Association. Then, she swept through the games room where gin rummy duked it out with canasta for supremacy. Her next stop was the large activity room where half the residents were shuffling through a line-dancing lesson. The singer's voice blasting from the stereo sounded inhumanly low. Darth Vader swinging a lariat sprung to mind though I wish it hadn't. I soon realized the instructor had slowed the CD down to one-third speed so her geriatric dancers could actually complete the steps in time with the song. After a final stop in the third-floor TV lounge where the old and the rested watched "The Young and the Restless," Muriel reappeared with the 100 signatures required to complete the nomination. We had liftoff.

She then gave me a thorough briefing on the state of the association's election war chest. In other words, she handed me a tired and tattered bankbook, showing a balance of $157.23. Excellent. That wouldn't even cover photocopying and file folders, let alone rent and telephone. I knew that filling the Liberal coffers in this community would not be easy. In fact, in Cumberland, we had a better chance of sighting Bigfoot than finding Liberal money. With no money, the McLintock campaign would be built on creativity, ingenuity, and parsimony—befitting, I suppose, a Scottish candidate. An idea for a low-cost campaign headquarters emerged from the fog in my head.

While getting around was difficult, Muriel did have time on her hands. I still had my cell phone from the Leader's office and had negotiated some extra time before I had to return it. It would be our official, campaign-office phone number. I handed it to Muriel. She agreed to carry the campaign phone at least until we secured our headquarters. We agreed to meet the following evening—along with any volunteers I could muster—for our first campaign meeting. I hoped to have reached a decision on our campaign office by then.

As I stood up to leave, I noticed a young and attractive woman making her way through the room, exchanging hellos with the women and laughing with the men as she parried their advances. I could see why her arrival caused a stir. She had very short, sandy hair, framing a face blessed with symmetry, lovely green eyes, and a memorable mouth. For some reason, I'd always had a weakness for women with short hair. I really hoped it wasn't because my late mother had always worn her hair short (paging Dr. Freud). Anyway, as I followed her runner's body and her dancer's gait, it was clear she was accustomed to the attention and not bothered in the least. She wore those new low-rider jeans, a man's white, button-down, oxford-cloth shirt—untucked—sandals, and funky sunglasses, resting just above her forehead. I pegged her at about 28 years old. She sported no eyebrow rings, no tongue stud, and no tattoos, at least that I could see. She stopped in front of us, cradling a cribbage board in the crook of her arm.

"Hey, Grandma, sorry I'm late. I got hung up after class."

"Hello, Lindsay, dear. Whenever you arrive is the right time for me," Muriel answered. "I'd like you to meet Professor Daniel Addison. He's just started in the English department at U of O. He's also the Liberal campaign manager for Cumberland-Prescott. Daniel, this is my granddaughter, Lindsay Dewar," Muriel concluded with a sweep of her hand.

"Hello, Lindsay. Very pleased to meet any relative of Muriel's."

"Hi, Daniel, I've heard a lot about you," Lindsay said with a grin.

I looked at Muriel for signs of a conspiracy but could detect none.

"Don't look at me; I've never mentioned your name," Muriel replied with her hands raised in surrender.

Lindsay jumped in. "Jasper over there just told me all about your double-twisting gainer on the sidewalk yesterday," she ribbed. The old man, still in his peach safari suit, bowed slightly when I looked over. I wondered who within the Cumberland town limits had not yet had a laugh at my expense. "You sure made a splash with this crowd," she chirped.

"Well, it was more like a splashdown. But thank you for keeping the story alive. I was beginning to think my 15 minutes were up already."

She laughed. I laughed. Muriel laughed.

"Lindsay is halfway through her master's degree in political science. She's researching the role of the Senate," Muriel remarked.

"Oh, don't tell me; you're advocating an elected Senate," I suggested, trying to hide the skepticism from my voice.

She laughed again. "Nope, I think I'm the only one around who still believes in appointing the chamber of sober second thought. I've never been a fan of creating another House of Commons. One is quite enough," Lindsay said.

"Well, Ms. Dewar, then, we have something in common. I'm actually a big fan of the Senate just the way it is. It does some very good committee work that never gets enough air time," I offered. I think I caught her off guard. Recovering, she seemed pleased with my response; hence, I was pleased.

Muriel interrupted our mutual admiration society. "Lindsay, dear, what I neglected to tell you was that Daniel recently left Parliament Hill where he worked in the Leader's office for several years."

"Ah, so you've been paroled," Lindsay joked.

"Yes, in a manner of speaking, I have. But my debt to society will not be fully paid until after this election." It was time to go before I said something to threaten the reasonably good first impression I thought I'd left. Anyway, I needed to sit down with Angus to be briefed for my first class with the engineering frosh. I gathered the nomination forms from Muriel and offered my hand to Lindsay. "Well, I'll leave you two to your cribbage. Be gentle with her, Muriel. It was really great to meet you, Lindsay, and I hope Liberal tendencies run in your family. We could sure use the help on the campaign. Muriel, I'll pick you up tomorrow night at seven o'clock. We'll check out the headquarters and lay out the campaign."

"I'll be ready. Good night, Daniel," Muriel replied.

"Nice to meet you, Daniel," chimed Lindsay.

I sauntered out of the room, this time to only a smattering of applause from my adoring fans. In another week, I'll need to fall off the boardwalk into the water to restore my tragicomic standing at the Riverfront Seniors' Residence. Jasper gave me the thumbs-up as I hit the crash bar on the front door. I waved and was out.

"Okay, what am I in for?" I asked and looked at Angus, sitting on the couch in his living room. I again sat in the easy chair and sipped a Coke—the course syllabus open on my lap. Without answering, he handed me a large binder with many coloured tabs—week one, week two, week three, etcetera. I flipped through it and found talking points to carry me through the weekly lectures for the entire course. For the second time in as many days, the phrase *I am saved* shoved its way into my thoughts.

"This is perfect! How long did it take you to pull this together?" I inquired.

"You're holdin' in yer hands the product of nearly 20 years of survivin' this abominable class. I've taught E for E five times in two decades, and I'm sane today because of that binder," he noted. "The more you can lose yourself in those lectures, the less engaged with the class you'll need to be. Just ignore 'em and keep on talkin'. It's easier that way."

"How many students will there be?" I asked.

"Well, the course is mandatory for all 120 first-year engineers, but about half of 'em won't show up after the first class. If you don't feel like talkin', you can always lob a provocative question into the seats and let the discussion flow," Angus said.

I turned to the talking points for the first lecture and followed through them. They looked straightforward to me.

"Yer first encounter with the philistines tomorrow is not a full three hours but just an hour-long orientation so that you can introduce yourself, set the tone and direction, and get the hell out of Dodge."

By this time, Angus had arranged the chess board and was sitting patiently with black. I set aside his E for E bible and slipped into the seat with white. I'd been playing a bit online since my last encounter with Angus and felt a little more confident at the board. I remembered his comments about the shortcomings in my game and tried to avoid them this time around. I kept my queen on the back rank for an appropriate length of time. I paid more attention to my pawn structure—something I seldom did. I castled at the earliest opportunity, securely sequestering my king under the protection of three pawns and a rook. Finally, I was careful not to split infinitives, dangle participles, promulgate nonexistent verbs like *prioritize*, *access*, and *impact*, or end my sentences with a preposition. (That was a practice up with which Angus would not put. My apologies to Winston Churchill.)

I won the first game. Angus was steamed. I'd taken his queen with a clever little move where I sacrificed my bishop to check the king, revealing a threat to his queen by my rook. Of course, he had to take my bishop with his king (he was in check), so I calmly took his queen with my revealed rook. Nice. It was the kind of move you can pull on a player like Angus once. So I did.

I was still enjoying my victory and lounging on my laurels when he advanced his queen pawn to start game two. I could tell Angus was mad at himself for underestimating me. It took 13 moves for him to pulverize me in game two. A combination of his anger-induced determination and my game-one honeymoon hangover was my swift undoing.

We shook hands and decided we'd play the rubber match the following night after my campaign meeting. I asked Angus if he'd like to come to meet the campaign team.

"Oh, that's a shame, but I just cannae do it tomorrow night. I'm rustproofin' the steel plate in me head," he deadpanned. A simple "No, I don't think so" would have sufficed.

As before, he walked me down to the boathouse and disappeared into his workshop while I climbed the long stairway to bed. I was beat again that night.

The heating grates once again gave up the sounds of Angus working on the hovercraft and talking. I couldn't make out the muffled words, but the tone seemed friendly. I heard nothing for a long while as I lay down and closed my eyes. As I dozed off, again I heard faint weeping, drifting up through the vents.

◆   ◆   ◆

Diary
Tuesday, September 3

My Love,

I like to have a run-in with "the Rumper" at least once every ten years whether I need it or not. Today, I needed it. He is truly a stench of the first order. One of my favourite pastimes has become piercing his pomposity. I took Daniel to meet with Rumplun so that we could finalize my escape from E for E and start Daniel's incarceration. On instinct, Rumplun flexed his meagre muscles and flatly refused. As I'd instructed, Daniel sat silent as a dormouse while I pulled the dean's strings. When it was clear he was not to be moved, I slipped Montebello into the play and that rumphole rolled over and offered me his throat in short order. The forms confirming my release were dutifully signed and my sentence commuted. Daniel has no idea what's in store for him. I feel a wee bit bad about it. Ah, balls, no, I don't. I wish I did, but I don't. You were always there to help me with empathy. It's hard mustering it without you.

I confess I've given no thought to the implications of letting my name take up space on the ballot in a federal election. I was so focused on eluding E for E that it seemed a minuscule price to pay. In hindsight, it is quite possible that my single-mindedness crippled my capacity for rational thought. I've told virtually no one, and Daniel reports that the nomination forms are to be delivered to Elections Canada tomorrow. I suspect all hell may break loose soon thereafter. The only other person who knows is Marie-Josée Cousineau. I figured I owed it to the president of the university. She was perplexed but pleased. I suppose from her perspective, it's good news any time the profile of the university is elevated. Positive media coverage seems to be the currency in which the administration trades these days. Anyway, the 39-day countdown to the election, or E-day as Daniel calls it, is expected to commence the day after tomorrow. Fortunately, while Eric Cameron is a slippery scumbag, he's so far ahead in the polls he could die and still win.

I've now finished installing the integrated lift-thrust system in Baddeck 1. When I make some final adjustments to the port and starboard vents and complete the decking, I can rev her up and test her balance. I'm still a long way from launching her, but I'm pleased with the progress. I think I have a sense of how A. G. B. felt when he was designing and constructing his hydrofoil. The HD4 was an amazing achievement. A world water-speed record of 71 miles per hour in 1919! The world's myopic view of Bell solely as the inventor of the telephone sells a great mind very short indeed. He was a true Renaissance man.

Tomorrow, Daniel has threatened to tell me about my campaign even though the candidate has no role whatsoever. I don't even want to know.

It is always late at night, without the daily campus travails to distract me, when the shadow of your absence falls most heavily upon me. I cannot escape it. I am immersed in it. The emptiness, the flatness of life without you, is stark and profound. Like a desert. What am I to do?

AM

CHAPTER FOUR

Battle stations. The next afternoon, as my eyes followed the steeply raked seats all the way up to the top, I had a sense of how the Christians might have felt scanning the rabble in the colosseum before the lions were let loose. The analogy was more than architectural. In all, 120 engineering students populated the first-year class. As expected, given the course and the fact that the first class was just an orientation session, I confronted only about 80 students. About a third of them wore purple construction hard hats. I kid you not. The engineering pack mentality was alive and kicking. I just didn't want to be on the business end of the boot.

Both women in the class also wore hard hats, confirming their membership in the "if you can't beat 'em, join 'em society." My heart went out to them. I really didn't think, as many did, that male engineering students were bona fide misogynists. However, I did believe that they succumbed to peer pressure for sustained periods and honoured traditions that undervalued women and nurtured stereotypes, particularly where nursing students were concerned. One glance through the engineering-student newspaper, *The Pipe*, provided ample evidence.

I made the mistake of writing my name on the blackboard, followed by "Department of English." After ten fruitless minutes of trying to bring the class to order through more civilized means, I thwacked (intentionally) and broke (unintentionally) a yardstick over the lectern. It made quite an impressive noise, after which the students settled down—out of curiosity, I was sure, and not out of respect for authority. I apologized to the burly engineer in the third row who'd been struck by the jagged two feet of yard stick I no longer held. I handed him a Kleenex I found in my pocket and noticed that the bleeding stopped shortly thereafter.

"This class is English for Engineers in case that wasn't already clear," I began. "I'm Professor Addison. I am not an engineer … but I play one on TV." Not a ripple. It was so quiet you could hear my bowels clench.

"What show?" some smartass shouted. I realized in an instant the query was genuine, delivered in earnest.

"Don't worry about it. That was my poor attempt at humour," I backfilled.

"Will this be on the exam?" Again, straight-faced. Serious question. I weighed my options and decided to just ignore it. I'd decided to attempt the Socratic teaching method, which meant posing the right questions to prompt discussion and debate and delivering the students to enlightenment—or, at least, dropping them off at a gas station on the outskirts of basic understanding.

"Let me ask you all something. How many of you would rather not be here?" I surveyed the room, stopped counting hands at 63, and raised my own. "Perhaps it would be easier to ask how many of you are *pleased* to be here?" Again I counted. I lost count after two as there were just no more hands in the air.

"Could I see you two guys after class, please?" I commented. Though I was kidding, my two supporters in the back lowered their hands and nodded. They looked like quite a pair despite the distance between us. They looked like finalists in a Johnny Rotten look-alike contest.

"How many of you think that engineering students have enough to learn without having English foisted on you?" Blank looks. Rewind. "In this context, *foisted* kind of means the same thing as *forced*." I was going to use the word *synonym*, but it was only a one-hour class. The penny dropped for most of them, and again, a large majority thrust their hands in the air. I approached the tiered seats and pointed to a smallish fellow, who I thought I could take if I had to. "Other than your engineering texts, what was the last book you read?"

Smallish fellow thought for a moment before replying, "*Beam Me Up, Scotty* by James Doohan." I saw much righteous nodding behind him.

"Ah yes, *Star Trek*, featuring one of the most famous split infinitives in modern history," I interjected, trying to find some small patch of common ground with my audience. Again, blank faces. "You know, 'To boldly go' etcetera, etcetera." Nothing. Dead air. I waved the white flag and moved on.

"Okay, what about you?" I nodded to a skinny car guy, sporting a Corvette T-shirt, a Chevrolet cap, and long, stringy hair that was in desperate need of an oil change. "What have you read lately?"

"I just finished an awesome autobiography—*The Camaro Story*."

I chuckled at his little pun. He seemed puzzled by my reaction, and I realized he was utterly oblivious to his inadvertent wordplay. Okay, screw Socrates. He'd obviously never taught engineers. I turned my back on the class for a moment to gather my thoughts and then, once more, leaped into the breach.

"Let me take a stab at explaining why this course is required for engineering students. I hope you would agree that university shouldn't simply be a factory that churns out engineers or dentists or whatever specialized personnel society happens to need at the time. Universities should make us more worldly, teach us how to think critically, and prepare us to be responsible, well-rounded global citizens."

"Will this be on the exam?" someone interrupted. I ignored him and kept on.

"The word *university* means 'of many schools.' In the original vision of the university, students studied a very broad range of subjects—philosophy, history, languages, logic, mathematics, art, and science—all to earn a bachelor of arts degree. Students sampled *many schools* of thought. In the last half-century, we've drifted quite a distance from this historical model, and your very focused curriculum is a product of that evolution. Your course of study is, relatively speaking, very narrow. Yes, it's complex, challenging, demanding, and important, but it represents a very thin slice of civilization's vast field of knowledge. I make no judgments about that, but it is true." I stopped to see whether anyone was still with me. It was obvious no one was, so I continued. "English is the engineering faculty's one concession to the broader world. This course should be just as important to you as math or fluid mechanics because you cannot realize your full potential as engineers if you cannot communicate your ideas. And you can't communicate your ideas without a passing understanding of the English language."

"Will this be on—"

"No, this will not be on the exam! I'm just trying to get you all to accept the need to be here." Few did, it seemed. After such a promising start, the rest of the hour went straight downhill from there.

My two allies in the back appeared engaged unless their nodding was actually nodding off. After the class, they waited until the others had left and approached the front where I was deciding whether it was too late to get my old job back. The obvious leader of the two wore Stuart tartan stretch pants, a black Punk Lives! T-shirt, and two-tone Doc Marten stompers. A Ramones ball cap covered what turned out to be a hairless scalp. Sizeable black skull studs pierced both ear lobes. The other guy sported black and pink striped hair, coiffed, it appeared, with a weed-whacker. He wore those inexplicably fashionable low-slung, baggy shorts with enough room to cradle a cantaloupe in the crotch. His green boxers extended a full four inches above the waistline of his sagging shorts. But wait, there's more. A black on black Iggy Pop T-shirt and multicoloured bowling shoes completed the ensemble. A hoop through his lower lip, a safety pin in his nose, and an "I eat nails!" tattoo on the left side of his neck made him as approachable as a coiled cobra.

"Professor, you wanted to see us?"

"Actually, I just wanted to thank you for being supportive today," I replied.

"No problem, Professor. We actually wanted to speak to you. I'm Pete Cadogan, and this is Pete Martelli." We shook hands rather formally.

"Well, that should make it twice as easy to remember your names."

"Right. We called the Liberal headquarters in Ottawa about getting involved in the campaign in Cumberland-Prescott. We live there and hate that heinous anus Cameron. Anyway, we were told to talk to you. What a coincidence that we found you teaching our English class," Pete1 explained as Pete2 nodded like a bobble-head.

I'd pegged them as militant anarchists, but beggars couldn't be choosers. So there it was—a barely discernible silver lining, glinting in a black cloud the size of Saskatchewan. And I would take it. I would take it. "Hallelujah!" I shouted, startling them. I clapped them both on the shoulders in a way that I hoped they would consider avuncular and not weird. Pat Boone flanked by Ozzie Osborne and Sid Vicious. Nice. "Our volunteer ranks have just doubled." (Heinous anus?)

Muriel Parkinson, her right hand vibrating all by itself, sat on a slatted park bench in front of the Riverfront Seniors' Residence. When she noticed the twitching, she tried to quell the shakes with her other hand, leaving both trembling in unison. It was ten minutes to seven. I leaped out to escort Muriel to her chariot while Pete1 and Pete2 stayed in the back seat so as not to frighten the residents.

I'd broken the news of our "in name only" candidate to the two Petes on the way over. After some initial misgivings (actually, they freaked), I persuaded them to stay on the team. It cost me a weekly 24 of Molson Canadian, two tickets to PunkPunk-palooza, and daily chauffeur service to and from the campus. In return, they agreed to manage the door-to-door canvass, which was the toughest campaign job to fill. I wasn't exactly thrilled at the prospect of two Sex Pistol understudies canvassing for us, but I was out of options.

I made it to the bench, offered Muriel my arm, and we started across the sidewalk to the car. The rhythmic grip of her shuddering right hand felt strange on my wrist but, in another way, comforting.

"You've been very mysterious about our campaign headquarters. What have you got up your sleeve?" she inquired as we shuffled in lockstep to the car. I held my tongue.

We had almost reached the car when out of the corner of my eye, I saw Lindsay emerge from the building and bound down the steps towards us. She modeled different jeans this time along with what I guess women call a top—a word I've never been comfortable saying out loud—which was orange, sleeveless, and, well, tight. Her hair peeked out beneath a Toronto Maple Leafs ball cap.

"Grandma! I step away for two seconds, and you're halfway into an abduction." She smiled at me, and I briefly lost track of where I was.

"Relax, Lindsay. Can't an old woman paint the town once in a while?" Muriel joked.

"Hi again, Lindsay," I fairly blurted. "I'm just stealing Muriel so we'll have quorum for our first campaign meeting. I think we have room in our headquarters for one more if you've got nothing on for the next hour or so," I concluded, trying to be casual and, instead, sounding eager. Lindsay noticed the visually arresting Petes in the back seat and winced.

"You don't think I'm letting her ride in a car with Daniel and the delinquents without her trusty chaperone, do you?" she replied. While I helped Muriel into the front seat, I heard Lindsay open the back door.

"Shove over, boys; I'm coming aboard." They shoved over all right.

Introductions were made all around, and the five of us pulled away from the curb. In hindsight, driving around with the entire Cumberland-Prescott Liberal brain trust in the same car may have been ill-advised. I decided to get started and turned off the radio.

"I call this first meeting of the C-P Liberal campaign committee to order," I announced as I headed out of Cumberland into the surrounding farmland.

"Why don't we wait until we get to the headquarters before we start the meeting?" asked Muriel.

"Ah, well, we're already at the campaign headquarters," I replied. Muriel and the others looked out the window at the farmers' fields ending in the river. Not a building in sight. "Actually, it would be more accurate to say that we are already *in* the campaign headquarters," I concluded and waited for the fallout.

With no money and few volunteers, we simply couldn't afford the conventional storefront headquarters—nor did we require it. My 15-year-old Ford Taurus station wagon, complete with balding tires, a coat-hanger antenna, suspiciously mushy spots in the floor, and a permanently lowered driver's window was to be campaign central—our HQ of no fixed address.

Lindsay started the barrage. "You can't be serious!"

"Where will we put the phone bank, coffee machine, and boom box?" asked the ever-practical Pete1.

"Yeah!" was Pete2's thoughtful and provocative contribution.

Muriel held her fire. The three in the back seat shot questions and comments for several kilometres as I waited for them to tire themselves out. We were in the northeast corner of the riding when the guns finally fell silent.

"Look, we're broke," I said, "but we do have an obligation to the party and to the people of C-P to run a campaign—a shoestring campaign maybe—but a campaign, nonetheless. With such a small team, a remote chance of victory, and a somewhat disengaged candidate, it makes sense to husband our resources." I spoke in a calm and measured tone, hoping to smother them with logic. Muriel tagged me and jumped into the ring.

"Let me read the subtitles for the rest of you," she started. "With five demented volunteers, no chance of victory, and an absent candidate, spending the $160 we have on storefront space makes no sense and would only cover 18 hours of occupancy, anyway."

I couldn't have said it better myself. I was encouraged by the begrudging silence behind us. "Isn't that what I just said?" I asked. "Anyway, I intend to position our headquarters-on-wheels with the media as another one of Angus McLintock's brilliant ideas. It's a revolution in campaigning that will allow us to take the election directly to the voters wherever they live in the riding. We have room in the back for all of our campaign necessities, and the car's just been tuned up and has at least another 200 miles left in her. So let's make them count."

Lindsay piped up next. "You mean you think you can load 2,000 lawn signs in the back of this beast? I thought men were supposed to have superior spatial abilities and a packing gene to boot. I say you've only got room for 10 or 12 signs."

"First of all, Ms. Dewar, based on recent polling, 12 Liberal signs in Cumberland-Prescott is five more than we need. Secondly, we actually aren't using lawn signs in this campaign, anyway. It was part of my deal with Angus," I revealed.

"No lawn signs in an election campaign? It's like Trudeau without the rose, Diefenbaker without jowls, or the Leafs winning the Stanley Cup. It's unnatural," Lindsay countered.

"We simply don't have the money, let alone the candidate's permission," I said. "I'm going to issue a news release, announcing our no-lawn-sign policy as part of Professor McLintock's deep commitment to reducing solid waste and protecting our environment. We'll make it fly," I insisted. "Besides, organizing the lawn-sign program is a colossal pain."

Muriel smiled as the back seat deliberated. I looked in the rearview mirror and saw the wheels turning.

"That might work," Lindsay conceded after a time.

"Cool," Pete1 offered.

"Yeah, cool," said Pete2.

A loud instrumental chorus of "London Calling" by the Clash broke the mood, causing me to veer onto the shoulder before regaining control. I liked the Clash, but this Muzak version was a travesty.

Muriel fished inside her aging Margaret Thatcher handbag and put the cell phone to her ear. "Cumberland-Prescott Liberal campaign," she intoned, using her political power-broker voice. She listened and rolled her eyes. "Ernie, you dirtbag, what do you want?" she growled in a striking impression of Roseanne Barr. I managed to stay in my lane this time despite the shock of hearing a kindly and perfectly mannered 81-year-old woman morph into a longshoreman. I heard snickering from the back seat.

"Of course, we're up and running, and we're coming to get you, so you best keep a weather eye open. Cameron is going down this time around. You're going to collapse under the weight of your own complacency," she snapped then listened with widening eyes to the response. "How dare you refer to me in that way? I know your parents. There was a time in this town when Tories were at least civil to Liberals. Thanks for marking the end of an era." She slammed the phone shut but then immediately opened it again and started dialing.

"Yes, I'd like to order 20 large pizzas, all with double anchovies. Of course, I'm serious. It's our campaign kickoff, and I've got 75 hungry volunteers salivating all over the phone bank, so shake a leg. Yes, 224 Riverfront Road. Yes, we'll pay cash. Yes, I'm Petra Borschart, Mr. Cameron's campaign manager. An hour is fine. Thank you," Muriel concluded and hung up. "Those assholes."

Muriel sat stone-faced with her arms crossed and her eyes aimed forward. I thought I detected a small curl of smoke issuing from her left ear, but I might have been wrong. The back seat had erupted in a gleeful cacophony. I was laughing hard.

When the ache in my side passed and we'd finished singing "For She's the Jolly Good Fellow," we completed our circumnavigation of the riding. The two Petes had grown up in Cumberland, but I still wanted us all to familiarize ourselves with the geography and diversity of the riding. Lindsay agreed to develop a canvassing schedule and a list of priority polls so that the two Petes could get an early start on door knocking. While we knew it was futile, we all felt enough loyalty to the broader Liberal cause at least to raise our flag in the campaign even if it would only ever fly at half-mast. Besides, the smug behaviour of the Tory camp that night lit a fire under us all. Anger is a powerful motivator.

With Lindsay and the Petes looking after the canvass and Muriel managing the campaign phone from the Riverfront Seniors' Residence, my first priority was to develop Angus's positions on the key local issues, run them by him, and then manufacture a reasonable facsimile of a campaign brochure. Without a flesh-and-blood candidate, the Petes at least needed a pamphlet to hand out.

With a few more organizational matters dealt with, I dropped Lindsay and her grandmother off, helping Muriel up the steps. She gave me a quick hug and promised to let me know if we received any noteworthy calls. Lindsay waved good night, one hand around Muriel's shoulders. Nice smile.

I drove the two Petes home and arranged to drive them back to campus in the morning as per our agreement. They lived together in a kind of bunkhouse behind Pete1's family home. They called it their "punkhouse." I'd checked with the admissions office after class that afternoon and discovered that both Petes had been accepted in engineering with academic scholarships on the strength of outstanding marks. Hard to see it in the package, but intelligence comes in diverse guises, including skull studs and lip rings. Their postgraduation job interviews would be interesting.

Angus kicked my sorry carcass all over the chess board that night. With election planning rattling around in my head, there was little room left to devise knight forks and impregnable pawn structures. Angus was in an ebullient mood, and I sensed it was due to more than the thrashing he was giving me.

"What are you so pumped about?"

"Beyond the satisfaction I derive from takin' the rubber match in our little world championship, I'm pleased because at two o'clock this afternoon, I was here, assemblin' the steerin' linkage on the hovercraft instead of spoon-feedin' Dr. Seuss to first-year engineers who know just enough English to order beer and to proposition nurses," he replied, contented.

"It wasn't so bad," I said. He fixed me with a steely gaze. "Okay, it was bad. Quite bad. In fact, very, very bad." He was delighted. "But on the positive side of the ledger, I did recruit two able-bodied volunteers to canvass on behalf of the newly confirmed Liberal candidate. You'll be pleased to know that there's little hope of them converting any voters to the Liberal cause. In fact, I figure most residents will call the police when they find the two Petes pushing your pamphlet on their doorstep. They are quite a sight."

Angus stood to refill his glass—Lagavulin again. There were three local campaign issues on which I needed positions for Angus. I figured this was as good a time as any to put them on the table.

"Angus, the national campaign understandably insists that all local candidates adhere to the party's positions on the major national and international issues be they economic, social, or just political. However, they do grant us some latitude on local issues, recognizing that their influence over your electoral fortunes can be profound."

He sank into the couch and rested his tumbler on his barrel chest. "All right, strictly as an academic exercise, what are the local issues that are likely to come up in this little campaign of yours?" he inquired with a little smirk teasing the corners of his mouth.

"Three major issues are in play: federal subsidies to prop up the Sanderson shoe factory in the southwest corner of the riding, the proposed Corrections Canada halfway house in Cumberland to ease the reintegration of paroled inmates into society, and I'll get to the third issue in a moment." I stopped and waited.

"What positions are you proposin' I adopt, Dr. Addison?"

"Well, there are 60 jobs at stake at the Sanderson plant. The federal subsidies will lower their costs and help make them more competitive on the export market. I think you should support the subsidies and pressure Eric Cameron to make them happen." I paused but then went on. "You know, Tip O'Neill, the famous U.S. politician once observed that 'all politics is local.' I think he was right." I stopped and waited while Angus pondered.

"No," he replied.

"Pardon."

"I said no. Let me ask you a question, Dr. Addison, English professor and political-organizer-at-large. Do you really believe it is in the national interest, *our* national interest, to pour tax payers' money into an inefficient and outmoded factory so we can dump artificially discounted shoes in other countries and compete unfairly with their strugglin' shoe factories? Hell, we even send some of those countries foreign aid. So we give with the right hand and take with the left. And we haven't even considered the environmental implications of supportin' a 35-year-old factory."

Now, I pondered. "Well, with the writ due to drop, I'm focused right now on your local interests here in Cumberland-Prescott," I commented. But it sounded weak to me.

Angus was talking again. "Every candidate in this country should be thinkin' first about the national interest, second about their constituents' interests, and third about their own interests. Everyone is more concerned with their own fortunes than with the nation's. That's the problem with the democratic institutions in this country. It's no wonder voters are cynical. Daniel, the national interest is not the sum of each ridin's interests or each MP's interests." He made this statement calmly, even casually, as if the words were self-evident and not worthy of special attention.

I had no idea he'd ever considered such matters. He laid bare the great paradox of Canadian politics. When not influenced by the need to be elected, a person like Angus was free to consider the national interest first. On the other hand, to be elected and earn the power and privilege to protect and promote the national interest, candidates often had to first support local-community causes that perhaps were not, in the long run, good for the country. As Winston Churchill once observed, "Democracy is the worst form of government, except for all those other forms."

I knew Angus was right. In this era of free trade, either we needed our factories to compete on an equal footing with other countries or we needed to retool for emerging industries where we could forge a competitive advantage. It was probably time for Canada to hasten its withdrawal from sunset industries and invest in sunrise sectors that promised long and bright futures. I knew he was right, but opposing the Sanderson subsidies would not be welcomed in Cumberland-Prescott.

"Okay, I accept your logic," I said, "but in the short term, I'm going to try to avoid this issue because although your position may be the right one, it likely isn't the winning one locally."

"I'm not advancin' a position based on the prospects of victory," Angus responded.

"I know, I know, I hear you. Okay, what about the Corrections Canada halfway house proposal? Cumberland City Council and Eric Cameron are on the public record opposing it."

"On what grounds?" asked Angus.

"Well, it's very simple. They just don't want it in Cumberland."

He was unmoved. "Well, I support the establishment of the halfway house for the same reasons I reject subsidies to the shoe factory. The halfway house has to be built somewhere. I assume its location was recommended for sound reasons by people who know more about such things than I. Cumberland should shoulder its share of the burden of rehabilitatin' and reintegratin' prisoners who have served their time. I say build it here; it's our turn. I might be a bit nervous livin' next door, but that doesn't mean it shouldn't be built." He sipped again, savouring the flavour of his homeland.

I confess I was quite impressed with his views and the conviction and clarity with which he presented them. I realized that I believed in the same principles and, in fact, had left Parliament Hill because of them. But I obviously had not yet fully shed the instincts and practices engendered by five years with the backroom boys.

"Let me guess the third issue," Angus interjected. "Ottawa River Aggregate Inc."

"Right," I replied. "They want to expand their aggregate operation on the outskirts of Cumberland, right on the river. It means 75 jobs for the next 18 months while the new addition is under construction and 50 new permanent jobs thereafter. Cameron has been a strong supporter." After local issues one and two, I was not surprised with his opinion of number three.

"No, I don't think so," he sighed.

Then I sighed. "Okay, strictly as an academic exercise, what is your problem with creating more than 100 new jobs in a town that could use some good news?" I inquired.

"Any more aggregate minin' on the shores of the Ottawa River would leave the land lookin' slightly worse than the lunar surface. The environmental impact would profoundly affect the habitats of several indigenous species of fish, amphibians, mammals, birds, and plants, not to mention compromise the water quality. The company is tryin' to escape an environmental assessment for the expansion and they're already fightin' four occupational-health-and-safety-code violations. Truck traffic in the proposed location is already dangerously heavy because of the neighbourin' beverage-bottling facility. The expanded aggregate operation would add six tractor trailers every hour of every day. Other than that, I have no problem with the proposal."

"I see you've been doing your homework. I thought you had no interest in politics," I said.

"I read the local papers, and I know a thing or two about water systems and how delicate a balance must be struck when tinkerin' with a river's natural state."

"Well, I can't very well argue with your high-minded philosophy, but as your campaign manager, I'm compelled to warn you that by espousing such positions, you may well cut your support from a few hundred votes down to a few dozen." Angus seemed very pleased at this prospect. I raised my glass towards him. "Here's hoping we can skate around these local issues." I rose to start my trek to the boathouse. "Thank you for the chess lesson and the civics class. I feel beaten down and lifted up at one and the same time." Angus was still grinning when I slipped out into the warm night.

There was one media call waiting for me when I made it to the boathouse. It was from André Fontaine, the senior news reporter for *The Cumberland Crier*. It could wait until the morning when the 39-day clock started.

◆   ◆   ◆

Diary
Wednesday, September 4

My Love,

Excellent day. I didn't even go into the campus but stayed and laboured with joy in the boathouse. More to the point, while I was doing that, Professor Daniel Addison was the one nearly having a stroke, courtesy of a hundred blissfully ignorant engineering students. I shudder at the thought of ever again facing those benign cultural pygmies. Give me graduate students in thermodynamics or even fourth-year undergrads in manufacturing processes, and I'm quite content. But not first year E for E.

I won't bore you with my technical travails, but I made considerable progress on the steering linkage today. I'm still working out how to operate the starboard and port thrust-vent rudders independently to enhance control, particularly at low speeds. I'm close but not quite there. Having only one engine simplifies the overall craft but introduces a new set of control complications.

Daniel was here for chess tonight and to discuss my positions on a few local issues for the campaign in which I'm not participating. I won the chess and the local issues debate—classic scenario where the community interest conflicts with the national interest. You know how I feel about that. The clowns that have run the country for the last two decades have dragged democracy through a sewer. There's no end to their conceit and arrogance and no beginning to their vision and intelligence. They simply do not, or cannot, see what is really happening. As Canadians' respect for democracy declines and their disdain grows, we tend to abandon the greater good, follow the politicians' lead, and grab what we can for ourselves. We give up and accept things as they are, leaving us trapped in a perpetual cycle of self-interest. That's what's happening in this country. Aye, it's a mess, and I abhor it. The writ drops tomorrow, but I'm just a name on the ballot, an ambivalent observer.

I know what you're thinking. It's easy to take potshots from the relative tranquility of tenured academe. Well, that's where I belong. I am a fossil, an old man out of his time and almost out of time. With two years till full pension, I'm going to stick to my knitting, keep my nose clean, build Baddeck 1, and wallow in your loss … every day.

AM

CHAPTER FIVE

This is "World Report" from the national news room of CBC Radio, for Thursday, September 5. I'm Elaine Phillips. Well, the Prime Minister revealed the worst-kept secret in Ottawa this morning. Canadians are going to the polls on Monday, October 14. The Conservative government is running on the federal budget of popular Finance Minister Eric Cameron. The polls as they stand now project a slim Tory majority, but much can change in the course of a campaign. The Prime Minister visited the Governor General early this morning to dissolve Parliament and start what will be a 39-day race.

The insanity, the surreal, the bizarre, had officially begun. I sat at my kitchen table, gargling orange juice and wondering how I'd managed to put myself in this ludicrous position. I was running a phantom candidate, in a cash-strapped campaign we were sure to lose, aided by an ailing octogenarian, her attractive granddaughter, and two pierced punks. Our campaign headquarters was comprised of a ready-for-the-scrap-heap Ford rust bucket and a government-owned cell phone. We had no lawn signs, no advertising, no marked voter lists, and one cheesy, desktop-published leaflet with no pictures.

It sounded like a sitcom that was cancelled after three episodes because it was just too far-fetched. I picked up the phone and dialed. "André Fontaine, please. Thank you."

"Fontaine," he said, rushed.

"André, it's Daniel Addison, returning your call. I'm the campaign manager for the Liberal candidate here in C-P."

"Right, thanks for getting back to me. So you've actually found a Liberal candidate to run against Cameron?" he asked.

"Yep, the nomination papers were submitted to Elections Canada yesterday morning, and his candidacy was confirmed by the afternoon," I replied. "His name is Angus McLintock. He's an internationally respected mechanical-engineering professor at U of O who's lived in Cumberland for the last 25 years. He's thoughtful, well versed on the issues, and eager to serve." I let my instincts do the talking.

"And you really think you can knock off Cameron?" he inquired without the decency of restraining his chuckle.

I sighed audibly and shifted into message mode. "Well, Cameron will be tough, but Angus does think he can win; otherwise, he wouldn't be in the race."

"Does Mr. McLintock have any history of drug abuse or mental illness in his family?"

"Very nice, André. Let's keep this friendly, shall we?"

"So you're the campaign manager, and you share his belief in the possibility of victory?"

"Look, anything can happen in politics and frequently does. So yes, I'm running the campaign, and to pre-empt your next question, no, I'm not on any prescription medication, either. We're running a serious, albeit somewhat underfunded, campaign. The people of Cumberland-Prescott deserve a real choice on October 14, and we're going to give them one." I was spinning so hard I struggled to keep my balance.

"I'd like to speak to Mr. McLintock sometime today if I could," André declared.

"Gee, I'm sorry, André, but I'm afraid Angus simply won't be available for interviews during the campaign. He's trying very hard to knock on every door in the riding. That's his top priority, so he has no time for interviews." (I know, when I die I'm bypassing purgatory and going straight to hell.)

"For a second there, I thought you said the candidate wouldn't be doing any interviews. I'm holding the phone closer to my ear this time, so can you pass that by me again?" He was getting hostile.

"Sorry, André, you heard me right. Angus is not your run-of-the-mill candidate, and he's set out his priorities. Look, I'll pass something along to you that we haven't yet announced. I'm trying to get a news release out the door, but I'm running out of time. So here's your Day 1 Liberal campaign exclusive. Angus is a staunch environmentalist with a particular interest in composting and reducing solid waste. Out of concern for the environment and our overflowing landfill sites—and out of respect for the enlightened voters of Cumberland-Prescott—the McLintock campaign will neither produce nor erect any lawn signs."

"Sounds like a desperate cost-saving measure from a campaign with empty coffers," he challenged.

"André, it's not about saving money; it's about saving trees and our dwindling landfill capacity. It's about saving our environment. If we're not part of the solution ... well, you know the rest."

"What's the URL for your Web site?"

"Web site? Umm, we won't be having a McLintock-campaign Web site, either." For some inexplicable reason, I'd completely forgotten about the Internet. It was time to strap on the skates. Silence on the phone. Like a rookie, I filled it. "Uh, Angus has been concerned for some time with kids' easy access to explicit and depraved content on the Internet. It really is a sewer, so we're steering clear of the Web."

"Nice one. Who's your writer?" he replied.

"Look, André, we're trying to do things a little differently and not just reproduce what every other candidate is doing." I'm usually quite a competent skater, but my attempted quad-toe loop on the Web question seemed to have ended in a face plant.

"What do you think about Eric Cameron?" André asked, mercifully moving to safer ground.

"It's going to be very difficult to dethrone Cameron. He's extremely popular with the voters, has a great human touch on the hustings, and has done a reasonable job with the government's finances though I'm convinced a trained chimp could have eliminated the deficit in this booming economy," I noted.

"What do you know about Petra Borschart?" he probed.

"Very little except that I don't much like her," I commented. "She joined his team a few years ago and has enjoyed a meteoric rise to Chief of Staff. We tangled a few times on the Hill."

"Something doesn't quite fit for me, but I can't put my finger on it. She seems good and tough and clearly has a close rapport with Cameron, but it all happened very fast," André mused.

We talked for a few more minutes, and I hoped that I'd managed the call well enough to avoid an embarrassing story right out of the gate. Dealing with journalists required quick thinking and steady nerves. That morning, I had neither.

In fact, I knew a little more about Eric Cameron than I'd let on. One of the benefits of being a nice guy was that people opened up and talked even if talking was ill-advised. Across my years on Parliament Hill, I'd managed to weave countless threads of information on Cameron into … hmm … let's say, a poncho of political insight, to complete the textile metaphor. On first meeting, you're blown away by his ability to connect with you, to engage you, to make you feel like you're the only person in his world. The fifth time you meet him, it dawns on you that he has no recollection of the first four meetings; his star begins to lose altitude. After the tenth time you meet him, you want to wash your hands. He seems to understand that his halo can only sustain two or three meetings with the good citizens of Cumberland-Prescott before it starts to corrode. So he limits his contact with individual constituents to no more than a few encounters between elections so the voters are held in a kind of suspended awe that works quite well at the polls.

Of course, in politics, luck and timing are everything. Being named Finance Minister at the end of the worst recession since the 1930s and at the start of the greatest economic boom since World War II, reflected the charmed political life he enjoyed. He was one lucky bastard. If I could persuade him to pick my lottery numbers, I would. One might argue, however, that he was unlucky in love. Rumours of serial philandering had never been confirmed, but with so much smoke, there must have been a flicker of flame there somewhere. At any rate, the point was rendered moot five years ago when his wife had died shortly before the last election. They had had no children.

Not to be crass, but the death of his wife gave him an immediate 15-point lift in the polls. The glossy, front-page photos of Cameron weeping over her grave looked a little too perfect, a little too contrived for my taste. Then again, I've grown bitter, suspicious, and cynical. Not long after the funeral, Petra Borschart was promoted from junior staffer in charge of the Minister's dry cleaning to Chief of Staff. Given his national standing and seniority in Cabinet, he didn't need to clear major ministerial-staffing changes with the Prime Minister's Office as other ministers did. Now, the two were virtually inseparable. She had bought a house in Cumberland, spending Mondays through Thursdays on the Hill and Fridays in the constituency office. By all accounts, their alliance boosted his political fortunes. As the election gun sounded, Cameron was, without question, the most popular politician in the country, even more respected than the Prime Minister. I didn't trust him. I didn't like him. After talking to André Fontaine about Cameron, I decided I needed a shower and took one.

I checked in with Muriel several times each day—often just to hear her authoritative salutation. She had an outstanding phone manner. She gave great voice. If I told you she was the mother of James Earl Jones, you'd believe me (that rumour would certainly set tongues a-wagging at the Riverfront Seniors' Residence). She deployed "the voice" only on the phone. In person, she sounded as you might expect an 81-year-old woman named Muriel to sound. When I reached her, she'd only had one call—from André Fontaine the day before.

Thankfully, I didn't really have many faculty responsibilities until the next term beyond some meetings and informing Professor Gannon of my research intentions. I'd always thought "publish or perish" was just a cliché. Alas, no. I made the 30-minute drive to campus to pick up the two Petes. They were waiting at our rendezvous point in all their sartorial splendour. I truly thought the police would be well within their authority to arrest them both for disturbing the peace just for standing on the corner, minding their own business.

Pete1 wore some kind of fishnet shirt sprinkled with holes. He sported purple paisley short-shorts over orange plaid boxers that extended to just above his knees. He wore a different pair of Doc Martens this time—black and white striped with the word *Shitkickers* in red, stenciled on both toes. Even though Labour Day had passed, he wore a white belt in stark contrast to his black lipstick. With no hat, his cue-ball cranium gave him a particularly menacing mien.

Pete2? Where to begin? His hair was now lime green at the tips and red to the roots. As for his hairstyle, he eschewed the classic punk's longitudinal centre strip of spikes in favour of the modified lateral, double-ridge Mohawk. If you could take your eyes off his hair, you'd see a powder blue, frilly tuxedo shirt under pink, tie-dyed lederhosen. In a moving tribute to Canada, he wore Bauer Supreme hockey skates—minus the blades. I noticed no new piercings to speak of, though I confess, I wasn't too diligent in my examination.

Let's just say that Pete1 and Pete2 didn't exactly look like two upstanding citizens committed to serving the public interest by working within the democratic system. In fact, had I not known them, I'd have said they were on their way to a coup d'état or, at least, a sit-in. When I pulled up to the curb, they were both buried in their Applied Math 1J5 texts. When I asked what they were working on, they casually informed me they were applying the Frobenius method to solve differential equations. I never asked again.

As we pulled away, I noticed a makeshift banner, hanging from the top of the engineering building. Affixing it that high up on the front wall must have been a hair-raising stunt pulled by some intrepid engineering students. Far below on the ground, U of O maintenance workers were talking with considerable animation while unloading a ladder that was clearly too short for the job. Other passers-by stopped and stared. The banner, flapping in the wind, read:

Kick some Tory ass, Angus! Mech. Eng. rules!

News travelled fast. We drove to poll 31 in the southeast corner of the riding where a relatively new subdivision had sprung up since the last election. Lindsay had phoned me earlier in the day with a list of priority polls. Apparently, there was a vague rumour of a lone Liberal supporter living somewhere in the precincts of poll 31. Who needed marked voter lists when we had that kind of inside intelligence on the electorate? Such hearsay was all that was required to make poll 31 worthy of special attention. After all, if there were one Liberal, maybe there were two.

It was time to start the canvass. I hadn't yet been able to finish and print the lone McLintock leaflet Angus had authorized, so we'd snagged a stack of general Liberal campaign brochures from the party's national headquarters in Ottawa along with a few red T-shirts and threw them in the back of the car for future use. I parked at the end of the subdivision, grabbed some brochures, put on a VOTE LIBERAL button and jumped out. I didn't really feel comfortable, yet, suggesting that the two Petes dress a little more conventionally. I couldn't afford to lose them from the campaign by offending them, so I gave them buttons and told them to stay behind me to watch how I handled the first few houses.

I climbed the steps to the front door while my canvassing duo watched from the lawn. I looked at the name on the mailbox, rang the bell, and offered the two Petes a glance of encouragement as I heard the sound of shuffling feet from within. It was then that I noticed that Pete2 had removed his lip ring and had installed in its place the VOTE LIBERAL button. It hung on his lip like a big, angry abscess. I felt queasy, but the door opened anyway.

"Hello, Ms. Fitzgerald, I'm Daniel Addison from the McLintock campaign. I hope we're not interrupting dinner." The older woman was still chewing so I barreled ahead before she could answer. "Angus McLintock is your Liberal candidate in Cumberland-Prescott. He's very concerned with how Mr. Cameron has neglected the riding, and we were really hoping we could count on your support on October 14."

The woman looked over my shoulder, as did I, and we both saw the two Petes smile and wave. Unfortunately, Ms. Fitzgerald was seeing them for the first time. She gave a little ... *shriek* I guess is the right word, darted back inside, and slammed the door.

"Tory," said Pete2 behind me.

Our encounters with the next six houses unfolded in a similar fashion. Well, the last one was a little bit different in that a Mr. Canning released his German shepherd, Adolf, to see that we vacated the property in a timely manner. Adolf hurtled out the door with lips curled and teeth bared. I was sprinting to the car to check for a pair of clean underwear when Pete2 knelt down and made soft, mewling sounds in the face of the charging canine. Instead of Adolf eating out of my leg, Pete2 soon had the dog eating out of his hand—awesome skill to have when you're door-to-dooring in hostile territory. I wondered if Pete2's talent might be effective on irate voters. We'd have to wait to find out. An Ontario Provincial Police (OPP) officer rolled up in her cruiser, took one look at my canvassing colleagues, and reached for her Taser. It took me 20 minutes and two phone calls to persuade the officer that we were legitimately engaged in the democratic process. We were escorted back to the car and encouraged to take our leave.

I drove us to a far-flung corner of the subdivision, spent 20 minutes persuading the two Petes to slip on the Liberal Party T-shirts to moderate the punk-rock fashion tirade they made. The shirts were long enough to obscure their anarchist outfits. With some nudging from Pete1, we convinced Pete2 to shoehorn his Mohawk under an old Molson ball cap I found under the front seat. Looking at Pete2, the new lid only modestly mitigated the fright factor. I failed to negotiate traditional footwear even though I had a couple of pairs of ratty running shoes in the back. The two Petes had their limits, and I respected that.

Eventually, they got the hang of canvassing and even identified one voter who was contemplating thinking about giving consideration to perhaps revisiting her support for Eric Cameron. (High-fives all around.) Whenever a voter would ask to meet Angus, the two Petes, with unanticipated thespian skill, would immediately crane their necks to look down the street in search of the elusive candidate. When they would fail to locate him, they would simply tell the voter that Angus must have gone into one of the neighbours' houses for a chat but that they would try to get him back here soon. Believe it or not, Pete1 and Pete2 sold the story well, and the homeowners bought it.

By the time I'd paid for burgers and beer and dropped the boys off at the punkhouse, it was after nine-thirty. You never canvass after nine o'clock at night. When I got back to the boathouse, the light was on in the workshop. Through the window, I saw our candidate's legs, sticking straight up towards the ceiling, which situated his head somewhere underneath the dashboard of the cockpit that was slowly taking shape. I softly knuckled the door and entered. Angus was talking away, muffled by the cockpit's close quarters, apparently explaining what he was doing as if a colleague were standing nearby. We were alone in the room. I was only able to catch snippets of his monologue:

"Goin' to go with cable steeri ... rather th ... ually associated with hydraulic steerin'. What I wouldn't give to have you here to see this la—"

Then, he paused, wiggled his legs a little, and released another of his cataclysmic farts, accompanied by a loud groan of satisfaction. The man had a gift. As I held my breath, I prayed he would only ever use his power for the forces of good. I knocked with authority on the plywood panel that I estimated would be just above his buried head. That was a mistake. I assumed he'd heard me come into the workshop, but the convulsion that toppled his upright legs onto the side decking and wedged his head under what I think was the steering column was a clear indication that I'd caught him somewhat off guard. When he'd extricated himself, he wasn't exactly the picture of congeniality.

"Are you not familiar with the local custom of knockin' on the door before enterin'?" Angus snorted.

"My apologies, Angus, but I assure you, I did knock before I came in. I was certain you'd heard me. In fact, I thought you were talking to me. Who were you talking to?"

"It's none of yer concern, laddie. Now, hand me that spanner there, would you?"

I followed his extended index finger carefully as I wouldn't know a spanner from a drill press. I handed him the wrench, and he contorted himself again into the inverted vertical position. The legs of his work pants slid down his shins, revealing tartan knee socks, which in my mind, was taking one's heritage a little too far. Moments later, he reappeared, face reddened from gravity's effect on his circulation.

"We need to talk, Dr. Addison. I'm growin' a wee bit concerned with this election of yours," he started.

"What do you mean? It's Day 1, and we've only canvassed one-third of one poll and failed miserably to scare up anyone who even plans to vote Liberal. In fact, our crack canvassing crew was threatened nine times and forcibly removed from three properties. I think we're off to a good start," I replied.

"Well, you may think so, but somethin's afoot. The Board of Governors met today as well as the Faculty Association. Both bodies passed motions supportin' me candidacy and wishin' me well in the campaign. And then, a reporter from *The Fulcrum* cornered me at the bar in the Faculty Club and would not let me escape until I'd given her an interview. She is clearly going to write some fulsome puff piece on me for tomorrow's paper."

"What's the big deal about a couple of meaningless support resolutions and a positive profile in the campus newspaper?" I asked, truly perplexed.

"I'll tell you what the big deal is," he said with palpable anxiety. "There's far too much support gatherin' behind me. What if it spreads like the plague across campus and busts through into the broader community? That simply cannae stand, and we must put a stop to it."

Smiling at that precise moment was probably not the prudent thing to do. I couldn't help it. I chose not to tell him about the banner on the engineering building. "Angus, calm down. It's natural for your colleagues to want to express their support for a local hero who is stepping up to challenge the Cameron juggernaut. Did you think your candidacy would go unnoticed on campus?" I asked.

"You're getting a right laugh out of all this, aren't you? Well, it's not your name that's on everyone's lips at the university now, is it?" Exasperation personified.

"No, but it's my name in the course calendar next to English for Engineers, so whose fate seems worse to you?" I countered.

"*Worse.* There are only two fates under discussion," replied Angus.

"I said *worse.* I'm an English professor."

"Sounded like *worst* to me, but I'll take yer word for it," he conceded. "I just don't want the whole campus mobilizin' around me sham run for office. That wasn't part of our deal," he whined. "That story in *The Fulcrum* could really start to swing things me way."

Looking at his angst-ridden face, I decided against bursting our laughing at such a ludicrous notion. I was standing close to the large doors and didn't relish being tossed into the river, of which Angus seemed perfectly capable at that moment. I stifled my giggles.

"Angus, I'm your campaign manager. I will handle it. You need not worry yourself over glowing articles in the university rag. You want me to take care of it? Thy will be done," I concluded with a bow and a flourish.

Angus was mollified enough to return to his tinkering. I took my leave and scaled the staircase to my apartment. I pulled out last week's edition of *The Fulcrum* and scanned the masthead. I found what I was looking for, flipped through the yellow pages, and reached for the phone.

"Hello, I'm just checking in to see when tomorrow's *Fulcrum* will be delivered to the campus?"

The things campaign managers do to appease the neuroses of their candidates. I drove back to the campus at two forty-five in the morning. As I anticipated, at various points around the campus, I found bundles of *The Fulcrum* fresh off the printer's delivery truck. I doused the headlights on the Taurus or, rather, head-light, and pulled up to the curb. I didn't want to trigger a second print run, so I only loaded about three-quarters of the bundles into the back of the station wagon, leaving a lonely stack on the sidewalk. I drove around campus, repeating the procedure at each delivery location. By my estimate, instead of 10,000 issues of *The Fulcrum* distributed around the campus, only about 2,000 remained. Given the hour, I went about my clandestine task unseen.

The floor panel in the back of the Taurus wagon sagged under the newsprint burden. I prayed that I would make it to my destination without it giving way, depositing 8,000 newspapers onto the highway. Half an hour later, I pulled into the Prescott landfill site and joined three tractor trailers lined up for the weigh scale. The sleepy attendant, unaccustomed to family station wagons at that hour, just waved me onto the scale. When the light turned green, I drove around to a remote section of the landfill where I wouldn't be observed.

Before I started dumping the bundles, I pulled out a copy and looked for the story. I didn't have to look far. Dominating page two was a large colour photo of a somewhat younger Angus McLintock in full Scottish regalia. His grey hair tried desperately to escape the gravitational pull of his head, and his beard cascaded onto his chest like Montmorency Falls. The headline read "U of O's McLintock takes run at Cameron." Angus was right in one sense. The story was obsequious well past nauseating. I finished reading the piece, slipped one copy onto the front seat to keep, and returned to the back of the car to complete the job. The dome light cast an eerie glow over the scene and shed just enough light to guide me in finding an appropriate drop zone. The bundles cartwheeled down the slope, ending up under an overhang created by stacks of drywall, which were likely culled from a house demolition. I doubted the papers could be seen even in daylight. Done.

It was pushing four o'clock when I finally made the boathouse, hit the horizontal, and fell into an untroubled sleep. Perhaps it should have been troubled, but the night's deed paled next to the chicanery that was the daily fare I'd left on Parliament Hill. I slept a saint's sleep.

◆   ◆   ◆

Diary
Thursday, September 5

My Love,

The river looked beautiful tonight. It flowed at your favourite pace, the whitecaps just occasionally asserting themselves. Cat's paws added texture to the waves—musical in their movement. I could almost hear Smetana's symphonic poem *Vltava* in my mind's ear. I sat for two hours on the dock and watched the sun make its lazy descent beyond the western hills. I unfolded your chair and placed it empty beside me. I couldn't help it. Twice in that interval, without thought, I reached out my hand to the arm of your chair. I could almost feel your familiar, sweater-clad wrist beneath my fingers. You've left me in an abyss. I don't blame you. Who could? But here I am. Down deep.

After my river reverie, I spent three hours on Baddeck 1's control systems. I've decided to go with a steering wheel over the stick to make driving Baddeck 1 a more familiar experience for the average driver/pilot.

Great goings on at the U today. My reckless foray into politics, in name only I remind you, is proving to be more complicated than I had expected. (Although had I thought for more than 30 seconds before agreeing to Dr. Addison's asinine proposition, I'd have seen all this coming.) Colleagues in ones and twos popped by the lab today to congratulate me on my "courage" and "commitment." Other colleagues by the dozens assailed my choice of party. I felt I couldn't simply admit that the whole affair is just a stratagem to slip the noose of E for E. I mean, that wouldn't exactly cast me in a favourable light now, would it, and I do have to work with these people.

At any rate, the word is well and truly out. What an ass am I. The B of G and the Fac. Ass. actually adopted motions (unanimously!) to wish me well in my quixotic political odyssey (those words were not used in the resolution, but that's the gist). As well, a very young student reporter from the campus paper, who looked barely out of Brownies, interviewed me for nearly an hour. I dread the gushing drivel that may spill over the pages of *The Fulcrum* in the morning. I flatly refused to pose for photographs, and I'm quite sure they have none of me in their files. I'm hoping for a small item towards the end of the news section, but what do I know?

Daniel assures me I have nothing to worry about. The door-to-dooring is proceeding miserably, there's not a penny to the campaign's name, and the Tory machine is already running in high gear. Praise be!

I intend to steer clear of public places to the greatest extent possible in the next three weeks until I fly to Papua New Guinea at the end of the month. You remember the water-filtration system I've been working on. Well, we're actually going to build a proof-of-concept model in a remote village in PNG that could really use clean water. Right now, the villagers trek four miles to fill plastic jugs from a public well before walking home, their backs bending with the burden of clean water. I think of them when sitting by our majestic river's edge ... with your empty chair next to me.

AM

CHAPTER SIX

Other than three more near-arrests, courtesy of the two Petes' unorthodox canvassing attire, an editorial critical of Angus and the virtually unknown New Democratic Party (NDP) candidate for their low profiles, and a broken exhaust system in the McLintock-campaign headquarters, the first two weeks of the race unfolded without incident. Relatively speaking, it was smooth sailing without a dark cloud or a Liberal voter on the horizon. After the initial campus-based stirrings of support for Angus, he now seemed satisfied that there was no McLintock tsunami rolling across the riding. In fact, the Cameron team had taken to calling our candidate "Angus the Invisible." Fortunately, with the election outcome a forgone conclusion, no one bothered to organize any all-candidates meetings in the riding. What would be the point?

When driving through the riding, one was immersed in a monochromatic sea of blue as glossy Cameron signs stood like sentinels on virtually every lawn. Sometimes, having expensive signs featuring photos of the candidate posed a few problems. Some juvenile vandals had drawn garish moustaches and blacked-out teeth on a large and growing number of Cameron signs in several different sections of the riding. The effect was quite comical and earned a front page photo in *The Cumberland Crier* along with an editorial decrying the assault on the Cameron campaign. Petra Borschart and her obedient young team of Tory brownshirts were incensed and, for some reason, suspected the McLintock camp. I looked into it and was able to confirm that we had nothing to do with it. After all, ours was a high-road campaign with a focus on the issues. It was sheer coincidence that the timing and location of the lawn-sign enhancements paralleled the two Petes' canvassing schedule. Some thought we were just jealous because we didn't have signs of our own. Defacing Cameron signs was just not our style. The Petes and I conferred privately. Shortly thereafter, the unauthorized artistry ceased. If we were going to be annihilated at the polls, and there was no doubt of that, I wanted to be slaughtered fair and square. Head held high as it's lopped off, etcetera, etcetera.

Muriel, Lindsay, and I sat alone at a table for ten in the River Ballroom of the Cumberland Motor Inn for Eric Cameron's luncheon speech, sponsored by the

72

chamber of commerce. Every other table was packed to capacity. There was certainly no shortage of Cameron buttons, posters, novelty flags, T-shirts, and the ugliest hats I'd ever seen. Cameron's monotonous campaign theme song blasted over and over from 175 two-inch ceiling speakers in the ballroom's archaic sound system. It had the fidelity of a cheap walkie-talkie just heading out of range. "Cameron, Cameron, he's our man. Cameron, Cameron, takes a stand." (Yes, I'll take that Gravol now, please.) Torture on an endless loop.

We proudly wore our VOTE LIBERAL buttons, hence, our extra elbow room, not to mention our table's location. We were seated as far from the podium as possible while staying within the same area code. We'd also arrived just minutes before the scheduled start, so I admit that our timing might have been a contributing factor. As I passed Muriel a basket of stale buns as hard as lacrosse balls, I noticed with horror two lines of bouncy cheerleaders from Cumberland Secondary, forming at the main entrance to the ballroom. They were singing along to the campaign song, shaking their pom-poms and jumping up in the air, and landing, hands on hips, in the traditional cheerleader dismount pose. I looked around to make sure I knew where the washrooms were.

"What is this, the 1950s?" I asked.

"As a matter of fact, when Tories in Cumberland get together, yes, it is the 1950s," explained Muriel. "It's a humiliating period piece, an embarrassing time capsule with Cameron and Borschart at the helm."

"It's just plain creepy," said Lindsay with a shiver as she surveyed the scene. "It looks like they're all drugged or zombies."

Just then, the lights dimmed, and in partial answer to our prayers, the Cameron theme song faded out as the large projection screens on either side of the head table flickered to life. What followed was the most nauseating, gilded video portrait of the Honourable Eric Cameron that I could possibly have imagined. No, check that. I could never have conjured up such a fawning tribute. It included clips of his childhood, the young man going to university, his wedding day, his early campaigns, his inaugural speech in the House of Commons, his first budget address, and his international trips to meet foreign dignitaries. After seven minutes, it closed with shameless cemetery scenes at his wife's gravesite. The whole thing was set against a symphonic soundtrack scored for maximum emotional impact. I had to admit, it was a political tour de force that left many in the crowd weeping—even while our table was gagging. A still photo of Cameron hunched over his wife's headstone slowly faded on the screen while the soundtrack moved into a dramatic brass prelude reminiscent of Copland's "Fanfare for the Common Man," often heard around the Olympic Games. In this case, it felt more like "Fanfare for the Uncommon Sham." A single spotlight pierced the room, touching down at the main doors, accompanied by a voice not unlike that of famed ring announcer Michael "let's get ready to rumble" Buffer.

"Ladies and gentlemen, the Cumberland Chamber of Commerce is pleased to welcome the most popular Finance Minister in Canadian history, the long-time Member of Parliament for Cumberland-Prescott, and perhaps, just perhaps, our future Prime Minister. I give you our very own local hero and favoured son—the Honourable Eric Cameron."

As the campaign song restarted at full volume, the room, as intended, erupted in a rock star reception that I'm sure briefly worried the paramedics standing discreetly at the back of the room. It was quite a performance. Framed by vibrating cheerleaders, a smiling Eric Cameron, taking care to stay with the moving spotlight, worked the room like the master he was. He held one hand high in triumph and stretched the other towards as many enthralled voters as he could reach. Melee was an understatement; frenzy was a slow dance next to the bedlam in the ballroom as Cameron inched towards the podium. Ten minutes later, he reached his destination, and the ovation still showed no signs of abating. By this time, I'd fled to the bathroom, unable to stomach the total Tory orgy of Cameron's entrance.

In the men's room, I bumped into André Fontaine there to cover the Cameron speech. He seemed a little agitated. "Addison, I'm glad you're here. I've just seen something very interesting," he whispered even though we were alone in the bathroom.

"I'm in your hands, André." In retrospect, probably not the most appropriate thing to say to him as we stood side by side at our respective urinals. "I mean, I'm all ears."

"I just saw Cameron and Petra get out of his Buick in the parking lot. They were partially hidden between two parked cars and clearly thought they were unobserved. She was yelling at him and stabbing her finger into his chest and was obviously very angry. He just had this hangdog, ultrasubmissive look on his face like he was a six-year-old being chewed out by his mother. It was the strangest thing I've ever seen," he recounted.

"Carry on," I urged. "Then, what happened?"

"Well, then, he nodded his head a few more times while looking at his feet, she calmed down, and they walked into the motel as if nothing had happened. Very odd," André concluded.

I doubted it was any kind of prespeech pump-up ritual. Curious. When I returned to our table, Cameron was still trying to quell the clamour so he could actually say something. Eventually, the wild cheering dampened to the point that he felt comfortable starting in on his stump speech.

He spoke for 40 minutes without a single note in front of him. It was a perfectly balanced and nuanced mélange of substance, humour, self-deprecation, politics, and drama. He never missed a word, never messed up his timing, and never broke the magic spell he'd cast over the audience. It was the perfect campaign speech. I'd heard him speak before, but he was really at the top of his game this afternoon. The crowd hung on every word, every gesture, every smile, and every pause. He torqued the strings of our emotions until they were taut and tuned then played us like Yo-Yo Ma. Cameron never once mentioned his Liberal opponent. Why would he? Why should he? There was no need.

Throughout his remarks, Petra Borschart stood at the back as stiff as a Buckingham Palace guard and just as stone-faced. I approached her as the postspeech applause continued with no end in sight.

"Hello, Petra," I opened, standing next to her. She'd watched me as I approached.

"Hello, Danny boy," she replied with the look of someone whose patience was under threat. "I'd heard you were running the Liberal show in town, such as it is. Trying a little infiltration exercise today?"

"I bought a ticket just like everyone else, despite the food. You know what they say, 'know thine enemy.'" I waited but she just stared up at her Minister, who was still acknowledging the ovation. Completely at ease, Cameron pointed to certain people in the throng and pulled the trigger on his finger gun, swelling the chest of whoever was in range.

"He gave an inspired performance, Petra. You must be pleased," I said, filling the space between us. She turned to face me and put her index finger on my sternum, hard. I looked into the cold eyes of the most single-minded person I think I'd ever met. I was unnerved by what I saw.

"Danny boy, you ain't seen nothin', yet." With the kind of sneer normally reserved for professional wrestlers, only this one wasn't faked, she turned and headed up the side aisle to hustle Cameron out of the room. He was preaching to the choir, and it was time to go.

Muriel and I could see through Cameron's eloquent political theatre, but Lindsay had never witnessed one of his speeches. I could see it in her face. Shock and ahhhh shit, are we ever in deep trouble. We left right after Cameron did and before the lunch was served. None of us had managed to salvage any appetite.

I dropped Muriel back at Riverfront and armed her into a chair with a great view of the water while Lindsay stayed in the car in a loading zone to fend off

Cumberland's lone but zealous parking officer. I slipped back behind the wheel, eased into traffic to drive Lindsay home, and then on a whim, pulled up in front of Cumberland's only Starbucks.

"Feel like a latte?" I asked with my heart rate slightly elevated.

"I do, in fact. Good idea."

My heart rate burst through the "slightly elevated" threshold and entered the frenetic zone.

Lindsay snagged a table flanked by two soft and deep easy chairs—the kind you don't get up from without a good reason. I headed to the counter to order. I had my usual—tall, no whip, 2 percent hot chocolate—while Lindsay went with a grande, nonfat latte. Seven dollars and three minutes later, I handed Lindsay her cardboard cup and sank into the chair opposite her.

"Thanks."

We sat in silence for a few moments, and I feared we were heading for conversational purgatory. Then, she started us off. "So Professor Addison, how did you get so wrapped up in politics?"

"Hmm, how long do you have?" She smiled. "I was actually born into politics. But until about 12 years ago, I was firmly in the clutches of the Tory Party thanks to the 20-year indoctrination I suffered at the hands of my well-meaning but ultimately misguided parents."

She smiled again. "So you broke with the family and crossed the floor to the Liberals?"

"Something like that. What about you? When were you bitten by the bug?" I probed although I felt I already knew the answer.

"Do you really have to ask after spending time with Parkinson the partisan?" she asked, chuckling.

"She is amazing, isn't she?" I commented. "I just wish I'd known her when she was our candidate."

Lindsay paused and looked far beyond the walls of the Starbucks. "If she'd run in pretty well any other riding in the country," she said, "she'd have already had a stellar career in public service. As fate would have it, she was born and raised in precisely the wrong town for a Liberal set on serving. She was a wonderful candidate. She believed in public service for all the right reasons, and ran for office for all the right reasons. She lost all five elections because of geography and history, not because she was ever the lesser candidate. I doubt I'll ever forgive the people of this town for denying Muriel, and all of us, her dream." Lindsay looked wistful and almost angry.

"In a democracy, we tend to get the government and the politicians we deserve. Eventually, the voters of Cumberland-Prescott will come around," I commented, trying to look thoughtful without spilling hot chocolate onto my crotch. "Did you get your start in the Young Liberals of Canada?" I asked.

Lindsay snorted in derision, but it was as charming and endearing a snort as I'd ever heard. "I'm not a big fan of youth wings in political parties of any stripe," she explained. "I think they suck the public-service idealism out of kids and turn them into suspender-wearing, backroom political operators long before they're even out of university. It really bothers me that they learn how to stack delegate-selection meetings before they even really know what liberalism is. That's not who young people should be."

A woman after my own heart. "I hear you. I quit the campus Liberal association when a group of my overly partisan colleagues hatched a harebrained plan for a palace coup to take over the university's Progressive Conservative club—not my idea of democracy in action," I remarked. "What are your plans after you complete your master's?" I asked.

"Well, funny you should ask. I've been giving it a great deal of thought lately, and yesterday morning, it finally hit me with crystal clarity—I haven't the faintest idea what I'm going to do. In fact, I sometimes think I'm pursuing the graduate degree because I don't know what I want to do. A master's seemed like a worthwhile stalling tactic."

"In my humble, PhD-addled opinion, staying in school is seldom a bad idea regardless of the reasons. I don't think I really started to appreciate the university experience until halfway into my master's," I replied. "Perhaps you'll consider a stint on Parliament Hill when you're done?"

"I may give that a shot but would likely stay only for a few years. I worry about staying too long and becoming jaded and jaundiced for life. No thank you," she commented with a little shudder at the end.

"Been there. So much depends on for whom you work. If you managed to land a position in the office of a progressive, high-road, policy-oriented Minister on his or her way up, it could be a life-changing experience. Conversely, if you're stuck on the staff of a cynical, political opportunist, who sees his seat in Cabinet as a throne from which to serve his own political interests, that could also be a life-changing experience of a different kind. You'll grow old, withered, and tired well before your years. You'll also distrust any random act of kindness that falls your way. I've seen it transform perfectly normal, intelligent, nice people. They see Trojan horses in their sleep. It's not pleasant," I concluded.

"Well, it's a moot point for the time being," Lindsay said. "I really need to focus on my research."

"Right, what drew you to the Senate anyway?" I asked.

"Well, the House has been studied to death, and even with the growing interest in the Triple-E Senate, solid research on the chamber of sober second thought remains sadly lacking," she replied with authority.

"Even though I like the Senate as it is, I do believe its very existence in its current unelected form proves that we really don't yet have complete faith in the democracy we've created. If we did, we wouldn't need a second appointed legislative body to step in should the House of Commons spiral out of control," I posited.

"Hard to argue with that," she said, "but I think until we reform our first-past-the-post election formula, it remains possible, even likely, that with at least three viable national parties in the play, a government can be elected by a minority of Canadians. Something's not quite right about that. It's time we took a hard look at some form of proportional representation," she concluded.

While I did introduce the topic, I was not in the mood for a heavy debate on the state of Canadian democracy, so I just nodded in agreement and prayed for a switch to a less taxing subject. She seemed to sense this and duly shifted gears.

"How are you finding your faculty responsibilities so far?" she inquired.

"Well, I'm a little surprised that they're not more onerous than they've turned out to be," I replied. "I'm only teaching one class this term—first-year English for Engineers. It's a little like force-feeding ballroom dancing to sumo wrestlers. They don't understand it. They're not very good at it. They don't like it. And it's not pretty. Other than that, I keep office hours four hours each week and will soon submit my research proposal to the English department. As soon as it's approved, I'll need to get started on that. I have three courses to teach next term. All in all, it's been a rather smooth transition, notwithstanding the minor distraction of a federal election."

And then, she hit me right out of the blue.

"Grandma told me on the sly that you'd broken up with your girlfriend recently and had sworn off women." She gave me a look that might have been sympathy, but my powers of perception had been temporarily knocked off line.

"Really?" I softened my initial deer-in-the-headlights countenance. "Well, I just told her that so she wouldn't think I was coming on to her when I really was just looking for her help on the campaign."

"Right, good idea. She's always getting hit on by young, eligible English professors."

"That's the last time I bare my soul to an older woman," I said with mock indignation.

"She actually told me out of concern for your well-being. She was worried about you—living by yourself in a new town with no family nearby. That's how Muriel is. If she likes you, she looks out for you. And she likes you for some reason."

I admit it, I was touched. I really regretted not having met Muriel earlier. "Well, I do appreciate her concern—I think. My last relationship did end in a rather spectacular fashion. I walked in on my girlfriend and her boss when they were engaged in what was clearly not just a meeting of the minds."

"Ouch. I'm so sorry."

"Actually, in hindsight, I'm not sorry it happened. I regret I walked in at that precise moment. It is not the kind of image that fades with time. But I certainly don't regret finding out about it. It gave me the gumption to break out of the rut I was in and try something new. Okay, now that I'm exposed and vulnerable, what about you?" I asked, more than a little interested in the answer.

"Nothing too exciting on my end. I've been so busy studying and keeping an eye on Grandma that relationships seemed to have fallen off my radar. Besides, living at home saves money, but it isn't exactly on *Cosmo*'s top 10 list of turn-ons for single men." She sighed.

We talked for another hour about our families, what we liked to eat, what we liked on TV, what we liked in political leaders, and what we liked in economic policy and other similarly romantic notions. I didn't really care what we talked about, but our discussion seemed to migrate to semiserious subjects that required the coordinated firing of synapses in the brain to sustain the kind of positive impression for which I was aiming. Fortunately, mine seemed to be firing well enough to keep me in the play. I drove her home without any major gaffes, provided you don't count shutting the car door on her foot. She was spared major injury, and I, major humiliation by the rusted-out door panel that simply collapsed around her well-padded leather shoes, almost without her noticing. I offered silent thanks to the corrosion gods before slipping behind the wheel.

It's likely obvious by now, but for the sake of clarity, yes, I was officially reconsidering my relationship moratorium. We Liberals do have some experience being flexible about our commitments.

The time was nearly two-thirty in the afternoon. I drove to campus for my scheduled office hours to permit my eager young flock of engineering students to ply me with questions about their assignment, provided they didn't ask "will this be on the exam?" The Taurus backfired as I pulled into a parking spot adjacent to the arts building. The noise sounded like a Howitzer, and several students and a few faculty members took cover.

My office, such as it was, overlooked the main quad from the fourth floor. It was small by any standard, measuring about nine feet by eight feet. The walls consisted of painted concrete block. Replace the desk and bookshelves with a cot and a sliding barred door and you'd have Alcatraz circa 1949. Nevertheless, I was quite happy with it and felt a rush of pride as I turned on the lights, unloaded my laptop, tried unsuccessfully to adjust the Venetian blinds, and settled behind the green metal desk. I checked my voice mail and found only one message. The message was from one of my engineering students, who was having trouble locating W. O. Mitchell's *Who Has Seen the Wind* in the library. After replaying his message a few times and listening carefully, I diagnosed his problem. I called the sad sack back, getting his voice mail.

"Hello, Leonard, it's Professor Addison calling you back. You'll find *Who Has Seen the Wind* under M for Mitchell, not O for O'Mitchell. He's Canadian, not Irish. Looking forward to reading your book report."

I sat for my requisite two hours, trying not to think about the campaign. I focused on finishing the academic research proposal I owed Phil Gannon. I planned to continue my work in the study of Canadian comedic novels. It was a relatively untouched area of study. I laid out my research intentions, indicating what academic papers might flow from my work and what journals might be targeted for publication. I considered noting my intention to write a book as well but felt it was a bit presumptuous at this stage. By five o'clock, I was satisfied with my document and e-mailed it to Professor Gannon. In the entire two hours I stayed in my office to serve the needs of my young engineering charges, nary a student darkened my doorway. This concerned me as their first assignment, a book report, was due within the week. As the deadline loomed, I felt sure there'd be a lineup for my sage advice or, at least, a couple kids explaining why their reports would be delayed. But no. Disquieting to say the least.

I picked up the two Petes on campus, and after they devoured two large pizzas, I dropped them off as planned in poll 14, conveniently located within walking distance of their punkhouse. They would canvass till nine o'clock and then walk home, saving me a trip. I arrived at the boathouse at around eight o'clock, tired and replete. I'd snuck a few pieces of pizza for myself.

Angus saw me from his workshop as I mounted the staircase and waved me in. The hovercraft was really taking shape. He claimed he was still weeks away from any meaningful testing but was happy with his progress. The skirt was fully attached all the way around the craft's perimeter. The decking was very nearly done, closing in the hull, and the vent thingies that traversed the hovercraft from front to back on either side looked finished to my untrained eye. The small rudders in each vent opening were now linked to the cockpit through thin metal arms, cables, and guide wheels. The dashboard and steering wheel made the cockpit look not unlike that of a car. There was no seat, yet, but two mounts seemed ready to bear a bench across them. I could also see what I assumed were two foot pedals—one on either side—on the floor under the dashboard.

"It's looking great, Angus," I said and meant it.

"Aye, she's comin' along. But I'm at a damnably tedious part of this business and am lookin' for a break. Fancy a game?" With eyebrows arched, he pointed through the large, opened doors to an old and battered chessboard that was supported by a small table on the dock, jutting into the river. Dusty chess pieces were set up, poised for play. He'd obviously been waiting for me, and I confess, it made me feel good.

"So how goes the great campaign?" he inquired jovially as we sat down at the board and started the game. He took white, and I took black.

"Well, two weeks in, we've hit about 2 percent of the houses in the riding. At this pace, I expect the two Petes to be able to knock on maybe 5 percent of the doors by E-day. So all in all, I'd say your chances of victory have improved from 'don't make me laugh' to 'you must be kidding.'"

Angus tilted his head back, giving me an excellent view of his cavernous nostrils, and laughed long and hard. "Splendid! Well said. That puts a tilt in me kilt," he chortled and pushed his king pawn ahead two squares.

"Yes, I thought you'd be pleased," I responded, pushing my queenside bishop pawn up two squares. Sicilian again.

"What about me fledglin' campus support? Is anythin' likely to come of it?" he asked, I think genuinely.

"Your ties to the university will undoubtedly score us some support, and as your chief scrutineer, I may even be forced to take off my shoes and socks to tally your vote total," I replied. Angus just giggled and shook his head as he slid his bishop into the fray.

"We went to hear the enemy speak today at some chamber-of-commerce love-in. If I had to take every meal with a side order of Eric Cameron, I'd waste away to nothing. Kills a Liberal's appetite cold," I reported.

"Aye, he's an enigma, that one," commented Angus. The sun had set by now, and our game was lit only by the light spilling onto the dock through the workshop doors.

"Enigma?" I repeated, not quite understanding.

"Aye, I've known a few politicians in me day through me wife, and though many of them seemed slick and shallow on the surface, when I got to know 'em, they turned out to be good, hard-workin' folks who really seemed to care about their country. But our Mr. Cameron is a paradox. He seems humble, honest, and genuine at first glance, but underneath it all, he is a self-absorbed, conceited, and contemptible blackguard," Angus observed.

I'd never considered this perspective, and as I turned it over in my mind, I decided Angus might well be right. Before I could respond, Angus stepped in again.

"Aye, the man's an ass with the Midas touch. His luck has to turn sometime. He's led too charmed a life until now. I know his wife passed on, but theirs was a loveless marriage, sure as guns. What's more, he seems to have done well enough as a widower, may God forgive me."

While I was mulling this over, Angus forked my queen and bishop with his knight. Shit, shit, shit. My chess-playing skills—and I use the term loosely—simply could not support a second train of thought while the game was in progress. I looked three moves ahead and saw his unstoppable checkmate, so I toppled my king in surrender. It was the only honourable thing to do. With magnanimity absent without leave, Angus leaped to his feet and clapped his hands together, accompanied by what I can only describe as a war whoop.

I confess I've never really been comfortable in close proximity to a naked man. So when Angus stood in the darkness on the dock and pulled off his clothes, I thought his victory celebration was a bit over the top. When his staid white and blue striped boxers hit the planks, the full moon (in the sky) made his stout, pale body seem even whiter than it already was. He gave me a wink and trotted off the end of the dock into a reasonably competent shallow dive. In a few, strong strokes of front crawl, he was lost from view, except when he occasionally glided through the narrow, shimmering trail the moon had draped across the river.

I waited until I saw him heading back to the dock before I put away the chessboard and pieces and moved the table back into the workshop. I left him standing on the dock, still naked and unabashed, studying the stars. I brushed my teeth, tossed my clothes on the chair, and slid between the sheets. By this time, Angus had returned to the workshop where I could once again hear him mumbling in one-sided conversation. I listened for the now-familiar descent from talking to weeping, but it never came.

◆   ◆   ◆

Diary
Friday, September 20

My Love,

It's a beautiful, clear night, and I've just taken a plunge in the river the way we used to. Dr. Addison, whom I just whipped in chess, seemed a little uncertain as I doffed my clothes, but he'll get over it. My whole body shrank as I hit the clean, cool water. As I swam out into the river, the moon illuminating my path, I swear I could hear you and feel you next to me. If only I could see you. Is that too much to ask? After a time, Daniel left us alone and retired to his loft. I'm now wide awake thanks to our dip. When I finish this entry, I'll spend another hour on Baddeck 1 before trying, against all odds, to sleep without dreams.

Chess tonight was grand. Daniel was clearly distracted by trying to carry on a conversation while playing. I was merciful and put him out of his misery in short order. Notwithstanding his lapse in concentration tonight, he plays methodically, like an engineer. I can see him weighing the implications of every move I make before considering and making his own. He is patient when he must delay his own strategy to defend against mine. A worthy opponent. A satisfying win.

The cockpit, dashboard, and control systems are all finished—though untested. However, there remains much to do as the boring and the mundane overtake me. I must remove the engine, flip over the hull, and apply three coats of marine antifouling paint so that Baddeck 1 at least tends towards watertight. Given my inferior carpentry skills, this will be an ambitious endeavour with limited chance of complete success. With paint brushes already dirtied and the air choked with fumes, I plan to paint the rest of the craft at the same time so that I only have to clean up once. Neither my laziness nor my distaste for painting has diminished since you left.

Daniel reported today that the campaign is just the exercise in futility I had hoped. He attended an Eric Cameron luncheon speech today. I know what you're thinking. I shouldn't use *Eric Cameron* and *luncheon* in the same sentence. You're right. Daniel confirmed that the three lonely Liberals in attendance completely lost their appetites. Little wonder. Cameron is a buffoon—suave, smooth, and debonair—but a buffoon just the same. But what am I, with my name on the ballot in an election I cannot, dare not, win?

I know I am offending democracy, but under the circumstances, I'm losing little sleep over it all. Aye, I guess I, too, am a buffoon. But you must shoulder some of that blame.

AM

CHAPTER SEVEN

With two weeks to go, our small but committed team had settled into a comfortable routine and rhythm that bravely but barely kept the Liberal cause alive in Cumberland-Prescott. The two Petes sustained their valiant canvassing and managed to bring their own special brand of political punk advocacy to neighbourhoods in every region of the riding. Their presence in some ultraconservative areas was tantamount to two unarmed Nazis, strolling through downtown London at the height of the blitz. Yet, they persevered. I'm still trying to divine what kept them going day after day. Perhaps I was just naïve, and they were only looking for better marks in English, but I don't think so. They were already among my top students. I marveled at their equanimity in the face of, at best, guarded ambivalence and, at worst, naked hostility. I knew how demoralizing it could be to spend two or three hours each day selling something that no one was buying. In most ridings in the country, canvassers would encounter a supportive Liberal voter every few houses. In Cumberland-Prescott, it was more like every few days.

Muriel spent her time working the phones—correction, phone—and annotating the official voters list, which was now available following the enumeration process. Lindsay continued her examination of the polls, using the returns from the previous election to identify any pockets of Liberal support. She also laid out the McLintock pamphlet I'd written. She was a whiz with Photoshop and had inserted a doctored photo on the front panel that showed a thoughtful Angus deep in discussion with our party's leader. Of course, the two men had never met nor even been in the same room together. At least, the leaflet voters crumpled up and tossed back at the two Petes finally featured some local content.

I helped out with the canvass and did my best to keep morale boosted above mild depression. I also stayed in very close contact with the national campaign to make sure they knew we were doing our part.

On E-day minus 14, I parked in the lot on Slater near Metcalfe just behind the modest building that served as the national campaign headquarters for the Liberal Party of Canada. I'd just dropped the two Petes off on campus and was right on time for a meeting of campaign managers for the eastern-Ontario riding. We had these little get-togethers every two weeks so that the national leadership could keep its finger on the local pulse and so we could benefit from the alleged insight and expertise of the senior campaign strategists.

I took my regular seat around the vast boardroom table with my back to the large second-floor window. I was easily distracted by the human and automotive traffic flowing past and would rather look at the wall opposite and the framed photo of the Queen and Pierre Trudeau, signing the Constitution on the lawn of Parliament Hill. Six other local campaign managers joined me on my side of the table. I knew them all—four women and two men, representing two Ottawa ridings and four more rural constituencies. I liked three of them (idealist policy wonks) and could take or leave the other three (cynical political operators). We left the other side of the table free for the big wheels of the party.

Fifteen minutes after the meeting was supposed to have started, Bradley Stanton, the Leader's chief of staff and deputy campaign director, and Michael Zaleski, the president of National Opinion and the Liberal Party's pollster, sauntered in and sat across from us. I wasn't Stanton's biggest fan. He'd been almost solely responsible for the decision in the dying stages of the last campaign to "'go negative" and hammer away at rumours of the Prime Minister's failing health. The PM had lost weight and had looked a bit gaunt. As it turned out, the Conservatives set us up by starting the whisper campaign themselves, hoping we'd take the bait. Stanton didn't just nibble at the worm, he swallowed it whole along with the hook, line, sinker, and half the rod. As soon as our declining-health-innuendo ads hit the air, the Tories rolled out the truth about the PM's recent weight loss. A videotape released to the press gallery showed the Prime Minister weight training, running, and (wait for it) sparring in a boxing ring as part of his three-month-old fitness regimen. The final insult? Well, with four days left in the campaign, while our reprehensible ads were running, casting doubt on the health of the Tory Prime Minister, he actually ran in the National Capital Marathon, finishing in just over three hours and forty-two minutes, coming in twelfth out of 469 runners in his age category. Overnight, the Liberal four-point lead in the polls evaporated to be replaced by a three-point deficit. Our majority government became theirs because of Bradley Stanton's "do whatever it takes to win" approach. He gambled; we lost, which for staunch Liberals across the country meant that Canada lost.

I knew Zaleski, the pollster guru, reasonably well and had worked with him a few times when slaving over the Leader's response to the Government's last Throne Speech. After all, I wanted to hit the right buttons with Canadians—support the Government on measures enjoying considerable public approval and bash the Tories on those that did not. He seemed a nice enough guy, but I worried that he was better at delivering the advice the Leader *wanted* to hear rather than what he *needed* to hear.

In a glance, they took us all in and then focused on me. Neither of them could stifle the early tremors of a smile. "Addison, good of you to take the time away from your close race in C-P," opened Stanton.

"Bradley, always a pleasure," I replied. I thought his sarcasm was a little out of line given that having me find the candidate and run the campaign had been his idea in the first place. I thought he owed me.

"Look, we might as well get started," Stanton said. "Thanks for coming. This won't take too long. I'm going to give you an update on the national campaign and what we're discovering on the ground. Then, I'm going to ask Michael to share the national numbers with you and how they look on a riding-by-riding basis in the constituencies for which you are responsible."

When he'd finished this preamble, Stanton sat down for the rest of his talk. "The Leader is doing a great job on the trail. We've got the reporters on the bus eating out of our hands. His rural and urban stump speeches are both going over well, and our 'time for a change, a change for our time' line is taking root. Nice turn of phrase, Addison," he commented with a nod in my direction.

I actually thought the line was a little trite and not clever enough when I first penned it, but the Leader had really taken to it. The success of such lines is really all in the context and delivery. The right speaker, in the right setting, at the right point in a speech, with the right crowd, could carry it off. Otherwise, it could go over like a concrete zeppelin. To his credit, not to mention his speech writer's, the Leader seemed to be making it fly. In what little media coverage of the national tour I'd seen, the crowds occasionally joined him in reciting the line. It made for solid TV in a Jesse Jackson "keep hope alive" kind of way.

I considered this somewhat of an achievement given the Leader's oratorical limitations. He spoke in a rather narrow band of inflection. So narrow that it often approached monotone. We'd coached him for hours on end with clandestine visits from Stratford actors, firebrand preachers, and even a popular professional wrestler known for his emotional and motivational prebout diatribes. Nothing seemed to work. Even when he managed to step up his performance, it was obvious that he wasn't comfortable in his own skin. Well, you work with what you have. The Leader did have several other redeeming qualities that I know I could cite if I thought about it for a time.

"That asshole Cameron's budget is our biggest challenge in the campaign," Stanton continued. "I've never seen such balanced and carefully constructed fiscal virtuosity. Canadians love the budget, and they love Cameron. Sorry, Daniel, but it's an incontro-fucking-vertible fact." He finished with his hands up in surrender. I've always found the use of profanity for effect to be a practice of the weak-minded. In Stanton's case, my theory held.

The woman next to me piped up then, mercifully leading us away from any more Eric Cameron idolatry. "Brad, on what issues are we finding traction?"

"Good question, Susan. In the jerkwater rural towns, the Leader is really hammering away on the Tories' plans to reduce and eventually eliminate any form of agricultural support programs in the name of free trade. We're getting a great response from the farmers, and the Prime Minister actually took a tomato in the forehead yesterday on the same farm in the Annapolis Valley that we'd visited the week before. In the urban centres, health care and federal support for cities are the hot buttons, and we're right there with our Smart Health and Smart Cities programs. I forget exactly what those initiatives are, but I'm certain they're groundbreaking, and they seem to be popular with the electorate," he remarked without even the decency at least to look sheepish.

Stanton stopped to take a swig from a bottle of Evian before he wrapped up his part of the presentation. "Finally, as I alluded to earlier, the Tories are really trying to ride the Cameron budget into the sunset, and that's what really worries me. I think you all know Michael Zaleski from National Opinion. He's going to give you a look at the national numbers before zeroing in on your ridings and, more importantly, your candidates. Michael."

Michael Zaleski, like Stanton, remained in his chair and just talked about the numbers. There was no handout, no PowerPoint presentation, just a stack of cross-tabs in front of him. I expected this. Polling numbers were hot commodities during campaigns, so it was not uncommon for the national campaign only to *talk* about the numbers even with insiders like campaign managers. History had shown that hard copies could easily go astray and perhaps fall into Tory hands or, worse, a reporter's.

"Thanks, Brad. Nationally, the numbers have stayed painfully stable during the campaign as if we weren't even fighting an election. We've been doing weekly tracking on our standard general-population national survey with a sample of 1,500 Canadians, large enough to give us reasonably accurate regional breaks. Of decided voters, the Tories have held steady at 43. We're at 38, and the NDP are at 19. What tells us that there is, in fact, an election up for grabs is that the undecideds have grown to 33 percent. Now, if we look at the demographic makeup of the undecideds, we see a preponderance of young- to middle-aged women and of immigrants who have recently become citizens. These two categories of voters among the decided electorate tend to vote as follows: Liberals 44, Tories 38, and

NDP 18, which bodes well for us," Zaleski droned on as he flipped through his printouts. I'd spent five years bearing witness to Government by poll and Opposition by poll. I wasn't sure I could take much more of election campaign by poll.

Unfortunately, my fellow campaign managers weren't quite so jaundiced. Noticing that they were still conscious, the polling pooh-bah went deep on the numbers while I drifted and counted the number of times he said "in terms of," an affected crutch phrase I'd come to loathe for some inexplicable reason. Instead of spending half an hour on pollster-babble, Zaleski could have summed up the numbers quite simply. If there were no knockout punches in the Leaders' debate the following week, it looked like the Tories would be re-elected with a slim majority or, at worst, form a minority government. With so little time left before the vote, it would be difficult, if not impossible, for the Liberals to turn enough minds. The only hope was a total flame-out of a scandal that might send the Tories into free fall at terminal velocity—our own faint hope clause.

I tuned back in when Zaleski started into the riding-by-riding breakouts. I admit I was curious about the numbers in Cumberland-Prescott. As I expected, he offered up the results for the other six ridings first, leaving my freak show until the end. Things looked quite good in the other campaigns. In the two Ottawa constituencies represented in the room, we were ahead in both by reasonably comfortable margins. The favourable ratings of both of our candidates had improved since the start of the campaign. In fact, the Ottawa Centre candidate had doubled her positive ratings after a rather lacklustre start. Short of catastrophes in getting out the Liberal vote, these two urban ridings were ours to win. This was particularly impressive as entering the election, we'd been neck and neck in both. It reminded me that it really was possible for individual campaigns to overcome national trends and assert some local control. Yes, the coattails effect was alive and well as local candidates rose and fell on the performance of their Leaders. But we did have some influence over our destinies at the grassroots level.

"In the four rural ridings here this morning—we'll get to you in a minute, Addison—we have four very tight races that could go either way. And we seem to be moving in the right direction in all of them," Zaleski noted.

Zaleski then proceeded to break down the data for the other campaign managers. The room hung on every number as if the words came straight from God. Predictable. In modern Canadian politics, the pollster stands first in the line of succession should God ever be unable to perform his/her righteous duties. The Z-man, as Zaleski was sometimes called (much to my nausea), reviewed the individual candidates' numbers before noting how crucial these six ridings were to our national electoral fortunes. Stanton couldn't resist jumping in for a little ham-handed pep talk.

"So it's absolutely critical that you six really bear down in the last two weeks. Winning your seats would be huge for us. We're in a fight to the death, and victories in your ridings could push us over the top. We must win all of your seats. Defeat is not an option." (I was close to hurling at this point.) He actually punched his fist into his other hand when he made this last statement, reminiscent of a Batman and Robin exchange. (Holy blowhard, Batman!) I know I should have kept my yap shut and let him finish his very, very bad Knute Rockne impression. But then again, I really didn't like Stanton.

"You've given us the national picture," I said, "but how do our numbers look in the seat count analysis across the country. That's what really matters on E-day. Michael, I assume you've run those results." I turned to Zaleski and tried to look earnest. My fellow campaign managers nodded in agreement.

"Of course, we've run those numbers," Zaleski started as he flipped through the large stack of computer printouts in front of him. "The seat analysis shows that we're likely to—"

"Hey hey, Michael!" interrupted Stanton. "We agreed we weren't going there in these briefings." Stanton glared at him and then at me. "Let's just move on to the train wreck in Cumberland-Prescott, shall we? The rest of you are free to go unless you want to hear about the state of affairs in Canada's safest Tory seat." His tone was frigid. No one left.

"Michael?"

"Right. Cumberland-Prescott. Well, it's not a pretty picture for the Liberal cause. Never has been, as you all know," Zaleski said.

"Let's just hear the numbers, shall we?" I prodded gently.

"Well, of the decided voters, which constitutes 90 percent of those eligible, 92 percent are for Cameron, and the support is rock hard. When we really get into the numbers, we've found only a handful of NDP supporters, all of whom seem to be related to the candidate. As for the Liberal candidate—" Zaleski consulted his notes again. "One Duncan Angus McLintock, our extrapolated numbers tell us that approximately 350 voters correctly identified him as our candidate but that only 127 say they'll vote for him. The lion's share of our support is firmly rooted in the over-75 demographic with another pocket among those with more than two postgraduate degrees. If the undecideds break down on election day in the same proportions as the decideds, we should finish with somewhere just south of 140 votes," he concluded in a tone that might as well have just voiced "ashes to ashes, dust to dust."

"Have we moved up or down since the campaign started?" I asked.

"Masochist," Stanton whispered not quite under his breath.

"Ah, well, Muriel Parkinson earned 3,600 votes last time around, so I'd say our support has dropped significantly since you signed up Mr. McLintock," reported Zaleski.

Thanks. The other campaign managers and the party's pollster kept their heads bowed in classic funeral-visitation style as they filed past me and out the door.

"Addison, would it be helpful if the Leader paid Cumberland-Prescott a visit in the last week of the campaign?" Stanton inquired. "He and your Angus McGillicuddy could do some main-streeting—rally the troops, as it were."

I was nearly certain he was just kidding, but in case he wasn't, I needed to play it right. Angus wouldn't even be in the country next week. "It's *McLintock.* Kind of you to offer, Brad, but I really don't think a tour stop in Cumberland is a good use of the Leader's time with one week to go in a close election. Better to have him in the neighbouring ridings where he could really tip the balance our way," I replied.

"Oh, I wasn't offering up the Leader. I was just asking whether you thought it would be helpful. Keep smiling, Addison. It's not over until the ballots are counted." Stanton chuckled as he made good his escape, leaving me alone at the table.

I found Muriel in her usual spot by the window, a marked-up voters list on her lap and my old cell phone implanted in her ear. She took one look at me, ended her call, and waved me onto the couch beside her. She turned over the voters list she was calling but not before I'd seen the sea of blue from the highlighter she held in her hand. Two other apparently exhausted blue highlighters rested at the bottom of a nearby wastepaper basket while brand new red and orange highlighters remained in their unopened packaging on the side table next to her. No need to open them.

"Daniel, whatever is the matter, dear boy?" she asked, patting the seat next to her—a paragon of grandmotherly sympathy. "You look like crap!" I was always caught off guard when she slid into sailor mode.

"Hi, Muriel," I replied, sinking onto the plastic-encrusted cushion. "I've just come from national headquarters for a little peek at the numbers. We're doing well across the country and in the eastern-Ontario ridings. However, that's the end of my glad tidings. Angus seems to enjoy the support of half of your housemates, but that's about all. Cameron owns the entire riding."

"Well, of course he does. Where have you been?" Muriel poked.

"I know, I know, but it seems so much more depressing when the cold, hard numbers are thrust in front of you. And I assure you, they're very cold and very hard."

"Don't get so wrapped up in it. It was doomed from the start," she soothed. "'Twas ever thus. This isn't about winning. It's about making sure the cause is well served in an admittedly quixotic quest. I never once allowed myself even to contemplate the possibility of winning. If I ever had, I'd have been lost."

I smiled and gave her frail shoulders a quick squeeze. I could feel the involuntary vibrations of her Parkinson's.

"You know, Daniel, I love my granddaughter very much," she started in a serious tone.

"Muriel, we went to Starbucks to talk about the campaign. It wasn't a date," I pleaded.

"You misunderstand me, college boy. It's been awhile since she's been out with anyone. She's so focused on her schoolwork and my well-being. I'm worried about her. She's not getting any younger."

"Please, Muriel, she's only 28. She's pursuing a master's in political science. She's intelligent, quick-witted, confident, and beautiful to boot. I don't think you need to worry about her. She'll do just fine."

"Well, I'm glad you think so. If I were you, I'd consider asking her out again. I have a feeling she'd say yes."

"Muriel, we're not in public school. I'm not going to pass you a note to give to her." I feigned disinterest for as long as I could, which was about nine seconds before turning towards her again. "Okay, you got me. What do you mean you think she'd say yes if I asked her out? Has she been talking about me? If so, I need all the details just so I don't put a foot in the wrong place, like, in my mouth."

"I'm not about to betray her confidence any more than I already have. Let's just say I see a spirit and an energy I haven't seen in her for a long time. I don't think it's because she's studying the Senate or visiting me and my merry band of aging lechers, who shamelessly ogle her whenever she's here. And if you mention one word to Lindsay about this, don't bother coming back here."

"You've been very bad, Muriel. And I thank you." I was surprised and pleased. It's always easier to navigate the shoal-infested waters of the early relationship when you have insider assistance reading the charts.

Something caught her attention out the window, and I followed her gaze. I heard her sharp intake of breath. She seemed transfixed by something along the banks of the Ottawa River.

"Well, dip me in chocolate and call me candy," she said as she shook her head, still looking out the window.

"What?"

"Do you see that big, old, dead tree on the shore there?" she asked and pointed.

I found it. "Yep."

"Do you see that long tree branch that's now floating down the river?"

"Sure do."

"Well, that huge, dead limb has been hanging out over the river, threatening to fall, ever since I came here. I've watched it bend over in the west wind. I've seen it bowed so it dipped into the water under the weight of a heavy snow. I've even been sitting here when kids have swung on it, trying to break it off. Against all of those trials and probably many I haven't witnessed, that tenacious limb has just held on for dear life, refusing to fall. Who knows how many years it's been swaying there on the verge of collapse. Well, I just watched it fall all on its own. No wind, no snow, no kids—just age and gravity."

"It's surely a sign," I said in mock reverential tones.

"Don't you make fun of me," she snapped, cracking me lightly in the ribs. For all I knew, she'd hit me as hard as she could.

"So sorry," I said, my hands in plea position, "I wasn't mocking you. I'm a believer in signs, too. What do you think it means?"

"I have no idea, but it seems so odd that after all that limb has been through, it would just up and fall completely on its own." She continued her vigil until the limb floated out of sight, heading east before she looked at me. "It could mean something as basic as all that was is no longer."

I returned home to the cacophony of a revving engine, reverberating through the walls of the boathouse. When I looked in the window, I was greeted with yet another bizarre sight. The craft appeared to be hovering with its skirt fully inflated, looking like a giant inner tube surrounding the entire vessel. From my vantage point outside the door, I could just see Angus's legs, emerging from underneath the near side of the hovercraft. By my reckoning, this would put his head directly under the fan and engine mounted on top. His legs weren't moving, and for all I knew, he'd already been decapitated. I opened the door, unsure of what to do next. Option one was to crawl under the craft and check on Angus. Option two was simply to head upstairs and forget what I'd seen. Option two won by a landslide, but I found enough balloting irregularities to throw the legitimacy of the vote into question.

On my stomach, I easily wriggled under the pressurized skirt. It gave way lightly, spilling air around me as I inched underneath. The noise was fearsome. There was some light underneath, shed through the fan housing. In it, I could see with considerable relief that Angus had not been eaten by the evil hovercraft but was calmly working on the scoops that could swing down into the air flow and redirect it through the side vents on top of the hovercraft.

I could tell by the way he banged his head on the underside of the hovercraft when he saw me that he hadn't expected us to meet in this particular location. He waved his wrenchy-thingy at me with some menace. Eventually, I figured out he wanted me to return to my normal upright position outside the confines of the hovercraft's air cushion—what he called the *plenum*. I slid back out and was brushing the sawdust off my jeans and sweater when he appeared at my side. He reached into the cockpit and dialed back the engine until it stopped. The craft immediately settled onto the floor of the workshop as the skirt billowed out, now free of the solid form it was given by the rushing air.

"That's twice now you've snuck up on me, Addison! A third time will find you in the river," he bellowed.

"I'm sorry! I thought you were dead, crushed by the weight of your own masterpiece. What would you have done if you'd walked into the workshop and seen my prone and stationary form, sticking out from underneath as the engine roared?"

"I'd have dropped a ball-peen hammer on yer crotch and told you to get the hell away from me hovercraft."

"All right, all right, I give up. You think I enjoyed crawling into the belly of the beast to save you? In the future, I hereby promise not to attempt a rescue regardless of your predicament," I intoned with due solemnity and my right hand raised.

He softened, and a flicker of a smile flirted with the corners of his mouth. "Aye, but you did see the height of tha' cushion, dinnya?" His smile germinated as he asked.

"I sure did. It was flying high. It's amazing, Angus. Congratulations."

"Aye, the cushion pressure's even higher than I'd calculated, and the skirt leaked not a molecule of air."

"Except when I crawled underneath."

"Aye, but that's behind us now, laddie."

We sat out on the dock, he with a shot of Lagavulin and I with a cold Coke. The river moved with gentle purpose towards the east. I told Angus all about the briefing session with Zaleski and Stanton, including the dismal and still declining

Liberal support in Cumberland-Prescott. Angus was utterly exhausted and quite short of breath when his laughing jag eventually slowed to a dull chortle. The Lagavulin spread in a wet splotch across his flannel work shirt where he'd dumped the scotch in the throes of hilarity. He finally grew silent save for his wheezing.

He could tell that I was not pleased by his over-the-top reaction. "I'm sorry, but I couldna help meself. Besides, I should be more upset than you. I know plenty more than 140 people in this town. I thought me support would be at least up around 275," he sputtered before convulsing again in poorly restrained giggles.

"Yuck it up all you want. It's no skin off your hide. But I still have to face my former colleagues in the Leader's office, and I can tell you, my stock is in free fall."

"Are you absolutely sure about the numbers?" he asked after a while.

"Plus or minus three percentage points 19 times out of 20," I sighed.

Angus nodded with some finality. We sat in relative silence for a time as the sun traced its arc towards the west.

"So when do you leave for Papua New Guinea?" I inquired.

"I'm off the day after tomorrow until very late the night of this blasted election. And doonae think me timin' is coincidental. Me bags are packed, me passport is primed, and I've already booked me a cab to the airport," Angus explained with some satisfaction.

"Angus, I would have taken you to the airport," I commented.

"Not in that death trap on wheels you won't. Besides, what if there's a campaign meeting scheduled in the back seat at the same time. I wouldna want to take HQ out of commission even for an hour," he mocked gently. "It's kind of you to offer, Daniel, but I'm takin' no chances."

"Well, after today's sobering lesson in public opinion, you can leave with a clear conscience. Nothing threatens Eric Cameron's coronation. He will have succeeded in hoodwinking 38,000 voters yet again, and there's absolutely nothing we can do about it. I feel about as useful as a seamstress in a nudist camp," I said.

"Aye, I've never been to a nudist colony," Angus remarked with what appeared to be genuine interest.

I had a night of marking ahead. My E for E students had handed in their first assignment the week before, and I had studiously avoided reviewing them. I just wasn't sure what to expect, based on how the classes were proceeding. I bid Angus good night and climbed up to my apartment. By ten o'clock, I was halfway through the book reports. Most were as I expected—pathetic. But occasionally, I found a diamond in the rough or, as it turned out in one case, a *diamonoid*. A particularly obnoxious and boisterous engineer, who usually sat amidst a cabal of disciples, had apparently read—and had written a book report on—John Irving's *A Prayer for Owen Meany*. This book was one of my favourite novels, and I was intrigued, if not a little suspicious. His book report was outstanding. He picked up some fine nuances in the characterization and provided compelling comparisons and contrasts with some of Irving's other works, notably, *The World According to Garp*. I was impressed, but my spidey senses were tingling to beat the band.

Have I mentioned that Google is a wonderful thing? I typed a particularly cogent and well-crafted sentence into the powerful search engine and banged Enter. Busted. In seconds, several different versions of the essay appeared in an orgy of plagiarism. He was smart enough to hijack an appropriate essay but not smart enough to realize that I would know he couldn't possibly have written it. Plagiarism is a big deal at universities. Just ask Dean Rumplun. I had the authority and the evidence to put this guy on probation, if not out the door. But I also had the power to be lenient and forgiving with a student whose engineering career could be crippled by one youthful indiscretion. After the quick chat I planned to have with him, I figured he'd be a little more attentive in class and hoped his acolytes might even follow suit.

As I lay in bed, Angus was still engaged below me though mercifully, the ear-splitting engine remained idle. As usual, I could hear him chatting away in an almost jovial tone. Beyond his muffled musings, the only other thing that seeped into my room through the floor vents was the paint-peeling stench of one of his flatulent depth charges. I'd heard the noise but dismissed it as a particularly sonorous boat horn out on the river. I opened the window, gathered the quilt around my nose, and drifted off.

◆   ◆   ◆

Diary
Monday, September 30

My Love,

In one more day, my neck will be free of this election millstone. Papua New Guinea beckons, and I will answer its call with featherlight feet and a happy heart. My equipment left last week via a U.S. Air Force Hercules cargo plane courtesy of a former student who now enjoys daunting responsibilities in the upper echelon of the American military. I had to transport my equipment in a rented cube van to the Canadian Forces Base at Trenton where my saviour aircraft was participating in joint exercises. But it was well worth the boring drive to know that I'll have all I'll need awaiting me when I arrive in PNG.

Poor Daniel. He was a mere shell of his usual self tonight after some meeting he'd attended at Liberal headquarters in Ottawa. He'd been briefed on the current polling results for Cumberland-Prescott, and it wasn't pretty. Tee-hee. After he materialized beside me beneath Baddeck 1, scaring the bejabbers out of me for a second time in as many weeks, he shared the blessed news with me. It turns out that after the election, I could probably throw a dinner party in our own house for every voter who supported me and still have room for the NDPers, too. Such is Eric Cameron's hypnotic hold on the good people of this riding. Praise be and spread the good news!

I did have another pleasant and lengthy phone conversation with Muriel Parkinson this afternoon whilst making final preparations to test Baddeck 1's cushion pressure. We've spoken a few times over the last few weeks. You likely remember her name. Muriel was my predecessor carrying the Liberal banner in the last five—aye, five—federal elections. A glutton for punishment to say the least. She called in search of your boathouse bunkee Dr. Addison. Charming, forthright, and quite the pistol to boot, she whiles away her days in the Riverfront Seniors' Residence, reading every word you've ever published. An unabashed disciple of yours she is. And who can blame her? She actually worked on Mackenzie King's staff when he reigned in Ottawa. We spoke of many and sundry things and were of like mind on most. She was unaccountably tolerant of my sham run for office, for which I was grateful, and said so. I freely confess I was quite taken with the old mum. Quick witted, silver tongued, with a bracing impatience for lesser lights. She'd have served us well were it not for that little matter of a century and a half of Tory bedrock protecting the seat.

Though I expect you were watching, Baddeck 1 rose from its haunches today and hovered in all its glory, reaching an altitude of 25 inches. My decision to enlarge the skirt has given me an unanticipated additional three inches of lift. (Cracking!) I was able to adjust the linkage I've concocted between the thrust scoops and the throttle so that I can maintain a constant hover height even while diverting some of the air flow for thrust and control. I think I noted this little problem in an earlier entry, but its significance bears repetition. I'm quite pleased with the solution and myself for uncovering it. Mr. Bell is smiling down on me. When I get back from Papua New Guinea, I'll begin the painting.

I confess that my spirits have been higher in recent weeks. Why, I cannot say. I miss you more than I ever imagined I would when you were still languishing and suffering in our sunroom. But the jagged edge of mourning has dulled recently, and I'm at a loss to explain it. Perhaps I shouldn't try. Perhaps I should just embrace it in the hopes that I'm not being teased, only to plummet back into the abyss next week. It is no diminished measure of my love for you that I am feeling better. I know you understand that. I know one should not feel guilty when passing from grief's raw and vicious first stage into the slow and unyielding throb of the second. Yet strangely, I do sometimes. Aye, I do. Now, I can almost hear you scoffing.

AM

CHAPTER EIGHT

"I've marked your book reports, and you can pick them up on your way out. Some of you did very well for engineering students immersed in calculus and chemistry. Others of you made solid efforts but missed the mark by varying margins. I appreciate the time you all committed. I think as we get into the coursework, the remaining two assignments this term will come easier. You might even enjoy them," I concluded, setting off a chorus of groans and head shaking.

It had been a somewhat encouraging session. After the nadir of my third class a few weeks ago, which had attracted only 37 students, I'd worked hard to make the lectures Angus had already outlined for me my own. I took the same approach I'd adopted to speechwriting for the Leader. In speechwriting, audience analysis was critical. You had to get into your audience's collective head to know how to engage and hold them. In drafting speeches, I often took as much time thinking through the knowledge, needs, hopes, dreams, opinions, and attitudes of the audience as I did crafting the actual words to be delivered. This up-front analysis almost always paid dividends. In my experience, the toughest speeches to write were those destined for very diverse audiences where capturing one listener, by definition, meant alienating another.

My particular audience of first-year engineers was homogenous to the point of monolithic, which made my job of holding their attention at least a little easier. In what little time I had left over from the campaign, I developed my lectures around engineering-related storylines and illustrations while still honouring the key literary themes Angus had outlined. My lectures improved, word spread, and my audience grew to respectable proportions. Even so, I was never able to convince all of the engineers enrolled in the course to attend one of my lectures—probably a good thing.

I tried to tap into the engineering part of their brains while making clandestine incursions into their latent artsy side. One day, we talked about the design and construction of the Bloor Viaduct, spanning Toronto's Don River Valley, as the bridge to Michael Ondaatje's masterpiece, *In the Skin of a Lion*, which featured this architectural wonder.

In another lecture, we discussed marine engineering and how sailing ships at the turn of the twentieth century were reinforced for arctic exploration to withstand the blunt trauma of pack ice. This was my subterfuge to introduce Wayne Johnston's excellent novel *The Navigator of New York*. The way I saw it, if you found the front door locked, sometimes you entered through a side window.

I looked up into the heaving sea of students as they gathered their belongings and headed towards the table by the door where I'd laid out their marked book reports. I found him where he usually was, at the centre of attention.

"Mr. Hawkins, a word, please."

Jeremy Hawkins, my creative Internet specialist and John Irving aficionado, descended the steps towards me. He couldn't quite mask the look of disquiet on his face. I couldn't quite mask the look of disdain on mine.

"Yes, Professor?"

I handed over his unmarked book report, which was likely drafted at some U.S. university by an impoverished English graduate student out to make a few bucks through the wonders of e-commerce. I kept it short.

"I know the Internet has made our lives much easier. But it is not just a boundless fount of information. It is also an unprecedented temptation to those looking for the easy way out. At this university, documented academic dishonesty usually means expulsion. You've got three days to hand in your own book report," I said with an extra dollop of gravity. I took his plagiarized work back from him. "I'll hold onto this in the meantime. Have a nice weekend." I smiled as he backed away, shell-shocked. I confess I derived modest satisfaction from bringing him down a few pegs. He deserved it.

The two Petes were waiting for me in my office after class, looking as disconnected from mainstream society as two people could possibly be. I won't dwell on their apparel yet again beyond saying that the most conventional clothing on either of them was Pete2's neon green tartan kilt. It matched the colour of his triple-rowed Mohawk perfectly, which I'm certain was just a coincidence. It also hurt my eyes. As for the rest of their ensemble that day, I wondered how long it took them to get dressed and whether power tools were required.

"Hi, Professor," greeted Pete1. Pete2 nodded salutations, content as usual to let his friend handle the vocal work.

"Gentlemen."

"Thanks for the good marks on our reports. You didn't have to do that, you know. It's not why we're working on the campaign," Pete1 said a little awkwardly.

"And just to be absolutely clear, it's not why I gave you both good marks, either. Don't go around thinking you can score better marks by canvassing for

Angus. That is just not on," I replied, feeling defensive. "Both of you did very well on your assignments. Pete1, your look at Robertson Davies' characters in … in … which Deptford novel did you read?"

"*World of Wonders*," he offered.

"Right. Your analysis was very strong. And Pete2, for someone who so often lets others speak for you, you certainly had a lot to say in your report. Plus, you happened to choose one of my favourite authors."

Pete2 handed me what looked like a first edition of Donald Jack's hilarious *Three Cheers for Me*, the subject of his book report. I also had a first edition that looked very much like this one.

"Thanks for the book," said Pete2 in his characteristic low, nearly monotone drawl.

"He borrowed it when we stopped by your place last week to pick up more pamphlets," Pete1 explained as if he were Pete2's personal translator.

"You're welcome," I replied. "My library is your library."

I had been serious. Both of their assignments were well above the class average and may even have approached the standards of a fair-to-middling grade-twelve student. That's one of the problems with engineering. Senior-high-school students intent on engineering careers had little room on their timetables for anything other than science and math courses if they hoped to be accepted by a good university. They simply had no time for history, English, art, and other important courses. It really showed in the E for E reports I'd just marked.

"Let's go, guys. I'll drop you over in poll 19. You can change on the way," I suggested.

Both Petes had resigned themselves to toning down their appearance when door-to-dooring. To this end, I always carried Liberal T-shirts and ball caps in the Taurus. I pulled over and parked as the boys scrambled out with buttons and leaflets. They looked pumped for another evening of hostile rejection, perhaps highlighted by one neutral encounter with a still-undecided-but-possibly-Liberal-leaning voter.

"Okay, guys, you know the drill. Angus is actually in a different hemisphere right now, but as far as the voters you'll see tonight are concerned, he's just in a different part of the riding. Clear?" I asked.

"Clear, boss man," replied Pete1 with the standard nod from Pete2.

"Now, I really think we're starting to get our message across, and we have you two to thank for that. We're just three days out now, and we want to keep the pressure on until the polling stations open. Politics is a very unpredictable game, and anything can happen." It wasn't exactly a Vince Lombardi, pregame barn-burner speech, but we were all pretty much tapped out by that stage.

"We know the score, professor. We can make it home from here on our own, so we'll see you tomorrow." Pete1 waved me off as they made their way up the front walk of the first house. I jumped back into the car and made a hasty retreat, unwilling to witness the reaction of what statistically speaking was almost certainly a Tory voter.

Three more days, and I would be free. Humiliated, embarrassed, disgraced, but free. I knew that no one in the Leader's office or at national campaign headquarters who was taking their medication as prescribed expected anything other than another Eric Cameron landslide. But I also knew the power at the centre was looking for progress, forward movement, some indication that we'd kept the Liberal flame aflicker to be kindled into a winning inferno in some future election. As far as I could tell, we'd snuffed out the lonely little fire and had flooded the whole riding for good measure. Smokey Bear would be proud. The party brass would not.

It was seven-thirty on the Friday night before the Monday election. I wasn't quite home yet and was listening to "As It Happens" on CBC Radio when my cell phone rang. "Hello."

"Addison, is that you?" It was André Fontaine, out of breath as usual.

"Yep, what's up, André? Looking for an invitation to our victory party?"

"You know where Petra Borschart lives, don't you?" he hollered. I could hear crowd noises in the background.

"I think so. She's on Welland Avenue, isn't she?"

"Yeah, 65 Welland. Get over here right now. Right now!" He hung up.

I closed my cell and drove right past the McLintock boathouse towards the quiet residential community where Petra lived on the west side of Cumberland. I realized my stomach muscles were clenched. André was an excitable guy, but he seemed utterly possessed on the phone. It made me nervous.

What happened next made me throw up. And, oh yes, what happened next also changed Canada.

We interrupt this program to bring you a special news bulletin from "CBC Radio National News." Less than one hour ago, Finance Minister Eric Cameron escaped from a fire at the home of his chief of staff, Petra Borschart, in Cumberland, Ontario. Neither was injured in the blaze, but both have been detained by police as part of a pornography investigation.

Eyewitnesses at the scene report that the Finance Minister and Ms. Borschart escaped from the house in rather unusual attire. Videotape shot moments ago and transmitted to CBC television news via satellite shows Mr. Cameron wearing only a studded, leather cummerbund, chrome handcuffs, alligator clips attached to his chest area, and a studded, leather choker with a three-foot leash attached at the other end to the wrist of his chief of staff. The satellite videotape shows Ms. Borschart wearing a revealing rubber bodysuit. Both Mr. Cameron and Ms. Borschart were transported in the back of an OPP cruiser to the regional detachment in Cumberland.

Video equipment and hundreds of apparently homemade, sexually explicit DVDs were also found at the scene in what police are describing as a sexual torture chamber in the basement of the house. There are unconfirmed reports that the Finance Minister and Ms. Borschart are both featured in at least some of the DVDs.

Firefighters report that the blaze started in an upstairs bedroom when a window air conditioner shorted, igniting the curtains. The fire was quickly extinguished. Stay tuned to "CBC Radio National News" for up-to-the-minute developments on this breaking story. I'm Daniel Lessard. We now return you to regularly scheduled programming.

In the middle of the news bulletin, I managed to bring my car safely to a stop though in hindsight, I should have chosen my parking spot with more care. Mrs. Kravchuk, the owner of the large, blooming, and as I discovered later, award-winning forsythia bush on which the Taurus came to a rest, was not happy. The situation didn't improve when, in the midst of her titanic tantrum, I barfed out the driver's side window onto the crushed yellow flowers that were sticking out below.

When Mrs. Kravchuk was finally placated or, more accurately, sedated, I carefully backed off her beloved bush and tore over to the scene of the fire. Bedlam greeted me along with André Fontaine. He was completely beside himself. A boisterous crowd filled the front lawn of the Borschart residence and seemed to feed off the bright lights and TV cameras. Thick, dark smoke still hung over the property, adding a surreal and supernatural aspect to the scene.

"Holy shit, holy shit, holy shit, Addison, it was simply unbe-fucking-lievable! I'll never forget it for the rest of my life. Mark my words—this will change the face of Canadian politics. I heard the call on my police scanner and got here before anyone else. I saw the whole thing with my own eyes," he blathered, frothing at the mouth.

"Whoa, André. Calm down," I said. "Take it easy, man. You're halfway to a seizure."

"Well, then, I'd die happy because I was here the moment Eric Cameron's guise of perfection fell away, revealing dog collars, nipple clips, and a sordid taste for S and M. I was actually here when a woman in a crotchless, rubber bodysuit pulled a revered Canadian icon off his lofty pedestal by a short, leather leash," unloaded André with a faraway look in his eyes.

"I hope you're going to write that down, André. You've got some good lines there," I noted, trying not to think about what was really happening here.

André babbled on about this being his Watergate, but I tuned him out and tried to take in what I saw around me. As I surveyed the scene, I wondered how so many people had shown up so quickly. I saw people crowding the sidewalks and spilling out onto the streets. With 150 or so Cumberland citizens squished onto Petra's front yard, the place looked like a little slice of Woodstock before the rains came. I asked a teenage boy what had brought out so many people so fast. He told me it had been years since the last good house fire in Cumberland, what with the popularity of smoke detectors and all. Apparently, everyone in the neighbourhood tended to follow the fire trucks in hopes of seeing the kind of blaze they used to have every couple of months in the halcyon days of yore.

"So they're all here to see a fire?" I asked, incredulous.

"Well, that's how it started," the boy said, "but we all ended up seeing something even hotter—that sexpot dominatrix, dragging some poor sap around on a leash. That rubber suit of hers had cut-outs in all the right places. The fire was out ten minutes after the smoke eaters got here, but the crowd was just getting warmed up," my informant told me. "When the news broke that Eric Cameron was walking around in his birthday suit with a few clamps and clips and some leather, all hell broke loose."

To my utter horror, the crowd was now chanting "resign, resign, resign." By this time, I saw four satellite-television trucks with reporters doing on-the-spot, live segments. André Fontaine was in his glory. He was being interviewed by the national networks as the guy who'd broken the story with his brief but hard-hitting piece that had been posted on *The Cumberland Crier*'s Web site within 20 minutes of his arrival at Petra's house. He'd written the piece and had transmitted it on his BlackBerry. Betacams were crawling all over the property. Despite the ubiquitous yellow police tape, several camera operators and reporters had crossed the cordon and were now in the infamous S and M cellar. The only police in the area at the time of the fire had already left with the ruined and under-dressed guests of honour.

I felt someone's hand squeeze mine and turned to find Lindsay at my side with her other hand in the crook of Muriel's arm, lending her stability. I must have looked shocked.

"What? Why should we watch it on Newsworld when we're only three blocks away and can see it live?" Lindsay said through a broad smile.

Muriel just shook her head in astonishment. "I've known for the last 15 years he's had a bolt loose somewhere. But I never expected he'd Hindenburg like this," she commented. "I've always said he was a slave to public opinion, but I never guessed he was Petra Borschart's slave at the same time," she said, unable to hold in a rather inelegant guffaw.

I noticed Muriel was holding a nondescript, unlabeled DVD in her left hand. "Muriel, please tell me that you're on your way to the video store to take back a couple of Bob Hope-Bing Crosby road movies," I said with trepidation.

"Oh, this may not be a road movie," she quipped, "but I think it's going to be a classic nevertheless. The common room at the lodge is going to be filled to capacity tonight. Fortunately, all of us are over 18."

"No no no! Please tell me that you're not holding an Eric Cameron amateur sex flick. You weren't rummaging around in their basement brig, were you?" I asked, still incredulous. In fact, I suspected that incredulity would be my constant companion for some time to come.

"André Fontaine slipped it to me. He told me that after five elections, I'd earned a sneak peek at the real Eric Cameron. Very decent of him, I thought," she replied, holding the DVD close to her frail chest.

Fontaine must have pilfered the DVDs from the sex cellar before the police arrived. Now, I had crossed the threshold of high anxiety into the zone of abject terror. If André and Muriel had sex movies that starred a groveling and submissive Eric Cameron, others surely did, too. Though I studiously avoided thinking about the night's consequences, my body seemed to understand the implications. I started shaking uncontrollably.

"Are you all right, Daniel?" asked Lindsay, still propping up her grandmother, who was shaking with glee as much as with Parkinson's. "You look like you're about to pass out."

"Well, I've had better days—like the time I fell out of a tree as a kid and broke my wrist and my femur," I responded. "I'm praying this will die a quick death and that the media will move on to something else," I said, considering the seismic shift in the political landscape that might have been triggered by a small electrical fire in a nondescript Cumberland home.

I had to get out of there. The growing and chanting crowd was pushing my anxiety level from "very concerned" to "deeply troubled." I thought it prudent to take my leave before it reached "meltdown."

Soon, there was nothing left for the camera crews to shoot beyond the rebellious rabble and the firefighters coiling their hoses; the fire was, by then, long extinguished. I made sure Muriel and Lindsay were safe and content. I learned that *content* was an understatement. In fact, they were safe and deliriously happy.

I turned to go when Muriel sounded an ominous note in a voice distorted by laughter. "Daniel, time to start thinking about Plan B."

I simply waved and backed away, effecting calm though my pulse was pounding. As I hustled to the car, my life actually flashed before my eyes. Until that moment, I'd always thought that phrase was just a cliché. In review, I thought my life looked quite impressive, at least until I reached the fire scene at Petra's house. I slid behind the wheel, fished out a sprig of forsythia that was digging into my neck from beneath the headrest, and turned the key. In the crowd-cramped road, I executed a perfect seven-point turn and headed home.

Surely Muriel was overreacting. The Honourable Eric Cameron was the most popular politician in the country, perhaps in Canadian history. He had such an enormous balance in the political-goodwill bank, I figured nothing short of necrophilia before a live studio audience would threaten his re-election. The good people of Cumberland had displayed, election upon election, their unreserved contempt for anything or anyone remotely related to the party of Laurier and Trudeau. Five times vanquished, Muriel should have known that better than anyone. What were the voters going to do—toss their lot in with Absent Angus? I thought not. Not in this riding. Not in my lifetime. Nothing like clear thinking to calm jangled nerves.

I was feeling much calmer by the time I parked and dragged myself up the steps into the boathouse. Eric Cameron would apologize humbly and masterfully like the virtuoso spin-meister he was and sail to another victory with a substantial, if somewhat reduced, plurality. The die was cast. History and momentum were on his side, and the election was only two days away. He'd blundered badly but would survive. Angus was safe; therefore, so was I.

My breathing slowed to normal. The planets returned to their time-honoured orbits. The river just beyond my window still flowed to the east. All was right with the world and still would be come election day. Feeling restored, I settled into the easy chair and flicked on the television.

What an idiot I am.

I'm Peter Longwood. Welcome back to "CBC National News" and our special live coverage of the firestorm engulfing the Conservative government and its popular Finance Minister.

I couldn't look away though I desperately wanted to. It was a train wreck in slow motion, and I felt like the conductor.

Eric Cameron is in police custody at this hour along with his chief of staff, Petra Borschart, following a fire at Ms. Borschart's Cumberland residence. The video you're seeing was shot by CBC earlier this evening at the scene. We advise discretion as some of these images may be disturbing to some viewers. As you can see, Mr. Cameron and Ms. Borschart escaped from the fire, wearing very little. Based on their distinctive attire and many hours of video footage found at the site, it appears that the two were engaged in—

I came to my senses and changed channels to escape my misery. I made the mistake of turning to CTV, then to Global, then to the multicultural network, and finally, to the local rural cable station—nothing but leather, leashes, and a nearly naked Cameron. I'd never really thought about how the Finance Minister might look *au naturel.* Why would I? But in strange times, the mind works in strange ways. Would he be a little flabby? Did he have chicken legs? A noted intellectual, he was obviously well-endowed upstairs. And by the way he, in the political sense, liked to swing his big staff around, I think most Canadians assumed he was quite gifted downstairs, as well. Enquiring minds want to know. Such is the undeniable curiosity that dwells in us all. Well, truth be told, though there was a chill in the air, Cameron wasn't half the man I thought he'd be. (Forgive me, but several million Canadians glued to their TVs made the same lewd observation of Cameron's shortcomings and, within minutes, clogged the Internet with crass, little jokes about it.)

In an admittedly desperate attempt to escape the wall-to-wall coverage, I actually switched over to the American Fox News Network. I was never a regular viewer of what Fox called news.

… electrical fire upstairs triggered panic downstairs in what has been described by Canadian media as a sexual torture chamber. Apparently, a dominatrix dragged Canadian Finance Minister Rick Cameron from her den of discipline by a leather, studded leash. The Minister escaped without a shirt on his back but with alligator clips on his front. The lifesaving dominatrix turned out to be—

Maybe I'm stating the obvious, but there is something very comforting about the fetal position. The stunning footage of Cameron and Borschart being led away in handcuffs (which they may well have enjoyed, for all I knew) didn't look quite as sinister from my curled-up position on the hardwood floor. I heard a soft moaning and spent a couple of minutes identifying the source. It was I. Eventually, I grew uncomfortable. Even in the fetal position, three and a half hours on hardwood can take its toll.

It was midnight when I collapsed into bed. My only solace—Angus was not burning the midnight oil in the workshop below. I realized that my earlier sanguine analysis, preserving a still comfortable victory for Cameron, may have been pure delusion sprung from wishful thinking. The curse of the sunny optimist. When I really stripped away all the trappings and distractions from the crisis, I realized we might be in a wee spot of trouble. Strike that. We were very likely in deep, deep shit. All would depend on how the story played out nationally, and just as importantly, how it unfolded in Cumberland. Cameron had a great deal of support that could be siphoned off long before his seat in the House of Commons was truly threatened. My neck was really in the hands of the voters of Cumberland-Prescott. If they failed me, my neck would then be passed into the hands of one Duncan Angus McLintock, and I had a reasonably good idea what he would do with his formidable paws. My fate was left to the voters' collective capacity for patience, understanding, and forgiveness as they weighed the sins of the Honourable Eric Cameron. I would also rely on their distaste for all things Liberal.

And what really was Eric Cameron's great sin, anyway? So he liked to be ordered around while wearing leather. So he liked to grovel at the feet of a rubber-clad she-wolf. So he liked to attend to the needs of said she-wolf in front of a camera while being whipped with a riding crop. Was that so wrong? Was that so very different from the life of the average Canadian voter that it might have some influence in the privacy of the polling booth? He didn't intend for his proclivities to become public. He practiced his little, sordid secret in the privacy, or more accurately, the captivity of a private home. Were not Canadians all about tolerance and acceptance? Did we not have a proud history of progressive and enlightened views on sexuality? To paraphrase Pierre Trudeau, the state had no place in the private sexual torture chambers of the nation. Was this really such a big deal?

In the face of such ubiquitous media coverage, one thing was certain. Unless you happened to be in a remote corner of Papua New Guinea, you would certainly have heard all about Cameron's self-immolation.

◆   ◆   ◆

Diary
Friday, October 11

My Love,

I have truly enjoyed my time in this remote corner of Papua New Guinea. It is a unique slice of the world completely at odds with our own. Where we have our blessed technology and all the modern conveniences of life in millennial North America, the lever and the yoke remain leading edge here where I write these words. Where we drive on smooth, wide asphalt highways that link one mall to the next, a cow path takes me from the village shanties to the nearly arid fields where struggling crops are grown on the village outskirts. Where we pass hundreds of strangers on our streets with nary a sidelong glance, let alone a greeting, it takes me a half hour to walk the hundred metres to the village square for all the friendly banter and offers of food I encounter. How can people with so little give so much? It is a humbling and grounding experience shared by all too few from our part of the world.

We've made tremendous progress on the water-purification system here since my arrival. Our experiments in the lab have translated better than expected into this real-world setting. We've made a couple of adjustments to valves and have added better filters to accommodate the perpetual dust that hangs in the desiccated air. Other than that, the 200 people in this village now walk 40 metres for a plentiful supply of fresh and clean water rather than the thrice-weekly four-kilometre trudge they've faced before. As well, these parched pastures can now be irrigated, increasing agricultural efficiency, not to mention yield quality. The people here are amazed at the change in their world our work has wrought. They are also grateful beyond measure. They have placed me on a pedestal at a frightening altitude. I have tried to convey that my reward is in witnessing the change in their quality of life, but it is to no avail. It leaves me feeling uncomfortable at best, embarrassed at worst.

However, I do feel renewed and totally rejuvenated. I've spent the last four days training two young men and three young women in the care and maintenance of the system and in the critical weekly testing of the water quality. If the filters are not carefully monitored and become clogged, impurities that can carry nasty bacteria can find their way into the water supply. Educating these five eager young people is critical to the long-term success of the system, the cleanliness of the water, and the health of the villagers. Better to teach them to fish than to deliver a skid of tuna and then bail out. Upon my return, I have some new ideas I intend to explore on how the filtration system might be expanded to serve larger but similarly challenged villages. With adequate clean water, there may be a chance to nurture the seeds of industry, exports, and perhaps even self-sufficiency.

You would have loved it here with me in this faraway land. I would have loved it, too. There is a fledgling movement towards equality though still in its nascent stage. The men are still the decision-makers, but I see among the women, particularly the younger, a growing sense of their own, if not, power, at least leverage. The exercise of their leverage is manifest in modest ways, but the ripples of which you so often spoke are evident for all to see.

Aye, you're right, I'm feeling stronger, and my dark times are fewer and shorter. But I find I do need at least your spirit with me.

AM

CHAPTER NINE

You know how sometimes, after a really bleak and demoralizing experience, when all hope seemed lost, you awake from a fitful sleep to a sunny morning and just like that, the world doesn't seem quite so malevolent? When after what seemed dark and depressing the night before isn't nearly so threatening in the light and warmth of a new and promising day? Well, that didn't happen to me. When I awoke the morning after the real Eric Cameron was laid bare for all Canadians to see, I had absolutely none of those redeeming and hopeful thoughts and feelings. None. Nada. Zilch. I was positioned directly in front of the fan, and a whole lot of shit was arcing my way.

So, already depressed and anxious, I opted for the full-meal deal and turned the TV back on. Lucky for me it was still tuned into the Fox News Network. As I waited for the pharmaceutical commercial to finish (10 seconds of product promotion, 50 seconds of detailed descriptions of side effects), I wondered how on earth things could get any worse. How about like this?

> *We are back on "Fox News Saturday." I'm Aaron Olson, and we are going deep on the sex-crazed Canadian Finance Minister. Fox News has obtained exclusive footage recovered from the scene of yesterday's fire in Cumberland, somewhere near Ontario, showing Finance Minister Eric Cameron engaged in very naughty sex games with his chief of staff and dominatrix, Patty Boochard. Joining me now to guide us through this extraordinary video is noted sex therapist Judith Humphrey, whose particular specialty is S and M. Hello, Judith, and welcome to "Fox News Saturday."*

I'll spare you the blow-by-blow (literally) analysis provided by the inimitable Dr. Humphrey. I initially thought it was satire—a big joke. But no, for the 34th time in the previous two weeks, I was wrong. My fervent hope that only André Fontaine and Muriel Parkinson had copies of Cameron's amateur sex-slave videos was faint and fading fast. If Fox News had footage, every media outlet in Canada and most in the United States had it, too. Preceded by a parental discretion warning, the American network aired the entire 17-minute video of Cameron and Borschart well on their way to sadomasochism nirvana. With an endless stream of expert colour commentary from Dr. Humphrey, it was kind of like watching an NHL hockey game, except this action was much rougher and the players were wearing next to no equipment.

A quick surf through the other channels, American and Canadian, confirmed my worst fears. They were all running unexpurgated footage (each station apparently with a different video) starring Eric Cameron and his sidekick (an apt term in three different clips). I had no idea Canada boasted that many bona fide sex therapists to play the Howie Meeker part as the video rolled.

Satellite trucks were still staked out in front of the Borschart home. At least three networks had set up anchor desks and were presenting their entire newscasts from her front lawn as if it were the site of some natural disaster. I knew this story had legs when four out of five networks developed scandal-specific graphics and theme music to enhance their ongoing coverage of what had been coined "Leathergate." Coining a phrase usually meant the media were in for the long haul. You didn't "brand" a scandal unless you were going to ride that horse for a while. Another indication was one network's use of the positioning phrase "a scandal for the ages." Great, just great. On the bright side, to the best of my knowledge, no reporter at the scene of the fire or in subsequent coverage had yet uttered, "Oh, the humanity," but it was still early days.

Were I still working on the Leader's staff, I'd have been doing handsprings at the prospect of seeing Cameron finally go down—in flames—with a huge explosion and fireball, sending shrapnel careening through the Tory Party. But I was no longer on Parliament Hill. I was in Cumberland, impaled on a long-shot crisis so unexpected, Vegas bookies would need a supercomputer to calculate the odds. While Liberals across the country convulsed in glee, I was torn between hara-kiri and the Witness Protection Program. I turned off the TV and weighed my three options:

Option One: I could fill my pockets with stones and pull a Virginia Woolf in the Ottawa River. No thanks, I've always been terrorized by the thought of drowning. There's just something about not being able to breathe. I cannot envisage a more horrible way to go. It was just slightly worse than being strangled by an aging and demented Scot who'd gone plumb postal.

Option Two: I could hightail it out of Dodge and lay low until the count was in. No, I don't think so. I had too much at stake—like my future, for instance.

Option Three: I could cling against all logic, evidence, and common sense to the faint and wispy hope that the Tory vote in Cumberland-Prescott was so rock solid that Cameron would still win. Local Tories could then pursue a recall and force a by-election to crown a new Tory MP.

I went with door number three. Rather than sitting on my hands, I decided to do what I could to right the good ship Cameron. As you can imagine, for me, this was very much counterintuitive—a "man bites dog" story, you might say. The worst part was that I had to turn my back on a possible Liberal victory in the safest Tory riding in the country. But I had to honour my promise to Angus McLintock that he'd still be an engineering professor on October 15.

I called the two Petes, and with a little cajoling, they revved up their home computers, as I did mine, and we sprung into action. We started by setting up scores of different hotmail accounts and sending dozens—no, it was hundreds—of e-mails to editors, producers, and assignment editors in respected media outlets across the country. We put heavy emphasis on newspapers, radio stations, and television stations that served eastern Ontario in general and the Ottawa area in particular. Although I phrased our message in countless different ways, I made the same, single point relentlessly: "We've all seen just about enough of Eric Cameron's cameo performances. He is a great Canadian, who deserves some respect and understanding from the media."

Blah, blah, blah. You get the idea. I had no illusions that we'd make much of an impact, but it gave us something to do, and at that point, I was ready to try anything. Among the three of us, we sent upwards of 500 e-mails to the same 40 or so media outlets in about two hours. Pete1 and Pete2 were a little perplexed at the whole exercise but pitched in, anyway. We received few if any answers in the first hour, but as our messages piled up in the media's inboxes, we did prompt a reaction. The responses were classic: "We welcome your comments and appreciate the time taken to share your views with us." Etcetera, etcetera. I knew the style well. After all, I'd started in the Leader's correspondence pool where I daily crafted such messages by the dozen.

Next, I drove over to the Borschart house and, as campaign manager for Angus McLintock, did live interviews with each of the networks still camped out there. I was magnanimity personified. I went on at length in each interview about Canada being different from the United States and that this was not how we treated our respected political leaders when they erred. I took such a high road that vertigo was a clear and present danger. I spoke with passion about Eric Cameron's stellar record of public service and declared that it should not be dismantled on live television over what was strictly a private matter between his chief of staff and him. I decried attack-dog journalism. I talked of high-minded ethics, the pressures in public life, and the need to search our hearts for understanding and forgiveness. It was great TV, and the networks were dying for material.

Who would have expected the local Liberal campaign manager to be the lone voice of support for a defrocked Tory Finance Minister? When the anchors commented, which they all did eventually, that it was strange to hear me defend Cameron on the eve of the vote, I climbed still higher, noting that this was much bigger than a single election. It was about the decency of our society and the civility of our democracy. I even invoked Angus's name, claiming that he was very troubled by the media's reaction to the Cameron affair and that he was not interested in winning if it marked a watershed in the decline of our democratic values. Eric Cameron had given much and deserved better. Blah, blah, blah. I was quite proud of my performance.

As expected, my phone was hot when I stepped back in the door. I knew what was coming. The Leader's chief of staff reached me first, followed quickly by the national campaign chair, and then by the president of the party. They were all livid and aghast at my unsanctioned performance. When the bluster and heat were removed, I was left with a clear chorus of "what the hell were you thinking?" I'd prepared for this albeit only as I was driving home with my makeup still fresh. I calmly and patiently walked them through my rationale. Even though I didn't believe my own words, I knew the political veterans on the other end of the phone would buy what I was selling. I was selling hope—the most sought-after commodity in any close campaign.

I told them Canada's most popular Finance Minister was already dead and buried. I told them that courtesy of Angus McLintock's assiduous campaigning (I had to stop and define *assiduous* for two of them before continuing), we were poised to capitalize on Cameron's flame-out. Therefore, in doing the interviews, I was merely staking out the moral high ground Liberals should always occupy. I reminded them that it was in keeping with the best traditions of our party. I told them it was Laurier's legacy. That was my message in a nutshell.

The Liberal campaign brain trust wasn't thrilled, but my point was made. And I hadn't even had time to sharpen my skates. I did get my wrists slapped for doing national interviews without approval from the Centre, but I was definitely operating in the "seek forgiveness rather than permission" zone.

Understandably, my political masters wanted me to kick Cameron while he was down. I was more interested in offering him the Heimlich manoeuvre and CPR at the same time. I, too, was running on the fumes of hope.

Finally, I issued a brief statement from Angus, reiterating my media message. In the statement, Angus announced that he would make no public appearances for the rest of the campaign out of respect for Eric Cameron's extraordinary contribution to Canada and out of disdain for the media's treatment of the former

Finance Minister. As part of standing in solidarity with Eric Cameron, I actually contemplated distributing a news release, revealing that Angus McLintock had also explored new sexual frontiers and could sympathize with the Finance Minister's position. (I know, I had gone completely off the air. I thought better of it long before my fingers ever hit the keyboard.)

By this time, the morning had become early afternoon. I was fine when I was busy. Running around doing interviews and fielding calls kept my mind in a more pleasant place. With the flurry of activity in the morning now behind me, I felt fatigue encroaching on my high spirits, and with it, returned the amorphous malaise I'd been trying to shed since the smoke cleared at Petra's house. At that moment, there was only one thing that could distract me from the gathering perfect storm. She knocked on the door at about two o'clock. Lindsay looked like she'd just stepped out of the shower, sans makeup, with her hair still damp. She wore those great jeans again, some sort of athletic sandals, and an oversize, orange golf shirt, untucked.

She'd called earlier and must have detected the crazed edge to my voice. She had ended the call with "I'll be right over." I'd hung up and realized I was looking forward to her arrival. Since our long talk at Starbucks some weeks earlier, I'd been so consumed with the campaign, not to mention the previous evening's "scandal for the ages," that we'd not advanced what I thought might turn into a real relationship. Of course, we both knew I was on the rebound—in a big way. Forewarned is forearmed. An image of Rachel flashed into my head, but I blocked her out with an imaginary rubber tree planted in my mind's eye.

"Hey, Daniel, turn on CBC. The PM is about to make a statement on the Cameron affair," Lindsay announced as she strolled into the boathouse and flopped onto the couch.

"Really? How do you know that?" I asked.

"I just heard it on the news coming over. I'm not sure why he's waited this long," Lindsay noted.

"They needed 24 hours to do a quick and dirty poll before deciding how to respond," I sneered. "Plus, the PM took a walk up the TV dial and was shaken by what he saw."

I plunked down beside her and tuned in CBC. As our legs touched, neither of us shifted to break the contact. A warm sensation washed over me. The TV flickered to life, and the Prime Minister emerged from 24 Sussex Drive, his face nothing short of ashen. Following his prepared statement, he would fly directly to Calgary on a government Challenger to be in his riding when the polls opened on Monday. The standard photo op of him casting his own vote was already arranged for the morning. He stood in front of a single microphone on the front steps of the Prime Minister's official residence, wearing a dark blue suit, white Oxford broadcloth shirt, and an ugly tie, knotted in a less-than-perfect single Windsor. (Prime Ministers really should always tie double Windsors.) All Canadian networks broke into regular programming to carry the PM's words live:

Fellow Canadians, good afternoon. In the last 24 hours, we have witnessed the sad and sorry end to a proud and prodigious public-service career. I'm as troubled, shocked, and disturbed by what I've seen as are all of you. When the news broke, my first priority was to reach and speak to Eric Cameron himself before I made any decisions. Unfortunately, that hasn't been possible. In fact, despite our best efforts to contact him, we simply don't know where Eric went after being released from police custody late last night. Speculation abounds, but one cannot govern on rumours and conjecture. What's important now is that we act in the best interests of our country. And that's what I intend to do.

I have relieved Eric Cameron of his Cabinet responsibilities and have expelled him from the Government caucus. I've spoken at length with the Chief Electoral Officer, and it is simply too late to remove his name from the ballot, or replace it, before Monday's vote. If Eric Cameron is elected, he will sit as an independent.

I've taken this action not because of what he has done in private with other consenting adults but because of the distinct lack of judgment he displayed and for exposing himself, the party, and the Government to ridicule and derision, bringing our entire democratic system into disrepute.

When the Prime Minister uttered "exposing himself," he winced slightly. Somewhere else, a lonely speech writer said, "Oops." The PM continued:

I do not condone what I've seen—what we've all seen. It flies in the face of our party's and our Government's deeply rooted commitment to moral family values. Eric Cameron's fate now rests in the hands of the thoughtful and fair-minded voters of Cumberland-Prescott.

I will not comment further on this unfortunate situation. It has consumed quite enough of our time and attention during what is a very important election. I intend to refocus my mind and energy—and I encourage Canadians to do the same—on the very real challenges we confront together as a nation. The platform the Government has laid before you will carry Canada into a new era of economic and social prosperity. Please consider the issues carefully because you will have your own say on Monday. Good day.

The Prime Minister folded his notes, turned on his heel, and walked back into the front door of the house he hoped to continue occupying for another four years. As a student of public speaking and a writer of speeches, I actually thought the Prime Minister had done very well under trying circumstances. I clicked off the TV and let my head loll to the right until it rested on Lindsay's shoulder.

"What am I going to do? Six weeks ago, I couldn't find a candidate and thought nothing could be worse. Then, Angus agreed to stand but only if I promised he would go down to defeat. Now, it's quite possible that the guy who ran to lose may actually win the damn seat. I've now discovered there's something worse than having no Liberal candidate."

"Would it really be so bad if Angus won?" Lindsay asked. "Isn't he just the kind of candidate you've always wanted to support? He speaks his mind, does the right thing, and is as honest as his beard is long."

"Yes, but he's halfway around the world, blissfully unaware that Cameron's star has not just fallen but been blown out of the sky, and he has no desire or intention to represent this riding in the House of Commons. He has his research, his water-filtration systems, and that hovercraft thingy right below us. He's 60 years old, looks like a vagrant, and is fond of late-night skinny dipping. He's not built to serve, he doesn't want to serve, and I promised him he wouldn't have to serve. No good can come of this," I moaned.

"Aren't you being just a tad pessimistic?" she persisted. "Perhaps if victory is handed to him on a silver platter, he may just say 'what the hell.' How often does an opportunity like this come along?"

"Lindsay, I've played chess and talked politics with him for hours on end. His views may be valid and just, but they are also naïve and innocent. Ottawa is a giant meat grinder that takes in idealism at one end and spits out cynical sausage at the other. I love him, but he's a relic. They'd have a field day with him on the Hill and in the House. Besides, he has a life here and doesn't want a new one there."

"I just think that in your zeal to find an escape hatch, you may be overlooking the perfect solution. If Angus does win, persuade him to serve. Marin Lee wrote in her last book that she always regretted not running for public office and trying to change Canadian society from within our democratic institutions. She spent her life on the outside. She made a real difference, but I can't help wondering what she might have achieved if she'd sat around the Cabinet table. Maybe Angus doth protest too much. It's worth a try, particularly if it's all we have," she concluded.

I knew she was right, but I was still stuck on trying to make sure that Eric Cameron somehow retained his seat.

"But what will you do if Angus wins and agrees to serve? He'll need a lot of help," she remarked.

"I can't even begin to wrap my mind around that one right now. I'm really focused on the here and now and making sure Angus doesn't arrive back here on Tuesday as the MP for Cumberland-Prescott." I shivered involuntarily. "Gives me the willies just to say it."

"Well, don't wait too long. The way this is all playing out, you may not have much time to make a decision," she said.

"I'm feeling a little claustrophobic, and I really don't think we're helping Cameron's cause stewing about things in here. Are you up for a late lunch?" I asked, hoping it didn't sound too much like I was asking her out on a date.

"Great," was all she said as she rose from the couch.

We went to Mabel's right in the downtown core of Cumberland. Lindsay ordered a Greek salad while I opted for a bowl of minestrone soup and the club sandwich. Just like our earlier get-together at Starbucks, time again stood still and flew by at the same time. We appeared to click on a whole range of different levels. At least, that's how it seemed to me.

To her credit, Lindsay knew I was carrying a lot of election baggage around with me, so she studiously steered our conversation away from anything related to Monday's vote. We talked about university, how her master's was going, and what she thought about tenure, capital punishment, and ketchup on macaroni and cheese. While we talked, a great weight lifted from my shoulders, albeit temporarily. At one point in our conversation, she rose to head to the washroom, and I stood up on instinct. When she returned, I again got to my feet and held her chair as I had when we'd arrived.

"Do you always do that?" she asked through a bemused look.

"My dear departed mother is always watching. She was a stickler for manners," I replied.

"You don't consider holding a woman's chair an anachronistic manifestation of a patriarchal society?" She was still smiling sweetly. I'd certainly heard this line of thinking before.

"I really hope and believe that feminism has moved beyond that," I started. "I remember attending a meeting of the National Union of Students in Saskatoon years ago when I was involved in student politics. On instinct, I held the door for a fellow delegate as we both headed into a lecture hall for an organizing workshop. She called me a misogynist at the top of her considerable lungs. That has stayed with me as a symbol of the misallocation of precious resources in the fight for women's rights. I was on her side." Lindsay nodded, and I continued. "Anyway, I've never considered good manners and equality mutually exclusive. Good manners may regrettably be an anachronism, but its roots are in common courtesy, not patriarchy. Here endeth the sermon," I concluded, praying we were on the same page. When I was nervous, I sometimes sounded like a Victorian novel.

"You're a very complex person, Dr. Addison," she said, still smirking. She rested her chin in her right palm and held me in a rather intense gaze. Hazel eyes. "Do you always talk that way?"

"Sorry, it's the curse of loving the language. I'm a charter adherent of the 'why use five words when 35 will do' school of English. As such, I'm often wrongly accused of high pedantry. I'm working on my ability to speak in monosyllabic grunts, but it's tough going."

More smiling. "We think very much alike," she said. "In fact, it's a little eerie. It's as if you've done some kind of a Vulcan mind meld on me. You haven't, have you?"

"Scout's honour," I replied.

She burst out laughing because I'd raised my hand in the traditional Vulcan split-fingered greeting when invoking Baden-Powell's promise. What a guy. What a wit. I figured I should strike when my stock was high.

"When all of this insanity is over, could we actually go out for dinner without my future hanging in the balance?"

"I'd like that." She beamed. I beamed. We were one big beam.

When I got home around six-thirty, the phone was ringing. I'd made the mistake of plugging it back in.

"Daniel? It's Michael Zaleski."

"Hi, Michael, what's up?"

"I thought you might be interested in some data I just pulled out of Cumberland-Prescott. Quite interesting."

"What do you have?" I inquired with a flicker of interest.

"We were in the field over the last eight hours, and the results are not yet conclusive. In fact, they're quite fluid. If the vote weren't until next Wednesday, I'd have held off until Monday to go into the field, but we just don't have the time. Anyway, the Cameron-sex thing is still developing, and so is its impact on the voting patterns." He paused.

"I'm still here, Michael. What do you have?"

"Well, Leathergate has already left a mark," Michael began. "Support for Cameron has plummeted with almost all of it now parked in Undecided. Because of the unique nature of Cumberland-Prescott and this particular situation, we added a new category to our standard voter intention question. Along with PC,

Liberal, NDP, and Undecided, we've added Spoil Ballot to give respondents another option. In view of time constraints, we were forced to start calling early this morning before many voters had fully considered what Cameron had done. His support was moving fast to Undecided, but there was virtually no activity in the Spoil Ballot column. But by late this afternoon, when the media coverage had just about reached the saturation point and the actual footage of Cameron and Borschart had been airing for several hours, we started to see heavy action under Spoil Ballot. If the election were held right now, Cameron would still win, but there're a lot of votes still camped in Undecided, and it's unclear how they'll break."

"Why would voters bother to spoil their ballots when they could just stay home and achieve the same thing?" I inquired.

"I'm guessing two reasons," he answered. "Number one: Opposition to the Liberal Party is so strong and so deep in C-P that voters want to register that they still refused to vote red. They want to rub our noses in the fact that even when voting Tory is not an option, they'd rather spoil their ballot than support a Liberal. Number two: Next to Prince Edward Island's Cardigan riding, C-P always has the highest voter turnout in the country. It's a tradition that's become a point of pride with the people of this constituency. We threw a question about this on an earlier poll. By spoiling their ballots, the good citizens of C-P are still considered by Elections Canada to have voted, thus keeping the high-turnout tradition alive." Michael fell silent.

"Right now, what's your best guess, Michael?"

"I wish I knew. It's going to be very, very close. It all comes down to where the Undecideds go and how the Spoil Ballots fall." He paused and then went on. "Angus must be excited."

"Oh yeah, he's flying high right about now," I said before thanking him and hanging up.

If the numbers broke the wrong way, Angus would land, see the front page of *The Globe and Mail*, and start planning his first homicide. If something didn't turn our way soon, I might even save him the trouble.

◆   ◆   ◆

Diary
Saturday, October 12

My Love,

I'm sitting on the plane in PNG, getting ready for takeoff. I was fêted last night and escorted to the airport, a four-hour bus journey, by virtually the entire village. I have been treated like a demigod, and it has left me feeling distinctly uncomfortable. The plane I'm on must be 50 years old if it's a day. It's an ancient, twin-engine Russian Aleutian. The port engine started normally, but three members of the ground crew literally had to spin the starboard propeller by hand until the aging radial engine kicked to life in a puff of black smoke and a backfire that sounded like the Amchitka Blast.

I have a long journey ahead of me with four different stops and an overnight stay in Honolulu. The last leg of my odyssey will take me from Hawaii through to Chicago and then finally, to Ottawa, landing around midnight on Monday. By Tuesday morning, I'll be battling jetlag and painting the underside of Baddeck 1 with dark blue marine-antifouling paint. I'll have a brush in one hand and a double Lagavulin in the other. I suspect it will take me several days to recover from the trip and not just because of the many time zones I'll have traversed. I'm going to ask two of my graduate students to come with me the next time when we've perfected the scaling of the water-filtration system to support larger populations. I'm also going to give Jim Kisoon at call at CIDA. I think this system may have beneficial applications in other parts of the developing world now that the pilot operation seems to be working so well.

When I awake on Tuesday morning in our bed, which I missed terribly while lying in an Australian Army surplus cot for the last two weeks, I'll have an extra spring to my step. I'll be free of this damn election business. From time to time over the last month, I've regretted my rash and impetuous agreement to let my name stand. But then, I think of Professor Addison, standing before a hundred first-year engineers labouring through the dark and nuanced style of Margaret Laurence, and I am at peace once again. I very much believe I got the better of the deal. Come Tuesday, I'll be free of politics and free of English for Engineers. Not so bad for the temporary use of my name. I've also improved my standing in the good books of the university administration. Having one of their own run was a source of pride, however misplaced.

It's been nearly two weeks since I've bathed satisfactorily. I may even dive off the dock before turning in when I get home. I miss our midnight dips. You'll join me, won't you?

AM

CHAPTER TEN

E-day, early dawn. I'd been awake for hours, listening to the river and the rain, trying to distinguish between them. As I lay, eyes open, chest tight, what I initially mistook as the soothing sound of the prevailing west wind turned out to be my own hyperventilation. There was barely a breath of breeze. Waking up with someone you love, or even being coaxed out of your nightly coma by a loyal and affectionate schnauzer, are comforting ways to greet a new day, provided the dog exercises restraint. Lurching into consciousness by the blaring alarm of your own anxiety, with dread as your only bedfellow, is somewhat less appealing. Welcome to my world.

It was a week before Thanksgiving, and I was having considerable difficulty counting my blessings. October 14 was to have marked the end of my foray into party politics and the start of my tenure-track tour of academe. Farewell party line and job insecurity, hello academic freedom and indexed sinecure. It was to have been my liberation day, so to speak. Instead, in knee-slapping irony, Eric Cameron's weakness for handcuffs and riding crops threatened to deliver me—bound, gagged, and struggling—back to Parliament Hill to resume my partisan bondage and servitude. Politics was the cruelest mistress of all.

I'd spent Sunday, the traditional day of rest, rocking and moaning, watching Newsworld, then rocking and moaning some more. I'd unplugged the phone again as its persistent ringing was quite a distraction from my rocking and moaning. The only tolerable part of the day had been the two hours Lindsay had spent holding me as I was rocking and ... well, you get the idea. Still no word from Eric Cameron or Petra Borschart—not even a sighting. I pictured them in an RV, her with hair dyed black, him with head shaved, driving maniacally towards the South Dakota Badlands or some other suitably isolated location, trying to outrun their humiliation. I, on the other hand, had considered, but rejected, plastic surgery (I have a low pain threshold) and had decided to face the music with neither blindfold nor cigarette. I'd gone to bed early Sunday night—around six-thirty—which may have been a factor in my early awakening Monday morning. That and the pulse-pounding, bowel-bending stress that came with knowing I may have ruined the life of a certain cantankerous and potentially violent old Scot.

I had not yet totally exhausted my dwindling stores of hope as I watched the sky lighten. Until the rain stopped and the sun finally asserted itself, I rode the pendulum back and forth, oscillating between "Eric Cameron can still win this thing" and "Angus, please put down the filleting knife." To ensure the former and forestall the latter, I sprang into action at the crack of ten forty-five with all the vitality of a pregnant sloth in a heat wave. I phoned in a shower and shave and forced down a bowl of muesli that pushed back the frontiers of tasteless. With nine hours until the polls closed, I still had stones to turn.

I started by calling Pete1 and Pete2. I told them to phone all known Liberals in Cumberland-Prescott and direct them to fictitious polling stations, a list of which I'd provided. The two Petes were a tad confused by my request, particularly when I suggested they not use their own names. But to preserve their sanity, they'd stopped questioning campaign decisions weeks earlier. They were nothing if not obedient though their blind acquiescence stood in stark contrast to their anarchic appearance. Cradling Molotov cocktails in their hands rather than telephones would have looked more natural. But beneath it all, they were solid, dependable, and dedicated volunteers. Eventually, they'd outgrow the Mohawks and piercings on their own terms.

About 23 minutes later, I received a call from Pete1—to clarify my directive further, I assumed. Nope. They were seeking their next assignment. They'd already finished calling all known Liberals in the riding and had time left over to frost their split ends electric neon blue. I then instructed them to use their voter lists to call all of the NDP supporters they'd identified when canvassing and to ensure that they voted. That would keep them busy for at least another 17 minutes. I then gave them the rest of the day off. Of course, I invoked our friendship when prevailing upon them to cast their own votes for the NDP candidate, Jane Nankovich. She was a little-known union activist from the beverage-bottling operation but would serve C-P admirably.

Lindsay had responsibilities on campus, so I was on my own for the day. Given my state of mind at the time, I would not have been scintillating company, anyway. In a moment when hope was briefly shocked back into normal sinus rhythm, I pulled a ball cap low and drove over to the NDP campaign headquarters. I walked with purpose into the election-day chaos. In C-P, chaos for the NDP was benchmarked at four volunteers, an overweight stray tabby, and Cat Stevens playing on a 20-year-old Radio Shack stereo. I'd have thought the Cameron crash-and-burn would have turned out more people. No reporters in sight.

By scanning the Bristol board charts and lists on the walls, I quickly found the corner of the room I was looking for and approached the clipboard-clasping, heavy-set woman who looked in charge.

"I'm here to drive, and my car is just outside the door," I opened, keeping the bill of my cap lowered.

With precious few volunteers, she took what she could get before it was gone; no questions asked. She handed me a list of voters along with their addresses and pick-up times and shooed me out the door. As I slipped out, I noticed an untouched plate of homemade granola bran bars, a clear contravention of the fatty-campaign-snacks code. No wonder they had trouble attracting canvassers. On the bright side, I suspect they'd lost no volunteers to constipation.

I spent the next three hours driving NDP shut-ins to their polling stations. For many of them, voting was a highlight of their year.

"Vote early and vote often!" cackled one withered, old man as he settled in the front seat of the Liberal campaign headquarters, his caregiver behind us in the back seat. After voting, he asked if I would drive them home along the water. Despite being somewhat behind schedule, we drove the length of the river that passed through Cumberland and parked for 10 minutes at the scenic look-off just beyond the town line. You could tell by his expression he didn't get out much.

I ended up chauffeuring 15 different NDP voters to seven different polling stations. To say that Jane Nankovich was a long shot to win was the understatement of the millennium. But driving aging lefties to the polls was better than sitting at home, catatonic and drooling. It was midafternoon by the time I'd done my driving for the socialist cause—just another bizarre episode in a constellation of surreal experiences. This campaign had completely extinguished my capacity for surprise.

She was in her usual spot, facing the river. I had expected to find her wallowing in melancholy. I couldn't imagine how it must have felt to have run in five futile elections only to sit on the sidelines in the sixth when the Tory juggernaut ran aground. Yet, there she was, wearing a look of triumph as she pored over *The Globe and Mail* opened on her lap.

"Hello, Muriel."

She hadn't seen me, and she jerked around. "Well, if it isn't college boy! You're just in time. I'm about to break into a rousing chorus of 'Oh Happy Day' and could use another tenor," she exclaimed, looking ten years younger. Depressed, she was not.

My eyes narrowed as I stared her down, trying to see beneath the surface. "So you're all right with all of this?" I asked as I dropped beside her.

"All right? If it weren't for the fresh gum on my shoe, I'd be flying around the room I'm so tickled," she bubbled. "Do you know how long we've waited for this moment? Do you know how good it feels to be sitting here on election day with a better-than-even chance of victory? I truly never thought I'd live to see this."

"Well, Cameron hasn't lost, yet," I reminded her. "I've been clinging for dear life to the far-fetched notion that he can still pull this one out of the fire. I can't imagine the people of this riding willfully electing a Liberal, notwithstanding the leather-and-leash business the other night," I commented in plaintive mode.

Muriel just shook her head—with purpose, not Parkinson's—her grin still intact. "Ring the bell and slather on the barbecue sauce; the Minister is well and truly done. Yes, if Angus wins, he'll be slipping into the Commons through the milk box. But this town takes its morals very seriously. A Finance Minister can't parade his block and tackle around for all to see and expect to win votes in this town, Tory or not," Muriel declared with authority. "Cameron is cooked."

"But there's no way they're going to vote Liberal or NDP. They'll hold their nose and mark the X for Cameron. The Tories can still win by default," I insisted.

"Well, you wait and see what happens. I think a lot of folks will be putting a giant X across the entire ballot. Spoiling your ballot is also a legitimate and time-honoured expression of democratic will. Mark my words, Dr. Addison, bad-boy Eric is going down tonight. Someone else will win—but only as the less interesting flip side of Cameron's defeat," she stated for the record. "For your sake, I'm rooting for the NDP, but my heart is with Angus. Poor old soul won't know what hit him when gets back. By tomorrow night, he may well be the highest-profile backbencher in the House." She dissolved again in laughter.

That was not what I wanted to hear. I revered her political instincts, but I was just unhinged enough to hold out some sliver of hope for the most popular Finance Minister in Canadian history. But she certainly was in a feisty mood.

"Now do you wish you'd run this time around?" I inquired as I rested my hand on the top of her wrist, feeling the metronome of her illness.

"Hindsight is for geezers with nothing left to live for," she spat. "I've completely lost interest in being elected and dealing with the piddling concerns and personal trifles of this sorry lot of voters. Let someone else expedite their passport applications and gun licences. I'm just as happy to sit here and read by this river for as long as I've got. What's more important is that right now, a 150-year-old dynasty is teetering on its pedestal. In less than five hours, we'll watch it crash to pieces at our feet. Who cares who wins? This time around, what really matters is who loses."

I was tapped out, grasping at anything, thinking about myself. "Angus is going to hurt me very badly if he winds up as the MP for Cumberland-Prescott," I whined.

"I think you've underestimated Professor McLintock. I've had a number of pleasant chats with him in the last few weeks, and I like him. You chose well, Daniel."

"Muriel, he only agreed to run on the condition of his guaranteed defeat," I moaned. "I'm no longer sure I can deliver my side of the bargain. He'll refuse to serve, and it'll be a monstrous embarrassment for the Leader and the party, to say nothing of me. I'll be run out of the party on a rail and will be a 'don't do this' case study in Liberal Campaign Colleges for years to come."

"Snap out of it!" she interrupted. "Have you spent any time with Angus? Have you talked to him about his views? Do you know anything about him? For mercy's sake, you've been living in his house for the last two months. Have you learned nothing about him?"

I held my tongue. Not that it was a struggle. I had no idea what to say.

"Daniel, based on my conversations with Angus, I think you may have read him wrong. I know he had no interest in running. Who would in this riding? But there's a man of principle lurking beneath that Scottish brogue and bravado. Marin Lee saw something there, and I think I may have caught a glimpse of it, too," she remarked. "He may well do you harm, but I would not assume he'll refuse to serve."

My puny and overtaxed brain simply could not assimilate this fantasy. I admit it. I thought her various medications might not have titrated properly that morning. I'd spent plenty of time with Angus—hours and hours. Hell, I'd seen him naked. I still thought assault and battery would be his likely reaction to winning the election.

I left Muriel to her river and her private thoughts of what might have been. Lindsay was going to spend the evening with her, watching the returns. I needed some time to plan my strategy although I still prayed I wouldn't need one. In any event, at midnight, I was heading to the airport to meet Angus and after that, perhaps my maker.

I had a very nutritious dinner of stale tortilla chips and mild salsa, and I had to force even that on my reluctant appetite. I'm not sure how old the chips were, but I don't think you should be able to fold them. After dropping several limp-chip loads of salsa on my pants, the floor, and my shoe, I resorted to a bowl and fork. Afterwards, à la Angus, I stripped off my clothes, checked to see that the coast was clear, and ran off the end of the dock in the gathering darkness. I hadn't been in the river for a few weeks, and in the interim, autumn had certainly taken a firm grip on the water temperature. In fact, it seemed to me that autumn's faltering grasp had already surrendered to winter's chokehold. Thankfully, sound doesn't travel well underwater, or I might well have violated several municipal ordinances. I shot back out of the water onto the dock, barely touching the ladder. Shriveled and shivering, but in a whole new zone of consciousness, I toweled off and dressed in election-night attire—sweat pants and a long-sleeved T-shirt. It would be a long night, so comfort was key.

I checked my voice mail before getting settled in front of the television and listened to 14 messages from various media outlets, begging me to tell them the location of our Liberal campaign party so they could set up their remotes and provide on-the-spot reports as the count came in. I fired up my laptop and crafted a batch—e-mail media statement, announcing that out of respect for Eric Cameron and the unique events of the past weekend, Angus would be watching the returns at an undisclosed location and would reserve comment until the morning. I hit Send and shut down (the computer, I mean; I'd shut down personally two days earlier).

I eschewed the election pregame shows and didn't turn on the TV until the polls closed at eight o'clock. CBC, Global, and CTV all led with Leathergate—excellent way to start. To my dismay, CTV actually devoted the bottom right-hand corner of the screen to what they called CTV Cameron Watch where viewers could monitor the changing Cumberland-Prescott vote standings as each poll reported. It was sort of like tracking my own vital signs as a life-threatening infection swept through my body.

CTV Cameron Watch (8:05 PM EST)
(0% of polls reporting)

Eric Cameron (PC)	0
Angus McLintock (Lib)	0
Jane Nankovich (NDP)	0

The other networks had screen crawlers along the bottom, updating Cumberland-Prescott every ten minutes or so.

When the coverage started in the Eastern Time zone, the Liberals had opened an early seat lead in the Atlantic provinces where we were traditionally quite strong. This surprised no one, least of all the political-pundit panels on each network, which was a staple of modern election-night reporting. As always, the political junkie's great anticipation of election-night coverage soon gave way to tedium as commentators tried to forecast trends based on a handful of polls reporting from a handful of ridings. "Well, in Athabasca-Ferguson, the NDP candidate has taken a commanding 12-vote lead over the Conservative incumbent with one poll reporting out of 45." Very enlightening.

I flipped through the channels and saw videotaped coverage of the Liberal Leader, voting in his own riding. It was the same contrived spectacle played out in constituencies across the country—the wave to the supporters, the presentation of the marked ballot to the proud poll clerk, the positioning of the initialed ballot halfway in the slot of the ballot box as the candidate smiles for the cameras, and the final, friendly tap on the top of the box to punctuate the ballot's induction into our democratic process. Absolutely riveting.

CTV Cameron Watch (8:30 PM EST)
(8% of polls reporting)

Eric Cameron (PC)	239
Angus McLintock (Lib)	176
Jane Nankovich (NDP)	203

So far, so good. I silently prayed and pledged to go to church every Sunday, but I confess I left my worship options open in case the other religious and pagan gods offered any eleventh-hour deals.

Lindsay called from Muriel's to compare notes. Nationally, it was shaping up to be a very close race as we had all expected. Lindsay voiced concern over the results in Québec that were now streaming in. We were doing reasonably well, but if we hoped to stop a Tory majority, let alone win a Liberal minority, we couldn't afford to lose many seats in *la belle province*. The Tories had already stolen two and were ahead in two others that we'd traditionally claimed for our side.

Interestingly, despite coast-to-coast coverage, the Cameron affair seemed to have little impact on the national standings—perhaps because the Prime Minister moved so quickly to cut his Finance Minister loose before the Government was dragged down, too. Lindsay reported that Muriel was in fine fettle, working both hands in the popcorn bowl, her eyes never leaving the TV screen. I mentioned that I was going out to the airport to pick up Angus. Depending on the changing numbers in the CTV Cameron Watch, I wanted someone to know where I was. I described what I would be wearing as well as the location of the minuscule Canadian-flag tattoo I'd had inked onto my left scapula after a night of revelry at the last Liberal Leadership convention. If Angus won, I thought she might need this information when filing my missing-persons report. Lindsay chuckled but then asked for clarification on my shirt colour.

Before hanging up, she passed along a message from Muriel. I was not, under any circumstances, to jump to conclusions on any matter unfolding that evening.

Suddenly, CTV Cameron Watch made a change in their reporting format that left me less than calm although I resisted the temptation to jump to any conclusions.

CTV Cameron Watch (9:00 PM EST)
(29% of polls reporting)

Eric Cameron (PC)	1,072
Angus McLintock (Lib)	984
Jane Nankovich (NDP)	961
Spoiled Ballots	4,337

I registered new respect for Michael Zaleski as his spoiled-ballots theory blossomed before my eyes. Muriel's reference from that very afternoon also echoed in my mind then settled in the pit of my stomach. I'd never considered spoiled ballots to be a factor of any significance, but I obviously should have. The CBC political panel was debating the significance of the rising spoiled-ballot count in C-P. With so much time to kill, no topic was too small. The CBC research team had been burning up the Internet and reported that as a share of votes already counted, the spoiled ballots were higher in C-P than they'd ever been in any riding in Canadian history. At this pace, they could approach 15,000. It concerned me and, I assumed, many other students of democracy that the winner of this race might be elected on the strength of 3,000 votes out of some 24,000 ballots cast or spoiled—not exactly a strong local mandate, but such is our imperfect electoral system. First-past-the-post strikes again. I wondered how Angus might feel about winning a seat in the House of Commons, knowing that less than 10 percent of his constituents had voted for him. Then again, I doubt his vote count would top his list of concerns. I somehow think he'd be stuck for quite some time on the part about his winning a seat in the House of Commons.

By this time, Ontario results were rolling in. In the national seat count, determining which party would form the Government, the Tories and Liberals were very close. With western Canada historically arid territory for Liberals, we had to make our numbers count in Ontario. In the first couple of hours after the polls closed, we were where we were supposed to be. My fellow eastern-Ontario campaign managers had all pulled out Liberal victories, adding two unexpected seats courtesy of Cameron's sex-slave sideshow.

CTV Cameron Watch (9:45 PM EST)
(88% of polls reporting)

Eric Cameron (PC)	2,691
Angus McLintock (Lib)	3,168
Jane Nankovich (NDP)	3,209
Spoiled Ballots	12,993

Shit. I started chanting "Jane, Jane, Jane" at the top of my lungs. Well, it might have worked. I lost my rhythm when the TV issued that annoying chime, signaling that some producer with a calculator, nerves of steel, and testicles to match, had decided to declare a winner even though thousands of ballots had yet to be counted. It was a point of pride among the networks to be the first to project winners and losers. Such a mentality also ensured it was a point of ignominy among networks when premature projections had to be withdrawn or corrected. I turned up the volume:

The CTV Decision Desk is declaring Eric Cameron defeated. His successor as MP for Cumberland-Prescott remains a mystery as a neck-and-neck battle plays out that may come down to the very last poll.

I switched channels. Within ten minutes, all three Canadian networks had buried Cameron, eulogized him, and then, for good measure, conducted gruesome autopsies to analyze and animate his political demise. As the pundits picked through Eric Cameron's steamy entrails, it was brought home to me once again just how cruel, ruthless, and brutal we are in the treatment of our politicians. Decades of tireless service, always putting the public interest first without even the whiff of impropriety is just so much dust in the wind if you happen to be caught just once with your hand in the cookie jar—or in handcuffs, as in the case here. Don't misunderstand me. I'm not talking about Eric Cameron and am certainly not defending him. I always suspected he was not what he seemed. But our history is littered with other outstanding public servants whose human frailty in a single moment of weakness erased entire careers of dogged devotion and selfless service to Canada and its citizens. For Cameron, the trip from revered to reviled was painfully short.

We wonder why we're unable to attract to public life the calibre of people we'd like to see. Well, we pry into their private lives, put their every move under a microscope, and subject them and their loved ones to the most invasive and penetrating scrutiny imaginable. Then, when we find the slightest little thing that even remotely resembles an infraction no more serious than leaving the toilet seat up, we eat them. We get the government we deserve. Yes, we want honesty, transparency, and decency in our politicians. To attract such qualities, we need understanding, sensitivity, and sometimes forgiveness in our voters.

I'm not sure how I got onto that. It was likely a self-defensive instinct to distract me from what was unfolding in the election. The west was now reporting, and the Tories were cleaning up. The margins were so high that winners were declared early. The polls in British Columbia had not closed, but CTV and Global had already declared a minority government for the Progressive Conservatives. Based on our slate of B.C. candidates, I was surprised CBC was holding off making it unanimous. Cumberland-Prescott was one of the few seats outside of B.C. still undeclared. It was almost over but oh, so close.

CTV Cameron Watch (10:40 PM EST)
(All but one poll reporting)

Eric Cameron (PC)	2,988
Angus McLintock (Lib)	3,614
Jane Nankovich (NDP)	3,627
Spoiled Ballots	14,661

The race for the Government is all but over with the Tories returned to power with minority standing in the House of Commons. But CBC Election Central has yet to declare the winner in the battle for Cumberland-Prescott. Simply put, the race is still too close to call. It all comes down to the ballots cast in the very last poll to be counted. We'll know shortly when the numbers arrive from poll 22 in the heart of Cumberland.

I knew without looking but checked anyway. Yep, it was just a formality now. I shut off the television, stripped down again, and slipped off the end of the dock. I didn't even register the cold this time. I had no shock left in me. I stroked strongly out into the river about 80 metres or so from shore. I bobbed in the water there for about 20 minutes. The lights in the boathouse looked so warm and welcoming. On the return trip, I swam for as long as I could underwater, reveling in that foreign world. I felt strangely at peace when submerged. But then, I'd surface again, and my nightmare would take over.

I stood naked on the dock, letting the cool night wind dry me. I was trembling with cold but stood there, anyway. In time, I pulled on my clothes, grabbed my car keys, and locked the door behind me. In the moon's dim wash of light, I could just make out the silhouette of Angus's beloved Baddeck 1 through the window as I passed by on the stairs. The Taurus started, eventually, and I pointed its front end towards Ottawa.

I met with the head of airport security, explained my situation with unvarnished honesty, and implored him on humanitarian grounds to grant my request. After two phone calls to his superiors and a mercifully cursory search (really, just a quick pat down), I was given a dummy boarding card. I passed through the metal detectors and climbed the stairs to the arrivals level. The flight from Chicago, bearing Angus, landed safely and on time, ripping away my last shred of hope. I felt oddly detached from the evening's events as if I were merely an observer rather than a very real participant with much at stake.

As I waited in the small arrivals lounge just a few metres from the door through which Angus would soon appear, I watched as a small army of reporters and cameras amassed on the far side of the security station. They saw me. I knew immediately that the mechanical-engineering department's naïve and ever-helpful administrative assistant had been naïve and ever helpful in providing flight information to the dozens of reporters who'd obviously called that day for the whereabouts of a certain Professor Duncan Angus McLintock. I chastised myself for not heading that issue off at the pass. I changed seats, putting my back towards the gestating scrum.

Angus emerged from the jetway in the middle of the pack of passengers. Not expecting me in the arrivals area, he didn't see me at first. Despite his long and arduous journey, he never looked so light on his feet, so animated, so congenial. The word that sprung to mind was *jaunty*. For the first time, I glimpsed the Angus free of English for Engineers and as far as he was concerned, now free of any political entanglements.

We made eye contact when he was about 20 metres away. I could tell that after taking one look at my weak, insipid, pathetic smile, he knew something was amiss. He dropped his carry-on bag and stood there with his hands in gunfighter, quick-draw position. The other passengers, eager for bed, streamed around him, sending him the odd glare, to which he was utterly oblivious. I watched as his facial colouring morphed from "Panic Pink" to "Raging Red" and then finally, to

"Ballistic Blue." Perhaps Crayola had an opening for someone like me. He knew in an instant. He knew.

"No no no no, you cannae be serious! Yer havin' me on, aye you are. Yer havin' a yank on me leg, aye you are. Shit, you cannae keep standin' there with that look on yer mug."

We moved to a deserted departure lounge farther down the terminal although we'd still have to run the reporters' gauntlet sooner or later or take our chances on the runway.

I explained exactly what had happened as calmly and clearly as I could while working around a lump in my throat the size of a small grapefruit. I'd brought the weekend editions of *The Globe and Mail*, *National Post*, and *Ottawa Citizen* with their graphic images to bring the fiasco to life. It wasn't a complicated story, and Angus was a quick study. I relayed the final vote count I'd recorded from the car radio and noted the likely futility of a judicial recount. I also pointed out the eight video cameras and about twenty-five reporters waiting at the other end.

Angus remained calm while he read the entire *Globe and Mail* coverage. He asked me a few questions and then seemed to drift into a Zen-like state. He went into the men's room for what seemed like an hour but was actually only about 25 minutes. When he emerged, he looked composed. He'd wet his hair and, using his fingers, had fashioned at least the beginnings of a part. He'd also meticulously removed all food fragments from his beard.

"Do I always cart around that much nourishment in me chin spinach?" he asked me as he tucked in his shirt and brushed his canvas pants.

"Well … well, yes … yes, you do. It's part of your charm," I babbled.

"Actually, it's part of me lunch and last night's dinner."

I honestly had no idea what was happening. I thought Angus must have been in some advanced state of denial; yet, he appeared calm and compos mentis. He looked down the terminal to the clamour of reporters, took three deep breaths, and headed their way.

"Whoa, Angus, what do you think you're doing? Where are you going?"

My endless stream of questions fell on the deaf ears Angus had only recently revealed through his hand-to-hair combat. He just kept striding towards the scrum. I had no idea what to do. Eventually, I fell silent and trudged behind him, bearing his carry-on. As we exited the secure area and confronted the horde, he turned to me. "You set 'em up, and I'll knock 'em down," he whispered.

He stood tall—for him, anyway—with his hands behind his back. I seemed to understand Angus though I didn't know how or why. I just knew what to do. I stepped into the scrum. The reporters clicked on their sun guns and hoisted their cameras to their shoulders. They thrust their microphones within inches of my face.

"Dr. McLintock will make a brief statement, but let's leave the questions until tomorrow, shall we. He's been flying for the past 19 hours, so please give him a break and let me take him home. It's Professor Angus McLintock, spelled M, little c, capital L-i-n-t-o-c-k. Angus?" I stood aside and felt my pulse pound. Not knowing what would happen in a tense situation always pushed my maximum-anxiety button. I went to DefCon 1. I was breathing hard but oddly also felt a wafer-thin gauze of serenity enveloping me, for which I had no explanation. Angus moved into position, and the reporters closed ranks around him. He bowed his head and closed his eyes for a few seconds, not in prayer but in preparation. He looked up and squinted briefly, adjusting to the glare of the lights.

"I'm new to this, so please bear with me. One hour ago, I was on a plane from Papua New Guinea where I spent the last two weeks installin' a new water-filtration and purification system for a village that heretofore had only limited access to clean drinkin' water. That is where I was. That is where me mind was. Like everyone else in Canada, I expected to walk off that plane free of any political encumbrances as Eric Cameron waltzed back to Ottawa as he always has.

"I freely admit that when I agreed to let me name stand as the Liberal candidate, I had no intention of servin', and no expectation of needin' to. I've heard me friend Daniel here say on more than one occasion that anything can happen in politics and occasionally does—like tonight, for instance. Rest assured, I'll not be throwin' me name around so cavalierly in the future.

"I like to think I'm an honourable man whose word is his bond. I hope me friends and colleagues would concur. I let me name stand on the ballot. Events have conspired to grant me the most votes. Unless someone named 'Spoiled Ballots' steps forward, I appear to have been elected for better or worse. And I'm quite convinced it's 'worse' if you want me view on it.

"In a weak moment of folly, I made a commitment. I stand by it and will serve though I'd certainly rather continue me engineerin' work, toilin' in relative obscurity.

"Let me congratulate Jane Nankovich for the campaign she ran. She undoubtedly did her supporters proud. I extend me heartfelt sympathies to Eric Cameron for the calamity that has befallen him. Whatever his extracurricular interests may be, he undoubtedly has served Canada well and deserves our respect, our gratitude, and in particular right now, our understandin'.

"For all me new constituents, I can only say I will do me best in a role for which I feel ill suited and unprepared. Whatever the situation, you may rely on me to be honest and direct. I shall never forget whose money the government is collectin' and spendin'. And I promise that I will always, always be guided by two immutable questions, posed, considered, and answered in this essential order of priority: Firstly, what is best for Canada? And secondly, if necessary, what is best for the people of Cumberland-Prescott?

"I guarantee that some, perhaps many of me own constituents will take issue with this approach and the positions and decisions it will sometimes yield. I can only suggest they will have a chance to vote for someone else in four years' time—perhaps sooner if we're all lucky.

"I want to recognize the long and distinguished service of Muriel Parkinson, who ran before me in the previous five campaigns. A lasting regret of mine will be that it is I and not she who stands before you now. While I am well aware of her famed organizational skills, part of me laments that she deployed them with such vigour and obvious success in poll 22, the Riverfront Seniors' Residence where she lives.

"Finally, I may need a few days to recover from me two weeks in a different hemisphere, not to mention from the surreal trip I've taken since landin' here in Ottawa. I seek yer patience and indulgence until I am feelin' meself again. In the interim, if you need anythin', you may contact me newly appointed executive assistant, or whatever his title should be, Dr. Daniel Addison. He helped me get into this situation, and he will be with me every step of the way on Parliament Hill. Good night."

I had to stop for a minute or two to sort through the jaws on the ground until I could find my own. Stunning. The reporters were transfixed. As was I—so much so that Angus's last sentence hadn't yet registered. André Fontaine just stood there blank-faced and dumbstruck. The scrum parted for us like the Red Sea for Moses. Come to think of it, Angus looked the part. I walked two steps behind as we made our way to the luggage carousel and then to the parking lot. I was trying to catch up, literally and figuratively. Seven cameras trailed us all the way to the car.

He spoke only once on the drive home and I, in a daze, not at all. "You'd best have left me plenty of Lagavulin."

CTV Cameron Watch (1:45 AM EST)
(All polls reporting)

Eric Cameron (PC)	2,992
Angus McLintock (Lib)*	3,703
Jane Nankovich (NDP)	3,639

Spoiled Ballots   14,662

* Declared winner at 10:55 PM

◆   ◆   ◆

Diary
Monday, October 14

My Love,

I'm at 29,000 feet, closing in on Ottawa, and I can't wait to get back. I didn't notice my longing for home whilst in Papua New Guinea. I was so consumed with my work and the deep and immediate impact it had on the villagers that I simply didn't notice I was missing our home. I'm utterly knackered after such a long journey. But I'm feeling like a new man with a new lease on life. Upon my return, the normal order of the universe will be restored, and I can resume my life free of the fetters of this damned election. My focus will be Baddeck 1 and my research. I also look forward to renewing my chess rivalry with Dr. Addison. I've missed our spirited matches these last two weeks.

The seat-belt sign has just bonged, so I must close this rather flimsy tray table and brace myself for landing. I'll complete this when I'm home—with you watching over me.

AM

Addendum (2:00 AM)
   Oh shite.

PART TWO

CHAPTER ELEVEN

I leaned against the stone wall on the other side of the corridor, watching the sign painter.

D. ANGUS MCLINTOCK
Member of Parliament for/Député de
CUMBERLAND-PRESC

Only the House of Commons would employ a commercial artist whose raison d'être was hand-stenciling the names of MPs in gold-fleck paint on the front doors of their offices. I watched as he worked meticulously to finish the final O-T-T as if it somehow confirmed as real what I'd hoped might be some particularly cruel nightmare. The irony was painful. I felt like the sad-sack inmate who had tunneled out of his cell only to miscalculate and surface in the gas chamber. Just a few short months earlier, I'd very nearly made a clean escape. Yet, here I was, back on Parliament Hill, atop my own personal pyre of politics.

While a weak and distant little whisper in my head argued for abandoning Angus and seeking political refugee status at the university, the whisper was quickly drowned out by a sanctimonious, annoying voice, delivering a will-sapping refrain of "do the right thing." Shit. I knew what I had to do. I just wondered what it would be like to flirt with being a jerk for once. I would certainly have been in good company. But I had gotten us both into this mess. I really had no choice but to stand by Angus in his hour of need. And how I wish an hour was all that was required. The way my luck was going, the next election might well have been five years off—despite the Government's minority status.

At least, the university had been reasonable, even generous. Both Angus and I had been granted open-ended leaves of absence with no loss in seniority and with our tenure status unaffected. Angus had his, and I was on a long road to get mine. My future seemed reasonably secure; it was my present that depressed me. On the brighter side of the ledger, neither one of us would be teaching English for Engineers. In a rather satisfying twist of fate, Dean Roland Rumplun had been forced to take over the class—the blind leading the blind. For Angus, the knowledge that Rumplun would be enduring the weekly torture of E for E almost made coming to Ottawa tolerable.

I was greeted by my former colleagues as the prodigal son, their smirking incredulity standing in for the fatted calf. Bradley Stanton, the weasel, offered muted congratulations, but the Leader seemed genuine in his praise for the "brilliant campaign" I'd run. My veteran status on the Hill conferred some privileges unavailable to the new kids on the block. I snagged us a choice office suite along the quiet corridor that ran the length of Centre Block behind the House of Commons and the Senate chamber. The suite was small but gave us a glorious view of the river. It was not unlike the vista offered up by Muriel's traditional vantage point in the lounge of the Riverfront Seniors' Residence some 30 kilometres east.

Not many MPs even wanted offices in Centre Block, opting, instead, for more spacious accommodations in the Confederation Building just to the west. But I wanted Centre Block. And in time, Angus would thank me. In the deep freeze of an Ottawa February, he merely had to saunter down the hall to the House for evening votes while many of his colleagues would be re-enacting Admiral Peary's North Pole trek to get there.

In the three weeks since the election, Angus had still not adjusted to his status as a Member of Parliament, not to mention his folk-hero notoriety. His extemporaneous, yet eloquent, airport soliloquy had endeared him not just to the press gallery but to millions of Canadians who watched, heard, and read it over and over through the media in the days that followed. The long-time parliamentary bureau chief for *The Calgary Herald* coined "Honest Angus," and the moniker stuck like a lamprey with nothing to lose. I must say it was a big improvement over "Absent Angus," with which we'd been tagged during the campaign.

True to his word, Angus slowly came to grips with the election's unlikely—check that, shocking—outcome. A few letters to the editor in the Cumberland newspaper decried the election of a Liberal on the strength of a piddling 3700 votes, calling it an affront to democracy. These were easily overwhelmed by the dozens of letters from Canadians who considered Angus to be just the sort of politician we needed—an honourable representative who spoke his mind and did what he said. His frank admission that he'd run with neither the intention nor the desire to serve, passed through the country's consciousness and out the other side with nary a discouraging word. And the skies were not cloudy all day. His honeymoon had started.

Angus had sequestered himself in his workshop in the immediate aftermath of the election, using me as his shield from the outside world. For an entire week, he spent his days painting his beloved hovercraft; I spent mine fending off reporters and getting high on the fumes rising through the vents in my floor. His contact with me in the first few days was perfunctory, even cool. It was clear he was wrestling with what had befallen him and was struggling to make peace with the hard-left turn his life had taken, with me at the wheel.

When his painting was done, he seemed to emerge from his funk, and our chess games resumed. In our initial contests, he crushed me with such relentless fury that I could only conclude it was his way of punishing me for involving him in this fiasco. While I felt justified in noting that no one had forced him into our little arrangement, I figured shoving that particular red-hot poker up his nose was ill-advised at best and suicidal at worst. I took my shellacking, game after game, with stoic good humour as Angus slowly burned through his considerable reserves of anger and self-pity. Eventually, he passed through the dark valley and emerged on the other side, showing at least traces of the personality I'd come to know, enjoy, and respect.

My agreement to return to Parliament Hill with him, as if he'd left me any choice in the matter, seemed to help put our relationship back on a tentative but promising footing. In the week following the election, Angus had studiously avoided newspapers, television, and radio. But I'd clipped and kept the stories chronicling his evolution from anonymous engineering professor to political giant killer. Most stories reprinted verbatim the remarks Angus made in front of the baggage carousel and conveniently overlooked that Cameron's demise had been wholly self-inflicted. Reading the coverage and how it developed over the days and weeks after the election was a case study in how heroes are manufactured out of media hyperbole, rose-tinted hindsight, and concerted lily-gilding.

We are all, to greater or lesser degrees, captives of our own egos. Angus, for all his hard-nosed honesty and honour, still lived with human frailties. During the second week following the election—his election—and after he'd soundly trounced me a dozen times or more on the 64 squares, I gave him the folder of clippings to read. Though he endeavoured to mask it, I could tell he was pleased and surprised that his predicament and response had been the subject of such positive, if exaggerated, comment. Though he scoffed and declared it all "drivel," I noticed that he'd read every article before delivering his faint and feeble verdict.

After carefully and sensitively managing Angus's moods and emotions for nearly three weeks, free from the prying eyes of the public and the media, I felt he was ready to venture into Ottawa and begin his new life. He was less certain but allowed himself to be cajoled into acquiescence.

Angus was sitting behind his standard-issue MP's desk, his back to the leaded window panes high above the river. His head was in his hands. His office was pretty well organized with only a few pictures on loan from the Parliamentary art collection yet to be hung. He looked as if he were at a funeral. Pale and stiff, he might have been at his own funeral. When I lost him in the black depths, one of my many jobs as his executive assistant was to drag him back up, boost his spirits, and force him to confront and, hopefully, accept his new reality. I called it doing a "Lazarus." It required delicate management of mood (his, not mine) and a passel of patience (mine, not his).

"Angus, we've got 20 minutes before you're due in the Clerk's office. Let me show you something I know you'll like," I proposed with the finesse of a neurosurgeon who knows his patient's head inside and out.

"Blow it out yer hindquarters! I cannae enjoy me wallowin' with you playin' cruise director."

I clearly had him right where I wanted him. "Come on, Angus. You're in Centre Block—the very seat of our nation's history. I guarantee you'll love what I'm going to show you. I know you, and you will want to see this," I persisted, carefully gauging my tone and words to yield the desired effect. I sensed I was close to reaching him. Reading and managing his temper really was an important skill, which I like to think I possessed in some modest measure.

"Was there a particular part of 'blow it out yer hindquarters' that left you confused as to me disposition?" he replied through teeth clamped tighter than canal locks.

I was obviously on the right path. Just a little more. "Angus, you need to buck up, and you need to trust me. You're in my house now, and I just want to show you a very special place. It's on the way to the Clerk's office anyway." Nothing. "Come on, Angus, you're about to embark on a completely new and rare experience that comes to very few Canadians. Please let me help you get off on the right foot. Now, let's go." I moved towards the door, hoping my very motion might help push him over the edge of agreement.

"Buck up and trust you? Get off on the right foot?" he said, hissing. "I've got a better idea of what I can do with my right foot if you come a wee bit closer. I wish you'd just shut up."

Brilliantly played. From buck up to shut up in two seconds flat. I stayed silent and trained a sympathetic gaze on him. It was my last gambit. Mercifully, he softened.

"Awright, awright, awright, if you'll stop yer yammerin' and give me a wee bit of peace and quiet, I'll come. But don't push yer fortune and challenge me good nature or there'll be more blood on the board tonight," he said, sighing. He stood up and shuffled after me like Eeyore off his medication.

We headed out into the hall and down to the central north-south corridor, running from the Peace Tower at the south end to two knobless, wooden doors at the north end. We turned left and approached the two doors, I walking with purpose, Angus slowing. Just as I was about to walk right into the beautifully carved wood (with the theme song from "Get Smart" echoing in my head), they silently parted, and we both entered my favourite place on Parliament Hill.

I stood aside and let Angus pass into the three-tiered wooden glory of the Library of Parliament. An alabaster statue of Queen Victoria towered over us in the centre of the circular library. A handful of staff laboured under her benevolent gaze. I fell silent and listened for Angus's reaction. I was rewarded by his sharp intake of breath at the sight of three levels of ornate, wooden shelves, which circled the perimeter of the room, and the arched windows in the domed, sky-lit ceiling. I'd entered that place dozens, even hundreds, of times and always felt a slight wobble in my knees as I passed over the threshold. As I anticipated, Angus was similarly moved.

"Consider yourself forgiven. It takes the breath clean away," he whispered, craning his neck and slowly rotating on the spot just in front of the beautifully carved counter sheltering the Dewey Decimal disciples who worked behind it. The head librarian gave me a wink, gathered Angus in her wake, and took him on a brief but engaging tour designed to entrance even the most seasoned bibliophile. Angus was duly enthralled. I could hear his endless stream of questions as I took my traditional place in the shadow of Laurier's plaster bust as I waited for Angus. Ten minutes later, I cleared my throat to gain the eyes of the head librarian. She escorted Angus to the door where I met them.

"Thanks so much, Lucille. I knew Angus would enjoy this place as I always have. I'm sure he'll be back, but it's time for his swearing in, and we shouldn't keep the Clerk waiting," I noted.

Angus thanked her as politely as his gruff manner permitted, and we passed back through the incongruous automatic sliding doors as if leaving the bridge of the starship *Enterprise* and not a pristine library constructed in the late 1800s.

"I've always felt at peace in there," I remarked as we strode down the hall towards the Clerk's office.

"Aye, it's a fine room, it is," Angus replied. "And I can go in there whenever the spirit moves me?"

"Whenever you please," I confirmed.

Someone I didn't recognize emerged from the Clerk's office as we approached. The mace lapel pin indicated she was a newly elected MP. We said hello as she passed and then slipped through the door she held open for us.

"Professor McLintock, I presume," said the Clerk of the House of Commons.

She was dressed in full regalia and with a sweep of her hand, waved us into a small ceremonial reception room from a bygone era, the centerpiece of which was a fireplace with logs blazing in its hearth.

"Aye, that is I," replied Angus as he extended his hand.

"Nice to meet you; congratulations on your election. You've caused quite a stir in the country," she commented with a gentle smile.

"As you may know, I had no intention of stirrin' anythin'. In fact, you might say I'm here under false pretences," Angus responded.

"Ah yes, but the people have spoken, and here you are."

"Well, a few of them have spoken, but I fear the vast majority in Cumberland-Prescott might rather I were somewhere else," he concluded.

She looked my way for the first time. "Hello, Daniel. How are you?"

We'd worked together over the years, particularly on the procedures in the House around the Throne Speech and budgets.

"I'm fine, Anne-Marie. A little taken aback by what has transpired, but that's politics," I answered.

"Well, it's nice to have you back. Now, why don't we proceed with the swearing in as we have eight more MPs to go before quitting time."

The House of Commons photographer positioned Angus in front of the fireplace, facing the Clerk.

"Did you bring your own Bible, Professor McLintock?" she asked.

"No, I tend towards agnostic," Angus commented.

"Well, you can use this one. It belonged to Wilfrid Laurier. We use John A. Macdonald's for Conservative members," she offered, handing Angus a well-worn, black, leather-bound edition.

"Fine. Thank you."

"The oath you're about to take is required under the Parliament of Canada Act. You may not enter the House of Commons before taking it. Please hold the Bible in your left hand, raise your right hand, and read the oath."

She held up a five-by-seven card, embossed with the official imprimatur of the House of Commons. Angus did as she directed while the trigger-happy photographer flashed away.

"I, Duncan Angus McLintock, do swear that I will be faithful and bear true allegiance to Her Majesty Queen Elizabeth the Second, Queen of Canada, Her Heirs, and Successors. So help me God."

"Congratulations, Professor McLintock, you are now officially a Member of the House of Commons of the Parliament of Canada," the Clerk intoned.

"Saints preserve us," Angus remarked in a doleful sigh.

I turned to the photographer for the first time. "When can we have access to the shots?" I asked. "We're going to need them soon for our first householder."

"They're digital, so I'll e-mail them to you when we're finished with the other MPs," he responded. "You'll have them by the end of the day."

"Perfect," I said and provided him with my e-mail address.

We were almost to the door when Angus piped up again. "Just before we take our leave, I reckon I should learn what I can about the procedures of the House before I'm in the thick of it. What would you recommend?" he asked the Clerk.

She was ready for the question and handed Angus a slim volume published by the Queen's Printers right in Centre Block.

"These are the Standing Orders that govern all that happens in the House. They define everything you ought to know about procedure from how question period works, to how many days we debate the Throne Speech. It is a clear and invaluable resource drafted to be accessible to the layperson or, in this case, a neophyte Member of Parliament. You may, of course, always call me or my staff with any queries you may have," she replied.

"I thank you."

Angus bowed slightly, and we stepped back out into the corridor.

"Let's make one more stop before heading back to the office," I proposed.

Angus seemed distracted but followed me, nevertheless. When he surfaced from his reverie, we were standing in front of the open main doors of the House of Commons. The guards on duty noted Angus's lapel pin and stood aside.

"After you," I said. "I can only go to the arch."

Angus walked in and stood on the green carpet, surveying the heart of Parliament. As I'd hoped, his standing there had the desired impact. The room is extraordinary in its design, power, and history. Even a visitor from another planet would know matters of great import unfolded in that chamber.

I watched as Angus took it all in. Although the seats had not yet been assigned, Angus seemed thrilled just to stand there. Eventually, he retreated and rejoined me.

"I still cannae believe I've a seat in that place. It's all a wee bit overwhelmin'. Humblin', in fact," he whispered.

"Indeed," was all I said.

We returned to our office where Angus broke out a new bottle of Lagavulin. He poured himself a generous measure and leaned back in his chair with his feet on the bare desktop. I sat in one of the 40-year-old guest chairs in front of him. The sun shone through the window behind, crowning his head in a beatific halo.

His cranial corona made the wayward strands of his frizzled hair look as if they were on fire.

"All right, you'd better tell me what's goin' on now that they've let me in here," he sighed as he downed half of his single malt in one gulp.

I leaned forward towards him, resting my elbows on my knees. "Okay, here's the deal. Like every other MP, the House of Commons provides us with a budget to run this office as well as your constituency office in Cumberland. The allocation is rather paltry and really only permits the hiring of two Parliament Hill staff and two constit staff." I stopped to make sure he was with me. He seemed to be. "I've already taken the liberty of hiring Camille Boudreau to help manage this office. The Leader's staff sent her over. She used to work over there but left when they no longer had room for her. I think you'll like her. I'm not certain she's an intellectual powerhouse, but on our budget, we should be happy with anyone who can read, write, and tie their own shoelaces. She starts next week."

He nodded.

"As for your constituency office, I've secured a small but adequate storefront space just off Riverfront Road. The price was right. After the landlord heard it was for your constituency office, he gave us a real deal—seems your honest and heartfelt little monologue on election night struck a chord with him. Anyway, Muriel is going to help us get it set up and will work afternoons when she's feeling up to it. She's also going to hire a full-time office manager to keep the trains running on time. The two Petes, who canvassed for you almost every day of the campaign, which should actually earn them the Order of Canada, are going to work part-time, their engineering studies permitting."

"Ah yes, the two Petes. I'd like to examine the structural engineerin' of their hair. The way they make it stand straight out from their heads seems to play fast and loose with Newton's truths," Angus observed.

I resisted the temptation to remind Angus that his own hair broke a few laws of its own. "Well, I'm sure they'd share their technique with you," I said. "We're actually very lucky to have them still on board. We can't pay them very much, but they agreed, anyway."

"Aye, I'll be sure to thank them. Without their tireless campaignin', I might well be havin' a nap right now or tinkerin' in me workshop, and that would be horrible," he spat in a tone I can only describe by using a new word I created for my own private use: *sarcaustic*.

I must confess I was shocked by how small our budget was. I'd grown accustomed to the more generous allocations made to the office of the Leader of the

Opposition. Now, I'd have to scrimp and save and actually pay attention to how much money we spent. Not a bad thing, I suppose, since it was public money.

"In addition to your salary of about $150,000, you'll also receive a housing allowance that will go straight into your pocket, assuming you're going to live in Cumberland and commute to Ottawa every day," I explained.

"Send the housin' allowance back," Angus commanded.

"I beg your pardon?"

"Canya not hear me? Send the housin' allowance back from whence it came. I don't need it. I won't be usin' it. And so it doesna belong to me. Send it back."

I should not have been surprised. I decided it would be a waste of time to pursue this further and made a mental note to call the House of Commons operations staff to see about reversing the housing allowance. While I wouldn't want Angus to know, I decided I'd quietly pass along this little public-minded gesture to a reporter or two in the gallery. It was good fodder for the McLintock myth-making machine.

"Thy will be done," I replied. "I trust you're happy to let me manage the staffing of both offices and that you don't feel the need to meet them first."

"Well, the horse is already out of that barn now, isn't it? That bein' said, I've neither the knowledge nor the inclination to be of much use on that front. That's why I've you," he declared. "How did you talk Muriel into puttin' in time in the Cumberland office?"

"I didn't have to ask her. She offered. In fact, it took me quite some time to convince her that she should be paid for her time. We'll get far more out of having her on staff than we could ever hope to give her in return," I observed. "If there were a Liberal volunteer hall of fame, she'd be a charter inductee."

"Aye, she's quite a lass. She called earlier on, and we had another nice chat. She was giving me pointers on the appropriate conduct of an MP," Angus mentioned.

"Was she looking for me?" I asked.

"I doonae think so. Yer name never came up," he said. "By the way, what in blazes is a householder?"

"Four times each year, the House of Commons pays for a mailing to all of your constituents to keep them informed of your tireless and constructive efforts on their behalf. We call that newsletter a *householder*. I'm big on photos because that's what constituents remember. Plus, the more photos, the less writing for us to do," I informed him. "Lindsay has already started to map out your first householder. I figure we'll send it out in about a month when your honeymoon with the voters may start to wane. When your profile is as high and as positive as it is right now, you can only go in one direction from there."

"Sounds like a brag sheet intended to serve to MPs' egos. I don't want ours to look like all the others. Let's really make ours useful, not a photo album," Angus directed.

"We'll sit down with Lindsay next week and kick around some ideas," I suggested. "It's late. I'll drive us home, we'll have some dinner, and then, I'll do my best to redeem my shoddy chess playing of late."

Angus downed what little remained of his Lagavulin and rose. "As grand a plan as ever I've heard," he answered.

I'd snagged a parking spot just to the west of Centre Block—another perk of past service. Though he tried to conceal it, I could tell Angus was pleased when several House of Commons' staff said "good night, sir" as we walked to the car. My cell phone rang as we reached the parking lot. It was Bradley Stanton, who'd resumed his role as chief of staff to the Leader of the Opposition following the election.

"Addison, are you still on the Hill?" he asked.

"Angus and I are just in the parking lot, why?"

"The Leader would like to meet your guy if you can come back in for a few minutes," Stanton said.

"Hang on a sec, Bradley." I turned to Angus, covering my cell's mouthpiece microphone with my thumb. "Our fearless Leader wants to shake your hand and bask in your glory. It'll only take a couple of minutes," I said.

His shoulders drooped. "Do we hafta? I'm beat, and the chessboard beckons," he scowled.

"Angus, he's the Leader of the Liberal Party and perhaps our next Prime Minister. When he asks for an audience, protocol—not to mention, courtesy—suggests we give him one. We'll be in the car in 15 minutes tops."

The Leader's office was also in Centre Block on the second floor. His office overlooked Parliament Hill and was a beautiful space with lots of carved wood and leaded windows. We were shown in. He was on the phone with his back to us, looking out the window. He finished his conversation and turned to find Angus and me before him.

"Duncan, my friend, how good to finally meet you," the Leader boomed.

I prayed Angus would not correct his split infinitive. The Leader did not take kindly to criticism. It made advising him a perilous task.

"It's nice *finally to meet* you, too," Angus replied, deftly rejoining the infinitive without burdening the Leader with any grammatical elucidation. "I go by Angus."

The Leader came around the exquisite wooden desk that once belonged to Laurier and gripped Angus with his habitual political handshake. It was much like any other handshake except with the addition of the strong, left-hand shoulder squeeze, connoting great friendship, respect, and affection for the person he's just met for the first time. The Leader had a tendency to invade your personal space when talking to you. From my vantage point, it looked as if his forehead actually came into contact with some of Angus's unruly locks. Even though Angus's hair was standing straight up as if straining to defect, the Leader was still right in his face. Angus tilted back to create separation.

"Angus you've done a great thing, knocking Cameron off his pedestal," the Leader declared.

"Well, the way I see it, sir, Mr. Cameron jumped off of his own accord. I just happened to be the least unpalatable alternative."

"Nonsense, man! Don't be so modest. You ran a great campaign. I followed it very closely. You deserve the accolades being heaped on you now. You've worked your way into the hearts of Canadians, and that usually takes years. Your victory was quite a coup and sets us up well for the next time around."

Angus just shook his head, the expression on his face eloquently asking "are you daft man?" My heart rate increased in anticipation of what might next fly from his lips.

"Since we're on the subject of nonsense, me campaign *and* me candidacy were not worth a tinker's curse—no offence to me colleague here," Angus patted my back in reassurance. "I dinnae win the damnable election. Cameron lost it, and no blatherskite's foolish ramblin's will ever change that."

The Leader was taken aback, unaccustomed to being contradicted. He turned to me with a "what gives?" look on his face.

"Ah, sir, *blatherskite* is a Scottish term of endearment. As you can well imagine, Angus is still coming to grips with our rather surprising victory," I skated, with very weak ankles.

"Understandable, completely understandable. It's been a shock to us all. But I have to say your little speech at the airport was a masterstroke. Daniel must have polished that prose for hours. It was brilliant," the Leader gushed.

I jumped in before Angus could tear the fabric off this meeting any farther. "Ah, actually, Angus is a wonderful writer and orator in his own right. I heard his speech for the first time that night when everyone else did. Angus was just speaking from his heart. There was none of my wordsmithing at all. It was completely extemporaneous," I clarified.

"Amazing. And I really do like the disheveled maverick look you've cultivated. The hair and beard are great—very strong and tough. Very 'bring it on' and 'go ahead, make my day.' Canadians really seemed to have bought it, you old rascal," he nodded and smiled conspiratorially.

We drove in silence for quite some time, and then, just as Cumberland hove into view, Angus weighed in.

"So he's the Leader of the Liberal Party."

"He wasn't exactly on his game today, Angus. I got to know him pretty well when I worked there, and he really is a good guy," I replied, feeling the need to defend my former employer.

"We don't need 'good guys' runnin' the country, Professor Addison. We need smart people who know what's what and aren't afraid to make the right decisions," Angus countered. "I dinnae get a good feelin' from him."

"Don't lock in your judgment, yet. He's done a good job. He just needs to surround himself with different people. He's got too many Bradley Stantons on his staff and not enough PLUs."

"PLUs?" he asked, looking quizzical.

"People Like Us."

I got whipped in our first two games but managed to draw the third. I retired to the boathouse, tired and uneasy. Angus had been sworn in. The Throne Speech was scheduled for the following week. I was back wearing my old life, but it somehow no longer fit.

◆   ◆   ◆

Diary
Tuesday, November 5

My Love,

I still cannot quite wrap my mind around it, but I was sworn in today as the Member of Parliament for Cumberland-Prescott. How did this happen? What am I to do? What would you do? Don't answer that. I actually know what you'd do. You'd jump in with both feet and crusade until you fell. Aye, that's what you'd do. I don't think I can muster the gumption to do it like you would, but I'll head down that road as far as my flesh and faculties will take me.

Young Daniel is coddling me like a new puppy even though I keep chewing the furniture and pissing on the floor. His shoulders weren't built for the guilt they're bearing. I'm still mad, but I know it's not his fault. If anyone's to blame, 'tis I. So quick was I to escape E for E that my judgment was clouded and my decision ill made. And now I sit in the damn House of Commons for my sins.

It's a wonderful chamber, it is. Glorious. I'm not keen on the green they've used for the carpet, but other than that, 'tis a fitting and worthy House. And the library we have there—I've never seen its likes before. It will make each day of my stay in Ottawa a little more bearable.

The Clerk gave me the Standing Orders that govern the goings on in the House. My methodical engineer's brain tells me that advantage in the parliamentary battle is conferred on those who know the rules of engagement. I'm told this is particularly so for a minority Parliament like this one. If I'm to spend time skirmishing there, and it seems I am, I intend to seize that advantage.

I confess that when I delve underneath the great shock and dislocation of the last three weeks, I'm forced to admit that a part of me, perhaps even a growing part of me, is excited at what the future holds while another healthy portion laments the loss of my old and comfortable life. And there's still plenty of room for dreams and memories of you. I've no choice in that matter. As I venture through the labyrinth of my new world, I'm guided by one simple question: What would you have me do?

AM

CHAPTER TWELVE

"You are the lab rat in what could be a classic experiment in Canadian democracy," I noted from the passenger seat as Angus drove us to Ottawa in his Toyota Camry. "I say that with great respect and regard."

"Aye, but I heard it with distaste and disdain," countered Angus. He gave me a withering look and held it as long as the road was straight.

"Seriously now, think about it. Perhaps for the first time in Canadian history, the voters have elected a Member of Parliament whose singular commitment is to the public interest, not his own, and the political consequences be damned," I continued. "You cannot be bought, you have no desire for re-election, you have no interest in higher office, and you don't care what people think of you. You actually do what you say. You are the mirror opposite of what Canadians have come to expect from their politicians. You are the antipolitician. In fact, my rudimentary understanding of physics suggests that if you were to collide head-on with a traditional politician, you might cancel one another out and both disappear in a puff of smoke," I concluded, quite pleased with my little theory.

What was the thoughtful and enlightened response of the newly elected MP from Cumberland-Prescott? He paused, looked pensive with brow furrowed like a freshly plowed field, and narrowed his eyes to slits. He then reached over and pushed in the cassette that protruded from the stereo in the dash. Out blasted the greatest hits of the 48th Highlanders. I've always liked "Amazing Grace." It's a very nice little tune. But played by 62 bagpipers at ear-bleeding volume in a subcompact car with a stereo of questionable fidelity, the tune lost some of its lustre. I turned down "Amazing Grace" until it was drowned out by the ringing in my ears. I let another 15 kilometres pass in silence before dipping my toe in the frigid waters again.

"I just think if more politicians adopted your approach, we'd be rewarded with better government and a healthier democracy."

"Me approach? What is me approach? I've only just arrived. Why not let me find out where the parliamentary crapper is before you declare me the cure for all that ails democracy," Angus commented with finality.

"Okay, okay, I'm simply saying that if you're the same person on the Hill as you were in the Ottawa airport on election night, we're in for an interesting time of it."

Angus just lowered his chin, nearly to his sternum, and shook his head. The simultaneous gesture translator in my brain came back with "haven't you done enough already."

"This from a man who promised me a Liberal could never win this ridin'. You need a wee credibility transfusion before your word carries much heft with me."

I held my tongue for the remainder of the drive while trying to coax vital signs out of my ego.

We had a busy day ahead. Angus had his first caucus meeting in the morning, about which I had considerable and justifiable anxiety. In the afternoon, the Usher of the Black Rod would bang on the front door of the House of Commons and then lead a ceremonial procession of MPs to the Senate where they would listen to the Governor General read the Government's Throne Speech.

While the House was in session, caucus meetings were held once weekly on Wednesdays. All Liberal MPs and Senators were supposed to go, but attendance was not taken and was frequently sparse. However, because this caucus meeting was the first one since the election, a capacity crowd was expected. Normally, political staffers, except for the Leader's advisers, were not permitted to attend; the Leader's advisers could pretty well do whatever they wanted. As a very recent émigré from the Leader's office, I slipped into the meeting unchallenged. As in similar situations, if you carried yourself as if you belonged there, no one said boo.

The Opposition caucus room was full of new and returning MPs. Several Senators also showed up, including the Senate Leader. A long table stretched across the front of the room, and theatre-style seating spanned the space from wall to wall with a centre aisle. The arched windows overlooked the front lawn of Parliament Hill while beyond, the Langevin Block, which housed the Prime Minister's Office, was visible on the south side of Wellington Street. The worn and seedy look of the green carpet was matched only by the beige drapes on five of the six windows. The sixth was curtainless although a naked steel dowel stood ready to do its part. Aging metal light fixtures painted a garish gold hung from rods in the ceiling and looked as if they were last dusted when Diefenbaker led the Opposition Tories in 1956. Within Centre Block, Her Majesty's Loyal Opposition lived on the wrong side of the tracks. Needless to say, the Government caucus room was in much better shape and was more lavishly appointed.

As agreed on the walk over, Angus and I separated on arrival. He looked good, for Angus, though a tad grumpy for a newly elected Member of Parliament. He was wearing one of two new suits I'd convinced him he needed. He'd tamed his hair, to the extent possible, and cleared his beard of food fragments as a dedicated farmer might have rid his field of stones. He took a seat close to the far wall near the front. Most others in the room were smiling and laughing. Excitement was in the air, and thanks to a carefully chosen breakfast menu (no turnip), I hoped Angus would contribute nothing else of his own. Many MPs approached Angus and offered spirited congratulations. There was much "David and Goliath" banter, which, I confess, had become tiresome by the morning after the election. Angus was polite but looked to me like he was awaiting a vasectomy. I lurked in the back, chatting up my former colleagues on the Leader's staff and trying to mask a growing sense of foreboding.

Bradley Stanton popped into the room, surveyed the scene, and leaned into the microphone on the front table.

"Awright, folks, listen up. The Leader is on his way, and as usual at the first postelection caucus meeting, he's bringing the press gallery with him. So let's be upbeat and act like we're spoiling for a fight and ready to bring down this evil Tory government."

A few muted cheers greeted his instructions before Stanton darted out of the room to pick up the Leader's posse. At that stage, Angus looked like he was about a third of the way into his vasectomy. He had low-to-no tolerance for political theatre and the kind of "optics" Stanton was trying to orchestrate. Ten seconds later, the Leader, with the look and gait of a man on a mission, strode into the room. The assembled caucus erupted into a "spontaneous" standing ovation, triggered by the frenetic applause of Bradley Stanton and his underlings in the wings. I stood and clapped, too. That was what one did. The Leader reached the front of the room and stood to face his adoring throng. He held his hands in the air in a half-hearted attempt to quell the commotion though we all knew enough to sustain it for several more minutes.

It took awhile before we all realized what was happening. The eight Betacams with their glaring sun guns were not trained on the triumphant Leader but had encircled the lone MP who'd remained seated while all others had leaped to their feet. Yep, much to the Leader's chagrin, and my misfortune, Angus was the centre of attention. Needless to say, it was not the desired "optics" for that particular photo opportunity.

Angus sat with his arms crossed, enduring the media's scrutiny before eventually succumbing to exasperation and invoking the classic "shoo" gesture with both hands as if to chickens in a barnyard. Great first impression. The Leader's communications director eventually corralled the reporters and moved them out of the room so the meeting could start. Stanton gave me a steely look, to which I responded coolly and maturely with a plaintive, schoolyard "it wasn't my fault" shrug, complete with retracted neck and upturned palms.

On balance, the meeting was mercifully uneventful, at least until the end. There was the requisite cheerleading and rabble-rousing in anticipation of the afternoon's Throne Speech. Stanton was first at the mic and talked about bringing down the Government at the earliest possible moment while steam still rose from the Cameron sex scandal. If we waited, the balance of politics in the country would eventually return to equilibrium, and we would have squandered Eric Cameron's one great mistake. Stanton argued that the motion accepting the Speech from the Throne was our first and best opportunity and that we should all be ready to vote against it.

The Leader echoed his chief of staff's views on the Throne Speech in a passionate and compelling speech that climaxed in a charge that the Conservatives lost the moral authority to govern in the final days of the election campaign. The Leader concluded by calling the Throne Speech the Government's last stand—its Waterloo—its Little Big Horn—its Alamo. We got it. I noted with some satisfaction that my replacement in the Leader's office was prone to hyperbole and overkill in his writing. Nevertheless, the Leader delivered the speech with energy and verve. Much whooping and foot-stomping ensued though Angus remained anchored in his seat. As the commotion died away and MPs sank back into their chairs, Angus rose from his.

I prayed he was just a little late embracing the caucus camaraderie and the partisan power of the moment. After all, as a rookie, his timing would be off until he found his feet. Right? Nope. Not only had he found his feet, he was on them.

"Sir, as you may recall, I'm Angus McLintock from Cumberland-Prescott. Nice speech—a wee bit over the top, perhaps, but a good effort. I know I'm new to this world, but how is it that we can, in good conscience, decide now to defeat the Government on the Speech from the Throne when we have yet to hear it and consider it?"

The Leader bristled but, to his credit, hid it well. Having worked with him for several years, I could tell he was irritated because the back of his neck was striated in at least four shades of pink. I'd seen the same colouring on Angus's neck—perhaps a small patch of common ground on which to build.

"Angus, I want to welcome you to the Liberal caucus and congratulate you on your extraordinary victory over Eric Cameron," oozed the Leader.

"Well, sir, I appreciate yer kind words, but after Mr. Cameron hit the airwaves in his leather, studded birthday suit, I figure a ceramic garden gnome could have taken the seat," replied a straight-faced Angus.

The room erupted in hysterics; the Leader merely smiled. "Perhaps, but don't sell yourself short. We all saw your brilliant airport speech; no pottery lawn ornament could have pulled that off," the Leader remarked, accompanied by a heartfelt chorus of "hear, hear" from the veteran MPs in the room.

"Well, sir, compliments aside, should we not hear what the Government has to say in the Throne Speech before we cast the first stone? Aye, I'm a newcomer here, so it may be beyond me ken, but I doonae think it wise that we oppose that which we havna yet heard."

Ever-thoughtful and logical Angus. He showed real courage to ask such a question in his first caucus meeting. Well, I suppose "courage" was only one of the possibilities, but I'll go with it. Angus would pay a price for his intervention, but wasn't that the reason he came to Ottawa—to challenge conventional wisdom and politics-as-usual? Most of my anxiety drained away and pride filled the void.

"Angus, of course we're going to listen to what the GG says. But my many years in politics and my knowledge of the Conservatives assure me that this Throne Speech will earn our contempt, not our support." End of story.

Angus nodded in comprehension, not agreement, and took his seat. The meeting droned on as the shadow cabinet was introduced. Bradley Stanton and some of his team were huddling in the back as lists of names were amended right up to the time they were passed up to the Leader. Unbeknownst to Angus, I had pushed hard with the Leader's office for Angus to be named to the House of Commons Standing Committee on Finance given his commitment to scrutinize every public dollar spent by the Government. I'd thought it was a done deal, but Angus may have undone it in his exchange with the Leader. Angus was the last MP appointed to a standing committee. He would sit on the Standing Committee on Procedure and House Affairs. How lame. The Centre had just sent a signal.

The irony was that Angus seemed very pleased with the appointment as it would afford him the chance to exercise his growing interest in parliamentary procedure. It appealed to the methodical engineer in him. I hadn't the heart to tell him he'd likely been demoted for questioning the Leader. He was utterly unaware that there were political implications for even the most innocuous actions. Support for the Leader was measured in exceedingly small gradations, and those in charge of calibration were more sensitive than drug-sniffing dogs.

At two o'clock in the afternoon, the Governor General settled into the raised chair normally occupied by the Speaker of the Senate and read the Speech from the Throne. Earlier, Angus had entered the House of Commons, walking in a way that I can only describe as reverential. He seemed reluctant to put all of his weight on his feet for fear the green carpet of this special place might take umbrage. His seat was on the far southern end of the second last row. He sat about as far as one could sit from the Speaker, but Angus was awestruck, nevertheless. He took two steps into the House, bowed to the Throne as tradition dictated, and climbed the gently tiered steps to his place on the backbench. I watched from the Members' gallery opposite him. He no longer looked like someone who was unhappy to be on Parliament Hill. He let his hands stroke the carved wood of his small desk before curiosity got the upper hand and he lifted the desk top and peered inside. Despite his off-the-rack grey suit and tartan tie (his idea though I tied the double Windsor for him), he still looked out of place in the chamber.

Shortly thereafter, Angus joined the rest of the MPs in the quick walk down the main Centre Block corridor to the Senate where they stood in silence behind a ceremonial bar, permitted to go no farther into the red chamber. I managed to snag a seat in the public gallery and probably had a better view of the proceedings than did Angus. When the Throne Speech began, Angus locked his eyes on the Governor General and seemed to enter a flow state as he listened and concentrated. Some MPs took notes as they stood and listened, but Angus did not. He'd read that parliamentary tradition handed down from Westminster disallowed notes of any kind in the House or Senate. But time moves inexorably on. Nowadays during question period, six-inch-thick briefing books rested on each Minister's desk. The "no paper" rule had long since been discarded as an anachronism. In his short time on the Hill, Angus had become a parliamentary purist of sorts and when in the House, kept his desk clear and clean.

The Governor General, a former Saskatchewan Cabinet Minister, wore a stately sapphire blue dress, fashionable high heels, white gloves, and a rather floppy and florid hat better suited for the big day at Churchill Downs than an afternoon in the Senate. The GG was three minutes into the speech before my mind finally swung from her chapeau to her words. I hoped I hadn't missed much.

As a partisan Liberal, the Tory Throne Speech, by default, began well behind the starting line. But despite my bias, it was not long before I was forced to concede the speech's brilliant writing and balanced content. Historically, Tory Throne Speeches and budgets have rewarded the rich by cutting taxes, liberated big business by eviscerating regulatory oversight, despoiled the environment by gutting legislated standards and enforcement, and shredded the social contract with those living in poverty. At least that's my detached and disinterested analysis. But this Throne Speech was obviously crafted by a party committed to governing from the centre and holding office for a long time, the minority Parliament notwithstanding.

It was a complex mobile of sated interests in perfect equilibrium. No one was overlooked. I mentally checked off the constituencies as they were rewarded with promises of new and enriched programs and supportive fiscal measures to be included in the Government's next budget, expected in February. The wealthy—check. The poor—check. Aboriginal Canadians—check. Women—check check. Big business—checkorama. Small business—checkerooney. Tree huggers—check. Organized labour—checkity check check. Amateur athletes—cheque.

Here a check, there a check, everywhere a check check. When it was all over, I could find no holes, no forgotten groups, and no chinks in the armour. To make matters worse, for the Liberals I mean, the Government decidedly did not project profligate spending in the "drunken sailor" tradition. Many of the measures reflected creative regulatory tweaks, redirected spending, and the odd tax expenditure that allowed the Government to claim fiscal prudence while appeasing virtually all interests. Despite the Tories' incessant campaign tax-cut rhetoric, I heard not a single, major tax cut in the speech for individuals or businesses. In fact, the speech even sounded a warning of an approaching recession and signaled the need for national belt tightening. In an oblique attempt to tarnish the chrome legacy of Eric Cameron and to distance the Government therefrom, the speech actually admitted there was room to improve fiscal management and strengthen fiduciary accountability to the people of Canada—a masterstroke.

From my vantage point, it seemed that the Red Tories, who might have felt quite at home in the conservative wing of the Liberal Party, had won the first battle in the inexorable and internecine war against the extremist conservatives who were so far to the Right they considered General Franco a bleeding-heart social democrat. The budget, traditionally due in February, would be the next battleground as the warring factions fought for control of the party and the government. This conflict of ideological interpretation lived in virtually all parties but was a particular scourge among Progressive Conservatives. I had heard rumours of in-fighting but the Throne Speech was the first hard evidence.

From my perch looking down on the Senate floor, Angus remained totally focused throughout the Throne Speech, nodding frequently as the GG read.

Afterwards, the MPs trooped back to the House of Commons where, in a tired refrain, both the Liberal and NDP Leaders viciously attacked the Throne Speech as if the Government had suspended democratic rule and declared martial law. Our Leader went directly to calling the Throne Speech an egregious abuse of power that would set Canada back three decades. The press gallery yawned—been there, done that.

That night, following the generally positive coverage on the Throne Speech (positive for the Government, I mean), CTV and CBC ran follow-up stories on Angus McLintock, a "compelling new figure on Canada's political landscape." Both stories reprised his now-famous airport speech and included the footage shot earlier that morning at the first Liberal caucus meeting. Much to Bradley Stanton's rage, there was not a single frame, let alone a separate story, on the Liberal Leader's return to Parliament Hill and bombastic assault on the Throne Speech.

My office phone rang the next morning and "B. Stanton" appeared in the ever-helpful call-display window. What an excellent way to start the day.

"Hello, Bradley, what can I do for you?" (Other than present my unprotected posterior for the tearing of a new and unwelcome orifice.)

"What are you up to, Addison?" he sneered.

"What do you mean?" I replied. "I'm just sitting here, banging out our Throne Speech response. Angus is up this afternoon after question period." I failed to mask the defensiveness I was feeling.

"I worked for two days to set up the Leader's photo op, and what do I see on the news last night—the shining knight, Angus McLintock. I'm getting a little tired of his profile. It's detracting from the Leader's and helping the Government," he explained in an icy tone. "The coverage you've been getting doesn't just happen. So consider this to be a directive from the Leader's office. Stop playing to the press gallery and start playing for your own team."

"Wait a second. You think I'm working the Angus angle with the gallery? You think I'm managing all of this from behind the curtain?" I asked, awash in incredulity. Usually, I was repulsed by confrontation, but I found myself enraged by Stanton's accusation. "Come on, Bradley, give me some credit. Angus is a force unto himself. I've managed to kill several stories already, but the guy is an ink machine. And believe me, he doesn't like it one bit. Since the airport performance, our phone hasn't stopped ringing. So you should stop insulting me and start thanking me there hasn't been more coverage."

"Insulting you?" Stanton retorted. "What crawled up your ass this morning? I'm just doing my job. I'm protecting and promoting the interests of my Leader and the party. When something or someone gets in my way, I get in their face. That's what I do. This is all about the Leader. So take a Valium." His tone became threatening. "Just keep your guy's head down so I don't have to call again or take other steps."

"What are you going to do, Bradley, kick us off Procedure and House Affairs?" I said, still spitting venom, but Stanton had already hung up. What an asshole.

I was incensed. Nothing was more important to me than getting the Liberals elected. You don't spend the years I had on Parliament Hill without yearning to govern. Living in Opposition was a will-sapping experience that could only be redeemed by power. The gift of governing was everything to me. So Stanton's accusation of grandstanding really stuck in my craw.

Still fuming, I finished Angus's Throne Speech response and took it to him in his office. He was hunched over his desk, engrossed in the House Standing Orders.

"Okay, here are your draft talking points for your Throne Speech response this afternoon. Following question period, you'll be the fourth speaker called upon to respond to the Throne Speech, so be ready. Have a look at your remarks and let me know if you want any changes."

I dropped the response on the edge of his desk and headed out the door to my office, which was on the other side of the open reception area occupied by our new administrative assistant, Camille Boudreau. She was a very timid young woman who was raised in a large rural family in the most remote quarter of the Magdalen Islands. Despite her shyness, she was smart and dedicated and seemed to have been inspired by Angus. Her three-month internship in the Leader's office had left her somewhat disillusioned (small wonder), but she had leaped into organizing our humble office with quiet energy and enthusiasm. She was perfectly bilingual, which really helped, as I was not.

Ten minutes later, a shadow cast by the overhead light and the unmistakable chaos of Angus's hair fell upon my blotter. It was not a happy shadow.

"What do you mean, givin' me this to say?" he asked, dropping the speech I'd written in my lap. "We had a long conversation about me views on the Throne Speech, and I doonae think it unreasonable for me to assume that some of them might have found their way into me response."

"Angus, the Leader's office has provided key messages and talking points for caucus members to use in their responses so that we create a unified front against the Government. We can't forget that we're part of a team here and that coordinated action is better than everyone going their own way," I suggested ever reasonably.

"Well, I'm all for teamwork but only if I happen to agree with the game plan," he replied. "You've put words in me mouth that exist neither in me heart nor me brain."

"Angus, you just can't praise the Government's Throne Speech up and down. It's not what Opposition parties do."

"Balls! Name me one thing wrong with the Throne Speech—just one thing!" Angus demanded.

"The only thing I can think of, and the only thing that really counts in the Leader's office, is that it's the Government's Throne Speech and not ours. We're Her Majesty's Loyal Opposition. We oppose things the Government does, everything the Government does. That's how it works. You can't mess with a political dynamic as old as the country." I pleaded with my heart, not my head.

"Aye, well that's one of the problems I aim to fix." With that, he walked back into his office and slammed the door. He wouldn't answer the door or his phone despite regular rapping and ringing. Needless to say, I was an assembly of anxieties as the clocked ticked. I understood what Angus was saying. If a Liberal government had introduced the same Throne Speech, I'd have been proud to support it. But it was our arch rivals' speech, not ours. I agreed the system needed to be changed. Hell, that's why I'd left the Hill in the first place. But change always came with a price.

I've never been a big fan of the scorched-earth approach, and I feared that Angus had his flame-thrower locked and loaded when he emerged from his office at one forty-five. Still eschewing paper in the chamber, I could see ink scrawled on both his palms.

"See you later," he said as he strode out the door and headed for the House. I scrambled to catch up.

"Angus, wait up," I chirped as I followed him out into the corridor. "I, ah, see you don't have your remarks with you. What do you plan to say?"

"I intend to give voice to me views on the Government's Speech from the Throne. I take it that is me right and duty as a duly elected Member of Parliament," he replied calmly as he walked.

"Angus, we can help change this place, but if we try to move too far and too fast, we may lose it all," I submitted. He stopped to face me.

"Well, young man, you seem to forget. Neither one of us has anythin' to lose. Neither one of us really wants to be here. Neither one of us likes playin' these asinine games. We both have secure jobs back at the university. So let's use this rare opportunity to shake the foundations and see what's still standin' when we're through," he said, trilling the *r* in *through*.

My head caught up with my heart. I could muster no opposing view. I just nodded in surrender. He was right. He knew it. I knew it. And what's more, he knew I knew it. His face cracked in a mischievous grin.

"Can you give me one good reason not to do what we both know is the right thing to do?" he asked.

"Good reasons? Other than party solidarity, there are none," I conceded.

"Not there *are* none. There *is* none. None literally means *not one*, so the verb is singular. A common mistake."

With that, he winked, turned, and disappeared into the chamber. I hustled up the white stone stairs to the Members' gallery, flaying myself for a grammar error I was forever correcting in others.

I felt as if I'd betrayed the principles Angus laid out in his airport message. His approach was just so foreign. I thought I'd let him down. I was clearly still at least partially captive to the last remnants of my political indoctrination years earlier. As I sat watching the debate unfold that afternoon from my perch above the fray, I was alternately proud of Angus and concerned for my own safety. Not to put too fine a point on it, I knew the Leader's office would be enraged when they heard about the inaugural speech of Angus McLintock. I suddenly felt queasy. Throwing up on the House Leader's rubber plant in the dead of night was one thing; projectile puking onto the floor of the Commons from the Members' gallery in the middle of the Throne Speech debate was something else again. I kept my head low and breathed deeply and slowly to quell my rollicking stomach.

Angus rose after two other Liberals and one NDPer had vehemently assailed the Government for its irresponsible and ill-conceived Throne Speech. Angus then stood in his place with no notes save for the hieroglyphics on his palms. He proceeded, not to applaud the Government, but rather to support the Throne Speech as a well-crafted, balanced, and progressive agenda that seemed more aligned with an enlightened Liberal platform than with the typical Conservative program that worshiped at the altar of free enterprise. He spoke eloquently, passionately, thoughtfully, and briefly, with no words wasted. After about ten minutes, he concluded his inaugural speech in the House with this:

"Mr. Speaker, tradition would have me oppose this Throne Speech for the simple reason that I sit on this side of the House. Well, I cannae yield to that ritual. There are many sheep from Scotland, but I'm not one of them. I will be supportin' this Throne Speech as it reflects the values and principles that, in me mind, underlie the Liberal Party and offer the greatest promise to the people of

Canada. Part of me job as a Member of this Parliament is to support that which earns me favour and to oppose that which does not. On the whole, this Throne Speech, despite its provenance, has earned me support. Mr. Speaker, another part of me job is to ensure that this Government fulfills the spirit, the letter, and the promise of this Throne Speech. Well, I can assure the Government that I'll be stayin' right here to keep their feet to the furnace. I thank you."

As you can imagine, the Government side of the House erupted in chants of "hear, hear," "come on over," and "cross the floor." The Liberal benches were perplexed but as a group tried to muster an impression that said "we meant to do that." Throughout the ten minutes of heckling and table thumping, an endless stream of Tory MPs approached Angus to shake his hand. Finally, about a dozen courageous Liberal backbenchers sidled over to him and offered congratulations. Angus looked distinctly uncomfortable. Mercifully, the Leader was not in the House for the remarks of the Honourable Member for Cumberland-Prescott. Eventually, the next Opposition speaker rose to thrash the Government yet again and restore the natural political order. Back to business as usual.

When we returned to the office, Camille waved 13 pink phone-message slips. Twelve from the Leader's office and one from Muriel.

◆   ◆   ◆

Diary
Wednesday, November 6

My Love,

Good fun today. I think I'm going to like being a Member of Parliament. I sat through my first caucus meeting yesterday, making few friends. I really do think our alleged Leader is a buffoon. He's just like most other politicians I've met. He is governed by polls and the press—the twin pillars of modern politics. Of course, the caucus was asked to oppose the Throne Speech even before we'd heard the wretched thing. I understand why. I just cannot accept it. What can they do, throw me out? Perhaps they can.

I gather the Leader's office, what I'm told is called "the Centre," has dragged Daniel through the ringer for my sins. And that was before I stood up in the house today and dropped the bomb that I'd be supporting the Throne Speech. After having heard it, I could do nothing but. It sounded to me like a speech the Liberals would draft; perhaps that was the intention. In any event, after I spoke, I was invited to join the ranks of the Government though I suspect tongues were firmly planted in cheeks. Even a few of my Liberal colleagues were prepared to be seen shaking my hand, which lifted my spirits. Strength lies in numbers, even small numbers.

Muriel called me tonight all atwitter at my speech. Even though she's been a loyal Liberal soldier for 60 years, she seems to think the party needs to have its cage rattled. Apparently, she's nominated me to do the rattling. As far as I can tell, she's utterly at peace with this unlikely turn of events. I admire her sense of purpose and perspective.

My anger with Daniel has receded though I still have to knock him about the head and ears when he slips back into his old way of thinking. I know he's with me, but I also know he's taking a beating from the powers that be, all on my account. They think he's orchestrating my maverick image. As you can appreciate, I'm not exactly a willing subject when it comes to image management. "The Centre" will learn this eventually and lay off poor Daniel.

I've a meeting upcoming with old-man Sanderson, at which I'm sure he'll ask me to support federal subsidies to prop up his factory. I can't do it, love. It just isn't right. But I do have an idea I'm hoping will take the sting out of my answer.

Will you keep watch over me, love? I'm in a foreign land, and your steadying hand is what I need.

AM

CHAPTER THIRTEEN

I spent the next morning, Thursday, on the phone, defending Angus and wondering how many abusive calls I could endure before I ripped the receiver's curling umbilicus from the base unit and hurled it out the window. At 10:17, I had my answer: 26. I actually only fantasized about chucking it out the window. I really wasn't capable of such rashness. The most I could manage was to unplug the phone and toss it gently onto the brown corduroy couch in my office where it landed softly, making no noise at all. I heard the jovial voice of Angus in his office, taking calls, too, though his tone suggested he was getting off easy, or was amused by it all.

Of the 26 calls I'd taken, 19 were from the Leader's office, including 4 from Bradley Stanton. Effective phone management is a critical political skill to have and to hone. In fact, telephone transactions, be they wooing or whacking, constitute a significant share of politics. I like to think part of my success on the Hill was due to my prowess on the blower. And in my experience, knowing how to "give" on the phone was not quite as important as knowing how to "receive."

Success often turned on how you handled a bad call, a mad call, a "this town ain't big enough for the both of us" call. When you exercised patience and restraint, listened well, issued soothing sounds at strategic junctures in your adversary's profanity-strewn tirade, and always maintained a relaxed and quiet voice, even the most crazed caller would eventually, inexorably, calm down and speak in reasonable, albeit tense, tones. In extreme situations, I would pull out all the stops and play Zamfir's greatest hits in the background, just loud enough to be heard on the line. Rest assured, the coma-inducing pan flute could quell the rage of a cornered gorilla. I used this calming telephone technique to defuse hundreds of irate calls; it worked even when I was the one who had screwed up and when temper tantrums were justified.

And then, there was Bradley Stanton, the smoke-snorting, fire-breathing, foulmouthed exception to my rule. To say he was angry that morning didn't quite capture it. At least twice during our phone calls, I feared he might be in the throes of a stroke. He'd hung up on me three times in paroxysms of rage before we'd finally finished our "conversation" on the fourth call. By that time, Angus was sitting across from my desk, chuckling, shaking his head, and once even giving me a thumbs-up, complete with manic smile and arched eyebrows. He really was enjoying himself. I hung up the phone, exhausted.

"I think it would be a good time for Brad to up the dosage of whatever medication he's on," I sighed, laying my head on my desk blotter.

"Doonae fret yourself, Daniel boy. Young Mr. Stanton's anger is the surest sign we're on the right path," replied Angus as if it was supposed to comfort me. "Have you seen *The Citizen* this mornin'?"

Uh-oh, I didn't like the sound of that. I'd glanced at the front page when we'd arrived, but with the phone ringing by the time I'd reached my desk, I'd been in the crosshairs ever since. Angus passed me the front section.

"Have a gander at A4," he directed with a mischievous grin.

With hands near trembling, I opened to the page: "Maverick Liberal Blazes Own Trail" read the headline. "Some backbenchers follow" read the subhead. My mind instinctively conjured up the next day's headline: "Liberal Leader Orders Former Staffer Crucified on Parliament Hill."

Obviously, Stanton hadn't seen *The Citizen* piece, either, or I would surely have heard about it in our morning calls. In fact, anyone in a 200-metre radius of my office could have heard Stanton's expletives, exploding from the telephone like bazooka shells. Salt in my wounds was the knowledge that *The Citizen* was owned by a large conglomerate of newspapers so that the "Maverick" article played in dozens of dailies across the country. Excellent.

The headline and subhead just about said it all. Angus was standing caucus discipline on its head by defying the authority of the Leader, the Whip, and the House Leader. Rogue MPs were nothing new. Virtually every caucus had one or two. What left me wishing I had some medication of my own, or anyone else's for that matter, was the final paragraph in the story, reporting that 11 other Liberal backbenchers would join Angus in supporting the Throne Speech. Emboldened by my neophyte MP, they parroted the rationale he had outlined in his speech. I figured that by nightfall, the Leader would have banished Angus from the Liberal caucus for his disobedience, leaving him sitting as an independent. But for some reason, that call never came. As I scanned the other papers in the office and flipped through the caucus clipping report that daily gave each Liberal MP political media coverage from across the country, an explanation emerged from the fog.

I read 4 editorials and 12 political columnists in various dailies across Canada, applauding the stand Angus had taken. I saw the adjectives "refreshing," "courageous," "honourable," and "honest" sprinkled throughout. Only one commentator took Angus to task for his breach in party discipline, noting that if organized political parties did not behave in an organized fashion, the whole democratic system might be thrown into disarray. As I listened to the radio talk shows and kept one eye on the television coverage on CPAC, this "blindly toe the party line" position gained no traction. Angus appeared to have considerable support among key political journalists, who played such an influential role in shaping public opinion. I began to see that the Leader could neither afford to rein Angus in nor expel him from caucus. Too much support was coalescing behind the shit-disturbing, pot-stirring, trouble-making, rabble-rousing MP for Cumberland-Prescott. I assumed Zaleski would be in the field with a quick poll in the coming days to see whether Angus was registering with voters beyond the insular world of Parliament Hill.

That afternoon, Angus was scheduled to probe the Government with his debut performance in question period. Most Opposition MPs used the term *probe* in the "alien abduction" sense of the word. But Angus adhered to the classic definition: to explore, examine, investigate. Televising parliamentary proceedings live from the House of Commons had forever changed the face of question period. Much of the decorum, protocol, and mutual respect within the chamber had died off as soon as the television cameras had turned on. Televising the proceedings was a challenging issue for those of us who wanted Canadian democracy to be more accessible, accountable, and for that matter, democratic.

In the pre-TV days of the House, question period actually had been an opportunity to challenge the Government, hold it accountable for its actions or inaction, and nudge reforms along the winding road to adoption. Now, the broadcasting of question period had completely reoriented the Opposition parties' approach. For the Liberals and the NDP, it had become a daily televised spectacle aimed solely at embarrassing the Government, securing the pithy sound bite on the evening newscasts, and looking good doing it. I suppose I need not point out that Angus hadn't exactly bought into the prevailing political imperatives of what was known as QP.

I was sequestered in my office, watching on television. Why be a sitting duck in the Members' gallery, inviting free shots from the Leader's staff? To the extent possible in influencing Angus and his actions, I'd instructed him to slip out right after QP and return to the office. I watched with tired ambivalence as our Leader and the NDP Leader asked their typically loaded but 100-percent-substance-free questions. I watched as the Prime Minister responded with shop-worn rhetoric nevertheless landing a few blows in the process.

Then, towards the end of question period, I heard my cue to put the phone on "do not disturb" and break into a cold sweat.

"The Honourable Member for Cumberland-Prescott," intoned the Speaker.

The camera swung up to the backbench as Angus rose in his place, no notes in his hand or on his desk. Recognizing that this was Angus's inaugural question in the House of Commons, several of his seatmates thumped their desks with open palms and cried "hear, hear."

"Mr. Speaker, 'tis the first time I've participated in the cut and thrust of question period, so do bear with me. I'm a wee tad nervous," Angus began.

Angus and I had gone back and forth on what question to ask and to whom he should pose it. Because Remembrance Day was quickly approaching, I'd suggested getting his feet wet by asking the Veterans' Affairs Minister about long-delayed funding for a war memorial in Cumberland. But Angus had already spoken to the Minister on this issue and had been given an assurance that the funding was forthcoming. So he thought it redundant to ask a question that had already been answered, particularly if it embarrassed the Minister who had approved the funding in the first place. No, Angus wanted his question to go straight to the PM. Excellent.

"Mr. Speaker, I've been sittin' quietly and listenin' carefully for the last three quarters of an hour, and it's now perfectly clear to me why this part of the proceedin's is called question period and not answer period. But hope springs eternal, Mr. Speaker. I have a question for the Prime Minister."

Angus's opening prompted appreciative snickers from the Liberal benches, stern harrumphing from the Government members, and a wry smile from the Speaker himself. In anticipation of what might come next, I merely clenched my sphincter so tightly it's a miracle it didn't fuse shut permanently. Clearly, I needed to work on my coping skills.

"Mr. Speaker, does the Prime Minister consider himself to be an honourable and trustworthy man, whose word is his bond?" Angus sat down and fixed the Prime Minister with a steely gaze.

The PM seemed taken aback by the brevity and simplicity of the question. Normally, Opposition members droned on and on before posing an unfathomable question that generally defied response. In reply, Ministers usually ignored the question anyway and seized the free air time to hammer home a few more key messages about all the wonderful things the Government was doing to make Canada a better place. Caught off guard, the Prime Minister hastened to his feet, looking as if he'd blown a tire somewhere on the road from perplexed to befuddled.

"Mr. Speaker, I appreciate the newly sworn-in Member's question and welcome him to this place. I want to assure him that this Government is committed to fulfilling the vision and the plan laid before Canadians yesterday by the Governor General in the Throne Speech. It represents a balanced response to the challenges we face as a nation, and I appreciate the support the Honourable Member yesterday declared for it." The PM took his seat and inserted his ear phone.

"Supplementary?" invited the Speaker. Angus again stood up.

"Thank you, Mr. Speaker. Well, it appears the Prime Minister has declared this chamber an 'answer-free zone,' but we on this side of the floor will keep tryin'."

"Hear, hear," exclaimed the Liberal backbench, accompanied by more desk drumming.

"Order, please, order. Supplementary?" The Speaker shut down the heckling Angus had triggered.

"Mr. Speaker, I am new to this game and perhaps am easily confused. So me supplementary question is simply this: Could the Prime Minister please clarify which plan his Government intends to pursue? Is it the carefully contrived and perfectly balanced Throne Speech we heard yesterday, or is it the Conservative Party's 'Blueprint for Canada' on which the Prime Minister and his candidates campaigned so slavishly a mere four weeks ago? Mr. Speaker, I ask only because these two documents present utterly divergent visions," Angus said before sitting back down.

Much hooting, hollering, and heckling ensued until the Speaker once again restored order. I unclenched and calmed down. Angus was finished on his feet for the time being. But the Prime Minister had yet to respond.

"Mr. Speaker, it is our responsibility on this side of the House to govern within the context of the economic and political conditions we confront at any given time. Since the election, it has become clear that the economy has not only slowed but has nearly come to a complete halt. The Throne Speech presented yesterday represents the Government's most up-to-date program for overcoming the economic challenges we now face as a nation. With this in mind, I am pleased to count on the support of the Honourable Member opposite. I also remind him that there is plenty of room on these Government benches to accommodate the Honourable Member at his convenience."

The Prime Minister sat down, the picture of smugness. His caucus rose in a standing ovation as the Speaker did his best to maintain at least a semblance of authority in the midst of such revelry. For a brief instant, the camera panned the

Liberal benches, and I caught a glimpse of Angus, nodding and smiling as if commending the Prime Minister's recovery.

"Well, that was great fun," noted Angus as he flopped down on the chair in front of my desk after strolling along the north corridor from the House. "The PM appeared ill-prepared for me first question but put me in me place on the supplementary, I thought."

"Well, I wouldn't exactly call your effort particularly sharp or penetrating," I commented, leaning back in my 1970s-era, purple swivel chair.

"Aye, but Daniel, I wasn't hurlin' a spear at him, I was simply askin' for a straight answer to a straight question."

"I get it, Angus. But there's no way your exchange with the PM will make the cut on any newscast tonight. It was just too bland and congenial. No one was mad. No one was upset. No one was insulted. It was altogether too civil to be of interest to the pack of wolves in the press gallery," I explained.

"Aye, 'tis a sad state of affairs when constructive and respectful debate is subordinated by cheap theatrics and mock outrage."

"Welcome to your new world."

It turned out I was wrong about what the media would choose to run that night. Angus did make the news in a CBC "The National" story on rookie MPs and how they were adjusting to life on the Hill and in the House. The reporter dwelled on the "Angus as maverick" angle and used a clip of his question in the House as corroborating evidence of his atypical approach. Unbeknownst to me, Angus had been intercepted as he left question period and scrummed about his thoughts on party discipline. His clip in the story that night sounded like this: "Aye, well, I am a member of the Liberal caucus, and I'm beginnin' to understand what that entails. But first and foremost, I'm here to serve the nation's interest—if that coincides with the party's fortunes, all the better."

Thanks, Angus. I turned off the TV and reached to unplug the phone just a few milliseconds after it started ringing.

Friday. Constituency day. Angus and I spent the morning on Parliament Hill but returned to Cumberland after lunch for our first official afternoon of constituent meetings. When we entered the Angus McLintock constit office, Muriel greeted us and we took in the repurposed Purple Rain Café that had folded a month earlier. A pair of red IKEA reception chairs flanked a white, plastic, modernist end table, circa 1961, on which were stacked back issues of *Reader's Digest* and *Today's Senior* magazines stamped with "Property of Riverfront Seniors' Residence." A leftover fluorescent violet counter that more closely resembled a runway stage in a strip bar separated the office's waiting area from its working space. We saw seated at a desk farther back a rather clean-cut young fellow I couldn't quite place, which troubled me somewhat since Muriel and I had done the hiring together. He gave me a friendly and familiar wave. A few Liberal Party posters left over from the campaign adorned the cheerful yellow walls. The faint scent of paint was only partially masked by the 13 solid air fresheners I counted in a quick scan of the front room. The painting party had adjourned at midnight.

When we had first arrived, Muriel had been leaning on the counter, talking on the phone, rolling her eyes, and shaking her head, yet sustaining a congenial and helpful patter. "That's right, Mr. Archibald, Eric Cameron is no longer your MP. Angus McLintock is." (Pause) "No, you'll have to deal with your paperboy directly on that. The federal government does not regulate delivery times." (Pause) "No, that's not a federal responsibility, either. Your driver's licence is issued by the Ontario government. Yes, I like the old blue better, too." (Long pause as Muriel lay her head on the counter while still holding the phone to her ear. Angus and I waited patiently, not daring to venture farther into the office until she had given us leave to pass through her checkpoint.)

"Mr. Archibald, I'm afraid I must take another call now, but if you turn the oven dial all the way around until it hits Broil and then bring it back to Bake, you should be able to brown the top of the macaroni while it's cooking." (Pause) "Yes, that's right, but you'll have to watch it carefully so it doesn't burn." (Pause) "Yes, I agree it's not the same without ketchup. Good day, Mr. Archibald."

She cradled the receiver gently but with blinding speed before making her way out from behind her desk to greet us. "Welcome, welcome, welcome," she bubbled. "Welcome to the 'Angus McLintock action centre.'" Muriel embraced us both in turn before taking Angus by the hand for a slow tour of his constituency office. I hung back, deciding I'd better introduce myself to the other staffer.

He looked up as I approached. "Hey, Professor!" The voice rang a bell. Red ink peeked out just above the collar of his dark blue turtleneck, and the pieces fell into place.

"No no no! No way! I cannot believe it!" I was reeling. Pete2 sat before me, looking more like Greg Brady than Johnny Rotten. His hair, though still longish, was precisely combed with a side part straighter than a skate blade. The turtleneck's long sleeves hid his epidermal arm art, and brown brogues rested peacefully at the ends of his grey flannels where Doc Martens usually scowled. It was a makeover worthy of its own MTV reality show. I just stood there and gawked as I rotated his office chair to take in the spectacle from all angles. "So this is the new Pete. What happened to the old one?"

I confess I was somewhat relieved when he pulled open his bottom desk drawer to reveal lime green stretch pants, an orange fishnet shirt, black and white saddle shoes, and a well-worn, blue tartan makeup bag.

"I really need the job. Plus, I'm scared of Muriel," Pete2 offered.

"So am I," I commiserated. "She's very fond of you, though. You'll learn a great deal from Muriel if you watch and listen."

Pete2 just nodded with a kind of goofy smile on his now utterly ordinary face.

I continued back to Angus's office, which stretched from wall to wall in the rear of the old storefront space. It was the only part of the constit office that was carpeted, courtesy of the very tight budget MPs were given to establish themselves in the riding.

"Old-man Sanderson will be here in a few minutes," noted Muriel as she shuffled past me on her way back to her post, using the wall to steady herself.

Angus was talking to a bookish young woman, who was dressed in what had to be a brand new, off-the-rack business suit. Her suit was clearly off the wrong rack as it looked at least two sizes too big. She moved a little awkwardly and seemed uncomfortable in her own skin as if she'd much rather have been wearing something else. Her tangled, jet black hair fell in a shapeless cascade around her shoulders. She looked like a junior engineering faculty member, attending her first off-campus business meeting after years of being sequestered in the computer lab—which made sense because that's exactly who she was.

Angus looked up when I entered. "Daniel Addison, meet Deepa Khanjimeer, an assistant professor in the computer-engineerin' department and the university's newest multimillionaire," Angus opened.

Professor Khanjimeer waved her hand to dismiss the comment before shaking mine. "Very nice to meet you, Daniel." She nodded vigorously and beamed.

"Nice to meet you, Professor. We're very excited about your work and how it might benefit the riding," I replied.

Professor Khanjimeer was the linchpin in a creative idea Angus had cooked up to deal with our little Sanderson Shoe Company dilemma. I was learning that Angus was a bit of a lone wolf. He'd been making phone calls to Deepa and Industry Canada officials for most of the week before he'd deigned to let me in on his thinking. Initially, when I'd heard his plan, I had thought it naïve and ambitious. (Working on Parliament Hill tends to limit your vision and push you towards the art of the possible, not the ideal, solution.) But the more I thought about his big idea, the more I liked it.

Muriel appeared in the doorway on the arm of a very short, elderly man, who was wearing a camel-hair top coat over a grey pinstriped suit. Despite the current style, he wore a three-piece suit with a small, gold chain that linked one vest pocket to the other. His shoes were so shiny they seemed to emit light rather than just reflect it. At the upper end, his lustrous bald pate did the same, encircled by a band of grey hair that neatly bisected his cranium.

"Gentlemen, this is Mr. Norman Sanderson," intoned Muriel before ushering him in.

I stepped forward and did what executive assistants do. "Mr. Sanderson, I'm Daniel Addison. You've met Muriel Parkinson already, I trust. This is Professor Deepa Khanjimeer from the University of Ottawa, and of course, this is Angus McLintock, to whom I think you've spoken on the phone earlier this week." I finished and shook his hand.

"Oh yes, Mr. McLintock and I have spoken, but I've still no idea what this meeting is about unless you've changed your tune on subsidies," said Sanderson, making no effort to soften his obvious impatience. "Eric Cameron promised me those subsidies, and our future depends on them," he concluded as we all sat down around the rectangular table opposite Angus's desk.

"Welcome, Mr. Sanderson. Let's get down to it then, shall we?" Angus started. "Do you enjoy makin' shoes, Mr. Sanderson?" Nice opening, Angus.

"What kind of a question is that? We've been making shoes in this town for 35 years. We've paid millions in taxes, employed hundreds of people over the years, and exported shoes around the world. Eric Cameron wore a new pair of our shoes for every budget he ever presented. Hell, we put this town on the map," Sanderson shot back.

"Aye, we know all that, but do you really enjoy makin' shoes, and do you really think it's the best way to invest yer time and money?" Angus persisted.

Sanderson's eyes narrowed and his voice grew steely. "I can't see what you're driving at, but I couldn't care less what we make so long as we're profitable. What is your point, McLintock?" he spat.

"Calm yourself, Mr. Sanderson. You've answered me question as I hoped you would," Angus soothed. "NAFTA and the World Trade Organization prohibit the very subsidies me predecessor promised you, and I'm not convinced they'd serve Canada well, anyway. Any country can make shoes. The real question in me mind is *should* Canada make shoes? In me world view, such as it is, just because we've churned out footwear for the last 35 years doesnae mean we should continue now that the landscape has changed. Without oversimplifyin' what I know is a complex policy area, perhaps, just perhaps, it's time we stopped makin' shoes and started makin' something else the world needs but can't get from lesser-developed nations. I gather it's called 'movin' into the knowledge-based economy.'" Angus paused but raised his hand to hold the floor. "Now, before you blow a gasket, let me ask Professor Khanjimeer to tell you about her work. And please be patient. There is a point to all of this. Aye, there's a very big point, and you, Mr. Sanderson, stand to gain. Professor?"

Sanderson looked affronted but held his tongue—probably because he'd never dealt with an MP quite like Angus. Deepa jumped into the fray, speaking slowly in self-conscious recognition of her Indian accent. "Mr. Sanderson, are you famil-iar with a company called Canatron?"

"Of course, I am. It's a Canadian electronics manufacturer. I read the business pages," Sanderson replied.

"Well, I have just signed an agreement to supply Canatron with a new, much smaller, and less expensive wireless router for networking computers. I've patented this new wave technology and have a five-year, exclusive deal with Canatron. This new device will initially be sold as a separate product, but eventually, Canatron wishes to supply all computer manufacturers with them so that notebook comput-ers will actually integrate the wave router to simplify networks further."

She paused and Sanderson jumped in. "That's all very fascinating, but what does that have to do with me and the price of shoes?"

"Mr. Sanderson, we'd like you to manufacture my wireless wave router in your factory," Deepa said. And the idea was out in the open for all to see.

I would be overstating it to say that Norman Sanderson freaked out—but only just. After crafting loafers and imitation Hush Puppies for 35 years, the idea of manufacturing leading-edge technology was so far off his radar that at first, he simply couldn't process it. (So where exactly in the shoe would the router be implanted?) But we wouldn't let him leave until he actually comprehended the plan and its implications.

At the end of the meeting, Angus tied it up into a nice, neat package. "So to bring it all together, while NAFTA and WTO consider the industrial subsidies you were seekin' to be a non-tariff barrier, they do permit grants for manufac-turin' transition to help older industries move into more sophisticated and tech-nology-driven product lines. Industry Canada offers just such a program of grants and interest-free loans to help the Sanderson Shoe Company retool and retrain to manufacture the most advanced wireless wave router available anywhere in the world. Me preliminary discussions with Industry Canada officials yield every rea-son for optimism, but only if you're with us. No jobs need be lost. In fact, based on the thunderous response to Professor Khanjimeer's discovery, expansion, mul-tiple manufacturin' facilities, global export, and a world-product mandate are the more likely outcomes. This idea is really a serendipitous confluence of timin', events, and people. In the interests of the employees of the Sanderson Shoe Company and the town of Cumberland, let us not waste this opportunity," Angus wound down. "Mr. Sanderson, what say you?"

Sanderson had overcome his initial incredulity at the scheme and was thinking hard. I knew his brain was firing on all cylinders because the once-shiny, almost chrome-like surface of his dome had dulled to more of a matte finish, apparently through sheer cerebral exertion.

"You'll have to give me some time to consider this and speak with my family partners about it," Sanderson said. "We need a much more fulsome discussion before we can decide. We've never ever considered such a radical course. But we've also never been this close to the edge before." Sanderson spoke in a tone that suggested he was still working through the implications feverishly.

"Well, you cannae take two months to reach yer decision. Canatron will not wait that long. So stiffen yer spine, sharpen yer wits, and let us know within the week, if you'd be so kind," Angus concluded. "Aye, and you might look up the word *fulsome* in the dictionary when you get home. You havna got it right."

Before departing, Norman Sanderson arranged a meeting on campus with Deepa for the following morning for a fuller briefing on the wireless wave router. I called in a few favours and coordinated a hasty meeting for Saturday afternoon with the Industry Canada director general responsible for the manufacturing-transition program. We also all agreed to keep our discussions under wraps. It would be hard enough to close this deal already without having it splashed on the front pages of *The Cumberland Crier*, not to mention *The Ottawa Citizen*.

Muriel leaned on his arm and cooed as she escorted a clearly shell-shocked Norman Sanderson to the front door. The rest of what little remained of the afternoon was consumed by more mundane but locally important meetings with constituents on topics that ranged from tax complaints and affordable housing to immigration problems and environmental policy. I sat in on all the meetings and noticed that Angus was more patient with constituents than I had expected him to be. In the end, nothing unfolded that afternoon that could compete with the Sanderson Shoe Company situation. Angus McLintock's inspired idea had "win-win" stenciled all over it. It was the kind of bold and creative gambit for which I'd entered politics in the first place. It suddenly dawned on me that I was actually having fun again on Parliament Hill even though I'd left the vaunted heights of the Leader's office to toil for a lowly backbencher.

I called Lindsay that night. We'd only seen each other sporadically since the election, but that fact had been driven only by our mutually hellish schedules. I'd been consumed with seeing Angus through his first days on the Hill and defusing the McLintock-assassination plots that were hatching daily in the Leader's office. Lindsay had actually been away in Mexico with her mother to escape the cold November winds that were snarling across eastern Ontario. Muriel had given them the trip as an early Christmas present. They tried to talk her into joining them, but she would have none of it. After all, who would organize the Angus McLintock action centre?

"Hey, stranger," I said when she picked up.

"Hi, Daniel, I was just thinking about you."

"Then, you've clearly received my telepathic messages." She laughed. "Welcome home. How was Mexico?" I pronounced it *Mec-kee-ko*.

"Mom and I had a wonderful time, and the weather was awesome. We ate, slept, swam, ate, and then, ate some more. I wouldn't want to live there forever, but a couple of years would suit me fine," she commented.

"Well, I'll look into consular openings first thing Monday morning."

"*Gracias, señor*. Muriel tells me Angus has not exactly embraced the path of least resistance since arriving on the Hill. How bad has it been?"

"Well, let's just say that Bradley Stanton has me on speed-dial so he can conserve his energy for yelling. But after living through the last week, I can't say I blame Angus. He wants to shake things up, cut a new path, and that's exactly what he's doing. This role of maverick staffer is actually kind of growing on me," I responded.

"Well, none of us should be surprised, I guess. But how are you really feeling about it?" she asked.

"I'm coming to terms with it, and I actually feel quite good about it. My role seems based on very different assumptions than when I worked in the Leader's office. But why don't we get together in the next couple of days, go out for dinner, and get caught up. You can tell me Mexican 'don't drink the water' stories, and I'll tell you 'how to enrage the Leader' stories."

"I'd like that."

We set it up for the following week and then talked for another hour about everything that was on our minds. Time passed unnoticed. It was just so ... comfortable.

◆   ◆   ◆

Diary
Friday, November 8

My Love,

This is much more enjoyable than I'd ever anticipated. Without the constraints that bind almost every other MP, I am free to go my own way, within reason. I felt some sympathy for young Daniel this week. I can see that he still hasn't yet shed the political instincts that ensured his survival and success when he worked for the nimrod occupying the Leader's office. I'm still taking the lead as he gets used to my unorthodox approach, but intellectually and morally, I know he's with me. He's just trying to catch up.

I asked the Prime Minister a question in question period yesterday and lived to tell the tale. If someone had told me three months ago that I'd soon be standing up in the House of Commons, trading barbs with the Prime Minister, I'd have thought it a load of bollocks. Yet, here I am. Anyway, I thought the PM disposed of me quite handily. I was not completely embarrassed, though. After a few more attempts, I reckon I'll be able to hold my own. I freely admit I'm quite taken with the House although beneath a veneer of civility, it's a seething snake pit, particularly in question period with the press gallery circling like hungry hyenas, waiting for blood to be spilt—anyone's. The great media machine must be daily fed.

Old-man Sanderson paid us a visit in the constituency office today. I've concocted a plan that I think will save the man's business, bring him riches that shoes never could, and provide sustainable employment in this riding for years to come. It all fell into place quite beautifully. I pursued it on my own early in the week but eventually brought Daniel in on it. Though Daniel was never explicit, his initial skepticism was palpable. His questions clearly betrayed a view that I'd bitten off more than we could chew. Perhaps we have, but my mouth is great and my appetite greater. Why not aim high? When I told him of my discussions with Monsieur Mailloux at Industry Canada, he started to come around and even grow a little excited though he maintained a calm exterior. After our meeting today, I think Daniel is fully on board and caught up in the chase as is Muriel, bless her heart. I've asked Sanderson for his answer within the week, but I foresee a response much sooner.

My early time in this new world has convinced me that the engineer's critical and methodical approach to problem solving is well suited to realms beyond the scientific. What are the knowns? What are the unknowns? What are the constants? What governing laws are at play? It's the scientific method brought to life in a different setting. Interesting. I have a speech to the Engineering Society coming up, and perhaps I'll explore these parallels further and work them into my remarks.

Shame on me. I've not lifted a finger on the hovercraft since the House opened this week. Much work beckons in my workshop and in my Centre Block office alike. I've a new life, my love—a life I'd once wished for you. You can still live through me.

AM

CHAPTER FOURTEEN

I was late. Our meeting with a delegation from the Alliance for Canadian Women (ACW)—the largest and most active lobby group for women's rights—was nearly over as I burst into Angus's office at two forty-five the next afternoon.

I was returning from Place du Portage, a government office complex across the river in Hull, where I'd been meeting with Industry Canada officials on the Sanderson Shoe file. I'd wrapped up the meeting at one-thirty or so, leaving plenty of time for the five-minute drive back to Parliament Hill and our two o'clock encounter with the ACW. I was halfway across the Alexandra Bridge when the articulated public-transit bus in front of me braked hard and swerved to avoid a lime green Yugo that had abruptly cut in front of it. Never having seen a Yugo actually driving under its own power, let alone weaving in and out of traffic at high speed, I could certainly understand the bus driver's surprise. As the two sections of the bus screeched to the left, a dump truck, which was clearly racing to a fire, nudged the back end to complete the now classic "three-lane bus-bridge wedge." The bus slid transversely across all southbound lanes and finally came to rest, its front squished against the east railing, its rear crunched into the west guardrail. It looked not unlike an elongated squeezebox, completely occluding a major traffic artery from Hull to Ottawa—the one I'd chosen as the quickest route back to the Hill. I slammed on what was left of the Taurus's brakes and stopped four and a half inches from the midsection of the bus and the wide-eyed woman in the window above.

Thanks to my recent stress-induced sphincter-clench regimen, I managed to maintain control over my bodily functions in a moment of life-threatening drama. As I surveyed the faces of other drivers around me, it appeared to me some were not as fortunate. Miraculously, no one was injured on the bus or in the 137 cars now compressed into an area designed to hold about 125 cars. There'd been no pedestrian casualties, either. While the Taurus hadn't been hit, I saw many fender-benders behind me on the bridge all the way back to Hull.

An hour later, I'd given a brief statement to the police, extricated the Taurus from the blocked bridge, and zipped back to Centre Block via the Portage Bridge to the west. I'm not sure what unsettled me more, the action-movie accident directly in front of me, or the thought of Angus on his own for 45 minutes in a meeting with Rhonda Atkinson—the charismatic and relentless head of the ACW. I'd had no time to brief Angus for the meeting. He was walking into a buzz saw, and it was my fault.

Not to put too fine a point on it, but Rhonda Atkinson was a passionate bully. No one was more committed to her cause; yet, in my view, she lacked the finesse to read the room and adopt the approach that would take her furthest in each situation. Rhonda had only one speed—full steam ahead and damn the torpedoes. In her 15-year reign as president, the ACW's annual lobby day on the Hill had evolved from a series of polite but pointless MP meetings into a cage-match marathon, for which politicians would train for weeks. Not only did Rhonda live by the phrase "take no prisoners," but legend had it she actually coined it years ago before politically knee-capping a member of Cabinet she had aptly dubbed the "Minister of Misogyny." She had put the ACW on the map as a potent and powerful lobby and had spearheaded dozens of legislative and judicial reforms to advance women's equality in Canada. She was a shining star in Canada's pantheon of advocates. I like to think of myself as a committed feminist. But Rhonda had a knack for making even the most progressive and enlightened man feel like a polygamous porn magnate fighting universal suffrage.

Camille shot me a worried look as I rushed past her desk and threw open the door to Angus's office. My worst fears were confirmed when the first thing I saw was Rhonda and Angus locked in mortal combat while the four other women in the delegation watched from ringside seats. They didn't need to help. Angus already looked overmatched. I'd been in several meetings where Rhonda had verbally abused MPs, but I'd never actually seen her physically attack one. She had Angus in a bear hug and was rocking him back and forth. Outdated and rather boring for the fans, that technique was still an effective submission hold. I half expected one of her colleagues to step up and count Angus out. I noticed a large hardcover book in Rhonda's hand that would make a formidable bludgeon. The fight would hardly be fair if she started swinging that weighty tome.

I was about to tag Angus and take my own chances with Rhonda—as any loyal executive assistant would—when I noticed that both of them were not actually grimacing in mutual combat but smiling in mutual affection. It was a subtle distinction, particularly in my frazzled condition. They were, indeed, locked in a bear hug, but not of the Hulk Hogan variety. Then, Rhonda misted up, and Angus followed suit.

"I am so touched and so grateful," she said, clutching the mystery book to her heart and dabbing her eyes with a Kleenex handed her by an ACW staffer. "I know you're with us, so let's stop convincing the converted and move on to some of your more patriarchal caucus mates."

"Aye, Rhonda, you're very kind to use such a benign term as *patriarchal*. *Neanderthal* is a compliment for some. But I know you'll set them right, and I'll work them from the inside as a fifth columnist in this most just of causes," Angus oozed as she gathered her papers.

Her compatriots rose en masse and filed out the door. Rhonda caught my eye as she passed me. "Hello, Daniel. You missed all the fun. You've got a real rough-cut diamond in him. Let him shine." She was still smiling and nodding her head as she disappeared out our door.

When I spun back to Angus, he'd already regained his composure and returned to the Sanderson Shoe Company initiative.

"Well, do you bring good news from Industry Canada, or is our little plan imperiled by bureaucratic ineptitude?" he asked.

"Wait a second. First things first. What just happened here?" I replied in a voice that occupied a higher register than it normally did.

"What are you on about, man? We just finished the ACW meeting. As you may recall, you were supposed to join me for it. No matter. It seemed to proceed well enough," Angus noted.

"I can see that, but how did it happen? Do you have incriminating photos? Did we just give the ACW a million dollars? Did you slip something in her coffee? What just happened here?"

"Hey hey, you doonae make jokes about drugged drinks when the availability of Rohypnol and the incidence of date rape are both on the rise," he thundered, shaking his head and looking as if bodily harm was in my immediate future. How did he know all that?

"I ... I'm sorry. I wasn't thinking about what I was saying," I stammered.

"Aye, that was painfully obvious."

"Look, I'm sorry. It's been a rough afternoon so far. I was almost killed in a spectacular bus crash on the Alexandra Bridge about an hour ago. And then, I finally make it back here, expecting blood on the floor, and find you're adjourning the inaugural meeting of the Atkinson-McLintock mutual adoration society." I sighed. "It's all been a bit too much to take in." I fell into the chair in front of his desk.

"Saints alive, were you injured?" he asked with what appeared to be genuine concern.

"No, I managed somehow to avoid T-boning one of those articulated buses as it wedged itself across all lanes of southbound traffic. But it did leave me somewhat shaken," I commented. "In fact, was I hallucinating when I saw Rhonda and you in some kind of platonic embrace?"

"Daniel, I've known Rhonda since she was a 23-year-old graduate student. Marin was her thesis supervisor, and for three summers, she lived in the very boathouse apartment you now occupy. I'm a great supporter of hers," Angus declared.

"But she can be so … so aggressive. So mean," I pointed out. "She's even got her detractors in the women's movement."

"Aye, but societal change hasn't often or, for that matter, ever come through polite and courteous discourse. That approach would simply take too long. Every social cause needs a 'Rhonda' to lead the charge," Angus argued. "And as for yer observation that she is not universally revered among her own constituents, if Marin were here, she'd tell you that the emergence of various factions within the feminist constellation reflects a social movement that is maturin' and is confident enough to nurture divergent viewpoints. This is the natural evolution of social change. It happened in the civil-rights movement, too. Malcolm X and Dr. King seldom saw eye to eye; yet each made important contributions to their shared cause."

He continued in this vein for some time, expounding on his theory of maturing movements. I thought I remembered something about this theory in an article Marin Lee wrote for *Saturday Night* magazine a few years back. But by then, I was tapped out and having difficulty processing his theoretical analysis. "What was the deal with the book Rhonda had?"

"I'd been remiss in not givin' it to her sooner. Before Marin passed on, she inscribed several copies of her new book to a number of women in positions of influence over the feminist cause. The inscriptions were deeply personal." He paused and bowed his head for a moment before continuing. "Marin was very agitated before inscribin' the books but seemed quite at peace when she finished. I think this last task signaled a passin' of the torch, but we never spoke of it before the end. I figured today was as good a day as any to hand over Rhonda's copy," he observed, looking as if he, too, were tapped out.

"Well, she was clearly touched. All I can say is that I've seen how Rhonda's enemies end up, so I'm delighted to count her as an ally," I concluded.

"Enough of this melancholia!" Angus suddenly decreed. "Pray tell of yer visit to our saviours at Industry Canada."

"Well, everything is 'go,'" I replied, "assuming Sanderson turns his back on 35 years of family tradition to manufacture a leading-edge technology he neither understands nor will ever use. He is your classic Luddite, a veritable tech-know-nothing. I think he probably contracts out the setting of his digital alarm clock."

"We're not askin' him or his workers to become experts in wireless transmission. He just has to see that this opportunity represents a much more secure and prosperous future than makin' unfashionable shoes on an assembly line that should be in an industrial museum," said Angus. "Do you think he's comin' around?"

"He's come a long way since our first meeting. Industry Canada has been very good about it, too. They toured the factory on the weekend. Apparently, the space, the workers, and Deepa's wireless wave router all seem to fit the criteria for industrial-transition funding. The one fly in the ointment is timing," I commented. "Deepa needs to show Canatron proof of manufacturing capability in the next eight weeks. To make that happen, Industry Canada has to approve the funding in the next week. Even if the paperwork were submitted today, that's an ambitious goal."

"So where does it leave us?" Angus asked.

"Well, I've already pulled together the paperwork after spending yesterday on the phone with Sanderson's CFO. So we need Sanderson to say yes today so we can submit the application and the company's audited financial statements no later than tomorrow. Then, it's up to you and the Minister to move it through the approvals process in record time."

To his credit, Angus stayed on the phone with Sanderson for an hour and a half that afternoon, convincing, cajoling, arguing, occasionally yelling, and then rebuilding trust until the recalcitrant, old industrialist finally arrived at "Yes." From the perspective of a distant observer, the decision was a no-brainer, but I could see it was a wrenching choice for Sanderson. Angus played it more sensitively than I'd ever thought possible. His approach presented an impressive display of patient persuasion and deft diplomacy.

"Now what?" asked Angus as he hung up the phone in triumph.

"You need to reach out to the Minister. She's tough and partisan, but only she can accelerate the funding approval to make our deadline. I'll try to set up a call with her and will send over the application to Industry Canada and the Minister's office right now."

As it turned out, the call could not be arranged until the following morning after caucus. I'd been dreading caucus after Angus's performance in his inaugural session the previous Wednesday. Though I didn't want to, I again stayed for the meeting. Angus was quiet through most of the meeting but perked up when the final agenda item was announced—the Throne Speech vote scheduled for that afternoon. The Chair of caucus and the Whip laid out the plan as the Leader looked on, nodding his approval. Finally, the Leader rose to close the deal.

"Friends, we have a historic opportunity today to send this Government packing. I know we've all just come through a tough campaign, but our polling confirms that the Cameron scandal hadn't fully taken root in the public's conscience by election day. It has now. The numbers say we'd win if a vote were taken today. In the minds of Canadians, Cameron's twisted morality seems to have cast doubt on everything he did as Finance Minister. Of course, a declining economy has helped, as well. But we must act quickly. Soon, Cameron's despicable performance will fade into the past. Our righteous indignation will dissipate. Our outrage will soften. And we'll lose this advantage and this golden chance. We must strike now. As of this morning, the NDP are with us. Friends, mark well this date in our history, for today's Throne Speech vote will be this Government's Waterloo."

Most of the room rose in a frenzied and mindless ovation of hooting, hollering, and that most fatigued political gesture, good old-fashioned back slapping. Angus just sat with his arms crossed and shook his head very slightly, wearing a thin smile. About six other Liberal MPs also abstained from the partisan histrionics. I sat at the back, programming 9-1-1 into my cell phone speed-dial and charting the quickest escape route. I knew that Angus wouldn't be sitting for long. Three, two, one … "Mr. Chair, Mr. Chair." Right on cue, Angus rose as the furor died down. The caucus Chair did his best to overlook Angus but eventually had no choice but to recognize him. It was hard to ignore a solid, bearded, wild-haired, aging Scot, waving both arms in an impressive display of semaphore. With a fluorescent orange vest and a couple of flashlights, he might well have been guiding in a 747.

"I'm sorry to urinate in the caucus coffee, but I am compelled to inform you that I'll be supportin' the Throne Speech as I committed to in the House last week. I doonae imagine you'll take kindly to me decision, and I lament this break in solidarity. But me conscience, not to mention common sense, leaves me no choice."

"How can you prop up this morally corrupt Government?" shouted an MP from the other side of the room.

"I doonae accept yer premise, sir, and nor should any of you who consider yourselves fair-minded. I'm votin' for the Throne Speech for three reasons. Firstly, it lays out a reasonable, balanced, and prudent course for the nation. And I defy any one of you to argue otherwise. Secondly, I said I would vote for it, inside the House of Commons and outside. And thirdly, defeatin' a duly elected Government because its former Finance Minister likes to 'do the dirty' in hand-cuffs and leather while bein' flogged with a ridin' crop is asinine, ludicrous, and everythin' betwixt." He bowed slightly and headed out the door. "Well, lads and lassies, it's been grand, but I've work to do."

Angus winked as he walked past me. I scrambled to catch up but not before the Leader, Bradley Stanton, and about 75 Liberal MPs turned on me and com-mitted assault with a deadly glare.

When I got back to my office, I shut the door and picked up the phone. Michael Zaleski answered on the first ring.

"Z-man, it's Daniel Addison. Look, I really need a favour," I opened.

"Hey, Daniel. I figured you'd have gone underground by now, maybe even had cosmetic surgery. You've got the Centre pretty pissed right now."

"Well, they won't be feeling any better after Angus shot down the Leader's pre-battle rally speech this morning. That's why I'm calling. If I were Stanton, I'd be thinking about expelling Angus from the caucus, and I'm sure he's under pres-sure on many fronts to do just that. So here's where you come in. If Stanton and I are going to play chicken, I need to know whether he's really going to go through with it or veer off at the last second. Can you help me out?" I fairly pleaded.

There was a long pause, which I took to be a good sign. I could hear him breathing deeper as he weighed his options. After a final sigh, he came back.

"You didn't hear this from me, but I don't think Angus is going anywhere. We just came out of the field, and your boy seems to be the toast of the country. The gen-pop numbers show Angus to be widely admired—a breath of fresh air at a time when public cynicism towards 'politics as usual' is peaking. The cross-tabs are interesting, too. Among Liberals, Angus enjoys very high awareness ratings and mega-strong support. What's more, he's incredibly popular among Tory and NDP voters, too. We've never seen that before. His appeal transcends party lines. If the Tories have run any numbers on this, they'll be hoping Angus is expelled."

I was stunned for the umpteenth time since meeting Angus. I'd been tracking the growing editorial support for Angus but hadn't counted on average Canadi-ans jumping on our bandwagon so early and in such force. The airport speech had started a snowball rolling down a slope. Now, a mere three weeks later, it seemed it was time to close down the mountain and call out the Saint Bernards.

Zaleski's voice brought me back. "Besides, with the seat count so tight, they'd be crazy to lose one and risk Angus joining the Government benches."

"Well, I doubt our Angus would choose that path, but your point is well taken. Michael, I really appreciate this, and you can count on my discretion," I said in all sincerity. I didn't really need the numbers to deal with Stanton, anyway, just the big picture.

By the time I hung up, I had three voice mails already. My half-hour call with Bradley Stanton went something like this: "You know, we're this close to kicking your ass right out of caucus! Danny boy, it's lonely as an independent. No one to talk to. No research staff. No clipping service. And it's worse than hell in the constit. You really want that?"

"Bradley, in case you didn't know, Prozac now comes in a convenient, one-a-day formulation." Nice light opening. "Come on, man, you know I'm not pulling his strings. I've got a guy who speaks his mind and is genetically programmed to do the honourable thing. I realize that makes him a freak on the Hill, but he is who he is. You can't change him. I can't change him. And I don't even want to."

"Don't give me that shit, Addison. Get him to use some common sense and be reasonable! That's your job! You're one of us!"

"Listen to yourself, Bradley. Angus is the only one around here who is using common sense. His position on the Throne Speech is eminently reasonable, and you know it." Time to fire a gentle shot across his bow. "And what's more, I think Canadians know it, too. I sense that people on the street like what he's saying and what he's doing. Maybe we can all learn something from him."

The same general exchange cycled through our conversation several more times at varying volumes and with ever more creative profanities but eventually tailed off. I knew the Centre was taking this seriously because I also had calls from the caucus Chair, the Whip, and eventually, even the Honourable "Dickhead" Warrington—our esteemed House Leader and accomplished swordsman and paramour. Ours was a short conversation that neither of us enjoyed. I half-expected Rachel to call, but she didn't. Perhaps she was busy calming down her boss.

By the time the full-court press had relaxed, it was nearly time for lunch, which I'm told is the midday meal though I hadn't recently enjoyed one. I joined Angus in his office for his scheduled call to the Industry Minister. I'd briefed the Minister's staff, and they'd prepped the Minister for the call. The planets seemed to be aligning. Angus dialed and was put right through. I decided not to risk listening in on the line and, so, could only hear Angus. At the last second, he covered the receiver with his palm and whispered to me. "What do I call her?"

"Minister," I whispered just in time.

"Minister, it's Angus McLintock. Good of you to take me call." (Pause) "Well, thank you, I'm enjoyin' meself despite me, shall we say, unanticipated victory." (Pause) "I gather you've been briefed on our little timin' problem. We have an opportunity to transform an outmoded shoe factory on its way down into a state-of-the-art technology facility that will produce an advanced wireless wave router to ease computer networkin'. It is a modern marvel of made-in-Canada ingenuity. But as usual, time is of the essence. We need Industry Canada fundin' approval under what I'm told is called the Industrial Transition Program in the next week or so to meet the ambitious retoolin' and production deadlines." (Pause) "Yes, yer officials have been very helpful, and the factory fits nicely into the program's eligibility criteria." (Pause) "Of course, Minister, I would insist on you makin' the announcement. I care not a whit about who gets credit for this." (Pause) "Yes, Minister?" (Pause) "Well, yes, as I said in the House last week, I intend to vote in favour of the Throne Speech this afternoon."

Uh-oh.

"But Minister, I'm not callin' to horse trade. Me decision on the Throne Speech is made. Please doonae approve the fundin' as some kinda payback for me support in the House. That's not how I operate. Approve the fundin' because it's the right thing to do." (Pause) "Aye, I've been gettin' a lot of that lately." (Pause) "When can you let us know, Minister? You'll understand that many jobs and livelihoods are hangin' in the balance." (Pause) "That's splendid, Minister. I'm grateful and so are the workers at the Sanderson Shoe Company. You have me gratitude." (Pause) "Yes, I'll be in the House. I cannae thank you enough."

He hung up and rushed to the fax machine. Two minutes later, the fax hummed to life and regurgitated a single sheet—the final page of the funding application with the Minister's signature, screaming at the bottom.

"Angus, you did it. I can't believe it, but you did it. You got the rusted and temperamental machinery of government to do your bidding. Congratulations!"

Then he did a strange thing. He hugged me.

By that time, the forces threatening us into defeating the Government slackened. I knew Angus was safe. I also believed that the Leader and the rest of the caucus would support the Throne Speech rather than risk parading cracks in the Liberal family for all to see. In the end, I was right about that. After Angus had left the room that morning, caucus debated for most of its three-hour meeting and ultimately, had succumbed to common sense. Late that afternoon, every single Liberal voted to accept the Throne Speech. The Leader appeared to be in pain as he spoke in the House. In his brief speech, he actually borrowed lines Angus had used earlier that morning in caucus. My, how that must have pained him. Only the NDP voted against the Throne Speech.

The next morning, my effigy burning in the Leader's office was further fuelled by a feature story in *The Globe and Mail*. I had steadfastly declined all media interviews the previous evening when rumours of Angus's role in the Liberal flip-flop on the Throne Speech seeped out after the vote. Obviously, someone in Angus's small but growing band of caucus allies was not so discreet and must have spilled the whole story. The piece in *The Globe and Mail* recounted the entire chain of events link by link in excruciating and, I must say, completely accurate detail. It covered the Leader's caucus rallying cry, the McLintock response, the behind-the-scenes expulsion threats, and the Leader's ultimate Throne Speech reversal. One large photo accompanied the front-page story—yep, Angus in full colour, speaking in the House during the initial Throne Speech debate. Just my luck, he looked great in the picture. Fierce and fiery. Almost noble.

I phoned Bradley first thing Thursday morning. Perpetuating my run of bad luck, he was there to take my call. "Bradley, it's Daniel." I barreled ahead without letting him start in on me. "I swear on a stack of Bibles that I had nothing to do with the *Globe* piece. I had no idea it was in the works. I returned no calls to *The Globe* or to anyone else in the gallery last night. I would not do that to the Leader or to you. The story came from someone else who obviously was in caucus yesterday. It's important to me that you know that I would not sell you out like that and neither would Angus." I paused to take a breath. "Bradley? Bradley? Hello?" Shit. And so it goes.

Another smaller but related story appeared in *The Globe and Mail* that morning. Eric Cameron and Petra Borschart had been located by an intrepid reporter, acting on an anonymous tip. They were living in a newly purchased beach house near beautiful Rum Point on Grand Cayman. They declined comment, but the neighbours described them as quiet, pleasant, and permanent, residents.

I picked Lindsay up on campus and then made the short drive to the ByWard Market and my favourite outrageously expensive restaurant in Ottawa, Le Jardin. Rachel and I had gone there often. It had been "our" restaurant. But just by sitting across from me, Lindsay shoved every thought of my ex into the deepest, nearly inaccessible recesses of my memory. She could do that without trying, without even knowing.

Our conversation ranged from books to politics to popular TV shows when we were kids to my new-found aversion to public transit. We spent fifteen minutes on our favourite *Saturday Night Live* sketches of all time. We seemed to be able to talk about anything with no pretense, no agenda, and no higher purpose other than just sharing the same space and sentences. Here was an intimacy I'd never before known. Though Le Jardin was packed, we were all alone. Later, I had no recollection of the food or even the bill though I'm certain both were remarkable if not extraordinary.

In a strange way, our comfort with one another was kind of what I'd always imagined it might be like to have a very close sister, though I was an only child. After closing down the restaurant, she suggested we go back to our local MP's boathouse and watch the stars from the dock. We went inside when frostbite threatened. After that, it wasn't anything at all like having a sister.

◆   ◆   ◆

Diary
Thursday, November 14

My Love,

This week's been a hell of a month. It's been nearly seven days since I last opened this folio. I must be more diligent, but I've been running low on time and consciousness.

Earlier this week, I had a relapse of sorts in what I'm told is called my "grieving journey." Rhonda was the culprit. She and her coterie of advisers came to meet with me as part of the ACW's annual National Day of Action. When my eyes fell on her for the first time since your funeral, I felt my healing heart take a turn for the worse. It caught me unawares and put me down for a moment. I think she noticed, but I doubt the others in the room did. When I saw Rhonda, I saw you. In years past, whenever she was around, so were you. My mind, on instinct, places the two of you together … always.

She learned much from you, but her "both barrels blazing" style was all her own and still is. I know you're proud of her achievements even if her path is not the one you might have chosen.

I finally gave her your most intimate parting gift. She read your long inscription right there in my office, unable to wait for a more private moment. She held herself together though we both shed a tear or two.

We didn't really have much of a meeting, which seemed to perplex her entourage. Having debated these issues with the two of you for the better part of two decades, she knows I am with her, as you are, too. The room was thick with your presence. So we mostly talked of you. I trust your ears burned and your face flushed.

Towards the end, Daniel breathlessly came upon the scene, fully three-quarters of an hour late. He knew nothing of our relationship with Rhonda and feared the worst, given her reputation as a bruising bollocks breaker. I set him straight thereafter. Another part of my life revealed.

A coup yesterday. We've managed to help that sourpuss Norman Sanderson switch over his archaic shoe factory to an advanced manufacturing facility to produce Deepa Khanjimeer's wave router. You remember Deepa. Brilliant mind. Our beloved government will be underwriting much of the transition costs to retool the plant and retrain the workers. And why not? In the span of about six weeks or so, the employees will go from sewing leather uppers to assembling high-tech gizmos—from soles to silicon without missing a paycheque. I admit to feeling a wee bit high on myself right now. You are free to bask in my glow.

More skylarking at our weekly caucus meeting yesterday. Our fearless but feckless Leader actually wanted us to bring down the Tories because Cameron likes his sex with a side order of spanking. It's clear to me who really needs the spanking. As you would know, I stood in my place, politely refused, and bid a hasty retreat. Alas, young Daniel is bearing the brunt of my obstinacy, but that's his job, I reckon. I hear him on the phone, taking body blows as he protects me from the powers that be. Much to my surprise, the scales eventually fell from our bumbling Leader's eyes, and he stood in the House this afternoon and publicly supported the very Throne Speech he'd privately exhorted us to defeat earlier that morning. Either no one has their hand on the tiller, or too many do. Neither augers well as this channel is strewn with shoals.

Muriel called tonight to let me know that Daniel is at this very moment dining with the young and talented lass Lindsay. Muriel is an inveterate matchmaker where Lindsay is concerned. She loves her granddaughter and has clearly given Daniel the coveted seal of approval. Though it's not exactly my field of expertise, I concur, for what it's worth.

Hallelujah! I actually managed a couple of hours on Baddeck 1 this evening. I'm very close to taking her out. I want to make sure the ice is strong before the testing begins in earnest. I'd much rather evaluate her seaworthiness in the tepid waters of July.

I'm on the edge of my sleep, my love. Are you still with me?

Aye, you are.

AM

CHAPTER FIFTEEN

In the morning, I drove Lindsay home. She kissed me before getting out. I stayed calm until she disappeared behind the front door of her mother's house. Then, I rejoiced at the top of my lungs in Stanley Cup Final overtime-winning-goal fashion. As my luck would have it, a middle-aged woman out for an early morning run, passed by my car at that precise moment. She leaped away, aghast. I remained in an advanced state of euphoria as her relaxed jog became a frenzied sprint in the opposite direction. What a beautiful day.

Even though the Commons sat Friday mornings, Angus was not on House duty nor were there any pressing votes scheduled. So we stayed in Cumberland for the day. Constituent meetings were only scheduled in the afternoon, so Angus and I hung out in his living room, enjoying the morning and the shards of sunlight scattered across the Ottawa River. The view from the front window peaked twice each clear day—once in the morning as the sun levitated over the eastern horizon and again at dusk when it sank beyond the shoreline to the west. It was not the actual sunrise or sunset that struck me but, rather, the very incandescence of the light playing on the water. Just as no two snowflakes were identical, the sun's river dance was never the same. Each wave, among millions, was unique.

An Oppenheimer blast of flatulence literally blew me out of my poetic reverie. Just as no two snowflakes were identical, each McLintock fart, among millions, was unique. I know. I was there for all too many of them.

"Oops! Sorry lad. Cabbage rolls at the parliamentary dining room yesterday," Angus confessed. "I knew I was teasin' a tiger, but I couldna resist them."

Angus waited in the kitchen for the fumes to dissipate before he dropped into the enveloping chair across from me in the room where we'd first met, the chess board between us. Our inaugural encounter seemed like eons ago, not a mere two months and a bit. He looked past me to some distant point.

"Well, I'd not have believed it when this calamity first befell me, but this new life of ours is not nearly the sharp stick in the scrotum for which I'd been bracin'," Angus offered before tilting a tumbler of orange juice down his hatch.

"I'm relieved to hear you say that. I quite like what we're doing despite the attendant hassles," I replied. "You're certainly not taking the easy path."

"Aye, 'tis the truth. But I'm counting on it bein' the right path," Angus said. "By the way, I'm nearly finished me speech to the Engineerin' Society for tonight."

Uh-oh. "I beg your pardon?"

"I said I've nearly finished draftin' me wee speech to the Engineerin' Society for tonight. Is yer hearin' givin' you trouble, man?"

"My hearing is fine, thank you very much. But I would have liked to have *heard* about this speech before the day it's to be delivered. I knew nothing about this," I complained. "I need to be in charge of your schedule. I need to assess what we're doing to make sure it's in your best interests. An important part of my job is to protect you."

"Ye gods, Daniel, it's only me faculty mates and some engineerin' students. It's hardly the Ku Klux Klan."

"Angus, it's fine. But I'd just like to know. There could be media there. You're not just an anonymous engineering professor any more. Right now, you're probably the highest profile politician outside of Cabinet, and your popularity's on the rise."

"Aye, that young fella from *The Crier*'ll be there. André … André …" Angus snapped his fingers and looked up as if the name he sought might be stenciled on the ceiling.

"André Fontaine," I offered. "How did he find out about this when I didn't even know?"

"I gather the faculty office sends out a notice of some kind to the community and that *The Crier*'s on the circulation list."

"Tell me more about this event. Who and how many will be there?" I asked.

"There's a quarterly dinner of the U of O Engineerin' Society organized alternately by the faculty and then the undergrads. I'd venture that forty or so faculty show along with perhaps 75 to 100 undergrads. Another 30 graduate students tag along as part of their faculty-ingratiation initiative. We convene in the Faculty Club dinin' room. People dress up a tad, and we gnaw on polymer poultry and sedimentary chocolate cake. And I don't simply mean the cake is layered but use the word *sedimentary* in its true geological sense."

"Is that just your fancy way of saying the cake is usually stale," I inquired.

"Aye, though *stale* is a grossly inadequate characterization. We once tested a piece in the lab, and its Brinell Hardness score was quite impressive."

"What's the room setup, and when do you actually speak?"

"If memory serves, we're in round tables of eight with a podium and a microphone that makes yer voice sound like you're talkin' from the command module in lunar orbit," he noted. "As to when I speak, I fear that's beyond me ken, but I reckon it's after dessert when everybody's loosenin' their belt a notch, sharing a belch, and nodding off."

"Head table?"

"Nope."

"Risers and a multifeed at the back for reporters?"

"Now, you've left me in the dust, laddie."

"I'll call the faculty office. I expect there might be a few journalists there tonight if your speech has had any kind of community promotion," I suggested. "Now, what were you planning to say in your 'wee speech'?"

"I'll pass it by you this afternoon when I've got it finished, but in short, it's a dissertation of sorts on a theory I've been workin' on."

I looked at him and elevated my eyebrows, prompting him to continue.

"Well, most people I've met since I naïvely stepped into yer political snare on October 14 have commented on how far afield politics is from engineerin'. Yet, in the last three weeks, I've found the exact opposite to be true. In fact, it's becomin' increasingly clear to me that the same laws and principles that govern science and engineerin' also preside over politics."

"Now, you've left *me* in the dust," I said, puzzled.

"Well, let me give you a few examples of the many I've pondered while observin' the political machinations in and outside the House these past coupla weeks," Angus offered. "Newton's laws of motion dictate much of what we know about our universe. Newton's first law says that an object at rest or in motion will remain in that state unless acted upon by another force. In politics, if a party is at rest—stalled in the polls, as it were—it will remain there unless it, or some other force, does somethin' to change its fortunes. Newton's third law says that for every action there is an equal and opposite reaction. Well, this plays itself out daily in the Commons. The Government makes an announcement, the Opposition responds, as the name suggests, in an opposin' fashion. When our world-class boob of a Leader asks a question, the Prime Minister immediately counters with an equal and opposite reaction—Newton's laws of motion. When I view it in this wholly familiar and comfortin' context, this game of politics becomes clear and comprehensible to me." Angus sat back, donning the grin of a child who'd just solved the Rubik's cube, something I'd never been able to do.

"So let me get this straight. You're applying the laws of science and engineering to understand and explain politics?"

"Precisely. And it reaches far beyond Newton's laws. I've done plenty of work over the years in materials science, explorin' and understandin' the physical properties of different materials to determine their ideal use in our world. A materials-science staple is load testin'. We apply stress, strain, and direct loadin' to various materials until they fail. Obviously, this has great bearin' on the development of strong and safe construction materials. Well, think about Government for a moment. Think about the Prime Minister assemblin' his Cabinet. As I sit through question period, I've already identified several Ministers the PM clearly did not load test adequately before appointin' them. At some time in the future, under a finite level of Opposition loadin', at least some of these Ministers will fail. It is inevitable."

I was not particularly oriented to the sciences, but I knew enough to grasp this fascinating concept. I'd always assumed politics was much more art than science. While I refused to accept that the weird and wacky world of politics could ever fit neatly into a theoretical framework, perhaps it could be at least partially explained and, more importantly, predicted and controlled through the prism of science. Fascinating, to a point.

"Very interesting, Angus, but a little inaccessible to the average Canadian, don't you think?" I suggested.

"Daniel, I'm not presentin' this theory at the Cumberland Fall Fair between the kids' sheep ridin' and the tractor pull. I'm talkin' to me people—engineers, scientists, and the complement of students who don't cap their dauntin' daily workload with a nightly six-pack of Labatt Blue."

"Fair point," I conceded.

"I'd never inflict this on a civilian population, but I do think me colleagues may well be intrigued. Usually, the speakers at these dinners are drier than the cake."

"When can I see the draft?"

"I'm just finishin' off the political applications of Boyle's Law and Bernoulli's Theorem. I'd say you'll have it shortly after we've strapped on the midday feed-bag if that will suffice."

"That'll be fine. I don't think we need to issue a news release and distribute the speech to the media unless you'd like to," I commented.

"Agreed. The scribes can come if they wish, but I'll not be panderin' to their needs. I've had quite enough coverage to last me at least till Robbie Burns Day." Angus sat up and faced me. "Have we time for a quick battle on the board?" he asked.

We played three games and didn't finish for an hour and a half. I'd planned on playing only one game but so disgraced myself with blunder after blunder that I needed two more games to secure elusive redemption. I lost, badly, the first two encounters but pulled off an upset in the third. I employed a neat little knight sacrifice that allowed my bishop to pin and then take his queen. Nice.

We spent the afternoon at the constit office. Both Petes were on hand, under cover, dressed to infiltrate mainstream society. They had adapted quite readily to the normal conventions of greeting and assisting constituents as they arrived. They had removed all earrings, tongue studs, nostril pins, and other body piercings and had stored them in two Styrofoam cups, labeled Pete1 and Pete2, on top of the toilet tank in the bathroom. They had hung two similarly labeled dark brown, plastic garment bags from the Arnie Bevan Men's Shop innocently in the front closet. I shuddered to think what surreal sartorial wonders lurked inside. The two Petes were heavy into midterms that week but insisted on doing their Friday afternoon constit shift.

The afternoon passed uneventfully with the typical array of constituent issues—passport applications, immigration matters, veterans' pension problems, and two complaints about the murky water attributed to the local aggregate operation. Angus was patient but direct in his dealings with his constituents and seemed quite at ease with his new role. I reviewed the speech he had drafted. He didn't know much about formatting the spoken word, but I must say, his writing was impeccable despite the esoteric topic. His words brought the subject alive with humour, anecdotes, and examples. I was impressed—again.

That night, I sat with Muriel and André Fontaine. Beyond the class I was teaching, I'd never been immersed in a sea of engineers and wondered if my arts degrees were plastered on my forehead for all to see. Everyone was pleasant though a few awkward engineers brought to life the socially inept science-nerd stereotype. Angus had badly undershot his attendance projection, obviously thinking he'd draw the same numbers as the dinner usually did. He failed to account for his newfound popularity on campus and beyond. Instead of 15 tables of 8, they were forced to set 25 tables of 10. This meant the last 40 people arriving were relegated to the reception area outside the dining room with an obstructed view of Angus through three sets of double doors. Thanks to my earlier call to the Faculty Club, two risers ran along the back wall and supported three camera crews, CBC, CPAC, and the local cable station. Not bad. I had warned Angus once in the afternoon and again as we'd arrived on campus that his audience was likely to be more heterogeneous than he might have thought. The president of the university was there. Two senior players in the Leader's office showed up along with one from the Prime Minister's Office. We had struck a nerve. I strongly suggested he "dumb down" his remarks somewhat so he could keep the entire audience with him and not just the engineering types.

I read in the program that the head of the Canadian International Development Agency (CIDA) was also an honoured guest. Angus had neglected to tell me that he was being presented with an award for this "enormous humanitarian contribution to the developing world through his breakthrough work in affordable, small-scale water purification." It seemed I was working for a saint. André and Muriel were impressed, particularly when I admitted Angus had said nothing to me about the CIDA honour. It occurred to me that he may simply have forgotten this aspect of the evening. His innate modesty separated him further from the pack of conceited, self-absorbed prima donnas with whom he shared the House of Commons.

To his credit, he did tone down some of the more technical aspects of his talk. I was gratified to hear an extemporaneous addition on the university education of engineers. He spoke passionately of the need to broaden the curriculum to redress the graduation of engineers who are experts in narrow technical fields but know nothing more about the world around them. He also encouraged the undergraduates in the room to get involved in other aspects of campus life beyond their studies. He even quoted Mark Twain, who once said, "I never let schooling interfere with my education." (Chuckles all around) Well, not all around. Dean Rumplun scowled in a corner, occasionally shaking his head in dismissal if not contempt.

Innately articulate in everyday conversation, Angus clearly understood that a speech from a podium in front of a large audience required something more. Through consummate and integrated use of voice, gestures, and eye contact, he held us all in the palm of his calloused hand. In unison, the crowd laughed when we were supposed to, nodded when we learned something new, and lamented the end, which seemed to come all too soon. The cameras and sun guns were trained on him the whole time as reporters scribbled furiously. And all this for a speech on how the laws of science also govern politics.

The award presentation followed a moving address by the CIDA head who described the profound impact of Angus's work in the third world. It was very impressive. We all lapped it up though Angus looked distinctly uncomfortable with the adulation that verged on idolatry.

Two hours later, I sat alone in the boathouse, watching the glowing and extensive news coverage of the speech as Angus laboured over his hovercraft below me. That night, I finally accepted that I might well be astride a comet.

Over the course of the weekend and into the next week, broader political developments were at play on the Hill and across the country. The economy was tanking, and the decline was happening faster than anyone had predicted. Many seemingly disconnected strands came together to braid what looked to be the early stages of recession. Hurricane Penelope had devastated oil production in the Gulf of Mexico the previous week. Then, OPEC had dithered on whether, how, and when to help out. As a consequence, in the space of three days, oil prices had soared to over $80 a barrel. The Canadian dollar was growing stronger against the greenback, not because of any inherent strength in our economy but because the U.S. numbers were dropping faster than ours. Our dollar hovered just below 90 cents American, so Canadian exports plummeted, our trade deficit skyrocketed, and our tourism sector suffered. To make matters worse, Stats Can had just released the October numbers. From the first of the month to Halloween, inflation had jumped from 1.9 to 2.8 percent while unemployment grew from 6.9 to 7.4 percent.

This news was not welcome for any federal government. The news was particularly bad for a minority Conservative government that had invested everything in the sound fiscal management and stratospheric popularity of its erstwhile Finance Minister—that is, until a poorly maintained air conditioner and flammable curtains turned Eric Cameron into a porn star.

It seemed that the chrome shackles found on the Finance Minister's wrists actually handcuffed the Government as well. To stem the tide of public outrage over Cameron's hobby, the Government had cut him loose in the dying days of the campaign. The problem was, the postelection polls soon confirmed that the Government was still at least a bull whip too close to the scandal. So after the election, as their numbers continued to sink, the Tories went one step farther despite their minority victory. They turned their back not just on Eric Cameron but also on the entire fiscal strategy he'd unveiled in the last budget. They took it right off the table. They threw the baby out with the bath water. They cut off their noses to spite their faces. All those clichés applied. Ultimately, the Government paid a heavy price for abandoning a perfectly reasonable fiscal approach after tossing Eric Cameron overboard.

To sum it all up, at a time when the economy appeared to be headed for the dumper, the Government no longer stood for any discernible economic policy. The Tories knew they were in deep. We knew it, too. The NDP would catch up eventually, but economic policy was not a particular strength of the third party.

The momentum gathered on the weekend and steadily grew early in the week. Saturday and Sunday editorials in most major dailies called on the Government to introduce at least a fiscal statement before the end of the year rather than cling to the traditional February budget cycle. The C. D. Howe Institute, the Fraser Institute, and the Conference Board of Canada all issued similar pleas on Monday, earning considerable media coverage. After all, it made news when the folks at the C. D. Howe were on the same page with the Fraserites. In a rare display of sound House strategy, every Liberal who rose in Monday's question period hammered the Government on its AWOL fiscal plan. Finally, the President of the United States delivered the fatal blow on Monday night. In a blatant and largely successful attempt to distract Americans from their own domestic travails, the President, in a speech on Wall Street, called Canada's ill-defined fiscal policy a potential threat to the economic stability of the G-8 countries. It was audacious. It was provocative. It was utter nonsense. But it also put the *hype* in *hyperbole* and played well on Main Street on both sides of the 49th.

As I watched the tail end of question period on Tuesday afternoon, the message on all fronts was the same. Canadians needed some reassurance that the Government, in the wake of the Cameron affair and the plummeting economy, was operating on a financial plan that ran deeper than "buy low and sell high." The Government was under unprecedented pressure to lay out, in clear, unequivocal terms, the economic plan that would carry the country until the budget in February. But pressure doesn't always have the desired effect. In fact, nothing tends to stiffen a government's spine and harden its resolve like an aggressive and relentless opposition. After all, human nature has always been a driving force in politics. As a species, we really don't like to be told what to do.

Picture the nasty and arrogant neighbour you never liked who demands that you stop hanging out your laundry on your backyard clothesline. Your billowing underwear is an eyesore he shouldn't have to look at etcetera, etcetera. Admit it. Even if you'd just purchased a fancy, new Kenmore drier, your first instinct would probably be to hang out every single pair of gotchies you could find, clean or not, and let them swing on the line permanently. In the same vein, Governments hate doing things that the Opposition parties—or anyone else, for that matter—have told them to do. The more sophisticated lobby groups are very judicious in how they use Opposition parties. If the lobby groups are smart, they realize that if they get the Liberals to demand it, the Government likely won't deliver it.

Sometimes, this phenomenon has far-reaching implications. In 1965, Prime Minister Lester B. Pearson gave a speech in Philadelphia in which he called on President Lyndon Johnson to halt the American bombing of North Vietnam. Legend has it that the President had been, in fact, just about to announce such a ceasefire when our unwitting Prime Minister pulled the pin and tossed in his grenade. As a result, Johnson felt compelled to sustain the bombing for several more weeks to avoid being seen to have acquiesced to the demands of his weak northern neighbour. Privately, the President was outraged and apparently told Pearson not to "come into my home and piss on my carpet."

All of this to say I was quite shocked when the Government caved that very day—folded like an origami master. Following question period, Roger Chartrand, the rookie Finance Minister appointed three weeks earlier to fill Eric Cameron's shoes, rose in the House.

"Mr. Speaker, in light of the volatile global economic situation that is undermining the stability of the Canadian economy, I rise today to inform the House that I will table an economic statement on Monday, December 2 at 4:00 PM, following the close of the financial markets. Thank you."

The Opposition benches erupted. The Government's hand had been forced, and a mini-budget, as it came to be known, was on the way. Or we were being played. I couldn't really tell which, but I knew what my gut was telling me.

Later that afternoon, Angus sauntered past my office and into his. He looked downright happy even though he'd just returned from the first meeting of the Standing Committee on Procedure and House Affairs. Often, coffee and a cattle prod were required to keep committee members engaged. But then again, Angus was not your typical MP.

"How was the meeting?" I opened as I lowered myself onto his couch.

"Fascinatin', utterly fascinatin'," he replied without the slightest trace of sarcasm.

"You were just at Procedure and House Affairs, were you not?" Just checking.

"Yes, of course." He shook his head dismissively. "I'm learnin' that the real power in this place is conferred on those who understand the rules of the House and how to use them. As far as I can tell from this first meetin', me wee study of the standin' orders has left me better informed on the rules than me more experienced committee colleagues," he declared with evident satisfaction. "In a minority situation, it strikes me that the future of this Government may well turn on House procedure."

"It may well," I agreed. "I must say I was a little surprised that the Government succumbed so quickly on the need for an economic statement. It was just too easy."

"Aye, I thought the Government rolled over and bared its throat without much of a tussle," Angus concurred. "Me thinks somethin's afoot."

That night, I stood bundled up on the dock, bathed in the powerful floodlights that hung under the eaves of the boathouse. I'd never noticed the lights before, but they illuminated about 1,000 square metres of the Ottawa River. The day's steady wind had swept the snow clear, leaving the ice solid, smooth, and shining.

I turned to see the hovercraft, still unpainted on top, roll down the shallow incline of the ramp towards the ice. Two small mover's dollies, one under the bow and the other under the stern, made the craft mobile while a winch and a steel cable kept the descent under control. As I'd been instructed, I steadied the stern and ensured that the rubber skirt did not catch on the ramp. Angus and I managed to extricate the dollies without incident, beyond my self-diagnosed hernia. Angus just scoffed and called me some obscure Scottish name I decided not to research.

Angus looked tense. He looked more nervous standing on the ice next to the hovercraft than he did standing in the House, challenging the Prime Minister. He gingerly installed himself in the cockpit and nodded my way. He hadn't yet installed the electric starter. So my job was to reach into the very scary engine compartment, pull the starter cord, and bring the engine to life while avoiding a triple-twisting face plant into the whirring multibladed fan.

"Contact!" I cracked as I leaned in to grab the handle.

"You're a right laugh now, aren't you? Just get the engine goin' and stand clear," Angus instructed.

I pulled, and the engine roared to life. It was loud. It sounded like a cross between a snowmobile and a municipal wood chipper. I hastened across the ice and climbed up on the dock. I wasn't really clear on what Angus had in mind. He was fiddling with something in his lap. Then, I watched as he donned a 40-year-old and very goofy-looking skin diving mask. When he looked over at the dock where I stood, I had to turn away. I was in a fit of hysterics, complete with watering eyes and vibrating shoulders. I gathered myself and turned to face him, feigning the denouement of a coughing fit. I waved, and he nodded again very seriously. I assumed the mask was in lieu of ski goggles, which made some sense in this arctic breeze. As well, if the ice beneath him ever gave way, at least he'd have a crystal-clear view of his plunge to the bottom of the river.

He reached for what I assumed was the throttle, and the engine roared louder. The black rubber skirt around the craft's perimeter inflated, and I watched as an invisible hand lifted Angus and Baddeck 1 off of the ice about two feet. It was hovering! The craft looked so much more impressive on the river's ice than on the floor of the boathouse.

Angus tinkered with the throttle, I assumed, to achieve the desired altitude. Then, I saw him shift both his feet and rev the engine a little higher. Very slowly, the hovercraft rotated on the ice, nearly in place. I noticed the vanes in the vents on either side of the craft moving slightly. Then, his feet moved again, and the craft stopped and rotated in the other direction. While obscured by his oversized diving mask, his broad smile was clear. Eventually, Angus pointed the bow towards the middle of the river, shifted his feet yet again, throttled up, and flew across the ice. He carved a long arc over the river, playing with the controls, getting to know his creation. He spent the next 20 minutes flying back and forth in the limited patch of light defined by the floodlights.

I watched from the dock, filled with an emotion I couldn't quite identify. I finally decided I was over-thinking it. I was simply excited, pleased, and happy for Angus. I was proud of him. He'd worked long and hard designing and then building his baby. And now, he was flying it, or whatever one does with a hovercraft.

Angus shot towards the shore at a speed that I found disquieting. About 50 metres from shore, his feet shifted, and the nose of the craft dipped slightly. Baddeck 1 slowed down though the engine roared at the same level. I now understood. He'd redirected all of the thrust out the front vents in the same way as a jet reverses its engines to brake upon landing. Unfortunately, stopping a speeding hovercraft on a frozen river taxes a commodity Angus had in very short supply that night—distance.

On the bright side, we didn't have to winch the hovercraft back up into the boathouse. I followed Angus and Baddeck 1 as they hurtled up the ramp and smashed into the south wall of the boathouse, narrowly missing the gas furnace. I scrambled up the steps, my heart in my mouth, expecting to find both the hovercraft and Angus in pieces. My heart soon returned to its traditional thoracic position. Angus exhausted his entire lifetime allotment of good fortune that night. I found him still sitting in the cockpit. His diving mask had shifted so that it was perfectly positioned over his right ear, the blue rubber strap deforming his nose. He was bent over in laughter, and then, so was I.

The crashing blow had been cushioned by the inflated skirt surrounding the vessel itself and by a fortuitously placed pile of rubber remnants left over from sewing it. Neither Angus nor his hovercraft was worse for the ride.

Angus removed the mask, stepped from the cockpit, and circled the craft in search of less-obvious damage. We found none. He sat back down on the starboard deck of Baddeck 1 as I closed the bay doors on the frigid night and doused the floodlights. He was clearly ecstatic with his first foray onto the ice though he kept his emotions in check. Neither of us had yet spoken.

"Well, she works," he whispered. "Aye, she does."

"Angus, you made a thrilling sight out there," I said slowly and quietly. "But I must say, you do need some practice parking. I'm just glad the big doors were still open when you shifted into kamikaze mode."

A sudden thought struck me, and I darted out the door and bounded up the stairs to my apartment. I found it at the bottom of one of my many memorabilia boxes with which I cannot seem to part—pieces of my life, kept and cherished to remind me who I am. I slipped back down to the workshop. I took the diving mask from his hand as he took what I proffered.

"I'd like you to have this and use this. It belonged to my great-grandfather," I said with reverence. "He wore it in the Great War over France. It was sent home to my great-grandmother with his personal effects after he was shot down."

With care, Angus pulled on the faded but soft-as-velvet leather headgear and lowered the flying goggles over his eyes. He said nothing but clasped my right hand in his while his left held my forearm.

◆   ◆   ◆

Diary
Tuesday, November 19

My Love,

Though I'm sitting on my old writing stool, I'm still hovering as high in the air as I was an hour ago. She's done, love, and she works. Oh, does she fly! It seems I've been toiling for so long on her. I never really had time to stop and think through *the* very moment. I cannot explain it, but I cried like a toddler as I flew over the ice. It was such a release; yet, I had only thoughts of you. My carrying on fogged up the bleeding mask, and I misjudged my stopping distance. The reverse thrust out the front vents worked very well, but I was just too close to the shore. But you lined me up with the ramp, you did, and we came to rest with nothing more than a wee head bash on the steering wheel.

She handles better than I dared dream. The side thrust vents grant remarkable control for a craft that makes no contact with the earth. I must only paint the top decking and the thrust vents now, and she's whole. I'm beside myself. She flies.

As well, I was able to retire my unwieldy diving mask though I'm sure I cut a fine figure in it out on the ice. Daniel, bless his kind soul, bestowed upon me this evening the very leather flying kit and goggles his great-grandfather wore in dogfights over France in the Great War. He flew the Sopwith Triplane, the Camel's forebear, in the famed all-Canadian "Black Flight." He shot down 42 German fighters but finally fell to Ernst Udet, second only to Richthofen in Allied kills. I was touched to my core.

I cannot turn my brain to politics tonight. There's nothing left for it. I will say I'm enjoying myself when I reckoned I never would. It is liberating when you answer only to what you believe to be right and just. How often do we enjoy such luxury?

I gave a little after-dinner address the other night at the quarterly ES dinner. It seems my unscheduled political sabbatical has caught the attention of some. The Faculty Club was brimming with folks I'd never met and who had never set foot on the science side of campus. I figure some of them think engineers drive locomotives. There were a few cameras on hand with their blasted blinders shining in my eyes throughout my little talk. I could barely see a yard before me. I prattled on about these connections I've been lately making between my old life and my new one. I'm finding that my beloved laws of science are not nearly so narrow but hold sway in other arenas. They gave me a little award for something. I could have done without that, but they're well-meaning, I grant them that. Enough of this marginalia.

I somehow feel as though I've reached the other side, crossed some kind of threshold. Can you make sense of it? I cannot fathom it, cannot see it clearly. I guess I'm not yet there. Tonight I'm tired and nearly content, yet never whole.

She floated and flew tonight. Aye, she did, my love.

AM

CHAPTER SIXTEEN

I sat across the table from Muriel and Lindsay. We were in Daley's, one of Ottawa's best hotel restaurants, just off the lobby of the Westin. Its proximity to Parliament Hill made it a gathering place for the political elite, at least when no tables were left at Mama Theresa's over on Somerset. We'd come on a whim after Muriel had spent the day in the Centre Block office. She'd never been.

Angus had fussed over her all morning, making sure she was comfortable. At one point, I feared she might swat him, but she knew his ministrations were well-intended. Muriel worked away on copy for our first householder, due at the Queen's Printers within the week. At about one-thirty, I took Muriel's arm and escorted her, at her own speed, to the Members' gallery across from where Angus sat. It had been years since Muriel had been in the House, and she craned her neck like a first-timer, taking in the polished chandeliers and ornate stone work.

"It really hasn't changed all that much since the forties," she noted, scanning the chamber. "The carpet is new, and the television lights make it much brighter. Other than that, I can almost conjure up Mackenzie King waltzing in to take his place."

At two o'clock sharp, the Speaker rose from his throne, prompting six young pages, who had been sitting discreetly on the carpeted steps below, to rise in unison.

"Statements by Members," he intoned. The Speaker immediately looked towards Angus. I had cooked this up with the Speaker's office earlier in the morning. "The Honourable Member for Cumberland-Prescott."

"You'd better not have," Muriel hissed as Angus stood up. As usual, his desk top was bare. He turned to face the throne.

"Blame Angus. I was just his indentured emissary," I replied. She scowled but returned her gaze to Angus below.

"Mr. Speaker, I rise today to recognize in our gallery a bona fide legend of Canadian politics. She is 81 years young with an unbridled zest for life I'd long to have at me age, let alone in 20 years. Muriel Parkinson toiled for Mackenzie King at his height and spent many an afternoon in this chamber observin' these honourable proceedin's from where she sits today. Since leaving Parliament Hill followin' King's tenure, there has been no more stalwart a Liberal in this land than Muriel

Parkinson. Many Honourable Members will know of her exploits on the campaign trail. When no other Liberal would, five times she stood for public office against withering odds. Mr. Speaker, Muriel Parkinson's dedication to public service is reflected today in her indispensable role as me personal adviser and grand marshal of our constituency office in her beloved town of Cumberland. She already enjoys me respect, admiration, and affection, but Mr. Speaker, I submit she deserves the same from the House this afternoon."

A chorus of applause, "hear, hear," and enthused desk thumping followed. My discreet index finger on her hip prodded Muriel to her feet where she waved with palpable modesty before sinking back into her seat. The Liberal side of the House was on its feet. I clapped, too.

"Codswallop," was all she said under her breath in the midst of the ovation. But her eyes betrayed pride and gratitude as they found Angus below.

"Order, order, please," commanded the Speaker as he held up his right hand as if in benediction. "The House welcomes and thanks Muriel Parkinson."

Lindsay had been tied up, teaching a first-year poli-sci tutorial all afternoon but joined us later for dinner. She was crestfallen over missing Muriel's tribute in the House. Angus had a rare evening committee meeting he was loathe to miss, so just the three of us went to Daley's.

Muriel's eyes were alight as the menu competed with the assembled "politerati" for her attention. Four Cabinet Ministers, a former prime minister, two senior political commentators, and three ambassadors were on hand, making it a rather slow night for people-watching.

For Lindsay's benefit, I provided a detailed account of Muriel's triumphant return to the House, complete with dead-on impressions of Angus, the Speaker, and the cacophony of "hear, hear" and bongo desk drumming. I had brought the statement Angus had written (he wouldn't let me near the drafting of it) so that I could give Lindsay the most accurate simulation.

I was just closing with the Speaker's final comments when our harried waiter happened by. Or perhaps it was his tag-team partner who administered freshly ground pepper with a deft twirl of his right hand. I was having some difficulty keeping them straight.

"Order, order, please," I performed in my most authoritative voice. To my chagrin, I was interrupted before I could recite the Speaker's final line for my rapt audience.

"I'm sorry, sir, please bear with us. I'll take your order as soon as I'm able. We're quite busy tonight," replied the waiter before hustling over to another table.

Our burst of laughter earned us some annoyed glances from neighbouring tables, but nothing could dampen our spirits that night.

Except perhaps Rachel Bronwin. Yep, *the* Rachel Bronwin. I caught sight of her dining in a quiet corner with the Honourable "Dickhead." Lindsay noticed the altered look on my face and followed my gaze.

"Is that her?" she asked.

"Yes, that is she," I replied, unable to hold back from correcting the grammar mistake daily made by the vast majority of Canadians.

"Well, she's certainly an attractive gal," offered Muriel.

I didn't think Rachel had seen me yet. I thought it was time I closed that book. "Would you excuse me?" I said as I pushed back my chair. "If waiter guy returns, I'm having the strip loin, medium rare."

By that stage in our respective relationships, Lindsay and Muriel had both heard the late-night rubber-plant-rendezvous story in about as much detail as decorum and good taste permitted. Worried looks played across both their faces.

"Calm yourselves. I'll be right back," I assured them. The concerned looks persisted. "Don't worry. You know how I detest confrontation."

I strode out of the restaurant and across the hotel lobby to the elevators. I ascended three floors, walked along the corridor, found what I was looking for, and returned to the restaurant. After a quick briefing with the bartender, I slipped him a twenty and returned to the still-befuddled Lindsay and Muriel.

"What's going on, Daniel?" Lindsay asked, looking skeptical. "Are we about to be thrown out?"

"No matter," Muriel piped in. "I've been thrown out of nicer joints than this." That seemed to slacken the tension. I smiled sweetly and took her hand in mine.

"Fear not. I'm merely putting the past where it belongs—behind me. So it's easier to focus on the future if that's not too maudlin an explanation."

Lindsay, Muriel, and I all watched as the bartender took a glass of white wine on a tray over to where Rachel and "Dickhead" were engrossed in quiet conversation. She looked up, puzzled, but took the wine glass and placed it before her. He then handed her the rather large DO NOT DISTURB sign I'd pulled from a doorknob on the third floor. He pointed towards us, and Rachel eventually caught up. When Rachel's eyes fell on our table, the three of us as if on cue, yet, utterly spontaneously, raised our glasses in a toast to her.

We watched the penny drop. Rachel threw down the sign and pushed back her chair with such force that it toppled over, landing on the foot of an older man at the next table. She walked away from us towards the lobby and was halfway there before

"Dickhead" processed the scene. He shot a malevolent look my way as he trotted to catch up to Rachel. The three of us again raised our glasses to him as he blew by.

"Was that good for you?" Lindsay asked with a mischievous glint in her eye.

"Oh yeah, I think that went quite well," I responded.

"Game, set, and match," was all Muriel said with her glass still raised.

"I think I've changed my mind," I commented as I reopened the menu. "I now feel like having the filet of catharsis with a side of flambéed 'just desserts.'"

We had a wonderful meal that night and laughed more together than we ever could have apart. I regretted that Angus had missed it in favour of tedious debate over procedure and the Standing Orders.

I escorted Muriel into the Riverfront Seniors' Residence while Lindsay waited in the idling Taurus. "Thank you, Daniel dear, for a wonderful day and a delightful time tonight. The dinner was perfect in every way," she said as she hugged me. "I'm so glad Lindsay was there to see that little harlot's exit."

"So was I." I kissed her cheek and moved towards the door.

"I'll let Lindsay's mother know she need not leave a light on," Muriel offered with a lascivious wink, and I was out the door.

Angus and the Minister of Correctional Services both held those cheesy silver spades used in all ceremonial sod turnings. With Eric Cameron replaced by a Liberal, Cabinet had quickly approved the federal halfway house for newly paroled inmates to be erected on the southern edge of Cumberland. It had been on the Government's books for the previous three years, but Cameron had easily wielded enough power to stall and, given enough time, even kill the project. With that obstacle eliminated and Angus supporting it, it was sod-turning time, accompanied by the *de rigueur* grip-and-grin photo op with the Minister. It would make satisfactory fodder for the still-unfinished householder.

The Minister looked a little nervous as she stepped up to the microphone after tossing her shovel full of dirt to one side. Attending the ceremony were about 20 supporters, 5 or 6 journalists, including 2 cameras, and 60 or so angry citizens of Cumberland, protesting the halfway house. Regrettably, the "not in my backyard" syndrome was a common enough malady in Canadian society, bred through the arrogance and apathy of affluence. According to several independent studies, including one paid for and discarded by the Prescott Coalition Against Crime, Cumberland was ideally suited for the halfway house. The town offered a reasonably prosperous local economy; a local police detachment, featuring a team of parole officers; adequate distance from the criminal temptations of the big city; and a local community college to help equip parolees with the skills they would need to integrate more easily into today's society. It just made sense to build the facility in Cumberland, full stop. But when ex-cons are involved, logic seldom prevails in the chosen community.

The Minister spoke only briefly, skipping several pages of her prepared address, and looking longingly at her Lincoln Town Car and driver parked 14 feet away with the engine running and the rear door open. Despite the efforts of her political staff to stimulate applause at the end of each paragraph by clapping like crazed wind-up monkeys, the booing and heckling still drowned her out. She turned her desperate countenance to Angus as a tomato hit the lectern and splattered over the platform party. I was standing off to the side and eluded the tomato shrapnel. Ever chivalrous, which he argues in no way conflicts with feminism, Angus stepped forward to stand at the podium, shielding the Minister.

"Hey hey, that's enough of that if you value yer throwin' arm, laddie," exclaimed Angus. I was forever counseling Angus not to threaten constituents with physical assault, but my pleas went in one ear and out the other. "Now, let's all take a breath and calm down. I want to assure you that the process and the exhaustive research undertaken to identify Cumberland as the ideal site for this important correctional facility were above reproach. I've reviewed it meself and have spoken at length with the Minister and her senior officials. As citizens of this great country, we all bear obligations that reach beyond payin' our taxes. And one of them is welcomin' this halfway house and the men who will pass through its doors to this community," Angus said in his best Obi-Wan Kenobi voice.

That's when the melon flew. "Incoming!" someone cried.

A less than athletic protester had thrown an overripe cantaloupe at the Minister while still holding onto his large and heavy RAPISTS OUT OF CUMBERLAND placard. Under such circumstances, John Elway would have had difficulty making such a throw. The cantaloupe arced gently towards the stage where Angus caught it deftly before it reached its mark. A great many lazy Edinburgh days of cricket played in the shadow of Arthur's Seat engendered excellent hand-eye coordination. Before either Angus or the protestor knew what was happening, the newly elected MP for Cumberland-Prescott hurled the cantaloupe right back with pinpoint precision. It burst on the forehead of the placard-bearing agitator, coating him and everyone else in a five metre radius with nearly rancid juice. About a thousand slippery seeds exploded from the melon-on-melon impact, lodging in hair, moustaches, ears, and even a few nostrils. When the seeds finally settled, I noticed that the offending protestor sported nearly half the remaining cantaloupe shell on his head like a gladiatorial helmet. Ivan Reitman could not have created a more cinematically comical scene.

I was quite sure that throwing rotting fruit at your own voters was not recommended in the re-election handbook. I hoped the Betacams had been packed away before the melon melee ensued. Upon closer scrutiny, both cameras were right in the fray. By the cantaloupe entrails on each camera, I figured they were close enough to have shot some award-winning footage. By the time the OPP arrived from the doughnut shop two doors down, Angus had safely escorted the Minister to her waiting getaway car, and she had left in puff of tire smoke.

"Well, your guy likes to keep things interesting. I'll say that much for him." André Fontaine approached. I reached out and removed the chunk of melon rind that rested on his shoulder beyond his peripheral vision.

"Hello, André. Just another day in the exciting adventures of Angus McLintock," I replied, hoping he was in a good mood. Unfortunately, the tone of media coverage and the story angle itself were often directly influenced by what kind of day the reporter was having. But it was what it was.

"I'm impressed with your man's arm, not to mention his quick hands."

"Ah well, he's the product of a misspent youth on the cricket pitch," I explained. "I suppose you're running with this, eh?"

"Well, I'm torn between writing up this little event—you know, where our new MP beans a constituent with a rotten melon—or going with a story on the Legion bake sale I visited this morning," he mused, trying his best to look undecided. "It's a tough call. See ya, Daniel."

He walked down the street towards the editorial offices of *The Cumberland Crier*. For the first time, I noticed the camera dangling off of his shoulder. Excellent.

"If some sod chucks a melon at me head, I'm gonnae return fire whether I'm an MP or not!" Angus bellowed.

We'd made it back to his house and were again sitting in his living room.

"Angus, I hear you, but you must understand, you're held to a higher standard now. You must rise above the juvenile tactics of protestors and stay on the high road," I implored.

"Doonae be givin' me any bollocks about the high road! That's me song. Yer in me glen now. It's not whether you take the high road or the low road that counts. It's how you conduct yourself, whichever road you're runnin', that'll dictate who reaches Scotland first," Angus said in a hissing tone. He paused to take a breath before barreling on. "I was protectin' the honour of a Minister of the Crown, and I'll not apologize for layin' out a hoodlum with the very projectile he fired at her."

I raised my hands in surrender.

I needn't have worried. Angus had so high a balance in the Canadian Imperial Bank of Popularity that the extensive media coverage served only to burnish his image further. The videotape captured the snarling protestor taking careful aim and launching the cantaloupe with a look of rage normally reserved for the Intifada. The footage showed Angus stepping in front of the Minister, catching the melon, and throwing it back. It closed with Angus hustling the Minister to her car like a Secret Service agent blocking the sniper's shot so the President can escape in the bullet-proof limousine. He looked almost heroic. At least that's what 17 editorials in Canada and the United States said the next day. Larry King was quite effusive as well when he ran the video (though Angus declined the interview). He also said no to *People* magazine, *The New York Times*, and Oprah Winfrey.

There are some honest and upstanding politicians in this country who try every day to do the right thing, make the right decision, and choose the right path, yet still, seldom get it right. They're not dumb. It's just not that easy. Angus wasn't even trying, beyond just being himself, but could do no wrong. He didn't even want it, and he had it. The man was a walking news story. If you tailed him long enough, something interesting, if not breathtaking, was bound to unfold. It was a miracle the hovercraft story had not yet come out. I figured Angus opted for night testing to lessen the likelihood of media exposure.

Camille entered my office to alert me that our guest had arrived. I asked her to show him into Angus's office in a minute or two. Angus was at his desk, scribbling in the margins of the Standing Orders as CPAC droned in the background. I switched off the TV. "Are you ready? He's here," I said, casting a thumb towards the reception area.

"What are we doin' again?" asked Angus.

"Ottawa River Aggregate Inc. Remember?" We'd prepared carefully for this encounter.

"Aye, I remember, I remember," he said, annoyed. "I'm just yankin' yer leg."

I stood up as the lone suit entered. He looked to be about 50 but wore his hair slicked back with enough petroleum gel to heat Iqaluit for a week. I couldn't have afforded his black, pinstriped suit if I had sold the Taurus. A heavy, gold chain, hanging from his left wrist, occasionally banged against his large, gold cufflinks. A neon blue, patterned tie lay against his bright yellow shirt, kicking off a glare that hurt my eyes. He wore shiny black, pointy shoes. When I was a kid, we called them "nose pickers."

"McLintock?" said "Slick," turning to Angus. "Whoa, quite the beard you got there, big guy." His thick Southern accent grated like a circular saw in concrete.

Angus smiled congenially and shook his hand. "And yer name, sir?" inquired Angus, bordering on obsequious.

"Todd Haldorson from International Aggregate out of Cleveland. We own Ottawa River Aggregate and 127 other gravel traps around the world."

"Good day, Mr. Haldorson. We've been expectin' you," oozed Angus.

"Well, it's nice to meet the man who sent that Cameron fellow packing. But I gotta admit, Cameron was sure enough good to us—always helping us out of jams and the like. I'm kinda sad to see him go," "Slick" noted wistfully.

I stepped forward and held out my hand. "Mr. Haldorson, I'm Daniel Addison, Mr. McLintock's EA. Welcome to Ottawa."

"Yeah thanks, nice little town you have here," he said as he made himself comfortable on the couch. "Man, I've been trying to get in to see you now for three weeks, but that old broad at your other office doesn't seem to like me much."

"Oh, I'm sorry to hear that. We had no idea there'd been any kind of delay," I replied, feigning concern. Muriel knew what he was after and had kept him hanging. I was in the dark until I happened upon an errant voice-mail message on the constit office answering machine and realized what was going on. I sympathized with Muriel's viewpoint, but avoiding a meeting was really not an option.

Angus piped back in. "So, Mr. Haldorson, what brings you to Ottawa, and how can we help?"

"Well, let's get down to it, then. I like a man who can cut to the chase."

Angus and I took the two easy chairs facing "Slick."

"Well, gentlemen, the Ottawa operation has been providing gainful employment for the good folks of Sunderland now for five years," Slick opened.

"Cumberland," Angus noted with an ingratiating smile.

"What'd I say?" Slick asked.

"Sunderland," I replied.

He shook his head, mad at himself. "Ah hell, we got a little facility down in Sunderland, Texas. I'm always getting them confused. Anyhow, I got good news for y'all."

"Do tell." Angus again.

"Well, as we like to say at IA, 'grow or die.' So we're on the grow in Cumberland. The big boys in Cleveland wanted to shut you down, but I talked them out of it, provided we can build the addition and take advantage of what I guess they call *economics of scale*."

"I believe the term is *economies of scale*, but we understand." Angus was laying it on thick.

"Right, whatever. So it means about 75 short-term jobs to get the addition built and another 50 permanent jobs when it's up and runnin' on top of the 82 jobs already there. So it's what we call down in Louisiana a big win-win."

"Why, that's terrific news, Mr.... um ... Haldorson. I'd be pleased to help cut the ribbon," offered Angus.

"Well, you see, McLintock, if we don't get your help long before that, we'll be cutting jobs, not ribbons. To get the big boys to approve this plan, I promised that you and I'd work together to make a few things go away before we'd start pouring dough into an expansion," Slick said with no diminution in confidence.

Extraordinary gall. Here we go.

"Well, we are at yer service, Mr. Haldorson. What needs to be done to expedite this most generous investment?"

"Now you're talking, McLintock. Well, we got two little problems that need to disappear to keep the padlock off the front gate. First of all, some of our more militant worker types have taken some trumped up health and safety issues to the Ministry of Labour, and we're catchin' some heat. There's some hearing coming up, and I've told my guys in Cleveland that I'd fix it so the hearing never happens."

Angus was having so much fun he could contain himself no longer. "Blast those damned health and safety zealots! Do they have no idea what it takes to make a buck in this day and age? The bastards!" Angus clenched his fists in mock outrage. Slick was lapping it all up. No warning bells were sounding in his brain; it was full speed ahead.

"I like your style, McLintock. I really do. But there's more. We just had a little visit from Environment Canada the other day when we weren't exactly expectin' 'em."

"The dirty blackguards," Angus muttered under his breath. I coughed to stifle a giggle. I held up my hand, signaling that I was breathing again and that the meeting could proceed. This guy was nothing but a caricature.

"Anyhoo, those pricks at Environment said there's some kind of discrepancy between what we're dumping in the river and what we're reporting to them. I'm sure it's just some kind a clerical fuck up, but it would sure help if the local MP stepped in to 'clear the water' you might say," explained "Slick."

"Well, how about if I arrange to have the effluent limits lifted so you can dump whatever you like in the river?" Angus proposed in an aura of sincerity.

"You could do that? Well now, that would be fine, just fine. Hell, Cameron tried and said it couldn't be done, and he was the goddamn Finance Minister. I am surely pleased to make your acquaintance, McLintock."

For a moment, neither Angus nor I knew how to proceed. We thought for certain our dim guest would have picked up on the performance long before now, allowing us to deliver the real message. But he was still bathing in our little act.

"Hell, this is the best news I've had all month. I gotta tell you, if we weren't able to take care of those two little problems, the plant would be in shutdown mode," Slick commented in passing.

Angus took his cue. "How soon could you be gone?" Angus asked straight-faced. Slick looked at him but then chuckled in a "you almost had me there" kind of way.

"Damn if you're not a pistol, McLintock. So when can you get the tree huggers off my ass?"

"Answer the question, man. How soon could you pack up the plant and be gone?" Angus bore down on "Slick." who had finally noted the change in temperature.

"What's your game, McLintock? Am I reading you wrong? Where'd the guy go who was goin' to cut us loose from all that dang red tape?" Slick then smiled, still not quite sure what had just happened on the previously smooth road to regulatory subversion.

"No game here, Mr. Haldorson—just a little misunderstandin' on yer part. We have no interest in aidin' and abettin' a rogue company in ravagin' our river, scarrin' the shoreline, and endangerin' the lives of those who sweat for you," Angus said. "I hope the picture's becomin' a tad clearer for you now."

"You've been playin' me, you sorry-assed mountain man. Who the hell do you think you are? I come in here trying to save you some jobs, and you play the game and make nice, and now you're breaking my balls? What is this shit?" Slick was on his feet, spoiling for a fight.

"Sit down, Mr. Haldorson," Angus directed calmly. "I'm sorry we led you on, laddie, but we just couldna believe you were still with us. This isna the bayou, man. We'd like yer jobs but not if it means despoilin' the water and imperilin' the lives of the workers. Are you daft? Can you really get away with this elsewhere?" As he finished his battery of rhetorical questions, Angus tilted his head slightly to drive home the quizzical look on his face. It was a nice touch.

"Cameron never treated us this way," was all Slick could muster. "He would have whipped those crunchy granola Environment folks good."

"Aye, that he would have. He might even have asked them to whip *him* for a wee bit, too," Angus replied, stifling a grin.

Slick then walked out the door.

We called Muriel together on the speakerphone right after. From her earlier dealings with him, she'd already pegged him as a good old boy but was side-split when we recounted the confrontation. Before leaving, I called the workers' representative and set up a meeting for the following week.

That night, I actually helped Angus paint the top deck of Baddeck 1. I was what you might call a full service EA. I hated painting. But I was still juiced from our remarkable meeting and couldn't sit still long enough to read or watch TV. Besides, Lindsay was away at a symposium in Edmonton on the Triple-E Senate, not that she was a supporter, mind you.

Angus rested his single malt on the engine cowling, and we re-enacted the meeting, taking turns playing the role of "Slick." Angus finished his side of the craft and leaned back against the wall of the boathouse.

"I just cannae believe I'm enjoyin' meself so." He whistled as he cleaned out his brush while I concentrated on painting inside the lines.

Nice.

◆   ◆   ◆

Diary
Wednesday, November 27

My Love,

I've found refuge for my methodological mind in the Standing Committee on Procedure and House Affairs. As in engineering, in the universe of parliamentary procedure, there's usually a right answer and a wrong one. The more I immerse myself in these arcane and esoteric rules, the clearer it becomes that the Standing Orders best serve the interests of the Government and not the Opposition. In short, the rules are not intended to benefit the three major parties equally. Nay, it may appear so on the surface, but underneath throbs the machinery of politics, and the Government has the upper hand.

I've concluded that the greatest gift the Standing Orders bestow on the Government is the power to control the agenda, to manipulate the Order Paper to its own ends. For a majority government, this benefit is more tactical given that the governing party holds all the cards anyway. But in a minority situation, the authority to set the agenda becomes strategic and yields an advantage lost on too many of my colleagues. I'll be keeping my eyes open so as not to compound the Government's edge by being caught with my kilt around my ankles.

I needed your moderating influence yesterday. My temper reigned, and I took offence when an insolent galoot tried to take off my noggin with a cantaloupe. Yes, I do lead an interesting and varied life, do I not? Not to dwell on an incident I'd rather leave behind me, but I returned the melon from whence it came, and it met a sudden stop against the poor sod's skull. I'll never feel quite the same way about cantaloupe again. Daniel said I'm lucky to have escaped without an assault charge or at least without having to grovel in the House in abject apology. I shudder at the thought. But the cameras were rolling the whole time, and the resulting video has been rolling ever since. If one is keeping score of the editorials, most in the country seem to consider my deed a clear case of justifiable "meloning," unleashed in self-defence. I've wasted enough breath and ink on this trifle already.

Daniel joined me in the workshop tonight and actually took brush in hand to help paint Baddeck 1. I'd almost have preferred him to watch in view of his seriously stunted painting skills. He ended up with more paint on his hands, arms, thighs, and even a splotch on his ear lobe, than he did on the bleeding craft. At any rate, 'tis done now, and the dark blue looks lovely. As I'm sure you know, it's your blue though it's come to be mine, too.

I'm knackered after a frenetic day. I've not the brain to tell you about a classic meeting we had with the unevolved head of the gravel plant on the outskirts of town. What an oaf. If we don't ignore serious environmental and health and safety infractions, he'll stop the plant's expansion and shut the damn thing down. Knowing what an eyesore it is, I'd be happy if they ceased operations but for the loss of jobs. Well, there may well be good news on that front, too. After a call I've just had with Norman Sanderson and Deepa, I've another wee idea in the pot, steeping.

I've yet to fly on the ice a second time but am hopeful I'll have my chance in the coming days. I know you're watching over me.

AM

CHAPTER SEVENTEEN

On Monday, December 2 at 4:00 PM, Finance Minister Roger Chartrand rose in the House of Commons and executed a picture-perfect, inward triple-twisting, double flip-flop in the pike position. Rip entry, no splash. It took my breath away.

If the Red Tories had won the battle of the Throne Speech, the hard right supply-siders had clearly triumphed in the war of the mini-budget. The rumours swirling on the Hill had obviously been closer to the truth than I'd thought. In the previous few weeks, the Right-Left split in Cabinet had broken wide open from crack to crevice to chasm. The right wing had been incensed by the "candy-assed Throne Speech" and had dug in for a bloodbath on the mini-budget. As I listened to the Finance Minister's speech in the House, the victor in the latest clash of Tory factions was clear.

I could certainly understand the confusion washing over Canadians. It seemed impossible that the Throne Speech and mini-budget could have been penned by the same party. It was Jekyll and Hyde, Oscar and Felix, Leafs and Habs. An army of spin doctors could never shoehorn Chartrand's fiscal measures into the philosophical framework laid out by the Governor General four weeks earlier. Never mind the lipstick; it was still a pig.

On the eve of what appeared to be a continental, if not global, recession, the highlights of the minority Tory government's mini-budget came into view:

- Another ten-percent cut in personal income tax

- Another one-percentage-point cut in the goods and services tax (GST)

- A ten-percent cut in corporate income tax

- A ten-percent cut in fiscal transfers to the provinces

- A two-year freeze on federal spending

Bottom line? The tax cuts would cost the federal government about $43 billion while the spending freeze and provincial transfer rollbacks would save only

$35 billion. Math was never my strong suit, but didn't that still leave an $8 billion shortfall? Chartrand explained it this way as he closed his mini-budget speech.

"Mr. Speaker, these bold measures will not just help us weather the gathering economic storm but will actually stimulate growth. By putting money back into the pockets of Canadian businesses and taxpayers, we will reap more than we've sewn because the market itself is the very engine of efficiency. And the government is not and can never be. The market will close the fiscal gap but only if we cut taxes and liberate the resources the economy needs to fortify itself for the battle ahead. Mr. Speaker, Canadians want tax cuts. They deserve tax cuts. It's their money. They earned it. By honouring their wishes, we are building our economy and our nation."

I'll take that barf bag now.

The Tories were actually proposing a return to Reaganomics, voodoo economics, supply-side economics—whatever euphemism you liked. They were turning back the clock to the time of the old trickle-down theory that worked oh so well for low-income Americans in the 1980s of Ronald Reagan. Obviously, Milton Friedman had won "Economist of the Month" honours in the Prime Minister's Office. For Liberals, it marked a return to the "bad old days."

Mayhem ensued as a stunned Opposition tried to square the mini-budget they'd just heard with the Throne Speech a month earlier. Insults and profanities ping-ponged across the floor. From my perch in the Members gallery, I watched Angus as his facial hue spun through the colour wheel. I hadn't seen him look so enraged since I'd mistakenly drilled too far through the stern decking of the hovercraft and into his left thigh waiting below. (It was an accident—just a minor flesh wound.) He was on his feet even before the Finance Minister's cheeks met chair.

"Mr. Speaker, point of personal privilege!" Angus boomed above the chaos in the Commons. "Point of personal privilege!"

"Order, order, please!" cried the Speaker. "I can wait." He stood with his hands clasped before him surrounded by his obedient pages. Eventually, the ferocious uproar settled to a modest exchange of heckling.

"Point of personal privilege, the Honourable Member for Cumberland-Prescott."

You'd have thought I'd be used to this sort of thing by now, but no. My heart rate doubled as the scene unfolded below me in slow motion.

"Mr. Speaker, this Government has abused me privileges as a Member of this House. This Government lied to me, lied to his House, and lied to Canadians."

The *L* word was verboten in the chamber, and Angus knew it. The Speaker and the Government side of the House knew it, too. The response was as deafening as it was colourful. With everyone yelling at once, I had to rely on the official Hansard record for the next couple of minutes of the proceedings until the Speaker regained control:

"Shame, shame!"
(Inaudible) "… sanctimonious little—" (inaudible)
"Withdraw that remark, you snaky-haired hermit!"
"Take it back, gas bag! Take it back, you—" (inaudible)
"You're a pile of—" (inaudible)

"Order, please, order!" The Speaker waited like a veteran child-care worker. "Order! Thank you. The Honourable Member for Cumberland-Prescott has used language in this House that is unparliamentary, and I ask him now to withdraw his remark."

Angus rose, the picture of indignation. "Mr. Speaker, I have nothin' but respect for this place and have done me best to honour its traditions. Pray enlighten me as to me offence so that I can reconsider the offendin' words."

The Speaker stood again. "The Honourable Member should know by now that accusing the Government of lying is not permitted in this chamber. I ask him again to withdraw his remark."

"Mr. Speaker, I merely spoke the truth, a concept with which this Government seems wholly unfamiliar. I accept that it may, in the strict parliamentary sense, be offensive to use the word *lied*, as in, 'this Government lied to me, lied to this House, and lied to Canadians,' and so I should like to replace it with *misled*, as in, 'this Government misled me, misled this House, and misled Canadians.' I trust that is satisfactory." Angus smiled sweetly and resumed his seat.

It's hard to describe the outrage of the Government MPs and Ministers as they listened to these statements. Invective and vitriol arced from one side of the House to the other.

"Order, please, order! You will come to order!" shouted the now-inflamed Speaker. "The Honourable Member cannot simply replace one unacceptable term with another. Neither *lied* nor *misled* is acceptable in this place. The Honourable Member is again asked to withdraw the remark, or I shall have no choice but to name him and eject him from the House until it sits again."

Angus up again. "Mr. Speaker, I do apologize. 'Tis not me intention to test yer mettle nor the rules of this House. I'm a newcomer to this place and appreciate yer guidance. Is it acceptable to employ the term *dishonest* as in, 'this Government has been dishonest with me, dishonest with this House, and dishonest with Canadians?'"

"No!"

"How about *not forthright?*"

"No!"

"*Misrepresented?*"

"No!"

"*Played fast and loose with the truth?*"

"Enough! The Honourable Member will withdraw his remark or be named and ejected!" the Speaker thundered.

The House was actually quiet by then as this surreal scene played on. His point now irrevocably and indelibly made, Angus stood once again. "Mr. Speaker, as I said, I'm still new. Can you tell me what it means to be named and ejected for sayin' the Government lied to me, lied to this House, and lied to Canadians? Yer wise counsel will greatly inform me decision," Angus gushed.

The Speaker was one step from infuriated. He answered through gritted teeth.

"It simply means that you are named in Hansard and escorted out of the House by the sergeant-at-arms for the duration of the day's sitting. Now, I ask again, will the Honourable Member please withdraw his remarks?"

Angus wiped the smile from his countenance and drew himself to his full height and width. "Mr. Speaker, I'm grateful for yer illumination of the rules of order. I have too much respect for this House to allow this Government to sully its honourable traditions with deceit and subterfuge. It is the Government's dishonest conduct that is the true affront to this institution, not the words I've used to describe it. This Government has lied to me, lied to this House, and lied to all Canadians. I cannae shrink from that truth, and I cannae withdraw me words despite the high regard in which I hold this place."

Angus then sat back down with his arms crossed in defiance. Liberals cheered, Tories raged, and the NDP didn't quite know what to do. The Speaker merely shook his head and rose yet again. The pages got quite the workout, leaping up and down in time with the Speaker.

"I'm left with no choice but to the name the Honourable Member for Cumberland-Prescott and instruct the sergeant-at-arms to escort him forthwith from the chamber."

The sergeant-at-arms, who actually carried a sword in the name of parliamentary ritual, rose from his seat on the floor of the Commons and strode stone-faced to stand beside the offending Member. Angus slowly stood to wild applause from the Liberal side. The sergeant-at-arms moved his right hand, presumably to seize the left arm of Angus and place him in symbolic custody. The sergeant's hand shot back to his side after a steely glare from Angus. In the midst of a maelstrom of adulation and insult, Angus stared straight ahead as he stepped to the middle of the floor, bowed deeply to the Speaker, then turned and walked out of the House with the sergeant-at-arms doing his best to keep up.

I unclenched as the last vestiges of parliamentary decorum disintegrated on the floor of the Commons.

The broadcast news Monday night and the papers Tuesday morning were filled with stories on the Government's about-face budget and the Angus ejection escapade. The Tory strategy was clear. Bribe Canadians with our own money and then dare the Opposition to bring down the Government and its tax-cutting mini-budget along with it. The success of the Government's gambit turned on one of society's pernicious and persistent forces—greed. The mini-budget bore all the hallmarks of a cynical, manipulative, and desperate political ploy to help the Tories cling to power just a little longer. I had no doubt that the Prime Minister's Office had numbers showing significant public support for tax cuts. I also had no doubt that *The Globe and Mail* or *The National Post* would be in the field within 24 hours, giving us all access to public-opinion research, saying exactly the same thing.

But there was something big missing from the Tories' analysis and from the initial media coverage of Chartrand's speech. The mini-budget threatened to compound the Government's moral bankruptcy with financial insolvency. Giving the people what they thought they wanted would exchange short-term gain for long-term pain. But three weeks before Christmas, the Tory strategists gambled that the Liberals and the NDP wouldn't dare defeat the Government over a budget that promised to give Canadians back some of their hard-earned money—a reasonable view to be sure. But a marked paucity of reasonable people existed in federal politics.

According to Standing Order 84, the mini-budget would be debated in the House for not more than four sitting days, culminating in a vote. The House Leaders had agreed on Tuesday, Wednesday, and Thursday for the first three days. About a dozen MPs from all parties would be on an extended weekend Inter-Parliamentary Union junket in Victoria from Friday to Monday, so the final day of debate and the vote itself were scheduled for the following Tuesday, December 10. The Whip and the House Leader put out the call to clear the decks and be in the House for the Tuesday vote come hell or high water.

Ever transparent and mindful of his commitment to open communications, Angus asked me to organize a public constituency town-hall meeting on the mini-budget. Now, I felt quite confident that the people of Cumberland-Prescott wanted the money promised them in the Tory mini-budget. Conversely, their newly elected MP wanted to kill their tax cuts and their windfall. So Angus and I argued for a time over his town-hall idea. I could see little point in inviting dozens of irate voters to dump all over us in person when we could simply read their nasty letters in the comfort and security of our own office. But as usual, he was insistent, and I was respectful. I stopped after observing that hosting a town hall meeting on the mini-budget was tantamount to sitting atop a carnival dunk tank in Riverfront Park and giving each constituent five baseballs.

We'd organized no such open meeting since the election, so I was forced to concede we were due. I suggested he might consider wearing a raincoat and a catcher's mitt in case cantaloupes were still on special at the Cumberland Food Mart. I booked the West Assembly Hall of the Cumberland United Church for Friday evening. I then called André Fontaine, and he hooked me up with the advertising manager. I placed a quarter-page ad in *The Crier*, selecting a virtually unreadable font and the most boring layout imaginable in the hopes that no one would notice it. Luckily, André Fontaine wrote an entire article, promoting the upcoming meeting. Bless him.

At nine-thirty on Tuesday morning, Sid Russell, the unofficial leader of the workers at Ottawa River Aggregate Inc., arrived in our Centre Block office. He was tall and lean—about 50 years old—and styled his hair in a brush cut. He appeared to be solemn and tense. In the past five years, he and a few others had attempted to organize the workers but had not been successful. Through threat and intimidation, the management at head office had quashed the fledgling union drive well before it had left the starting blocks. We got him seated with coffee in hand before Angus took over.

"Well, Mr. Russell, I'm precious little good at gildin' the lily, so let me deliver the blow bare knuckled so it's quick and clear."

Sid Russell was fishing in his backpack for something but stopped when he processed what he'd heard.

"Mr. Russell, I regret to say that I doonae think yer aggregate operation will be foulin' the river for much longer. We've heard from the rogue who runs it that someone sittin' at head office in Cleveland has his finger on the button. 'Tis only a matter of time before the place closes. I'm sorry, but I cannae support suspendin' the effluent discharge rules just to keep the doors open or even to expand the facility. It just isna right."

I braced myself for the reaction, and by the look of Angus, he did, too.

"Mr. McLintock, I'm way ahead of you. I brought this to show you," he said, waving a VHS tape he'd finally extricated from his pack. "This has gone on long enough. Someone's going to get hurt, and I'm tired of shoveling dead fish into the dumpster."

Sid Russell had shot the tape himself with a Hi8 video camera concealed in a gym bag he had carried around the site. Grainy but clearly discernible images flashed across the screen. The scene was the interior of the facility, perched on the shores of the Ottawa River. It looked like my old residence common room at university after Homecoming weekend. Well, perhaps not quite that bad. We were looking at a workplace out of the early days of the Industrial Revolution. Workers straddled large holes in what appeared to be a rotting floor as they monitored the large and loose conveyor belt that bore mud and rocks from the riverbed. Windows were boarded up, leaving the workspace dim. Some workers wore hard hats and safety boots, but most did not. Sid Russell shook his head as he watched.

"We combine river water with chemical cleansers to wash the mud and sediment off the aggregate we excavate from the shoreline. Then, we dump the waste water right back into the river. The process has been approved by Ontario's Ministry of the Environment but only if we limit our effluent discharge to a provincial standard set when the operation was first certified," Sid explained.

"So what's the problem if MOE has approved it?" I asked.

He pointed back to the screen. At that moment, a pair of hands opened a padlocked door, and the gym-bag cam descended a rickety set of stairs. The camera steadied in front of a large-diameter pipe that angled down through the floor and into the ground below just at the northern wall.

"Well, we're pumping way too much shit into the river," he said matter-of-factly. He then pointed to the screen. "That there, gentlemen, is what we call the *shadow pipe*. We discovered it a month ago when a set of keys was 'borrowed' and copied so we could open that mystery door. The suits are so thick over there that they still don't know we've discovered their dirty little secret." He pointed again to the screen. "That there 24-inch pipe feeds effluent right into the river. There's another 24-inch pipe that runs along the outside wall of the building that also delivers crap to the water. The outside pipe is the one the Environment Canada guys test every month or so. They know nothing about the shadow pipe running beneath the floorboards right under their noses," Sid informed us.

"Are you telling me you're dumping twice as much chemically laced waste water into the river than you're permitted to?" I inquired.

"More than three times the limit," replied Russell. "The shadow pipe empties at twice the flow rate of the approved pipe. Every morning, three of us gather the dead fish before it gets light. Besides that, one of my guys tore up his knee pretty good last week when he went through the floorboards again. The place is a workers'-comp commercial waiting to be shot."

"Can ya leave us the tape, Mr. Russell?" asked Angus. "We'll need it to show the environment officials. You do realize we hafta take it to 'em, doontya?"

"You can have the tape. That's why I brought it. It's just gone too far. What do you figure's going to happen?"

"Well, I doonae know for sure, but I cannae imagine they'll let the plant operate after seein' yer little documentary. I am sorry," Angus said. "But doonae fret yourself just yet. You may not be out of a job for long if providence is with us."

I wasn't sure what Angus had in mind but held my tongue.

Sid Russell left half an hour later. He gave us the tape and agreed to bring the workers together that night for a clandestine meeting at Cumberland United Church. I called as soon as he left, and the elderly woman in the office was able to move the weekly senior's tae-kwon-do lesson to the Minister's lounge. She'd taken a shine to me when I had called earlier about the mini-budget town-hall meeting. This liberated the West Assembly Hall for our impromptu gathering of aggregate workers. If we survived the next month, I pledged to visit the church for a Sunday service and not just to book another room.

Angus and I spent the rest of the morning at the Department of the Environment in Hull. Our meeting with the director general of regional enforcement was arranged on very short notice. There's nothing like the promise of a whistle-blowing videotape to advance a meeting that might normally take weeks to coordinate. Our session with the director general started off slowly but gathered steam when we played the tape. They'd known something was amiss on the river but hadn't been able to prove it. Their frequent effluent test readings all fell within acceptable limits. They were stumped. The videotape revealed the smoking gun—a parallel but hidden effluent-discharge system that tripled the chemical concentrations released into the river.

The director general smacked his forehead in self-flagellation. He admitted his whole department had been duped by one of the oldest scams in the environmental degradation handbook. He looked angry.

The health and safety violations revealed on the videotape were sufficient alone to shut down the company, but the legal procedures through the Department of Labour would take a couple of weeks. So we opted for the much shorter environment route. Pending the signature of the Minister on a shutdown order, which they expected to secure by late afternoon, the gates to Ottawa River Aggregate Inc. would be padlocked the following morning—indefinitely. There'd be no warning. Cleveland would not be pleased with Mr. Haldorson. And Mr. Haldorson would certainly not be coming to the McLintock New Year's levee.

When we made it back to the Hill, it was nearly time for question period and the first day of debate on the mini-budget. Awaiting me was a voice-mail message:

"Addison, it's Bradley Stanton. Look, one of our more generous corporate donors is holding onto a big cheque for us until we clear up a little misunderstanding they seemed to have had with your boy, Angus. This has got to stop, Daniel. I'm now officially calling him 'Anguish' 'cause that's all he's meant to me since he arrived. Just sort out this aggregate company's environmental problem so they'll release the cheque, okay? You know we've got a big-ass debt to pay off from the campaign. Don't make me come down there, Danny boy. Are you reading me? Peace. Out."

Fabulous, just fabulous. I had just flushed what little was left of my political career down the secret secondary effluent-discharge pipe.

On Tuesday afternoon, debate resumed in the House on the following motion as dictated by Standing Order 84.(1): "That this House approve in general the budgetary policy of the Government." As a budget motion, it was, in fact, a vote of confidence in the Government. Defeat the motion and the Government would fall.

The Leader's office had already decided to try to bring down the Government based on its opportunistic, economically devastating, and utterly deceitful mini-budget. Christmas be damned and tax cuts, too. I knew of few, if any, dissenters in the Liberal camp.

During the debate, Angus spoke with passion for the full 20 minutes allotted to each speaker under the Standing Orders. It was not difficult for him to muster emotion when ripping the Government for leading us all on with the progressive Throne Speech only to pull the carpet out from under us with the tax-cutting mini-budget. He called it "duplicity of the first order." Tory MPs heckled like loud drunks at a down-market strip show. Hansard ensured the accuracy of my memory:

"Go ahead, make our day. We dare you to defeat these tax cuts!" (inaudible)
"Canadians want their money."
"Morons." (inaudible) "I smell a majority."
"Go on, vote it down, you—" (inaudible)
"We call your bluff, buffoon boy—" (inaudible)

Ah, the high dignity of parliamentary debate. We should all be so proud.

While Angus made some last-minute calls, Pete2 and I arrived at the church early to make sure it was set up as I'd requested. In other words, we set out the 75 chairs in theatre style and laid out four boxes of doughnuts on arthritic trestle tables at the back. We put another table at the front of the room from which Angus would preside over the proceedings. The fluorescent lighting buzzed above. By seven o'clock, 53 of the 82 workers had arrived, the most we could expect as the remaining 29 employees were toiling on the four-to-midnight shift. Most of the workers were men, but about a dozen women attended, too. The workers consumed the coffee but not the doughnuts. Anxiety and appetite were not very compatible.

Sid Russell and Angus were among the last to arrive and at 7:20, took their places at the front table. The murmuring died away. Much to my surprise, Norman Sanderson slipped into the room and stood at the back. He was smiling as he surveyed the room. So was Angus. He gave me a quick thumbs-up and got to his feet. Pete2 and I stood along the east wall, working our way through the doughnuts.

"Good evenin', all. I'm Angus McLintock, and I've finally accepted that I am, in fact, the Member of Parliament for Cumberland-Prescott. We're here this evenin' through the courage of Sid and many of you. We're here this evenin' to blow the whistle on an unsafe and irresponsible industrial operation that jeopardizes yer health and yer lives, not to mention our beloved Ottawa River. Now, I ask only one thing of you tonight. I need you all to wait until I've finished what I have to say before you rush to judgment. Can I count on yer patience to stay with me until I'm done?" A hum of assent accompanied nodding heads. "Very well, I'll not sugarcoat our news tonight. Yer lives are goin' to change tomorrow mornin'. You may not believe me straight off, but yer lives are goin' to change for the better. At eight o'clock tomorrow mornin', officials from Environment Canada will arrive at Ottawa River Aggregate Inc. and shut it down, probably forever." Angus paused to let that sink in. A smattering of gasps and head shaking ensued, but no one leaped up to challenge Angus.

"Now stay with me. Under the terms of the shutdown order, you'll all be owed severance as required by provincial labour statutes. I'd not bank on seein' that money any time soon, but it will eventually make its way to yer pocket. None of us should lament the long overdue passin' of this particular industrial blight. And we should hoist a glass that there'll be no expansion to make the curse worse. So ends the bad news." Angus again paused. Sid sat impassively with his hands clasped in front of him.

I figured Angus had just about exhausted the patience and self-control of the assembled future ex-employees of Ottawa River Aggregate Inc. He resumed his calm and clear soliloquy.

"Let me introduce the gentleman at the back of the room. He brings with him good news tonight to offset the bad. He is Norman Sanderson, who, until two weeks ago, owned and operated the Sanderson Shoe Company. When his factory reopens in about five weeks, shoes will no longer be rollin' off the assembly line. I'll let him tell you the rest. Norman?"

I'd figured it out before Angus had pointed out Sanderson at the back. I now knew who Angus had been calling as I'd left to pick up Pete2 to make it to the church on time. Norman Sanderson carried himself to the front of the room with a confidence, even a swagger, that had not been part of his repertoire when we'd first met him two weeks earlier.

"Good evening, ladies and gentlemen. I took over the Sanderson Shoe Company from my father 20 years ago. My best year financially was my first year, and even it wasn't so great. Ever since, I've managed a declining business in a declining industry. What it says to me is that modern nations with advanced economies probably don't need to be making their own shoes any more. I had difficulty seeing that for a very long time, but it's crystal clear now thanks largely to Mr. McLintock. In five weeks, the Sanderson Shoe Company will officially become Sanderson Technologies. In five weeks, we'll stop making shoes and start manufacturing an advanced, wireless, Internet wave router developed at the University of Ottawa. As of last Tuesday, I won't be able meet my year-one production targets unless I add another full shift right from the start. You see, the high price of oil has eliminated the import cost advantage our offshore competitors have always enjoyed. So we've just finished negotiating exclusive supply contracts with another six computer manufacturers, giving us deals with the top eighteen. Long story short, we're going to have trouble meeting demand, and we haven't produced a single unit, yet." The room was growing a bit restless.

"Yeah, but we just lost our jobs. Where does that leave us?" shouted a woman from somewhere towards the back. Angus stepped in to rescue Norman.

"Well, madam, if you're interested, it leaves every last one of you gainfully employed by Sanderson Technologies starting in two weeks. The work is safer and cleaner, the pay is better, and yer futures are brighter." Angus stopped to let it sink in.

The workers said nothing for about three seconds; then, they hooted and hollered and rose for a sustained ovation. An hour later, they were still completing applications. As a gesture of good faith, Norman's HR manager arrived to cut advance cheques to cover the new employees' first two-weeks' pay.

Despite the hour, Muriel arrived with Lindsay to witness the historic gathering. She beamed and shuffled over to hug Angus. She even planted one on Norman Sanderson, who looked pleased and shocked at the same time.

Once again, the pieces had all just fallen into place—all but one. I stepped out into the parking lot and reached for my cell phone. I dialed André Fontaine and bit into my sixth doughnut.

◆   ◆   ◆

Diary
Tuesday, December 3

My Love,

Though I can barely recall it after the day we've had, last night I actually finished the very last stroke of painting on Baddeck 1, including repainting every square inch done (badly) by dear Daniel. Though well-intentioned, what an offence he is to the workshop. Bell complained that he could find no skilled help in his day, too. Ah, Bell—to be sequestered on the shores of the Bras d'Or Lakes in that glorious summer home. It must have been idyllic. But I digress.

Daniel is about as handy as the Venus de Milo. Yet, he grows on me still. And he does play chess, which compensates for a great many shortcomings.

I've not yet put the hovercraft through its paces after my initial run across the ice. There's simply been no time. None. My mind has been elsewhere, dueling with a sticky problem. Modesty aside, I think we've sorted it out in a way that's beneficial to all but the rascals who caused the crisis in the first place. Alas, I'm too weary to dwell on the day's excitement. Suffice it to say, I think I did my job well today—my new job. We actually helped people today. We saved some jobs and protected our river, too. It feels good. Like a cool highland breeze on a sweltering day.

My blood boiled yesterday when the Government released its so-called mini-budget. It was supposed to breathe life into the Throne Speech by unveiling the related policies, programs, and funding. All they unveiled was the Government's duplicity and deceit. Aye, those are strong words, but I trust you were there to see for yourself. Was it not the height of arrogance? Was it not opportunism at its zenith? They're preying on Canadians who can no longer distinguish the blurred lines between self-interest and the national interest. One does not always support the other. The clearest examples of this dissonance are the ill-conceived tax cuts, through which the Government hopes to hoodwink the voters even as it bankrupts the nation. I say again—it is duplicitous and deceitful.

I intend to confront my electors later this week to help them to see that we all will pay later for the baubles the Government offers today. Daniel did not wish us to hold such an open and public meeting, but I'm actually looking forward to it. Caring little for how I'm viewed by my own constituents is freedom itself!

I do confess I am enjoying myself. 'Tis the most interesting sabbatical I've yet passed. I keep waiting for the wheels to fall off; but then, I remember that a hovercraft has no wheels, so perhaps I'm safe for a time.

Stay near and lend me your steadying hand when you're able.

AM

CHAPTER EIGHTEEN

It all went down the next morning right on script. I found the entire experience somewhat surreal. I felt as if a "movie of the week" were unfolding before my eyes. When Angus and I arrived at the aggregate operation, two OPP cruisers and an Environment Canada car were parked at odd angles in front of the gate as if they'd skidded to a halt like Starsky and Hutch on a raid. As it turned out, they'd just parked that way. A gleaming padlock and chain secured the large drive-through gates though a small walk-in gate remained open. The official, plastic-laminated shutdown order was fixed to the gate post with duct tape. About 40 workers, most familiar to me from the meeting the previous evening, huddled in small groups outside the gate, hands in pockets, talking quietly.

Notebook and digital recorder in hand, André Fontaine sat on the hood of his car off to the side, talking to several other reporters, all waiting for something to happen. Three satellite trucks with dishes elevated were also parked nearby. Three well-dressed and coiffed reporters with mics in hand were facing their cameras. I looked at my watch: 8:01. The reporters were obviously about to go live. I really had no idea how they caught wind of the shutdown story—none at all.

As Angus and I stepped from his Camry, the cameras turned towards him. In a stroke of cinematic timing, the director general of Environment Canada then emerged from the decrepit building and walked back to his car, flanked by two OPP officers. He waved to Angus and nodded in a "the deed is done" kind of way. He held a clipboard just like in the movies. Our slick friend, Todd Haldorson, walked four paces behind, waving a now-crumpled piece of paper and hurling obscenities at the DG's back. When the workers spied Angus and me, they started chanting, "Angus, Angus, Angus, Angus, Angus."

Slick looked our way, and suddenly, he no longer had the DG in his crosshairs. He rushed to the fence, gripped the steel mesh, and, well, snarled at us—I guess that's the best way to describe it. He looked not unlike the Tasmanian devil in a Warner Brothers cartoon—hyperventilating, eyes bulging, temples pulsing. His lip curled on one side like a Doberman's.

"You commie bastard! I shoulda known. Fuckin' red Liberals. You're pathetic," shrieked "Slick." He pointed to the locked-out workers. "Their jobs are on your head, mountain man."

Angus seemed almost serene as he looked at "Slick." "Dya mean their old jobs or their much better new ones?" Angus said quietly with the slightest trace of a smile. He turned and slid behind the wheel. I got in my side. There was nothing left for us to do there. I'd only suggested we go to make sure Angus was in the media's footage though that's certainly not what I told him. We then circled the gravel parking lot and headed back towards the road with the workers trotting along side, fists pumping the air.

"Angus, Angus, Angus, Angus."

Yes, the cameras caught the whole thing. I didn't even need to see the coverage. I knew how it would play out. I didn't need to see the coverage, but I kind of wanted to. So I clicked among Newsworld, Newsnet, and CPAC in my office while Angus sat in the Commons on House duty. The media fame machine had latched onto Angus and wasn't letting go.

Call display is a wonderful thing. Four times that morning, "B. Stanton" flashed in the little liquid-crystal window on my phone. The Liberal Party would be short one whopping corporate donation, and I figured Stanton would want to take it out of me in ways I cared not to contemplate. Four times, I let the phone ring and ring.

That afternoon, debate on the mini-budget resumed for the second of four scheduled days. Our Finance Critic, as was traditional, moved an amendment to the motion on the floor quite literally to turn it on its head and condemn the Government's financial plan. In addition, again as usual, the NDP introduced a subamendment to the Liberal amendment, which then became the central topic of debate for day two. Hard to keep straight, parliamentary procedure is not noted for its simplicity.

The Liberals and the NDP could not reach agreement on how to play the amendments and subamendments that always attend the central budgetary-policy motion. As a consequence, when debate ended late Wednesday afternoon, the NDP subamendment was defeated—to the Government's satisfaction, even amusement.

On Thursday morning, the papers reported on the first polls conducted to gauge public support for the Government's tax-cut budget. The numbers spelled out exactly what I expected and what the Government already knew. When Canadians were asked whether they favoured the mini-budget that left hundreds, if not thousands, of dollars (depending on income) in their pockets, a considerable majority said yes.

I've always thought that a democracy works best when its citizens are prepared to forego personal benefit to protect the collective interest. Unfortunately, with cynicism in our democratic institutions running at peak levels, the catchphrases were "everyone for himself," "look out for number one," and "take whatever you can get." This mini-budget symbolized and helped entrench this jaded, me-first mentality.

The poll, covered extensively in all major dailies, not to mention the broadcast media, revealed that Canadians wanted their tax breaks and wanted them now. The numbers softened when the mini-budget was placed in the context of an impending recession—but only slightly. If the Government were going to batten down the fiscal hatches as the bottom dropped out of the economy, let it happen after the public had taken back some its hard-earned, begrudgingly paid tax dollars. Putting no stock in supply-side economics, Angus was convinced that not only would the tax cuts fail to stimulate any meaningful economic growth, they would, in one fell swoop, plunge the country back into the dark days of crippling deficits.

Predictably, the Government embraced the new survey, trumpeted it from the rooftops, and flogged it shamelessly. By that evening, two more polls had been released, mirroring the morning survey's results. The regional cross-tabs revealed virtually no differences across the country. The polling results fortified the Prime Minister for the fight in the Commons and crystallized his belief that the Opposition would ultimately back down in the face of such overwhelming public support. With Canadians so strongly behind him, he was convinced his Government would carry the vote.

The debate on the Liberal amendment raged all Thursday afternoon. Dictated by the Standing Orders, the vote on our amendment was called for 6:00 PM. We lost it. The NDP MPs were still angry that we hadn't supported their subamendment and so voted against our amendment. They took their marbles and went home, leaving us alone to play with ourselves. Of course, the possibility existed, though I could never confirm it, that the Tories had bought off the NDP somehow. It had happened before.

We weren't exactly on speaking terms with the NDP, but I had hoped that making up was on the Leaders' agendas for the weekend. We were left with one more opportunity to defeat the Government. By unanimous consent, the fourth and final day of debate and the vote on the Government's budgetary-policy motion were set for the following Tuesday. If we voted together, the Government would fall, and it would be Happy Holidays on the hustings. If not, it would be a Progressive Conservative Christmas with the Finance Minister filling stockings with tax dollars. In either event, our New Year's resolution would have to be to play more nicely with the NDP or get used to life in Opposition.

Friday dawned crisp and clear. I was still having trouble with that evening's town-hall meeting, particularly after poring over the polls. On the drive into Ottawa, I appealed to Angus again while I still had time to shut it down.

"Angus, we now know where Canadians stand on the mini-budget," I opened. "And recent history suggests that support for tax cuts in Cumberland is likely the highest in the country. We know what they're going to say tonight. The only question is what are they going to throw?"

"Aye, I grant you that. We know what they're goin' to say. But that isna why we've called the meeting," said Angus.

On instinct, I nodded in agreement. I eventually stopped nodding as my thinking caught up. "So remind me again exactly why we've called this little gathering if not to solicit your constituents' views on the mini-budget?"

"I'm not lookin' for their input on this. Quite the contrary. Frankly, I couldna care less what me constituents think," Angus countered.

"Friendly suggestion, Angus? Keep that thought to yourself at the meeting," I counseled. "Some voters might not rush to embrace your isolationist perspective on democracy. Crazy as it sounds, some constituents might even think you should be interested in their views. I know it's a radical notion, but there it is."

"Sarcasm really doesna become you," Angus chided. "I believe I understand the traditional relationship most MPs have enjoyed with their voters, and I've little interest in perpetuatin' it. I was elected. I will advance me views as I see fit, guided as I always am by me conscience. This budget is a fiscal disaster, poised to wreak havoc on our economy and spill red ink all over the nation's books. Against that backdrop, I care not a fig for the selfish views of greedy constituents lookin' to cash in their tax cuts."

I held up my hands in surrender, at least until we drifted over the centre line. "Message received loud and clear. But my question stands. Why put yourself through a town-hall meeting that will probably degenerate into nothing but a Salem witch trial with you playing the role of lead heretic?" I asked.

"While I care precious little what the voters think, I do believe I've a duty to explain me views with clarity and candour," he noted. "And that's what tonight's about—educatin' the masses."

"Well, not to put too fine a point on it, let me be clear and candid. You're committed, you're compelling, and you're persuasive," I observed, "but tonight, you'll be standing between taxpayers and their hard-earned money. Tonight, if we're lucky, being right will only get you verbal abuse and maybe another melon hurler with a better arm. And if we're not lucky, well, I'll park near the door and leave the engine running."

"I doonae think yer givin' the great citizens of Cumberland-Prescott enough credit," Angus replied.

"Angus, you're tilting at windmills on this one. They don't want any more credit. They're looking for cold, hard cash."

By this time, I'd pulled into our prime parking space on the Hill.

"Very clever," was all he said as he climbed out and walked towards the back door of Centre Block, not bothering to wait for his loyal Sancho Panza.

Still, I stressed about the town-hall meeting. And I was right to worry. As with the meeting of the aggregate workers three days earlier, I arrived at the church an hour before the meeting. The two Petes were already there, disguised as normal citizens, trying to control the flow of placard-waving constituents into the room so we could arrange the chairs, two floor mics, and the podium at the front. Muriel and Lindsay had wanted to attend, but I had insisted they stay clear, given the fireworks that were likely to ensue. To my amazement, they reluctantly agreed.

I brought the coffee—decaf, of course—and doughnuts with me, courtesy of the local Tim Hortons, and not a moment too soon. Nothing calms bellicose belligerents like free food. And too, until we evolve a third hand, protestors simply cannot swig coffee, chew on Boston cream doughnuts, and pump a placard all at the same time—chapter 14 of the "Creative Crowd Control Handbook."

The church caretaker helped as we aligned the chairs and warmed up the temperamental PA system from the early days of radio. Eventually, even the most cantankerous constituents sank into seats. The church minister hovered at the back, wringing his hands and hoping horse-borne riot police were not in his future.

At ten minutes to seven, Angus made his entrance to a chorus of boos and foot stomping. Obviously, people could still stomp their feet while dipping their doughnuts. The vehemence of the crowd seemed to startle Angus—I could tell by the way his eyes widened for a split second before he gathered himself and headed to the front. I met him at the podium and smiled in a way that shouted "I tried to warn you." I tilted my head towards the emergency door with the crash bar at our end of the assembly hall. "The Taurus is just outside," I whispered. He nodded, looking grim. He'd actually thought I'd been kidding when I'd mentioned proximal parking in our earlier chat. Always be prepared. I leaned into the mic. "Good evening, ladies and gentlemen and—"

"It may be good for you, asshole, but we're pissed!" yelled an enlightened and courteous constituent.

Normally, such a rude heckler would be shouted down or at least "shushed" by others in the room. Well, we were a long haul from normal that night. Emboldened, the assembled throng cheered. I caught Angus glancing at the emergency exit.

"Um … welcome to Angus McLintock's first town-hall meeting, and thank you for coming." I'd reserved the room till ten o'clock, but at that moment, three hours seemed unduly long—torturously long. I improvised. "Just a housekeeping note, this room is booked at eight o'clock for a seniors' tae-kwon-do class. Now, I don't know about you, but I'm certainly not eager to anger a group of aging martial-arts experts, so we'll have to wrap up by eight o'clock if that's—"

"This won't take that long, asshole!" Same guy, same reaction from the crowd.

I saw André Fontaine in the back, standing because no chairs were left. He flashed me a grimace of sympathy and fingered the shutter button on his Canon Sure Shot.

"Ladies and gentlemen, I'll now ask Angus McLintock, MP for Cumberland-Prescott, to take the floor. Ang—"

"Oh, don't worry, asshole. He'll be taking the floor all right." That guy was beginning to bug me.

"Nice set up, laddie," Angus muttered as he passed me on the way to his crucifixion.

At the mention of his name, the crowd thrust their placards into the air—primitive but effective, handwritten signs. They never get old.

IT'S OUR MONEY!
GIVE IT BACK!
TAXES BAD! TAX CUTS GOOD!
KEEP THE PROMISE
$AVE OUR TAX CUTS!
Etcetera, etcetera

Angus stood at the podium and rocked back and forth, releasing anxiety from foot to foot. The crowd simply would not let him start. Every time he raised his hand or tried to speak, the chanting reignited. "Taxes, no! Tax cuts, yes! Taxes, no! Tax cuts, yes!" Their creativity left much to be desired. They even dusted off an old chestnut: "What do we want? Tax cuts! When do we want them? Now!" How lame.

Angus was about to blow. The crimson tide flowed up the back of his neck, and his knuckles oscillated from white to red as he gripped the lectern. He was ready to take them all on—just how you want your MP to react in such situations.

Thirty seconds later, the two Petes and I put the "crash" in crash bar and literally dragged Angus from the hall in a hail of doughnuts. We took several direct hits before we made it out the door. Angus had red jelly in the middle of his forehead and two honey-glazed Timbits enmeshed in his beard.

"Just be glad I brought doughnuts and not cocoanuts," I commented as we fishtailed out of the parking lot. In the rear-view mirror, I watched as Pete2 calmly pulled a half a cruller from Pete1's shoulder and crammed it in his mouth.

"Barbarians!" Angus exclaimed. "Whatever happened to respectful and civil debate?"

The two Petes sat in silence in the back seat, unwilling to enter the fray. We dropped them off at their punkhouse and headed home.

My heart was still pounding. "The next time you want to have a public meeting to explain your opposition to a Government policy everybody loves, let's just write an article in your householder and be done with it," I proposed as we climbed out of the car. "Think of the money we'd save on dry cleaning." I pointed to the four-inch blotch of chocolate on the left lapel of his ill-fitting blue blazer.

"Aye, you've made yer point. You need not pound it till it stops breathin'."

We parted paths in the driveway and headed for our respective sanctuaries. I dreaded the front page of the next *Cumberland Crier*.

The following morning, heavy overcast skies turned the frozen river slate grey. The wind had again cleared a smooth ice path in the middle that stretched as far as the eye could see in either direction. On that ice, a lead pass and a breakaway could take you all the way to Ottawa.

I cherished my Saturday mornings. I usually luxuriated in bed until about seven-thirty. (I'd lost the ability to sleep in when I had turned 30.) Then, at first light, I'd read whatever novel I had on the go for an hour or so. Then I'd get up, pull on sweatpants and a long-sleeved T-shirt, and settle into my leather couch in the living room to devour the newspapers. I loved the Saturday papers. That Saturday, though, I had a better idea. I really didn't want to open the papers yet, anyway—and certainly not *The Crier*.

I knew he was up. I could see his lights on inside. I wrestled both his latte and my hot chocolate into my left hand, freeing my right to rap on the door.

"Starbucks delivery," I said as he opened the door. He took the latte; I just caught the hot chocolate before it slid out of my hand.

"Ah, mornin', Daniel. I thank you. I could use a boost," Angus replied, waving me in.

I headed for the chess table and gave him a face full of arched eyebrows as I inclined my head towards the board. He seemed discouraged—a reasonable reaction to the previous night's debacle. Perhaps he'd already forced himself to peruse *The Crier*. I hoped not and didn't ask. To his credit, he nodded and took his place opposite.

As usual, I moved e2-e4. He replied with e7-e5 this time, and we were off. Through the centuries, chess has been a wonderful diversion. As the game develops, your cerebral resources, by necessity, shift from your problems in life to your challenges on the board. It is unalloyed escapism. By the time Angus skewered my rook on move 24, he seemed to have returned to his customary demeanour. In the succeeding two hours, he beat me twice while I actually took game three. Thrilling endgame. One of my real weaknesses is a pawn-heavy endgame. I always seem to mess up the late-game pawn advance and end up losing mine and promoting my opponent's. But that day, I managed to marshal my brain power and promote one of my pawns for a queen. Six moves later, I'd thwarted any and all attempts by Angus to move his pawns onto my back rank. He conceded.

"Well played, laddie," he offered. "It all turned on one move you made with yer king to protect that passed pawn about ten moves ago. From there on in, 'twas done."

"Yeah, but I'll be a basket case for the remainder of the day. I've not a single synapse of brain function left."

Angus looked past me out over the river with that faraway focus that made me think he was looking at nothing at all. "I really thought that if I could just explain the fiscal folly of the mini-budget that they'd be right there with me," he said slowly and quietly. "I obviously underestimated the power of a few dollars to blind reasonable people."

"In this selfish age, I suppose it is asking too much of voters to look beyond a modest windfall and consider its longer-term cost. We're really not built to think that way, yet," I suggested.

"Aye, and that's why it's in the public interest to elect someone who is built that way—someone who can help them navigate this twistin' road to understandin' and acceptance. That's precisely what I planned to do last night. I knew they were mad. But I thought I could turn 'em if I could just have their ears for a wee bit."

"Angus, you're really way out in front on this issue. I think we're going to need some time and some allies before people on the street come around. It doesn't mean we should stop fighting the tax cuts; it just means we should pick our spots and accept modest progress as success," I reasoned.

"Aye, I cannae argue with you. Feel free to remind me what it feels like to face a rabble like that the next time me confidence clouds me judgment."

"That's my job."

I finally grabbed *The Crier* at about two-thirty Saturday afternoon. It was just what I would have run were I laying out the front page. Staring back at me was a full-colour photo of Angus, standing in defiance at the front of the town-hall meeting. The infamous jelly doughnut was about six inches from hitting his considerable forehead. André had snapped the photo with such fortuitous timing that Angus's eyes were actually crossed, having followed the flight path of the doughnut till it was right above the bridge of his nose. It was the kind of image that might make it to the annual photo issue of *Life* magazine although I prayed not. The shot was as hilarious as it was brilliant if you didn't happen to work for, let alone be, Angus McLintock. The story, however, was reasonably balanced and conveyed the essence of our opposition to the irresponsible mini-budget. It was a good thing André had interviewed Angus before the fateful town-hall meeting.

I reached for *The Globe and Mail*. In its "Focus" section, the newspaper had gathered a panel of eminent economists and respected think tanks to assess the Tory mini-budget in the context of the deteriorating national and global economic situation. I hoped Angus had seen it. I also hoped every last one of the pack of town-hall protestors had read the extensive article. There's an old joke that tells of what happens when you put 10 economists in a room. Answer: You wind up with 11 different theories. Having worked with several economists in preparing the Leader to respond to past Tory budgets, I could vouch for the punchline's validity.

But across time, rare events united the most disparate collection of economists. The Tory mini-budget could now be added to that short list. The C. D. Howe Institute, the Fraser Institute, the Conference Board of Canada, the chief economist from each chartered bank, the former head of the Bank of Canada, and three former deputy ministers of Finance found common ground in denouncing the Government's mini-budget. Common themes ran through their arguments against the massive-tax-cut approach. I had never witnessed such solidarity among a group of economists.

Supply-side economics had met with some success in the United States during the 1980s, but that was when the American economy was just rebounding. The optimism of the Reagan revolution gave Americans permission to spend their tax-cut gains and boost consumer spending. In Canada, as the economy deteriorated, the economic thinkers on the *Globe* panel agreed that Canadians would not risk spending their tax-cut money but would, instead, shove it under their mattresses. The Government's promise that the budget would actually stimulate the economy required Canadians to spend their tax-cut dividends and spend fast. This assumption was dubious at best, ludicrous at worst. Other grounds for agreement among the panel existed, including a unanimous belief that a decade of deficits was inevitable under the Tory plan.

I hoped the piece would be the first of many credible and compelling assaults on the Government's fiscal ineptitude. Such thoughtful media analysis would certainly help to turn the tide of public opinion even against the promise of refunded taxes. But it would take time. With the vote set for Tuesday, we had not a moment to lose. At the very least, I hoped the elite opposition emerging in the media would help ally the Liberals and the NDP for the vote.

On Sunday afternoon, Lindsay and I drove through light snow to Ottawa to visit the National Gallery of Canada. Despite working in Ottawa for so many years, I was embarrassed to admit I'd never set foot in the place. For the uninitiated, the National Gallery is a wonderful introduction to the highfalutin world of art. My knowledge of art is somewhat limited—okay, very limited. Once past Picasso, da Vinci, Rembrandt, and the Group of Seven, I'm at sea. Lindsay knew much more than I and helped me keep pace with the walking tour, narrated on the electronic headsets we'd donned. Irrespective of my plebian appreciation for art, spending the afternoon with Lindsay was just the respite I needed.

Shortly after we entered the gallery, I watched through the glass walls as snow began to fall heavily. Two and a half hours later, after we'd viewed a touring photography exhibit and visited a special gallery dedicated to the works of Tom Thomson, we emerged from the gallery into what seemed like the second coming of the Ice Age. The storm had evolved into a full-on blizzard with gale-force winds. Massive snowdrifts had already formed wherever the gusts found room to manoeuvre.

We left the car in the gallery lot and finally caught a cab that shimmied its way south along the Queen Elizabeth Driveway. Taking twice as long as it might have on a clear day, we eventually made it to The Ritz, a comfortable Italian restaurant perched on the edge of the frozen canal. The storm had chased all but the heartiest skaters from the ice and explained the many unoccupied tables. We had garlic bread with cheese and held hands. I ordered spaghetti carbonara while Lindsay opted for mushroom risotto. We didn't really talk a great deal. We'd moved beyond that. Across the two and a half hours we spent at The Ritz, we watched the storm intensify and the growing drifts consume newspaper boxes and a couple of unlucky cars parked in spots that seemed to welcome the wind and snow.

By the time we paid and left the restaurant, the streets were pretty well deserted. I gave thanks for parking underground.

"I've never seen it like this. It's still coming down," noted Lindsay.

"Yep, it's quite the dump. Something tells me we won't be driving the Taurus back to Cumberland tonight," I said, curious about her response.

"Sounds like the snow storm corollary to running out of gas on a first date," she replied, still smiling. "Let's try the Château."

Though it was not particularly cold, the wind was unforgiving. There were few cars out and not a taxi in sight. So we walked up Elgin Street as it seemed more navigable than the canal. The sidewalks were completely impassable, so we stuck to the middle of the street, swinging wide around monstrous snowdrifts that rose out of the road at irregular intervals.

The Château Laurier was built on the eastern edge of Parliament Hill and the Rideau Canal. The Château was aptly named, featuring steeply raked, copper-roofed towers and limestone walls. For nearly a century, it had been the hotel of choice for political power brokers. I'd stayed there occasionally, too. The lobby was congested, but the line snaking away from the reservations counter moved quickly.

"Any chance?" I asked, leaning on the marble.

"I've got two rooms left," announced the desk clerk. "Would you like a view of Parliament Hill or the river?"

I was feeling kind of excited, not so much about another night alone with Lindsay, but just about sharing the whole stranded-by-snow scenario with her.

The room was perfect—old-world charm with new-world plumbing, not to mention those fluffy robes. Lindsay called her mother. I called Angus. He reminded me that André Fontaine was coming to the house in the morning for a long-arranged feature interview. We'd put him off as long as we could. Angus had gained enough perspective on the town-hall meeting by then to laugh at *The Crier* photo when he'd finally seen it. So the Fontaine interview was still on.

Lindsay and I ordered dessert from room service and turned the small loveseat around in the window so we could watch the ferocious storm's assault on Parliament Hill. I'm not given to using the word *cozy*. I'm just not a fan. But the shoe fit.

◆   ◆   ◆

Diary
Sunday, December 8

My Love,

Welcome to Siberia. I've seldom seen a storm of such relentless fury aided by such fierce winds. Heavy snow and a big blow is a potent, paralyzing tandem. I had planned to take another test run in Baddeck 1 this afternoon, but Old Man Winter's tantrum put the boots to that. Still, with what visibility the storm affords, I can see the winds are keeping the river clear and the ice smooth. Perhaps on the morrow.

You'll be pleased to know, though I'm sure you were with me, the gravel operation you detested so much was padlocked today by the Government's enforcement folks, and we had a hand in it. The outlaws were dumping far more toxic tripe into the river than the rules allowed. Why they'd be permitted to dump any at all is beyond my ken. They'll not soon be up and running again, either. In fact, I think it's well and truly over. God bless and good riddance.

Sanderson has granted jobs to every displaced aggregate worker and is still wanting. 'Tis a nice problem to have as the economy dips into a dive. The papers have been quick to cover me with glory; yet, without Deepa's brilliant mind, the win-win everyone's calling it would have been a lose-lose.

I confess my arrogance got the better of me on Friday at the town-hall meeting I insisted on convening—against Daniel's advice. I swaggered into the room, feeling like Moses bearing the tablets. I knew my constituents were mad and wanted the money the Government had pledged them. I reckoned I'd lay the logic before them and they'd see the light and throw rose petals at my feet. As it turned out, they saw red and threw doughnuts at my head. A wee miscalculation caused by my recently enlarged cranium.

I know I'm right on the mini-budget. The Government has made a cynical appeal to our baser instincts of greed and aggrandizement. It seems others with more knowledge of such things than I are now popping up to lend a hand. The paper today was full of smart people decrying the Government's gambit. Let more come forward before the vote on Tuesday.

I took Muriel to lunch yesterday, bless her heart and mind. That Parkinson's is a right bastard, it is. She knows where she wants to go, but her feet just can't get started. That problem would be the end of me, but she, at least figuratively, takes it in stride. She was mortified to hear of our narrow escape from the town-hall meeting and roundly chastised me for not thinking the whole thing through. She urged me to listen to Daniel. As a neophyte, I'm hardly in a position to know, but Muriel claims Daniel is one of the best and can help me dodge the slings and arrows of partisan politics.

We played chess this morning. I defeated Daniel in the first two games, and then, just because I'm such a treasure, I purposely messed up my pawn march at the end so that Daniel took the win. He needed it more than I.

Saints alive, the storm still rages beyond these walls. I fear I'll not be leaving this refuge tomorrow although I'm to be on House duty in the afternoon. Do you remember the day just after we moved here when the snow shut us down for nearly a week? We never stirred from in front of the fire. We had dry wood, candles, wine, books, and one another. We wanted for nothing. I can think of little else as this blizzard airs out its anger.

AM

CHAPTER NINETEEN

Ottawa is one of the world's coldest capitals, and we're used to it now. The snow falls early, often, and heavy yet slows the city rarely and barely. When I lived downtown during my years in the Leader's Office, I walked to the Hill every day. In the deepfreeze of winter, I legitimately feared frostbite during my two-legged, one mile commute. To avoid hypothermia, I would plot a route that passed through the lobbies of several office buildings and one shopping concourse. It was the only way to go—stretches of six or seven minutes of crystalline cold, punctuated by brief respites of welcome warmth. Few Canadians are more relieved to reach their offices in the morning than Ottawa walkers.

None of that prepared me for the city I surveyed from the window of our room in the Château Laurier on Monday morning, December 9. Flying in the face of meteorological convention, the high winds and heavy snow of the day before persisted throughout the night and still raged at sunrise, leaving the streets, buildings, and Parliament Hill itself virtually unrecognizable. The open lawn on which huddled Centre Block, East Block, and West Block, offered the perfect staging area for the gale-force gusts. In places, the drifts reached the second floor in all three buildings. The main door to East Block had disappeared beneath a steep slope of snow left in the wind's wake. I watched a small snowplow try in vain to clear a path from the Wellington Street driveway to the entrance of the House of Commons. It made it half way, slowed, struggled, and then stopped. It could go no farther. Steam or smoke or both rose from the stranded jeep. The driver smashed his fist onto the hood and trudged towards Centre Block, his legs disappearing with each step.

The Weather Channel promised relief in the early afternoon when the storm was to flag. Lindsay had nothing till two o'clock when she was scheduled to lead a first-year poli-sci tutorial. I assumed the university, like the rest of the city, would be shut down anyway. As agreed, I left her asleep as I made my way to Centre Block at around nine-thirty. By that time, a second, more powerful snowplow had completed the northwest passage to the Peace Tower and the doors beneath. The scene looked surreal.

I found very few people in Centre Block although the stalwart Commission-aires were on duty, protecting Parliament's perimeter. I heard nothing but dead silence, outside and in, as if I were there at dawn on Sunday instead of at mid-morning on Monday. I never really minded working the odd Sunday. With the phone silent and interruptions rare, I could usually achieve more in a couple of hours on a Sunday than I ever could in a full day during the workweek.

By noon, I noticed more activity in the halls but nowhere near the normal level. I kept the television in my office tuned to the local Ottawa CTV affiliate and watched as the cancellations rolled in. All primary and secondary schools were closed. Most child-care centres were closed. Libraries, community centres, municipal offices, and federal departments—all closed. Buses weren't running, either. The House of Commons would have to open briefly until unanimous consent could close it for the day.

Somehow, the newspapers had made it through the storm and to our office door. I flipped through *The Ottawa Citizen* and clicked through several other Canadian dailies on the Web. Influential opposition to the Tory mini-budget was mounting—first, the *Globe* panel on the weekend and now, scathing editorials in *The Citizen, Toronto Star, The Calgary Herald, Edmonton Journal, Halifax Chron-icle Herald,* and *The Winnipeg Free Press*. Favoured words included "opportunis-tic," "irresponsible," and the ever-popular "deceitful" and "cynical." Columnists also weighed in on both sides of the debate with the lonely two Government sup-porters crushed under an onslaught of informed and articulate opposition. It was the kind of coverage that could turn public opinion in a matter of days. I sus-pected anxiety levels would be running in the red at the PMO. They had clearly miscalculated the high backfire potential of the tax-cut mini-budget. It went up light and fluffy on December 2 but amidst heavy flak, was coming down fat and fast on the ninth.

At two o'clock, I called Angus. André Fontaine had arrived at noon for their nine o'clock interview. I was surprised he'd even tried the trip, but André wanted that feature piece, and he couldn't complete it without the interview. Angus didn't care. He was marooned at home, anyway. He told me they were having coffee and watching the storm as it finally abated. I had one eye on the television where the House of Commons materialized at about 2:05, following the daily prayer, which was not broadcast. My spidey senses were tingling.

"Hang on a sec, Angus," I said into the phone as I turned up the volume.

Liberal House Leader "Dickhead" Warrington had risen to seek unanimous consent to close the House due to the storm. Very few MPs were present in the chamber. The Speaker rose, looking bored. "Is there unanimous consent to suspend these proceedings until tomorrow at this same hour?"

A chorus of "Aye" rang out, and then, after a slight pause, a lone "Nay" sounded. The dissent came from the Government House Leader himself, who then stood to be recognized. "Mr. Speaker, we have a very full agenda, and despite the weather, I see no reason to delay this Parliament's important business." He then sat down. The Speaker raised his hands in surrender. Unanimous consent meant exactly that. One dissenting voice could turn back the majority. I lowered the volume on the ensuing boos and heckles and slid the phone back to my ear.

"Sorry, Angus, but the Government House Leader just killed the motion to suspend today's sitting."

"You mean the whole region is shut down, and he wants us to gather in the chamber and carry on as if it's just another day?" asked Angus.

"Yep, that's exactly what I mean." I heard nothing but Angus's breathing on the other end.

Finally, he spoke. "No no, I cannae believe they'd stoop to that depth."

"What are you talking about?"

"Daniel, the Government may be playin' us for fools. How many members do we and the NDP have in the House?"

"By the looks of it on TV, not very many. The Government benches seem a little fuller," I noted.

"Then, I suggest you get off the blower with me and get to the Leader's office. I reckon the Government's tryin' to force the mini-budget vote when they've the numbers to win it," Angus said, his voice rising. "The slimy sons o' brigands!"

"Angus, relax. That vote's not till tomorrow. There was all-party agreement on the debate schedule," I reminded him.

"I'm well aware of the schedule but you doonae understand what I'm sayin'. The tide is turnin' against the Government. I'm sure you've seen the papers this mornin'. They could lose the vote when everyone shows up tomorrow. But they could very well win it if it's held today when so many MPs are snowbound," he explained.

"But Angus, it can't be done, there was all-party agreement. They wouldn't dare mess with that," I countered.

"My boy, all-party agreement is a whisper in a wailin' wind to this Government. They're desperate. I've told you before, the rules of the house favour the governin' party. The budget motion is already sittin' on the Order Paper. The Government House Leader has only to call it, and the despicable deed is done."

Angus had become quite the procedure geek since joining the Standing Committee, but I was still unconvinced. "But that would mean violating all-party agreement, not to mention parliamentary tradition," I replied.

"Daniel, the way their mini-budget's unravelin', it may well be their only hope of survival. I feel it in me bones. They're about to swindle us."

It still sounded far-fetched but discretion was the better part of valour. I called and warned Bradley Stanton, giving Angus the credit for unearthing the Tory stratagem. He, too, was skeptical but had always survived by a "take no chances, take no prisoners" approach to politics. So the call went forth across the land to all Opposition Members, Liberals, and NDPers alike, wherever they were, to brave the blizzard and make it to the House by six o'clock. If the Government were actually going to renege on its promise and call the vote 24 hours early—on a snow day, to boot—I was convinced history would view it as the Pearl Harbor of political sneak attacks. December 9 would live in infamy in the annals of Canadian politics.

With so few MPs in the House, and even fewer Ministers, question period that afternoon was not the spectator sport it often was. The chamber was so sparsely populated that inexperienced backbenchers were called upon to pose the lead-off questions. It was generous in the extreme to say the questions were boring. Mildly put, the performance could have rendered a charging rhinoceros unconscious before the second supplementary. I stayed awake to witness the pivotal moment as question period drew to a close. The live broadcast of the House proceedings offered a very narrow slice of what was actually going on in the chamber. The cameras stayed trained either on the Speaker or on whichever Member was on his or her feet. Little else could be seen on TV. So I zipped over to the Members' gallery for an all-encompassing view and made it just in time. As the Minister of Veterans' Affairs droned on in response to what the clock confirmed was the last question, my heart rate rose as I watched the Government House Leader stand up and approach the Clerk's table. I was forced to concede that Angus might well have been on to something.

The Government House Leader finished his brief conversation with the Deputy Clerk, who was standing in for the vacationing Clerk, leaving the black-robed parliamentary expert looking as if he'd just slipped off his bicycle seat onto the crossbar below. The Tory House Leader resumed his seat, looking cool and calm. The Deputy Clerk conferred briefly with the Speaker, who listened but then shrugged his shoulders in submission. Following Routine Proceedings, the Speaker stood once more. "Orders of the Day."

The Deputy Clerk stood, holding the Order Paper, which vibrated in his trembling fingers.

"Order number seven, resuming the adjourned debate on the motion: 'That this House approve in general the budgetary policy of the Government,'" intoned the Deputy Clerk in a voice that sounded tense and taut. He repeated his words in French and then dropped back into his chair as fast as gravity permitted.

Understanding slowly dawned on the rest of the House. The Tories had laid down their cards on the Clerk's table in the calculated hope they had a winning hand. The chips would fall in a couple hours—but would the Government?

"Dickhead" was immediately on his feet, enraged. "Point of order, Mr. Speaker. Point of order!" he shouted.

"I ask the Honourable Opposition House Leader to calm himself and present his point of order," replied the Speaker, well aware of the ignominious precedent the Government was setting.

"Mr. Speaker, we had all-party agreement to conclude the mini-budget debate and vote tomorrow, not today. It is an unparalleled abuse of office, of our rights and privileges as Members, and of the traditions of this place. It is also an insult to the people of Canada. I ask you to intervene to set things right." "Dickhead" sat down and looped the small audio speaker over one of his elephantine ears to hear above the roar.

"Order, order. I remind the Honourable Opposition House Leader that while calling this motion to the floor today may well violate parliamentary tradition and violate all-party agreement, it does not violate the Standing Orders that govern all that is done in this place," the Speaker decreed. "Resuming the adjourned debate. The Honourable Member for Vancouver East."

With that, the Speaker sat down and a Tory backbencher stood and delivered a passionate and partisan defence of the Government's mini-budget.

So that was it. They had really done it—and on a day when the elements had stranded nearly half the MPs wherever they'd laid their heads the previous night. Travelling to Centre Block from outside Ottawa was impossible, and making it from within Ottawa was next to impossible. Most streets in the city were impassable and all major thoroughfares into and out of Ottawa were closed and not expected to be plowed and opened for up to 48 hours. The airport had been closed since late Sunday night, leaving many MPs trapped in their constituencies. By my informal head count during question period, the Tories had about 17 MPs while the Opposition parties mustered only about 13. The Standing Orders set quorum at 20, including the Speaker.

The time by then was close to 4:00 PM with the vote scheduled for 6:00 PM. Both the Government and the Opposition parties had about two hours to get as many of their MPs as humanly possible into the House. The life of the Government hinged on the vote. I rushed back to the office to work the phones. Time was very short.

When I phoned Angus, my call rang into his voice mail. I figured he was on the phone. I hung up without leaving a message and called the Leader's office. They already had a phone tree going. For the next hour and a half, Liberal MPs stuck in and around Ottawa made Herculean efforts to reach Centre Block. Two MPs who roomed together in a Hull condo found an open sporting-goods store and bought cross-country skis. They made it to the House in plenty of time, leaving their new purchases stuck upright in a snowbank next to the west door of Centre Block. An NDPer snowshoed two miles from deep in the Glebe and made it. A young Liberal MP in his first term, representing Ottawa-Gatineau, roared all around Ottawa on his snowmobile, dragging a trailer sleigh of sorts filled with caucus mates. He considered making the run to Cumberland for Angus, but a broken timing belt put an end to that icy side trip. The Tories had their own stories of derring-do as well. It was a race to fill the benches by 6:00 PM.

The speeches in the House that afternoon were as predictable as they were passionate. The Government Members defended their tax cuts with religious zeal while the Opposition railed against the Tories' audacious opportunism. Clearly, MPs on both sides of the House had been counting on another day of speech prep and polish. For every dozen well-crafted lines of oratory, I heard at least three stumbles, two sentence fragments, and a non sequitur. Even the Government Members had been caught off guard by their House Leader's procedural gambit.

The division bells rang at 5:45 PM, calling the MPs to the vote. I left the office and entered the public gallery at the south end of the House so I could count Members on both sides of the chamber. In the intervening fifteen minutes, I found it impossible to get an accurate read on numbers. Members were darting about, conferring with one another and disappearing behind the curtains that separated the House from the Government and Opposition lobbies. I gave up until the Speaker rose to bring the bedlam to order. Everyone took their seats, and virtually everyone in the chamber starting counting as the Speaker and the Deputy Clerk introduced the vote.

I'd smuggled a small message pad into the gallery and shielded it in my lap from the vigilant eyes of the two House of Commons security staff posted at either entrance. I finished my first count: Government 31, Opposition 38. I took little comfort in this margin. The Government House Leader and Whip looked too calm and confident to be seven votes short. They were playing us again.

The roll-call vote started precisely at 6:00 PM with the Speaker calling for the "Ayes." The Tory side stood. Starting at the north end of the chamber, as the Deputy Clerk read each name, the Members, in turn, sat down. As I expected, halfway through the "Ayes," I watched as the Government House Leader nodded once and seven MPs floated in to take their seats in the south end of the House, just in time to record their affirmative votes. The Prime Minister could not contain a Cheshire-cat grin. Government 38, Opposition 38. They had done it. They had their tie, and a tie was all they needed. The Speaker had made his own mental count and looked uncomfortable at the prospect of breaking the tie. But he would, without doubt. He was a loyal Tory soldier, and duty called.

The Deputy Clerk finished counting each standing Government MP and turned to the Speaker.

"And the 'Nays,'" invited the Speaker formally.

The Opposition benches rose, and the Deputy Clerk again started his roll call from the north end of the NDP and Liberal benches. I watched in hope and then in vain for additional Opposition Members to slip into the chamber to break the tie and wipe the smug smile off the Prime Minister's face. But we were stalled at 38. It was over.

About three Opposition Members were yet to be counted when I heard a commotion beneath me. What looked like an Arctic explorer, complete with heavy boots, snow pants, and a bright orange parka with a snorkel hood zipped to the hilt, stumbled into view on the floor of the House of Commons, dragging two Commissionaires with him.

"Unhand me. I'm to be here. I'm to be here!" he shouted.

He unzipped and pulled back his fur-lined hood, revealing soft, brown leather and aged goggles. As the zipper descended still farther, a grey and straggly cascade spread onto his chest. It could not be. But there he was. As the leather headgear was removed, so too was all doubt as to the identity of the intrepid traveler. I have never heard such noise in the House as I did at that moment. Movement to the right caught my eye. I looked over to the press gallery to see André Fontaine, dressed to tackle the final push to Mount Everest's summit, beaming my way. When he took off his soaking parka, his face appeared bright pink, and his eyes were streaming though not with emotion—apparently just from winter's wind. He looked like he'd just gone through a car wash on a bicycle. An ice-encrusted camera swung from his left shoulder. I was at a complete loss. I had no words, no explanation.

Below me, a dozen Liberal MPs gathered around Angus, hoisted him to their shoulders, and carried him to his seat like an Egyptian pharaoh. He did not seem happy about the antics and looked to the Speaker, who was still trying to restore order in the chamber, in apology. Before the vote could be resumed, the Government House Leader was on his feet. The Prime Minister was no longer smiling.

"Mr. Speaker, the Honourable Member for Cumberland-Prescott must not be permitted to vote as the roll call was already in progress."

The colour had drained from the Speaker's face as he summoned his Deputy Clerk for counsel. Whispered conversation ensued for several minutes. Throughout, repeated and emphatic head shaking was the Deputy Clerk's response. He returned to the table as the Speaker wobbled to his feet.

"The Standing Orders are silent on the matter, but we are guided by precedent. Provided the Member is in his place before the roll call is concluded, his vote is legitimate and will be counted."

"Mr. Speaker, I demand a formal ruling on this matter before we proceed," barked the Government House Leader. He was waving his hands, grasping at straws.

The Speaker rose again, steadier now. "I have just given the only ruling possible in this situation. In fact, my Deputy Clerk reminds me that last year, the Honourable Government House Leader himself sought and received this very judgment, allowing a tardy Minister to register her vote on her own bill. The vote will proceed." Live by the sword, etcetera, etcetera.

The Government House Leader had nothing in return. He bolted from the chamber followed quickly by the Prime Minister, the rest of his Ministers, and eventually, the entire Government caucus. The Tory benches were empty when Angus McLintock, reluctant MP for Cumberland-Prescott, took his seat after delivering the coup de grâce. Every scrap of paper on and in the Opposition desks was tossed into the air as if in tribute to the day's snowstorm. The noise was deafening. Angus sat calmly in the eye of a storm of well-wishers. The Leader himself was first in line to pump Angus's hand, afterwards locking him in a bear hug. The Speaker had already adjourned the House, no doubt to return to his Centre Block apartment and contemplate his less-than-promising future in the Progressive Conservative Party.

The Government had fallen.

The next morning, the following story ran on the front page of *The Cumberland Crier*. It was syndicated the day after in papers across the country and even in a few in the United States.

GOVERNMENT FALLS

Local hero rises ... on a cushion of air

by André Fontaine

Crier *reporter André Fontaine spent yesterday at the side of Angus McLintock as he made a heroic journey against daunting odds to cast the vote that brought down the Government. Here is his exclusive, first-hand account.*

Angus McLintock, rookie MP for Cumberland-Prescott, is a quick study. As yesterday's crushing storm finally relented, we were sitting in his living room on the shores of the Ottawa River. Our interview was interrupted when a phone call came from his executive assistant, Daniel Addison, on Parliament Hill. The Government had refused to adjourn the House even though the blizzard had marooned most MPs in their ridings. McLintock had been appointed to the lowly Standing Committee on Procedure and House Affairs and, with an engineer's mind, had immersed himself in the arcane world of parliamentary procedure. I could see the wheels turning beneath his unruly, grey hair as he listened to Addison. McLintock feared the Government was pulling a fast one and would call the vote on its controversial mini-budget that very evening, one day earlier than originally scheduled. McLintock was livid when he hung up the phone. "Our interview is over, but our time together is just beginning. On with yer coat and let's go," Angus instructed. The time was 2:10 PM.

The snow had slowed by this point and had threatened to stop all together. We fought our way through the waist-deep drifts to his boathouse and work-shop that sat right on the shore. Inside the workshop, a strange craft came into focus. When my eyes adjusted to the light, Angus stood before me and fixed me with a serious gaze. "This is a hovercraft. You and I are taking it up the river to Parliament Hill. There's a vote to be won, and I'll not sit idly by while an unscrupulous Government hornswoggles a nation." I was given no option. The time was 2:25 PM.

The high winds had left an enormous snowdrift angled up against the large boathouse doors. Our first task was clearing the doors. McLintock dug out two ancient snow shovels, and we set to work. The snow was heavy and had drifted halfway up the side of the building. I soon discovered, several feet down, that a ramp descended from the doors to the ice. It took us just over an hour and a half to clear the path to the river and break open the iced-over doors. I rested several times during this period, unable to sustain the back-breaking effort. McLintock worked steadily. I am 41 years old. He is 61. The time was 4:05 PM.

We then went back inside the workshop. He directed me to hold a light on the engine compartment so he could make some adjustments to the move-able vents housed beneath the motor and fan. He draped himself over the craft this way and that with not a grunt, a sigh, or a complaint. He also inspected the rubber skirt that surrounded the hovercraft. Finally, he led me to a closet in one corner of the room where he had stored winter parkas, ski pants, boots, mitts, and hats. Ten minutes later, we were both suited up. We opened the big boathouse doors, and the cold wind rushed in. The time was 4:56 PM.

He had me hook the steel cable to the eyebolt on the front of the hovercraft while he adjusted the winch. With enough slack in the line, we then pushed the craft along the floor of the boathouse on two dollies until the rear wheels started down the ramp. McLintock then winched the hovercraft onto the ice. Ten minutes later, we'd extricated the dollies and filled the fuel tank from an old, red gas can stored underneath the workbench.

"Are you ready for a wild ride Mr. Fontaine?" The time was 5:14 PM.

He stood next to the craft and pulled the cord and started the engine before climbing inside. Although cramped, the cockpit accommodated us both on a low-slung bench seat. McLintock directed me to pull up my hood against the wind. He slid what looked like leather flying headgear from World War I over his head and lowered the goggles to his eyes. Next, he pulled up his hood and zippered it all the way, leaving but a small opening through which he would navigate. Then, he patted my knee. "I thank you for coming. I doonae think it wise to make the trek alone."

At the time, I knew very little about hovercrafts, but the essentials became clear soon enough. He reached for the throttle, and the engine roared. At the same time, I could feel us rise up off the ice. The wind had kept the river clear of snow, and a runway of smooth ice stretched to the western horizon. Angus then moved his feet on two pedals beneath the dash and throttled up further. With the engine directly behind us, my ears were ringing. Slowly, we gathered speed, McLintock adjusting the steering wheel as the hovercraft skidded along the ice. The time was 5:26 PM and nearly dark. The vote was set for 6:00 PM sharp.

The flight in the hovercraft was cold, ear-piercing, and hair-raising, but beyond that, quite smooth. The plentiful snow lightened the landscape and gave us enough visibility to stay on course. Twice along our river route, low snowdrifts encroached on our ice path. Both times, we slowed down—McLintock's feet moving again on his pedals to direct some of thrust frontwards through the side pods. When we hit the drifts, the fan kicked up the snow, and we found ourselves in a whiteout until we'd passed over.

With Parliament Hill in sight in the distance, I noticed a patch of open water ahead where the current kept the river from freezing. McLintock saw it, too. Rather than slowing down, however, he gunned the engine. The craft hurtled over the water, spray flying everywhere. A moment later, we slid back up onto the ice on the other side, wet but safe.

"I'm not the best carpenter, you see, so stopping in open water is not in the plan. I doubt she's seaworthy, let alone watertight," he screamed in my ear above the engine's wail.

And then, we were there. He nosed into a snowdrift at the river's edge immediately below the Library of Parliament. He cut the engine, and we settled back to earth, our bow on the bank, our stern on the ice. The time was 6:12 PM.

"I fear we've missed our mark," was all he said before heading up the slope. The trees on the side of the hill kept the snow shallow on the ground, so scaling the heights was easier and faster than expected. I had some trouble keeping up with McLintock but was only ten paces behind when he was accosted outside the chamber by two House of Commons guards. He ignored them and barreled through the doors onto the floor of the House with a sentry on each arm.

Bedlam reigned in the House of Commons as this strange figure peeled off his parka and became Angus McLintock, Member of Parliament for Cumberland-Prescott. The time was 6:21 PM.

McLintock cast the tie-breaking vote, and the Government collapsed at 6:29 PM.

Four photos accompanied most layouts of André's story. The first one showed Angus sitting in his living room, looking as if he'd like to drop the camera from a great height. The second one featured Baddeck 1, perched at the top of the boathouse ramp. The third one was a shot from inside the hovercraft, looking out at high speed, the inflated skirt dominating the lower part of the photo. Finally, the fourth one showed Angus being borne on the shoulders of his caucus mates just before he cast his decisive vote.

I sat with Muriel on the same plastic-coated couch we'd first shared three months earlier. While we waited for Lindsay, she looked out over her river, *The Cumberland Crier* spread out on her lap, a stern Angus glaring back at us from the front page. She wasn't exactly smiling, but her look was one of deep contentment.

"You served your party well when you found him," she said, staring back at the photo of Angus. "What now?"

"Well, I figure the world returns to normal. To start, Lindsay and I are going to Quebec City for a long weekend to hibernate and vegetate. Then, I assume Angus and I will pick it up where we left off in September. We'll resume our interrupted academic careers, and the last three months will become a bizarre and exciting conversation piece for us both," I replied.

"You've got it all figured out, have you?" she said, her head moving slowly from side to side.

"Well, Liberals are already coming out of the woodwork now that this seat can be won. And we've always known how Angus feels," I said.

"Really." She adopted a tone that was the oral equivalent of rolling her eyes.

"Come on, Muriel, are you sure you won't go again? The seat's yours for the taking. We'd all be there for you."

"Bite your tongue! I'm done. I've told you that," she scolded. "Have you spoken to Angus about all this?"

"Not yet. He's sequestered himself in his workshop."

She turned to look directly at me, taking both my hands in hers. I could feel her Parkinson's travel from her fingers to mine and up through my arms.

"Daniel, I'll say it again—time to start thinking about Plan B."

◆   ◆   ◆

Diary
Tuesday, December 10

My Love,

It was like a dream, flying her up the river. I confess it was not the circumstance I'd have chosen for testing her, but I was left with no alternative. With a passenger, it was a wee bit more sluggish to respond to the helm and took longer to stop her, but that's par for the course. She did me proud. I'm in her debt.

By the bye, we defeated that rogue Tory government yesterday. It was a satisfying conclusion to Baddeck 1's dash up the river, not that I wasn't already chuffed enough. Everyone is making an uncommon fuss over it all.

That was one fierce storm we endured. Remember how we used to love just sitting by the fire and watching the storm lash the land and river? It isn't the same now.

I woke up Muriel when I phoned her late last night. She'll not do it. I tried and tried till I was blue. She'll just not do it again.

So what say you, my love? Do I seize the moment I've helped bring about and slip quietly back to the refuge of my university, my students, my research, and my memories?

No, I didn't think so.

AM

The End

978-0-595-42872-4
0-595-42872-X